POPULARMMOS

Popular MMOS (aka Pat) is one of the most popular YouTubers in the world. Pat and Jen (aka Gaming With Jen) created their *Minecraft*-inspired channel, PopularMMOS, in 2012. Since then, they have entertained millions of fans around the world with their gaming videos and original characters.

Pat and Jen live in Florida with their cat, Cloud. *PopularMMOS Presents: Enter the Mine* is their second book.

To my Nana. Can't wait for our next adventure.—D.J.

A special thanks to Joe Caramagna for all his creative help!

Harper Alley is an imprint of HarperCollins Publishers.

Popular MMOs Presents: Enter the Mine Copyright © 2019 by Popular MMOs, LLC. All rights reserved. Manufactured in China. No part of this book may be used or reproduced in any manner whatsoever without written permission except in the case of brief quotations embodied in critical articles and reviews. For information address HarperCollins Children's Books, a division of HarperCollins Publishers, 195 Broadway, New York, NY 10007.

www.harpercollinschildrens.com

Library of Congress Control Number: 2018966562
ISBN 978-0-06-289428-1 (trade bdg.) — ISBN 978-0-06-291529-0 (special edition)
ISBN 978-0-06-294024-7 (special edition) — ISBN 978-0-06-293357-7 (special edition)
ISBN 978-0-06-295022-2 (special edition) — ISBN 978-0-06-289429-8 (pbk.)

The artist used an iPad Pro and the app Procreate to create the digital illustrations for this book.
Typography by Erica De Chavez   20 21 22 23 24   SCP   10 9 8 7 6 5 4 3 2   ❖   First Edition

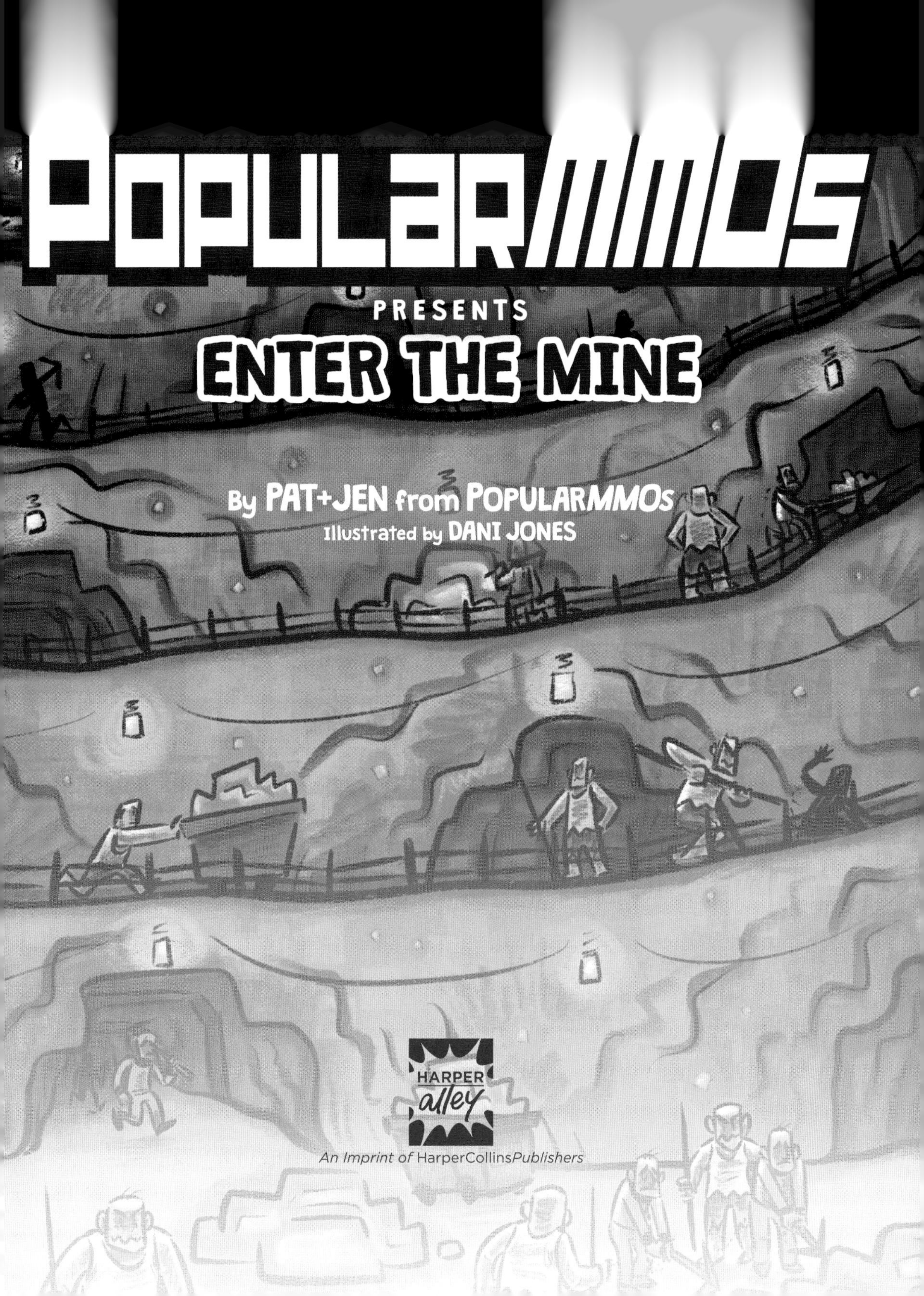

POPULARMMOS

PRESENTS

ENTER THE MINE

By PAT+JEN from POPULARMMOs
Illustrated by DANI JONES

HARPER alley
An Imprint of HarperCollinsPublishers

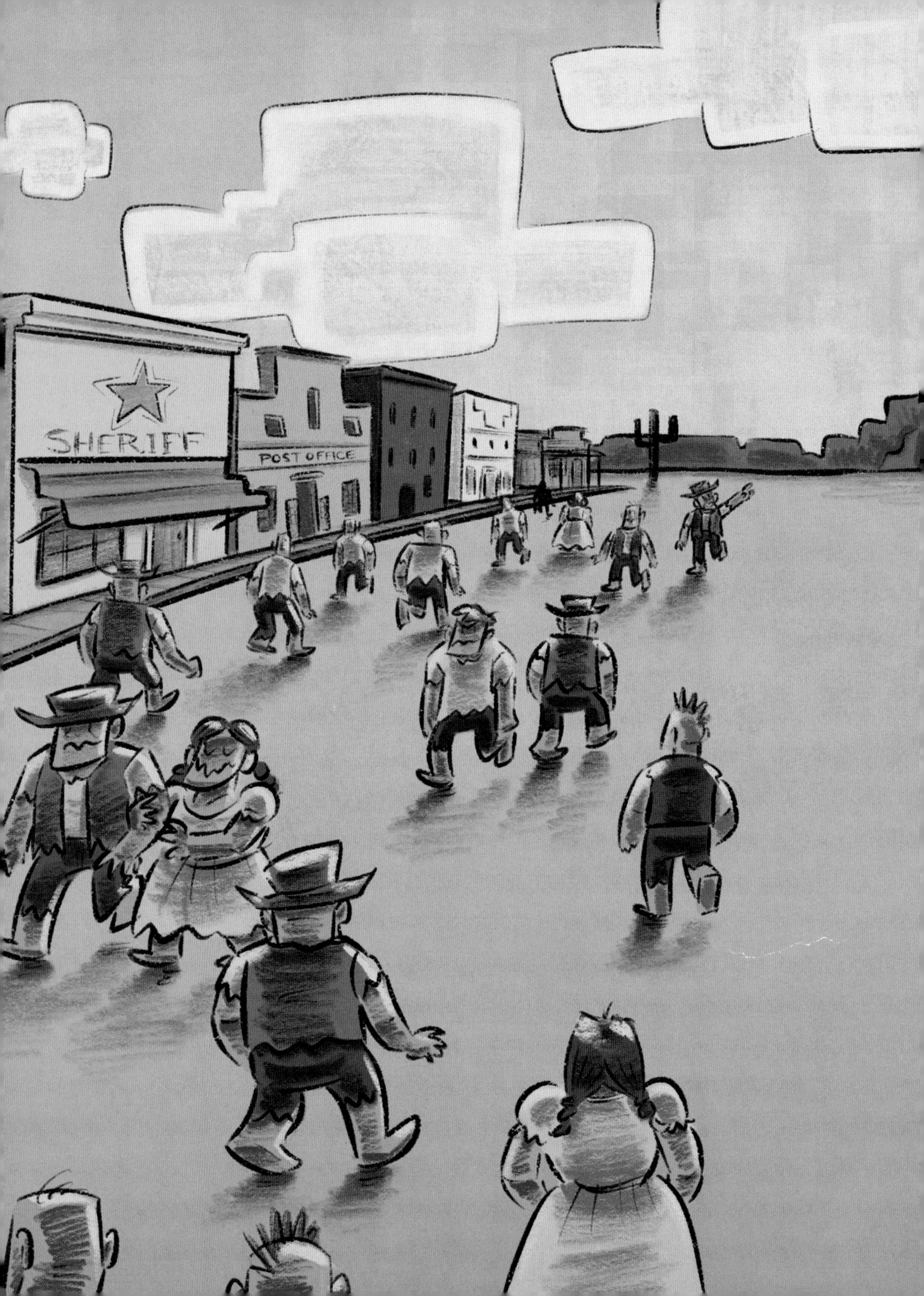
SHERIFF
POST OFFICE

Hey, what's going on, guys!

It's Pat and Jen, and we're so thrilled that you're reading our second book. It's another exciting adventure where you'll get to meet all your favorite characters from our YouTube channel. Of course, there's me and Jen and Bomby and Cloud, but this time, Bob, Hoss, the Mayor, Valentine, and more get in on the action. We all band together to stop Evil Jen's evilest plot yet—and worse, this time she has Evil Pat along for the ride!

We can't tell you how much we appreciate your support. Writing this book has been a totally amazing experience, and we can't wait to tell you how much it means to us both that you've decided to Enter the Mine along with us. We think you'll really enjoy this "explosive" new adventure—watch out for all the zombies and holes. We just hope you enjoy reading it as much as we enjoyed writing it. Being creative is what we are all about, and we hope that this book inspires you to be creative, too!

Have fun! Read on! And thanks for being a fan.

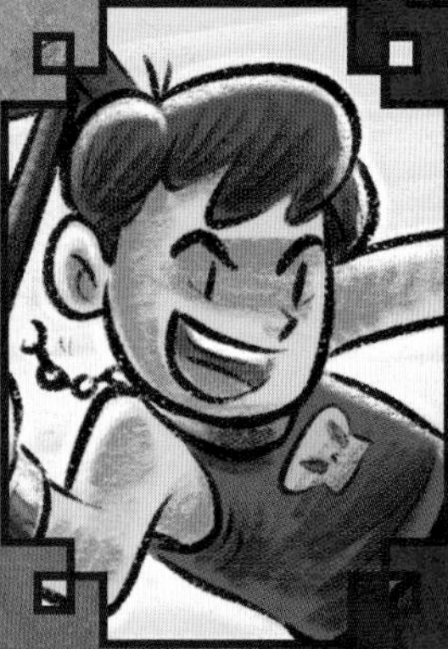

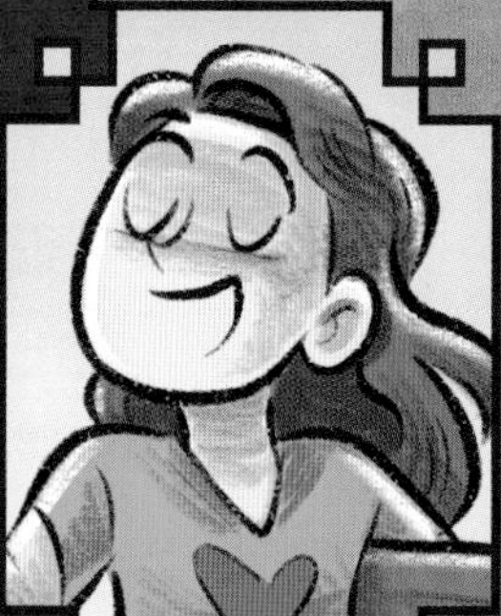

PAT & JEN

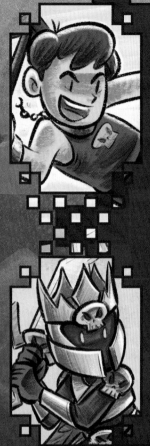

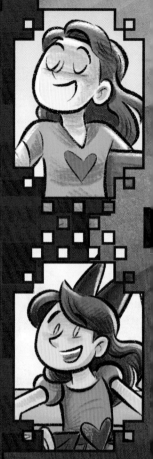

Pat is an awesome dude who's always looking for an epic adventure with his partner, the Super Girly Gamer Jen. Pat loves to have fun with his friends and take control of every situation with his cool weapons and can-do attitude. Jen is the sweetest person in the world and loves to laugh, but don't let her cheeriness fool you—she's also fierce. In fact, she could be an even greater adventurer than Pat . . . if she weren't so clumsy. Together, along with their cat, Cloud, they have a bond that can never be broken.

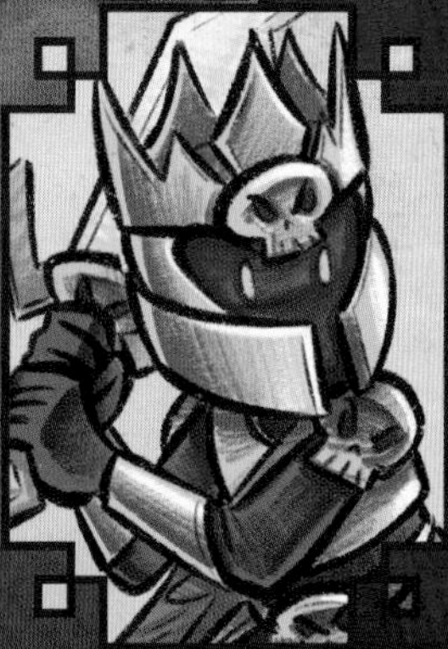

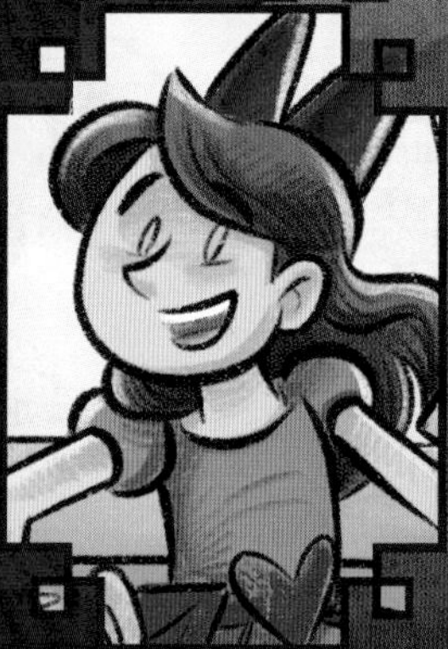

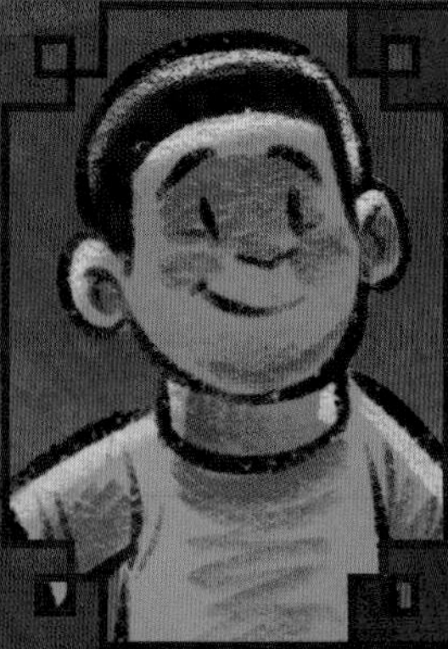

CARTER

Carter is Jen's best friend and biggest fan, but he doesn't seem to like Pat very much at all. Carter is also not very smart and sometimes carries a pickle that he thinks is a green sword!

CAPTAIN COOKIE

No one is quite sure if Captain Cookie is a real sea captain or if he just dresses the part. He doesn't seem to be very good at anything, but that doesn't stop him from bragging about how great he is! He's rude to everyone he meets but always in a funny way.

CLOUD

Cloud is Pat and Jen's white Persian cat. He may have a fluffy exterior, but underneath, he's all *savage*.

HONEY BOO BOO

Honey Boo Boo is a golem of iron on the outside but is all softy on the inside!

BOMBY

Bomby is somewhat of a pet to Pat and Jen but also Pat's best friend. You can usually find him by following the craters left by the TNT that he loves to watch explode.

THE MAYOR

The Mayor loves being the mayor and loves reminding everyone that he's the mayor, but doesn't seem to have much authority over anyone or anything.

VALENTINE

An elf and a master archer, he leads the revolt against Evil Jen's rule in the Underworld.

BOB

Bob is Valentine's best friend. After he is imprisoned by Evil Jen, he becomes the unofficial leader of the miners.

HOSS

Hoss claims to be a doctor but doesn't seem to know anything about what a doctor actually does. He's better at being a chef. Actually, he's better at doing anything than he is at being a doctor!

EVIL JEN

Evil Jen's favorite thing is chaos. She lives for wreaking havoc on the world. What makes her truly evil, however, is that she would take someone as sweet as Jen and become an evil version of her. She even looks *exactly* like her (just don't tell Jen we said that!).

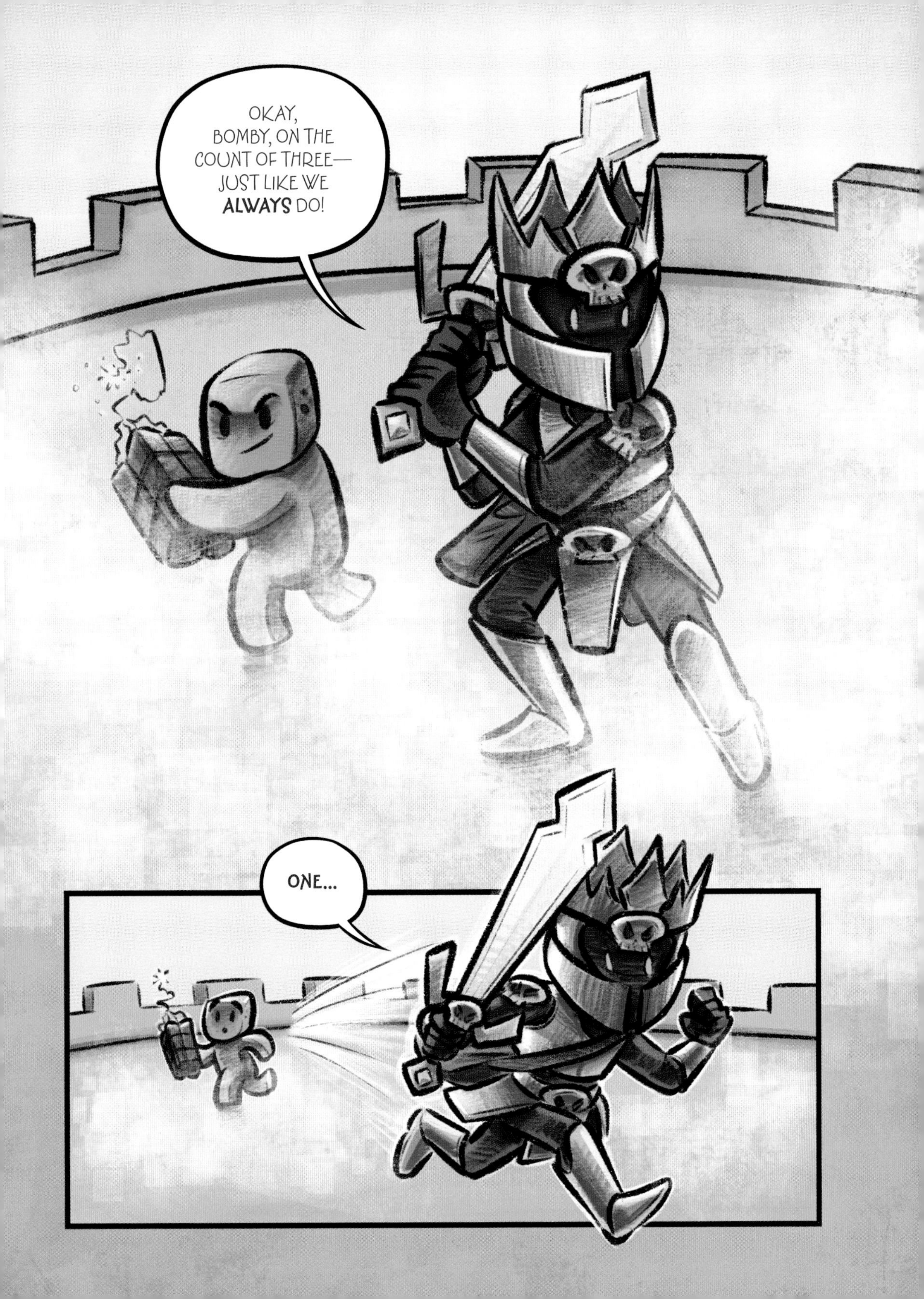
OKAY, BOMBY, ON THE COUNT OF THREE— JUST LIKE WE **ALWAYS** DO!
ONE...

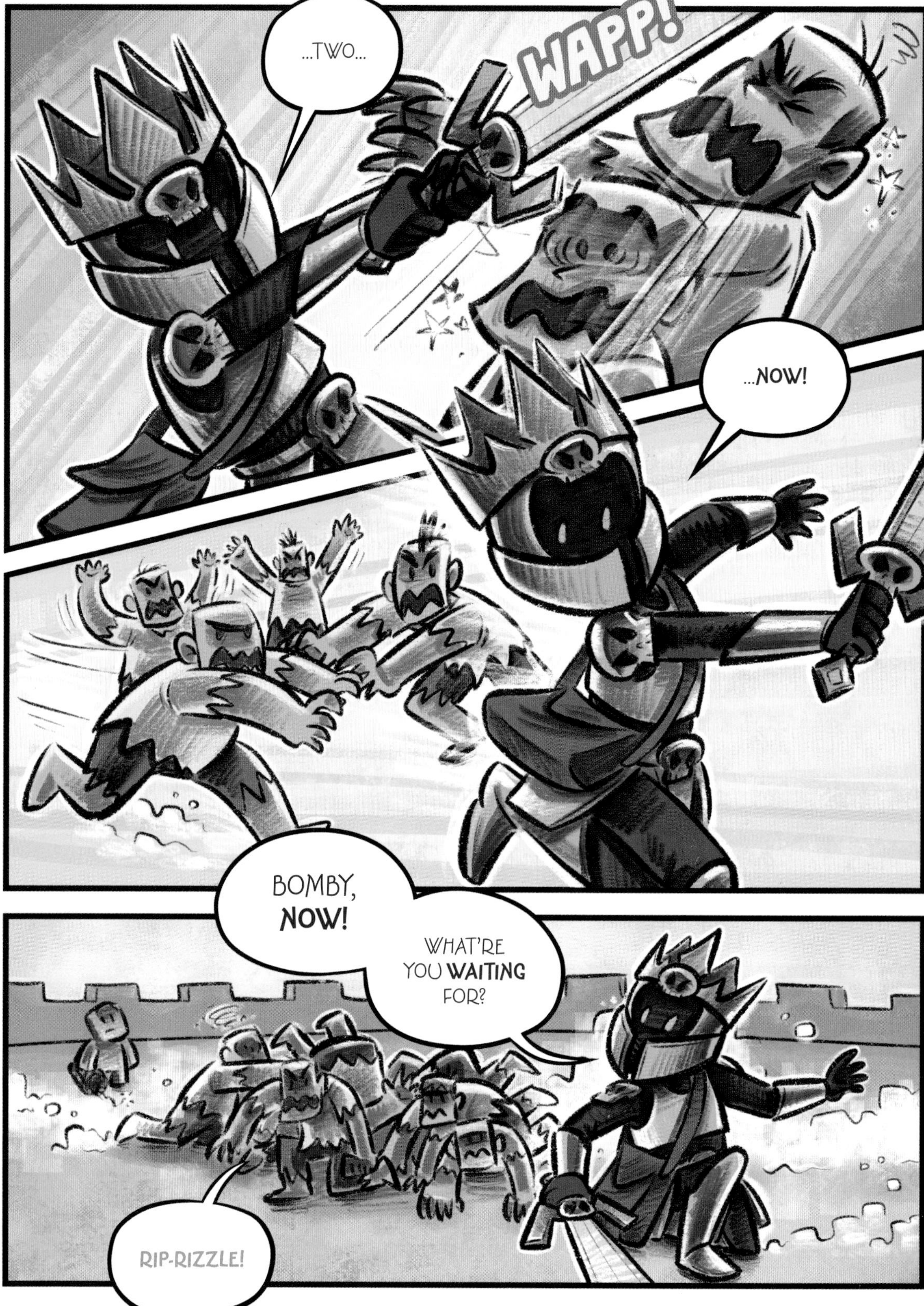
...TWO...
WAPP!
...NOW!
BOMBY, NOW!
WHAT'RE YOU WAITING FOR?
RIP-RIZZLE!

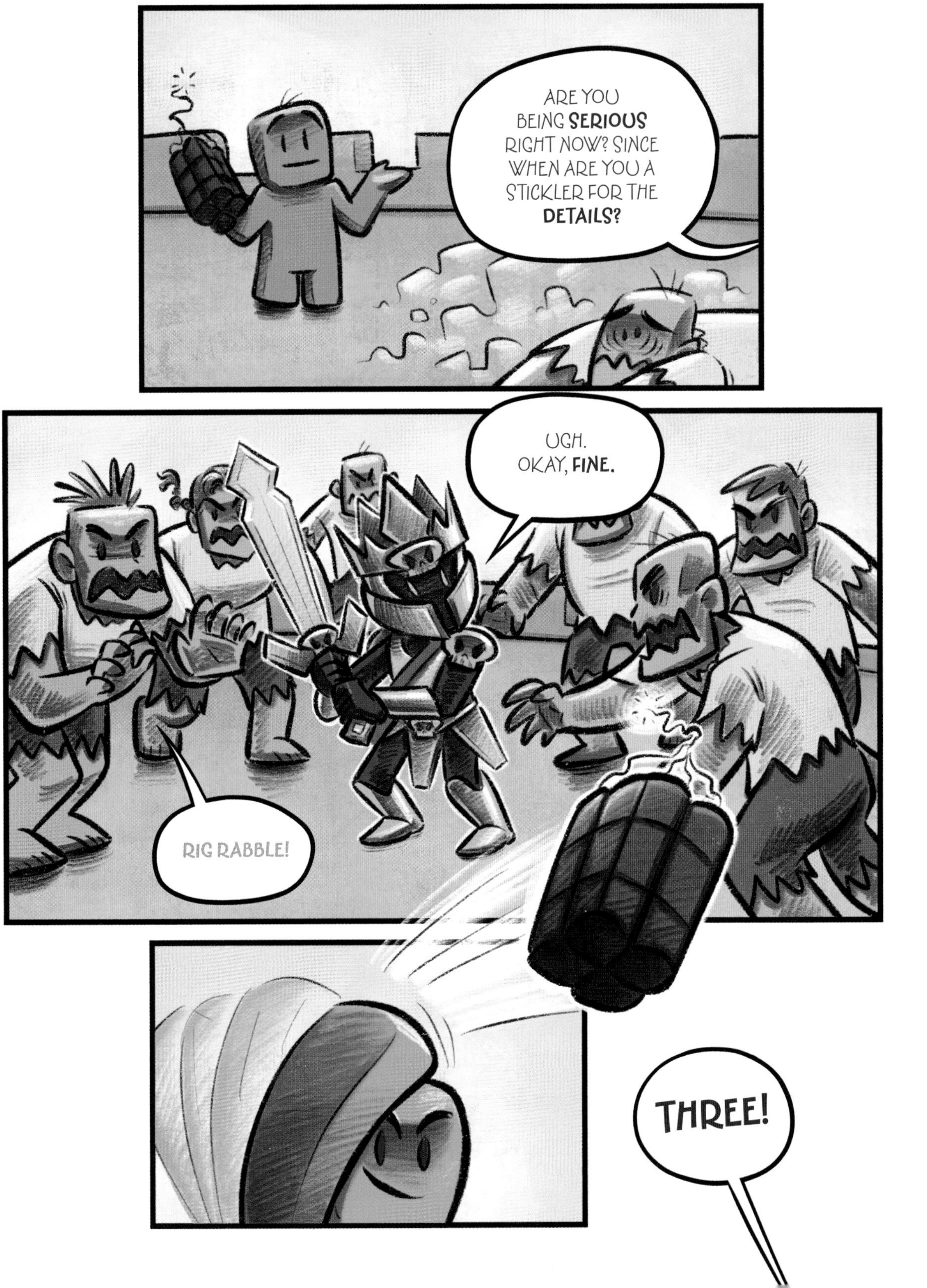
ARE YOU BEING **SERIOUS** RIGHT NOW? SINCE WHEN ARE YOU A STICKLER FOR THE **DETAILS?**
UGH. OKAY, **FINE.**
RIG RABBLE!
THREE!

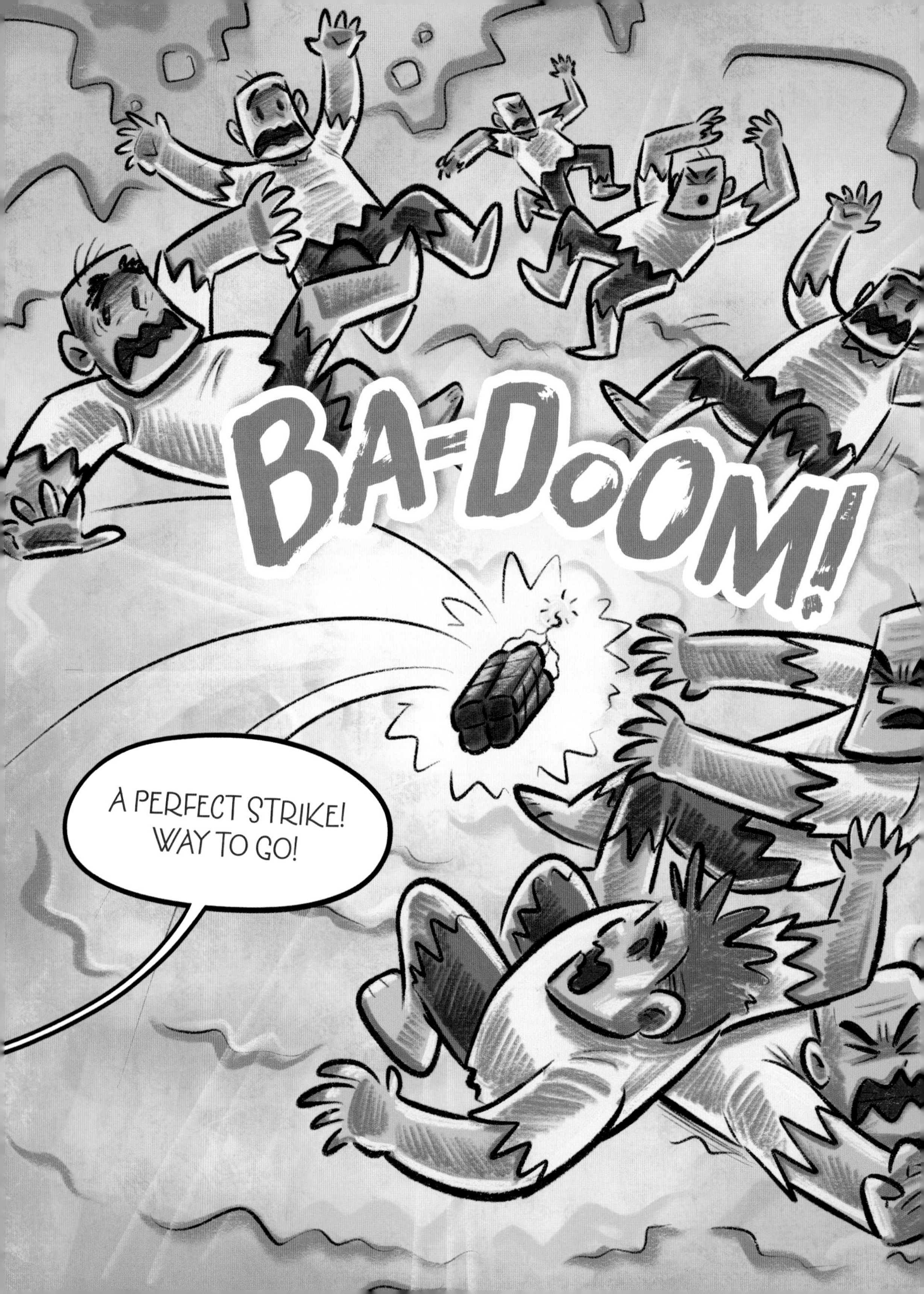
BA-D-OOM!
A PERFECT STRIKE! WAY TO GO!

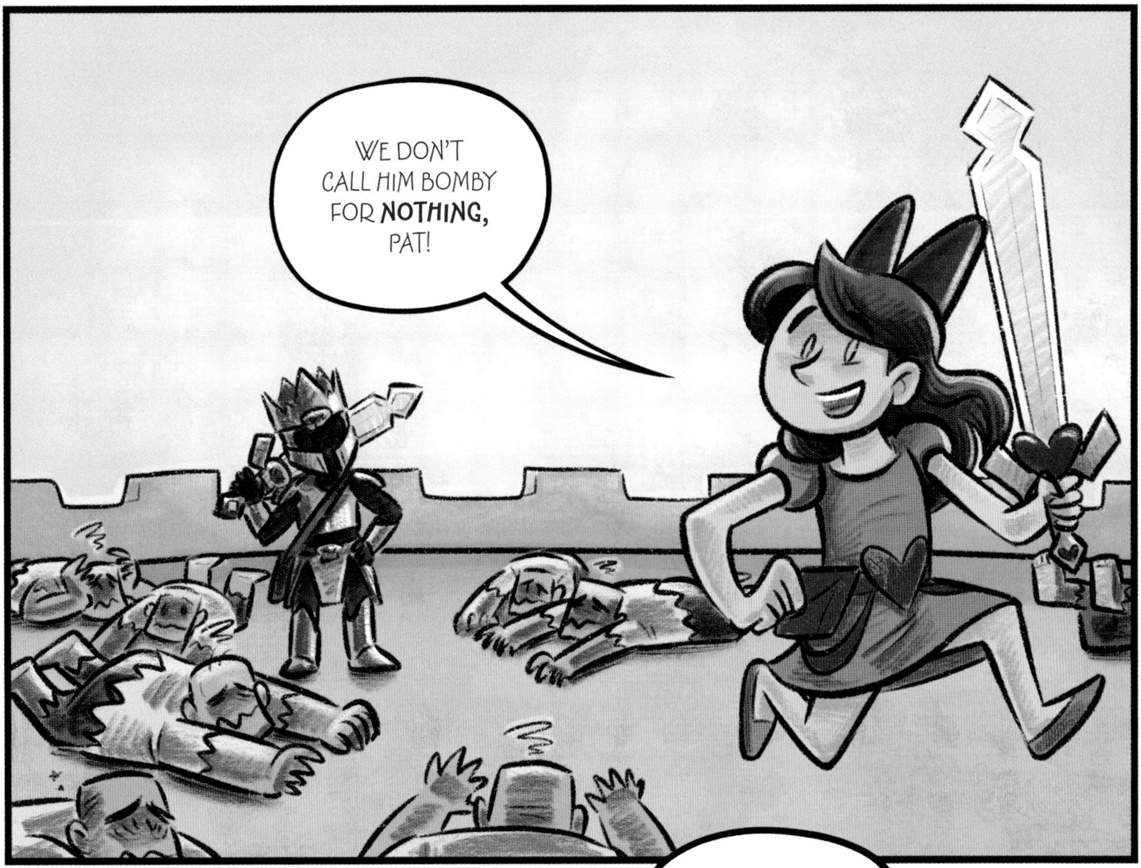
WE DON'T CALL HIM BOMBY FOR **NOTHING,** PAT!

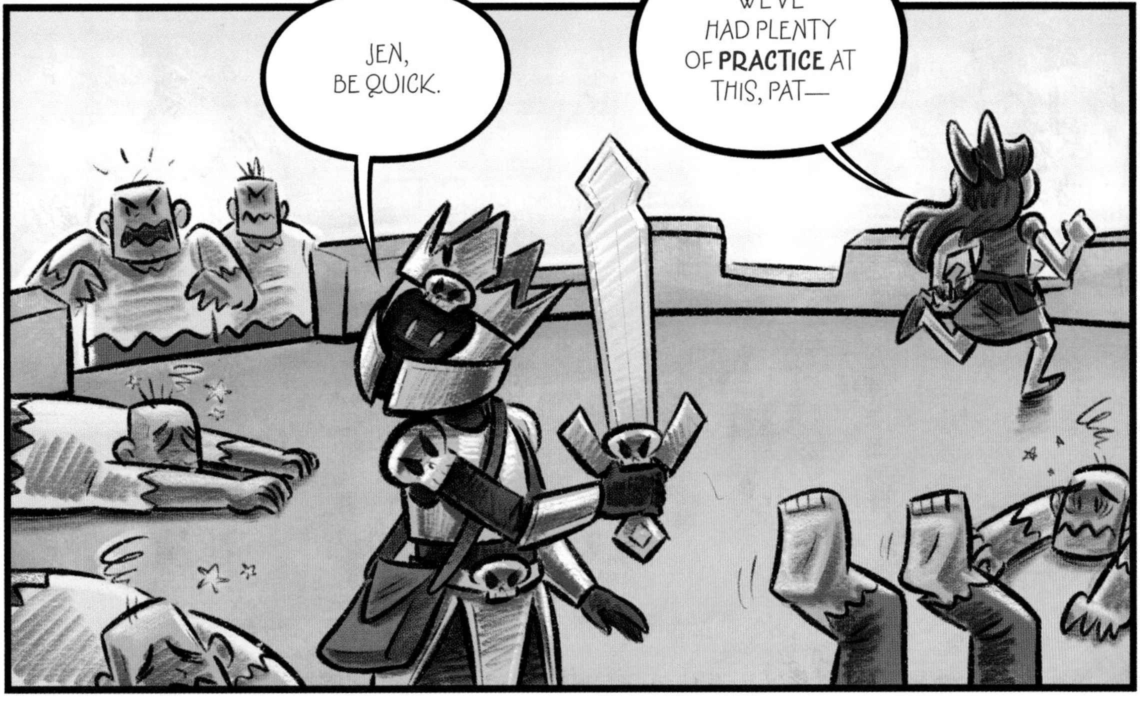
JEN, BE QUICK.
WE'VE HAD PLENTY OF **PRACTICE** AT THIS, PAT—

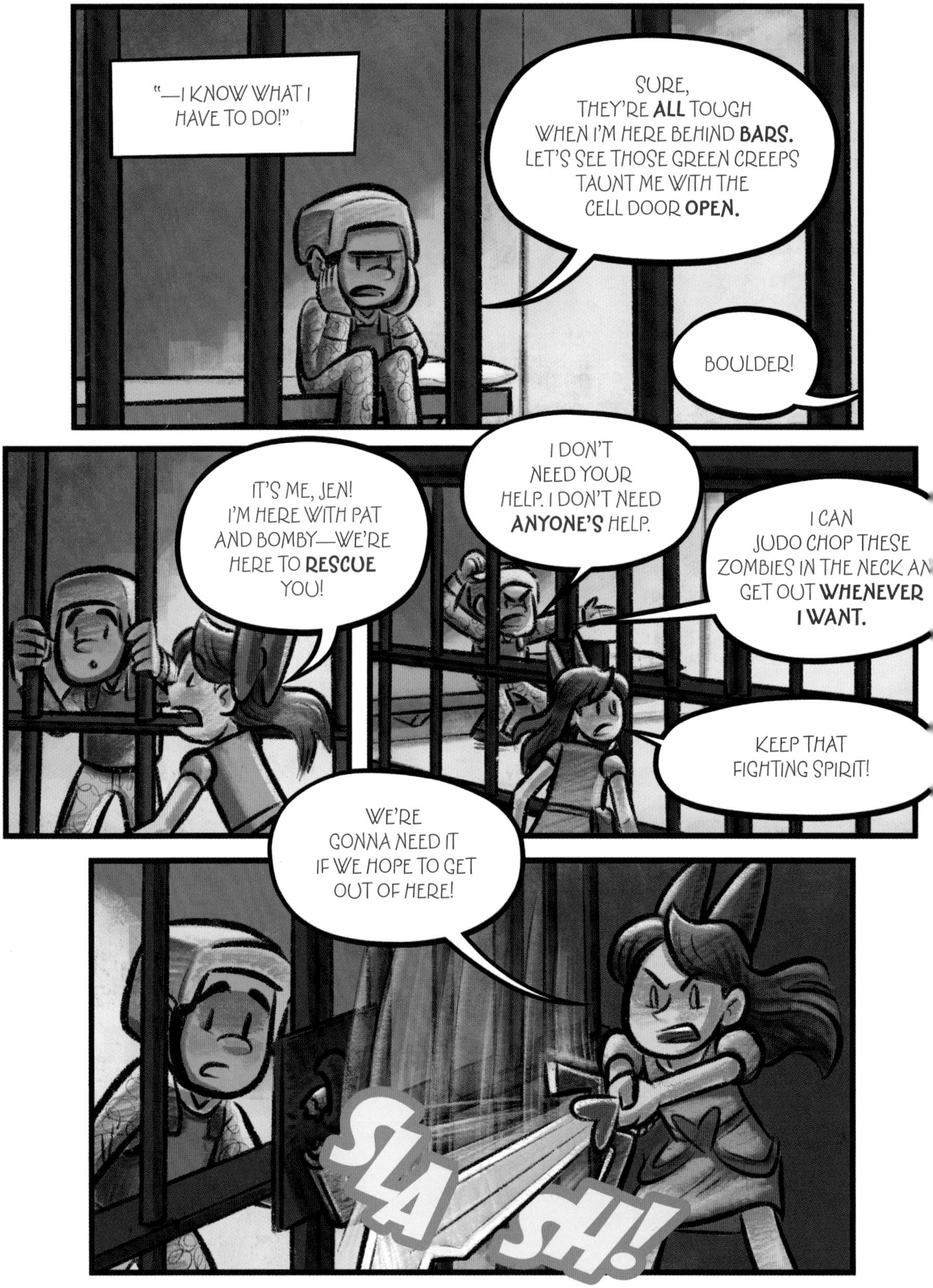
"—I KNOW WHAT I HAVE TO DO!"
SURE, THEY'RE **ALL** TOUGH WHEN I'M HERE BEHIND **BARS.** LET'S SEE THOSE GREEN CREEPS TAUNT ME WITH THE CELL DOOR **OPEN.**
BOULDER!
IT'S ME, JEN! I'M HERE WITH PAT AND BOMBY—WE'RE HERE TO **RESCUE** YOU!
I DON'T NEED YOUR HELP. I DON'T NEED **ANYONE'S** HELP.
I CAN JUDO CHOP THESE ZOMBIES IN THE NECK AN GET OUT **WHENEVER I WANT.**
KEEP THAT FIGHTING SPIRIT!
WE'RE GONNA NEED IT IF WE HOPE TO GET OUT OF HERE!
SLASH!

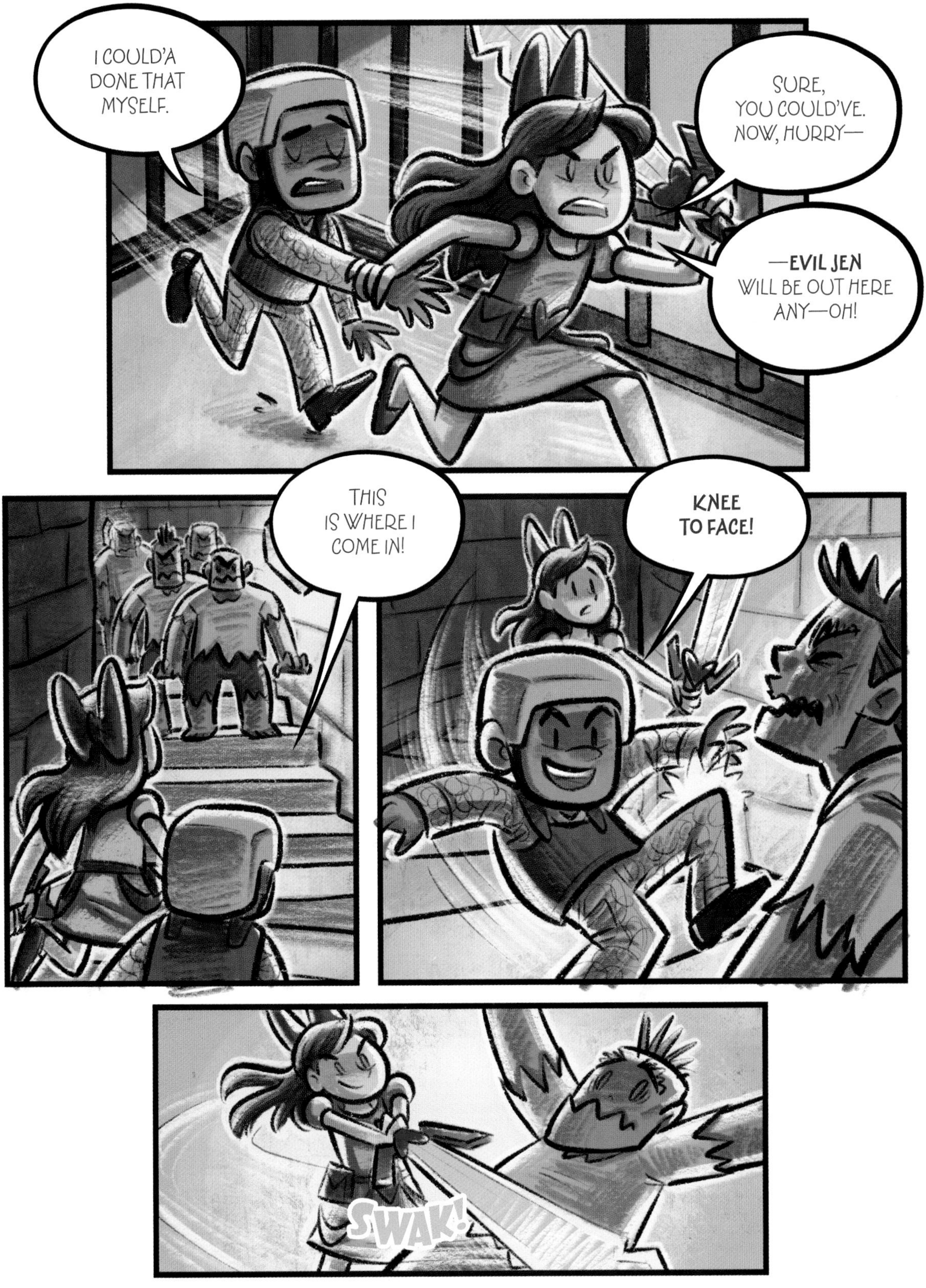
I COULD'A DONE THAT MYSELF.
SURE, YOU COULD'VE. NOW, HURRY—
—**EVIL JEN** WILL BE OUT HERE ANY—OH!
THIS IS WHERE I COME IN!
KNEE TO FACE!
SWAK!

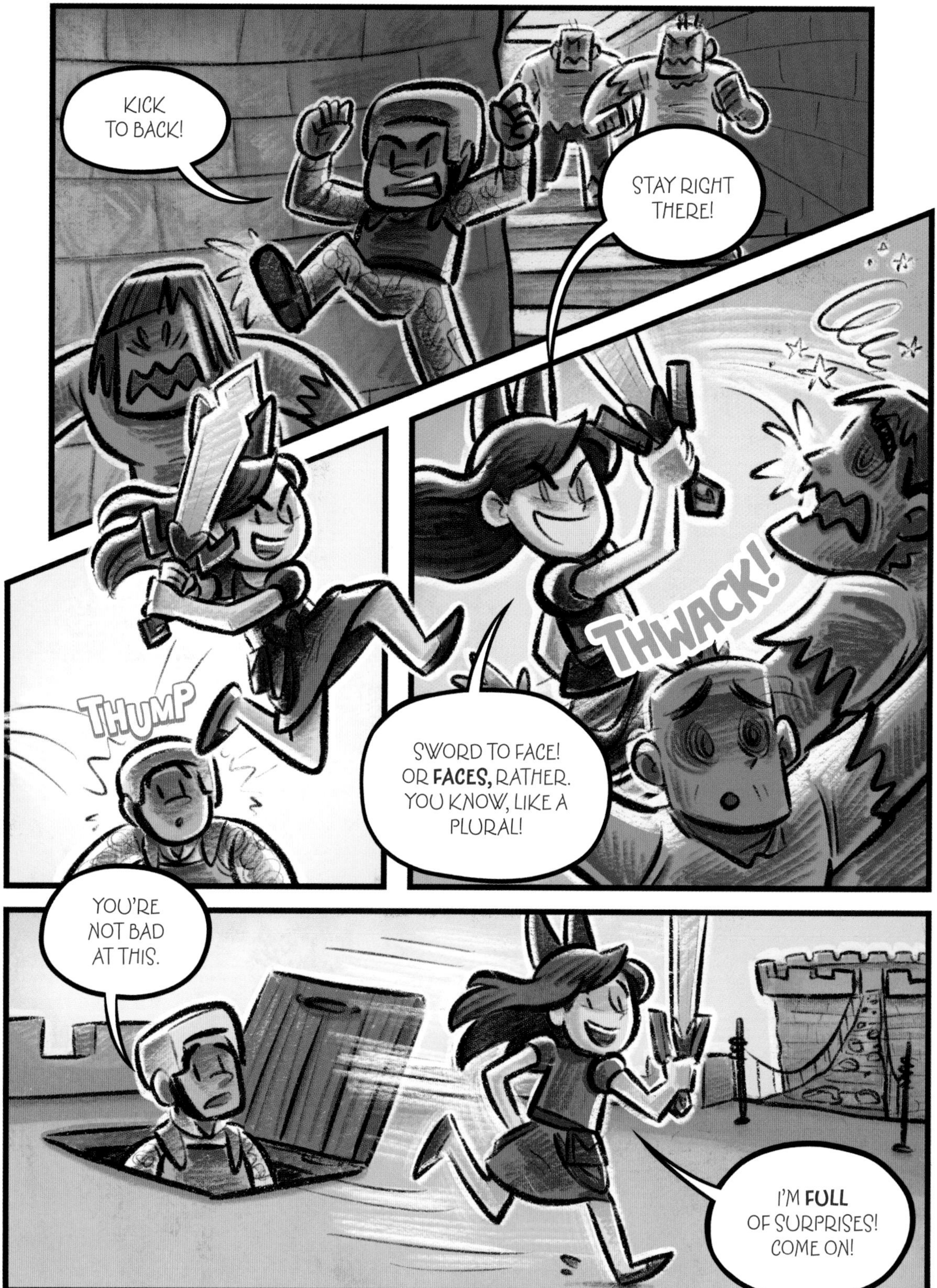
KICK TO BACK!
STAY RIGHT THERE!
THUMP
THWACK!
SWORD TO FACE! OR **FACES,** RATHER. YOU KNOW, LIKE A PLURAL!
YOU'RE NOT BAD AT THIS.
I'M **FULL** OF SURPRISES! COME ON!

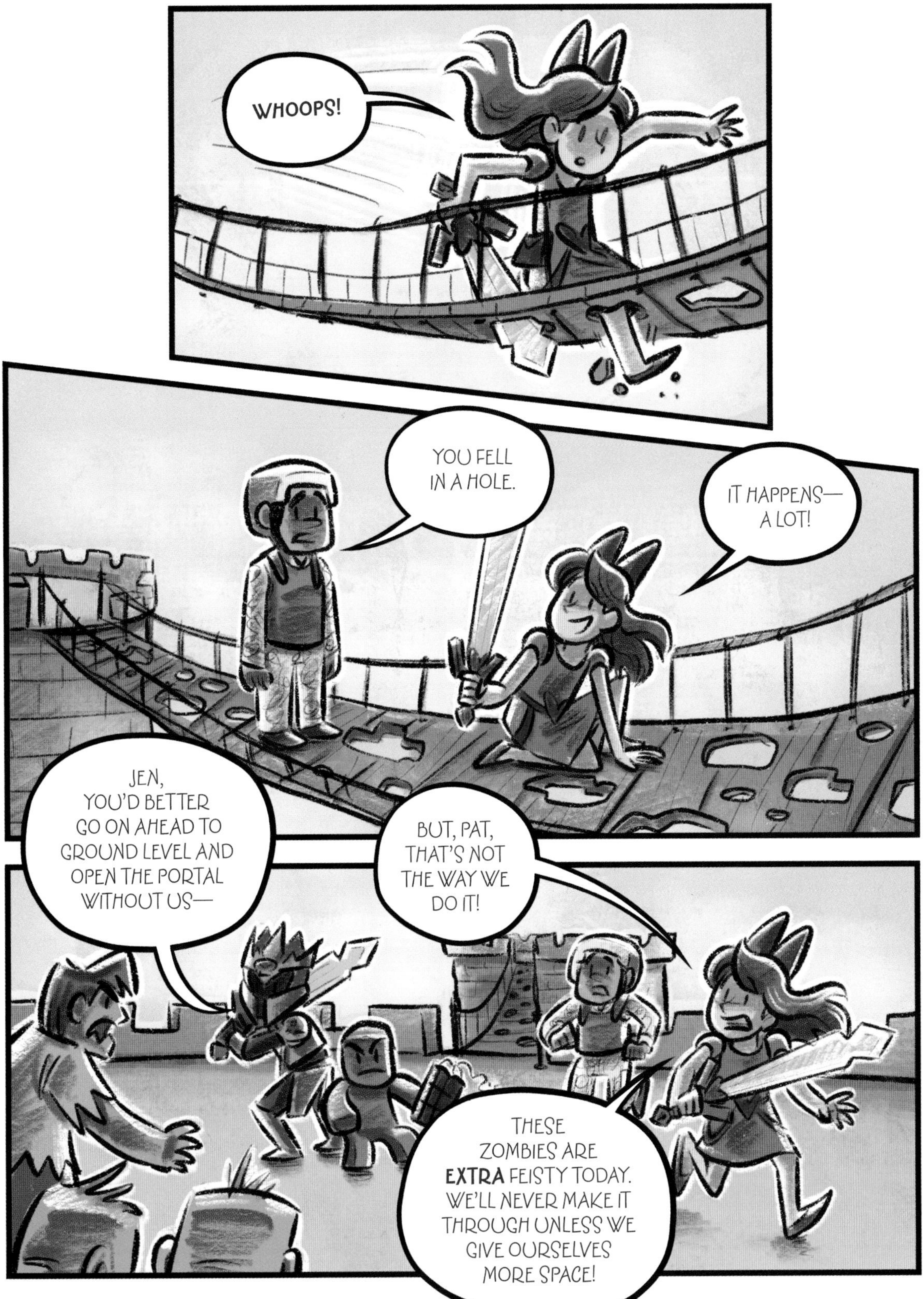
WHOOPS!
YOU FELL IN A HOLE.
IT HAPPENS— A LOT!
JEN, YOU'D BETTER GO ON AHEAD TO GROUND LEVEL AND OPEN THE PORTAL WITHOUT US—
BUT, PAT, THAT'S NOT THE WAY WE DO IT!
THESE ZOMBIES ARE **EXTRA** FEISTY TODAY. WE'LL NEVER MAKE IT THROUGH UNLESS WE GIVE OURSELVES MORE SPACE!

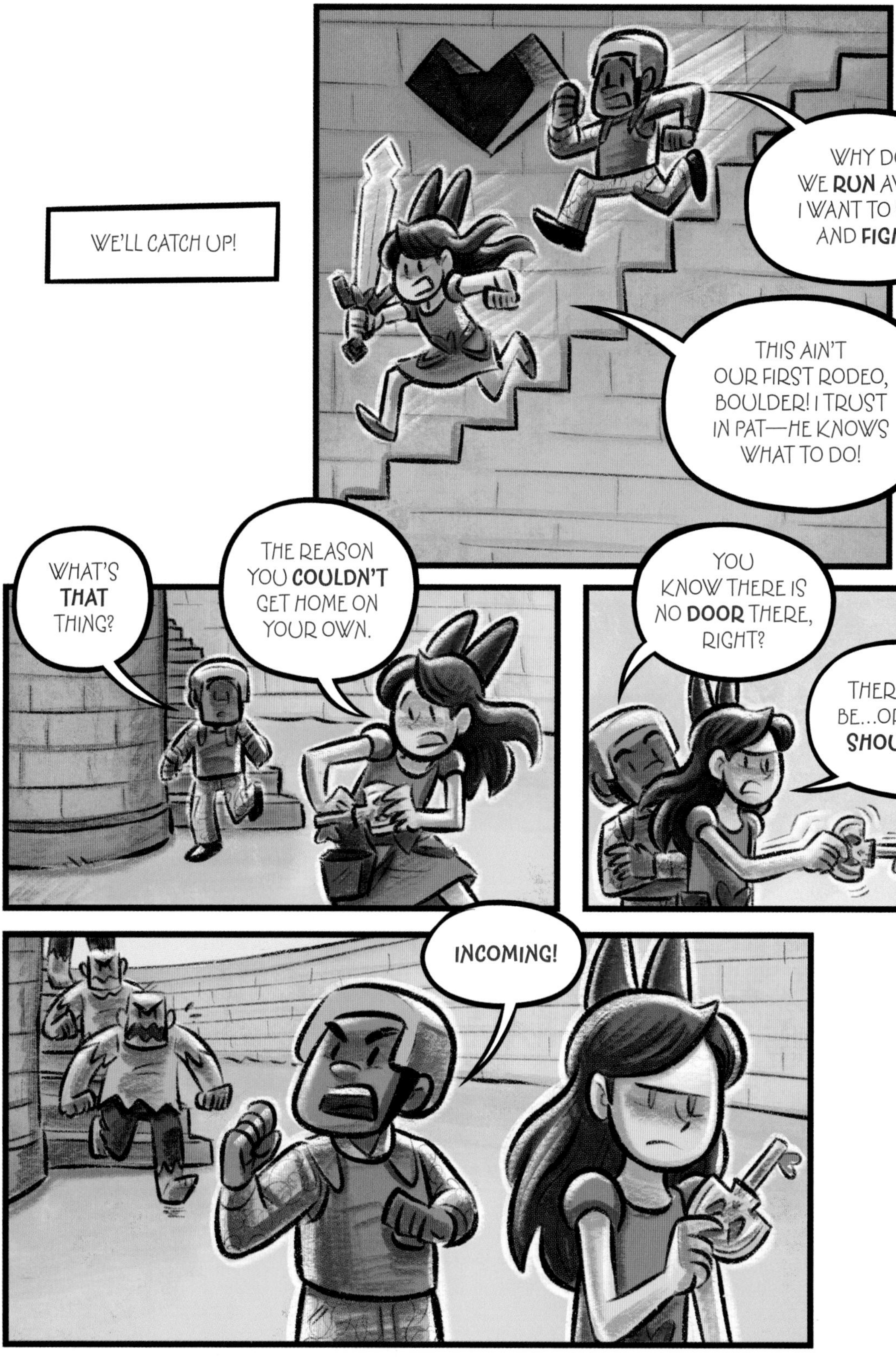
WE'LL CATCH UP!
WHY DO WE RUN AWAY? I WANT TO STAY AND FIGHT!
THIS AIN'T OUR FIRST RODEO, BOULDER! I TRUST IN PAT—HE KNOWS WHAT TO DO!
WHAT'S THAT THING?
THE REASON YOU COULDN'T GET HOME ON YOUR OWN.
YOU KNOW THERE IS NO DOOR THERE, RIGHT?
THERE WILL BE...OR THERE SHOULD BE!
INCOMING!

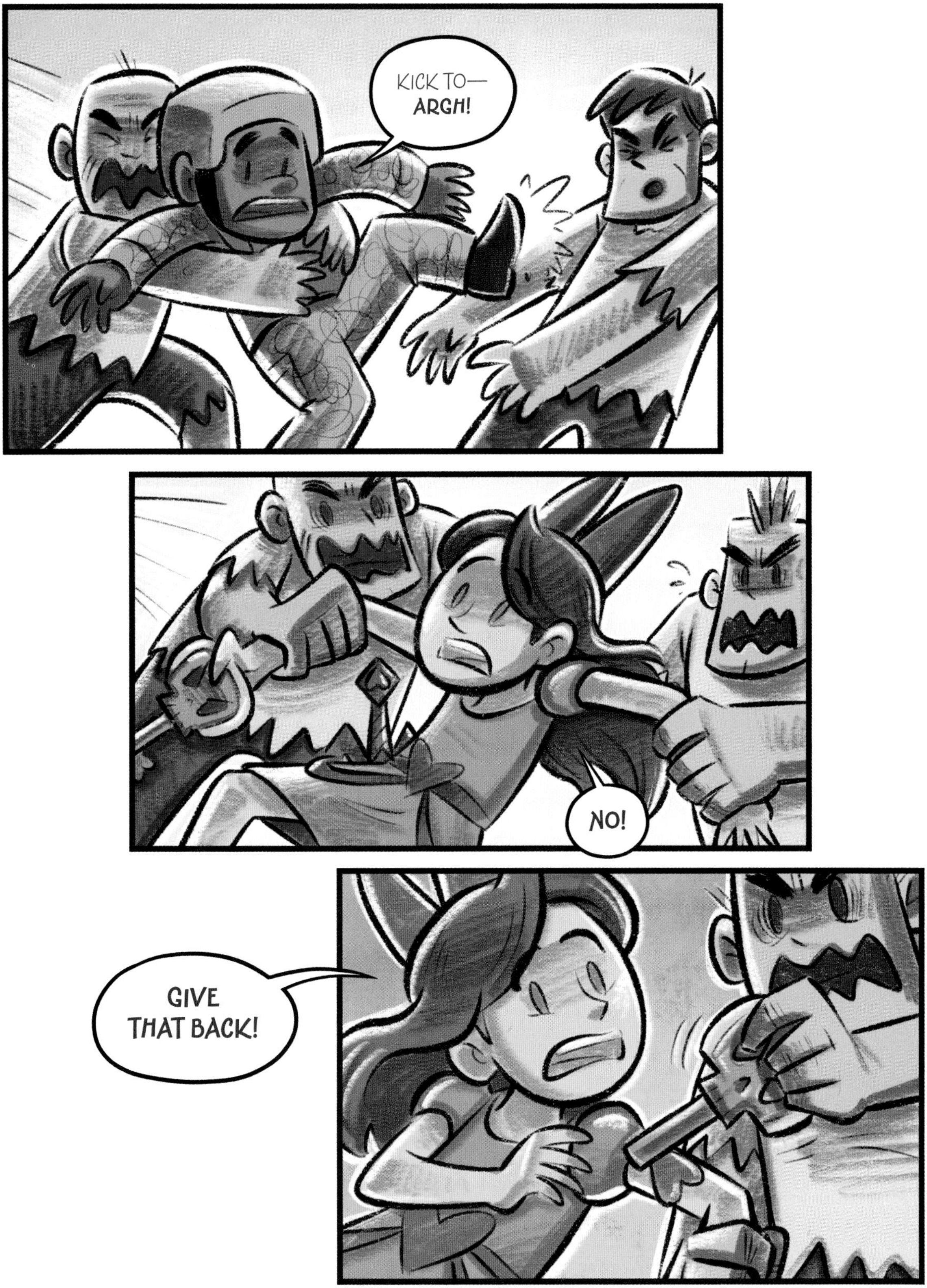
KICK TO—
ARGH!
NO!
GIVE THAT BACK!

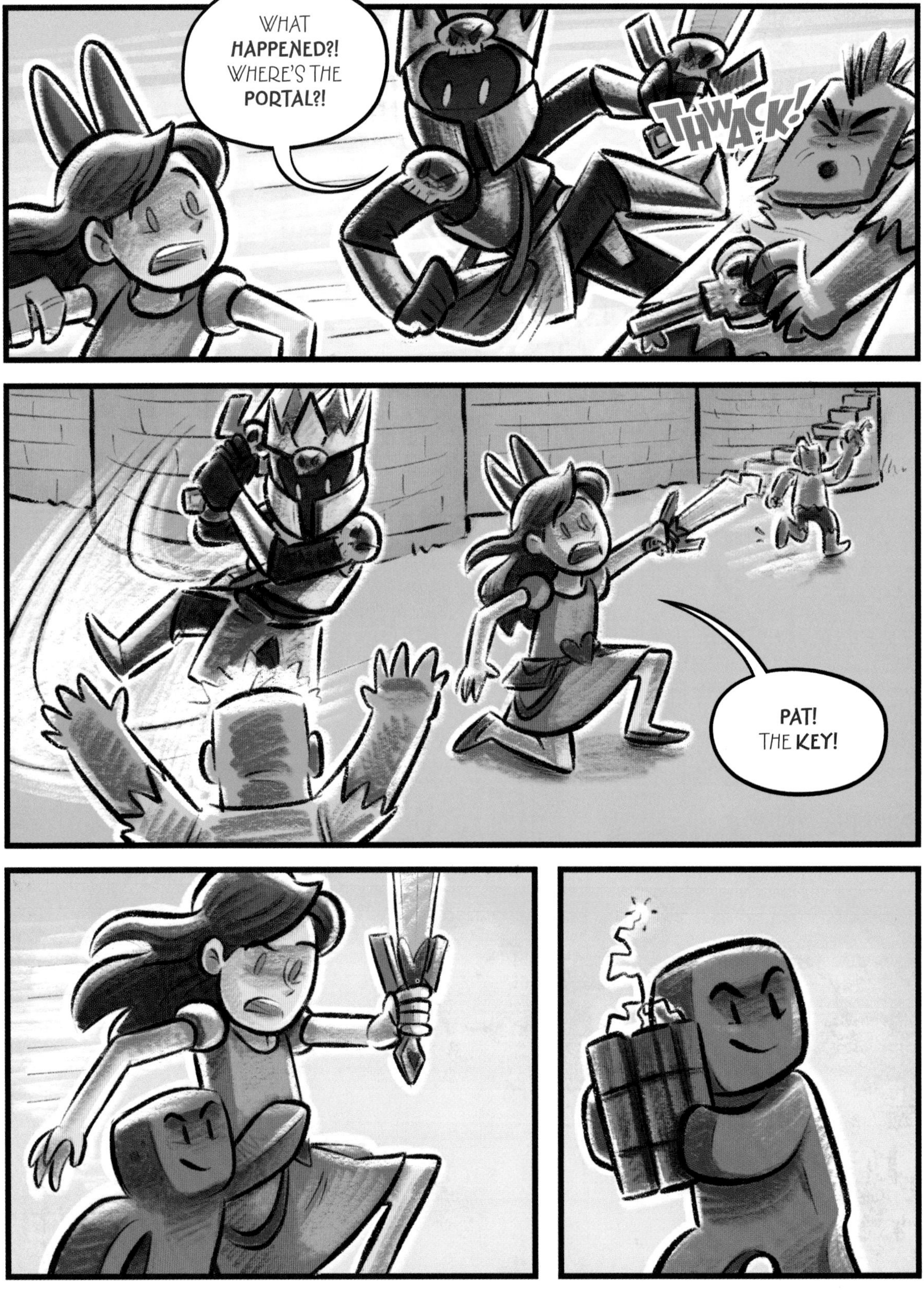
WHAT HAPPENED?! WHERE'S THE PORTAL?!
THWACK!
PAT! THE KEY!

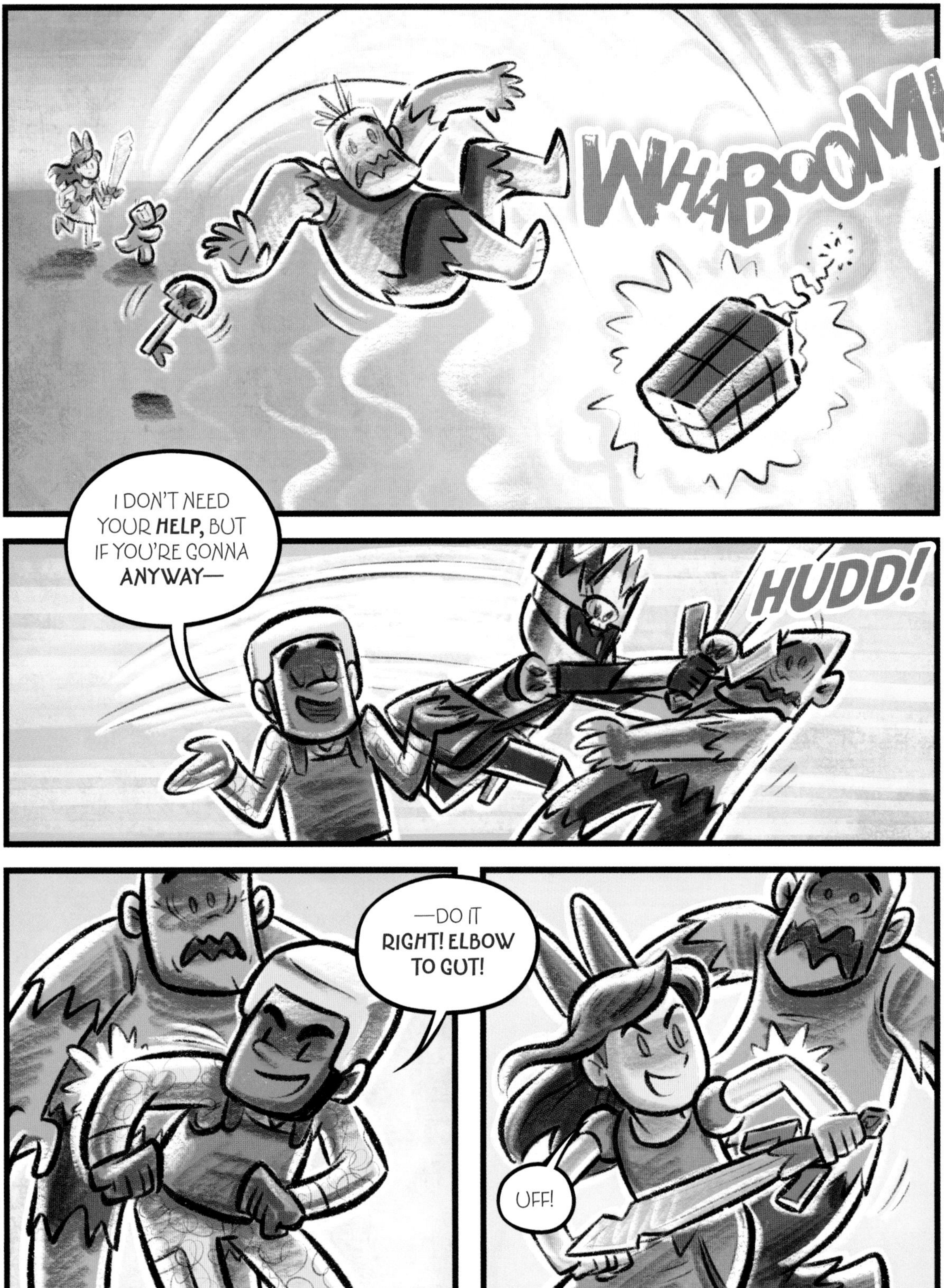
WHABOOM!
I DON'T NEED YOUR HELP, BUT IF YOU'RE GONNA ANYWAY—
HUDD!
—DO IT RIGHT! ELBOW TO GUT!
UFF!

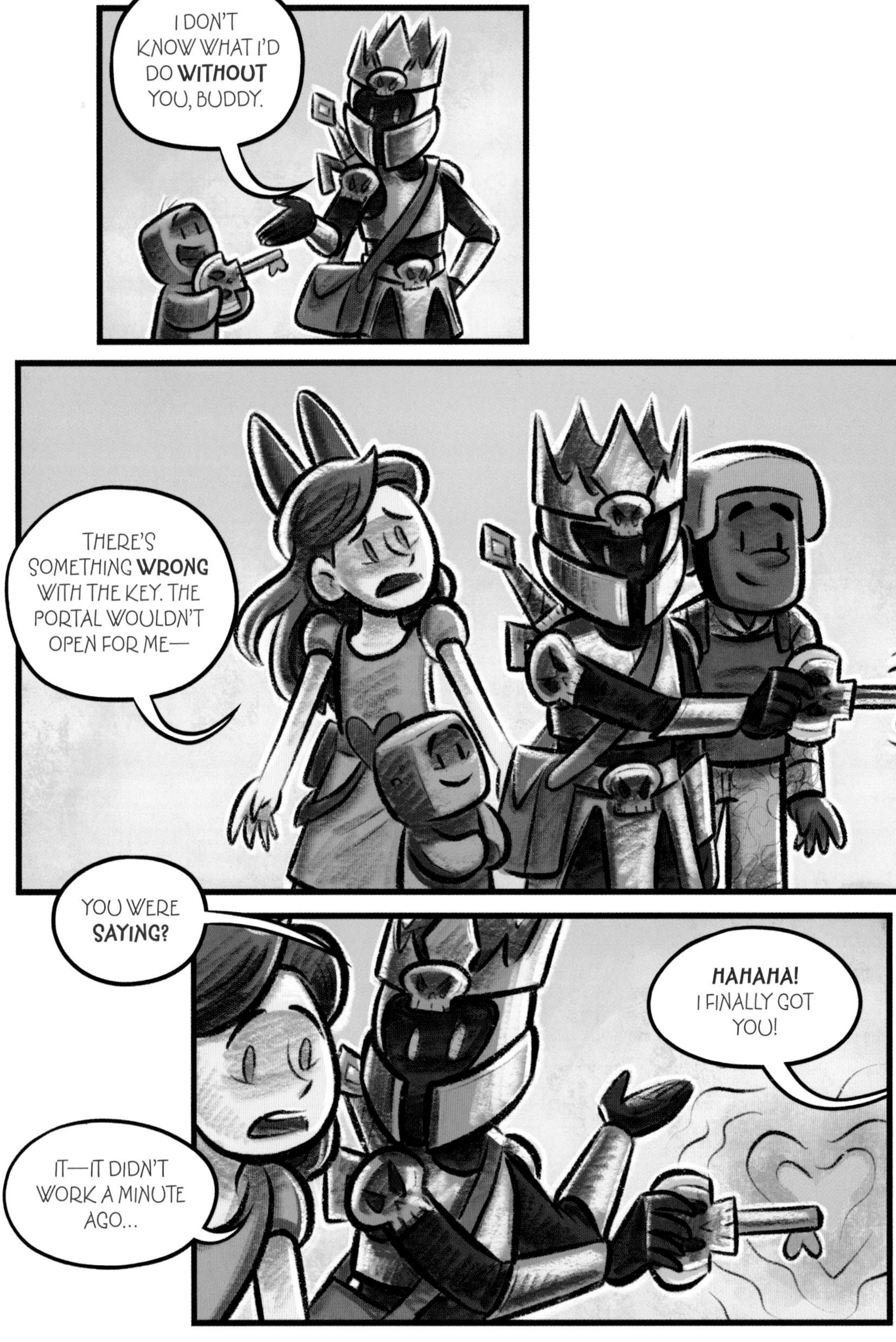
I DON'T KNOW WHAT I'D DO **WITHOUT** YOU, BUDDY.
THERE'S SOMETHING **WRONG** WITH THE KEY. THE PORTAL WOULDN'T OPEN FOR ME—
YOU WERE **SAYING?**
HAHAHA! I FINALLY GOT YOU!
IT—IT DIDN'T WORK A MINUTE AGO...

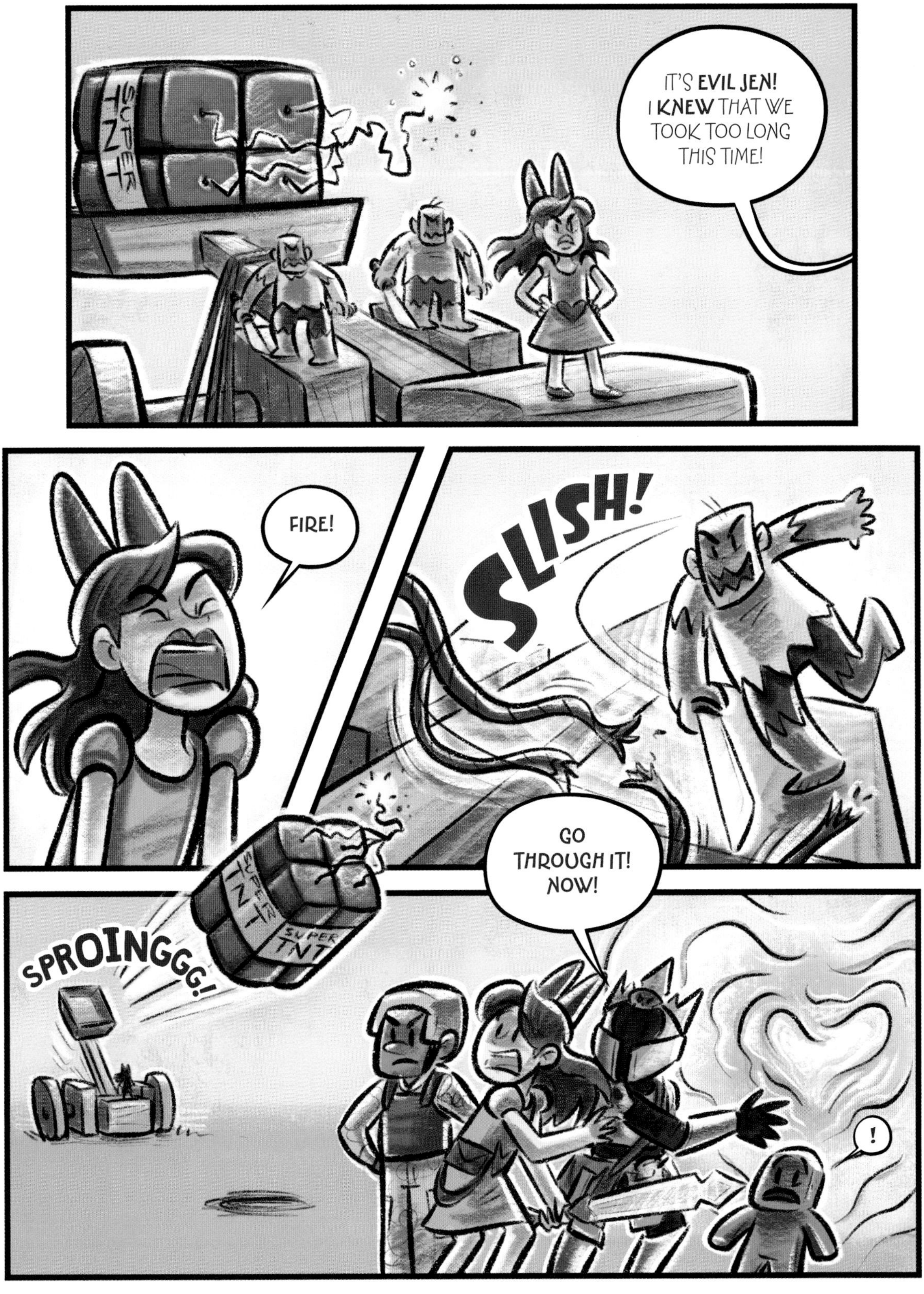

SUPER TNT
SUPER TNT
IT'S EVIL JEN! I KNEW THAT WE TOOK TOO LONG THIS TIME!
FIRE!
SLISH!
SUPER TNT
SUPER TNT
GO THROUGH IT! NOW!
SPROINGGG!
!

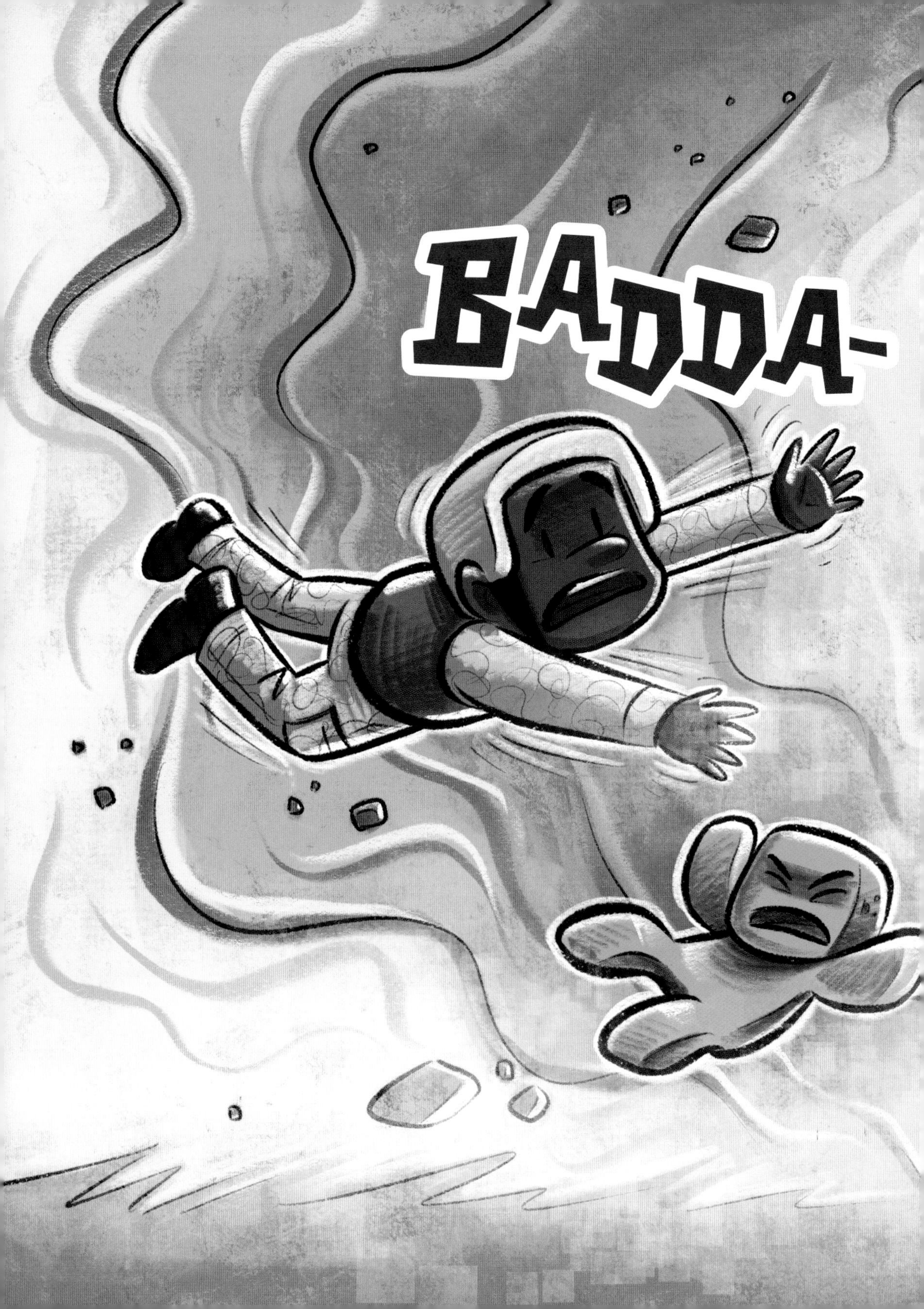
BADDA-

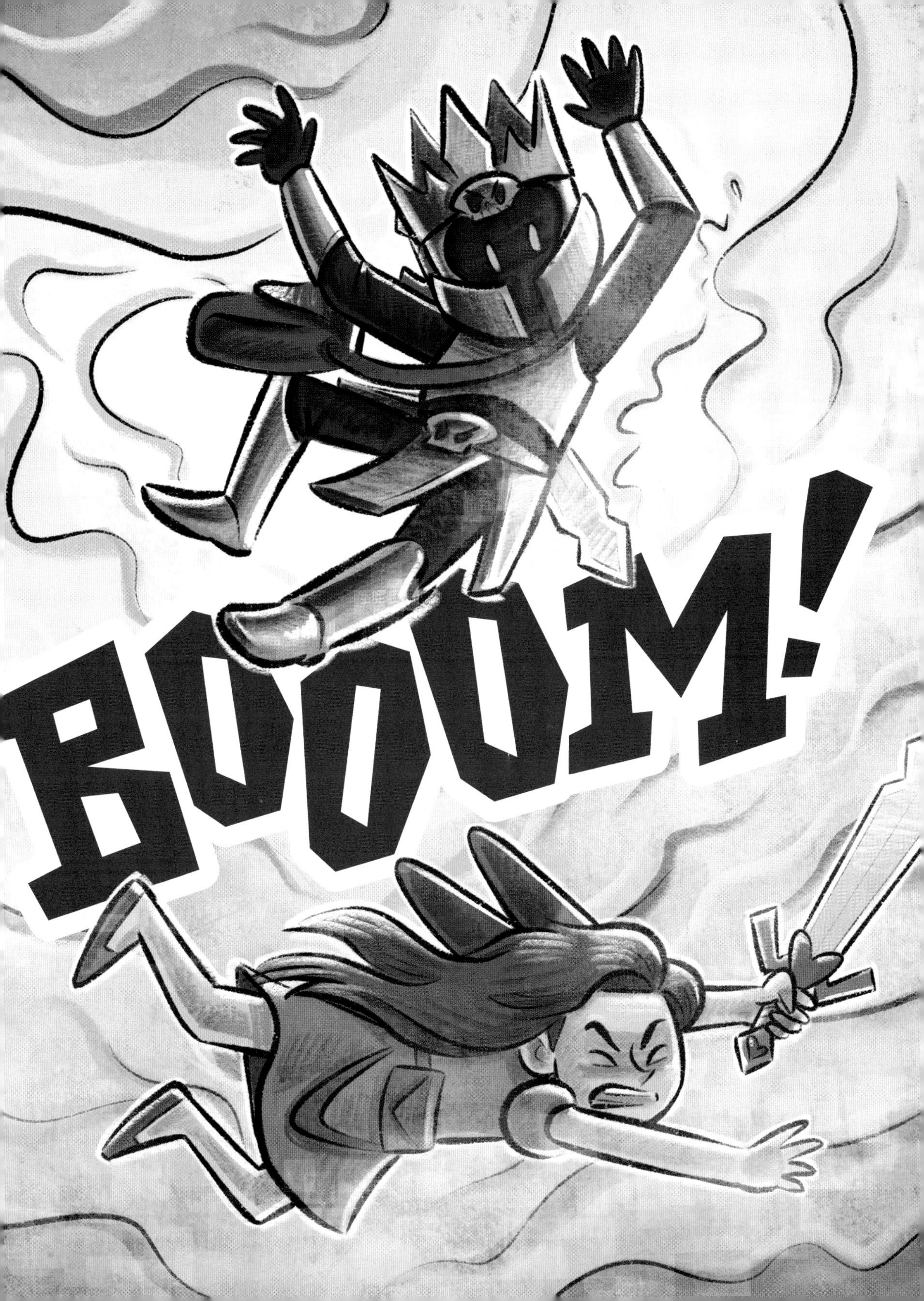
BOOOM!

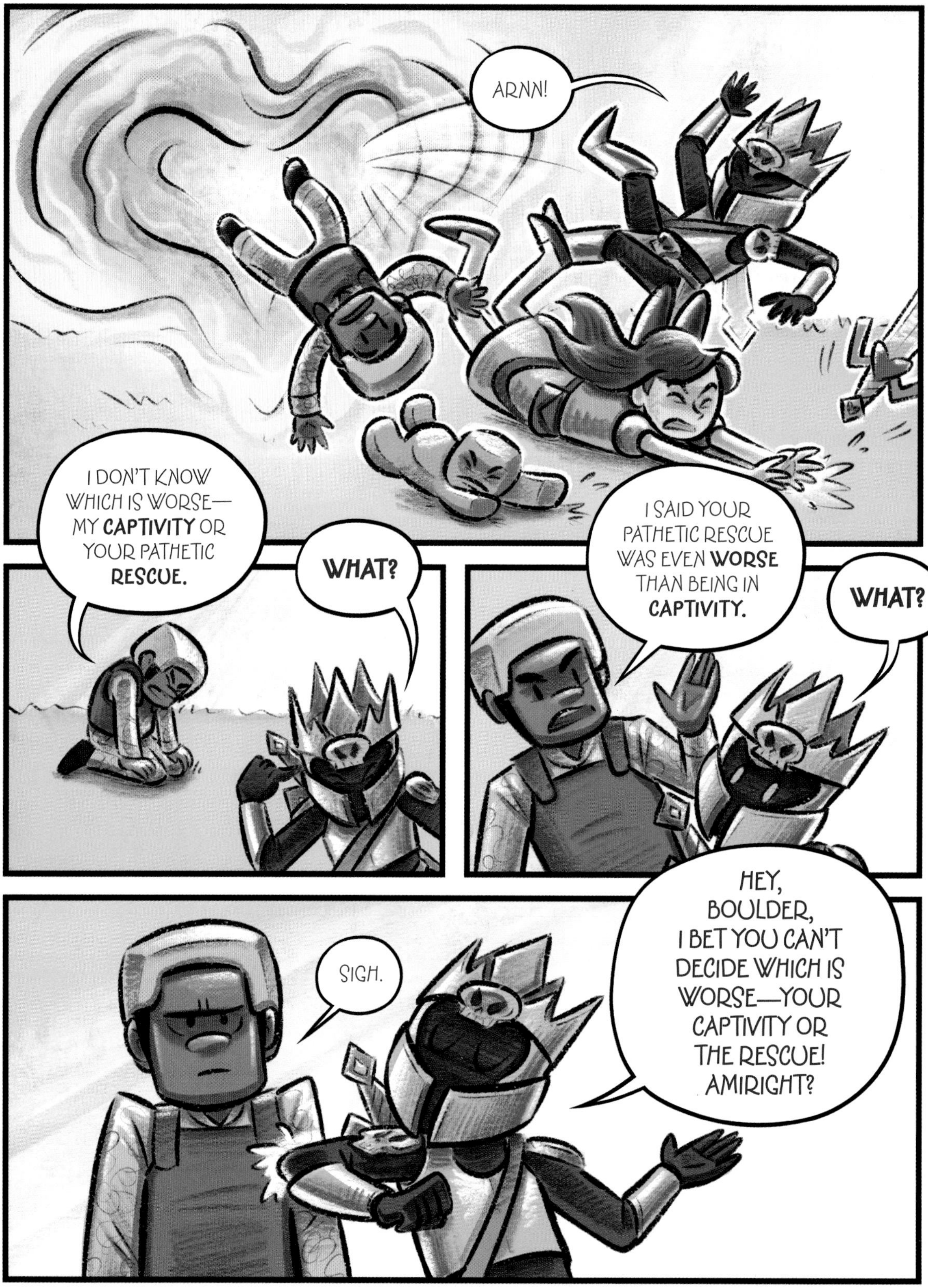
ARNN!
I DON'T KNOW WHICH IS WORSE— MY **CAPTIVITY** OR YOUR PATHETIC **RESCUE.**
WHAT?
I SAID YOUR PATHETIC RESCUE WAS EVEN **WORSE** THAN BEING IN **CAPTIVITY.**
WHAT?
SIGH.
HEY, BOULDER, I BET YOU CAN'T DECIDE WHICH IS WORSE—YOUR CAPTIVITY OR THE RESCUE! AMIRIGHT?

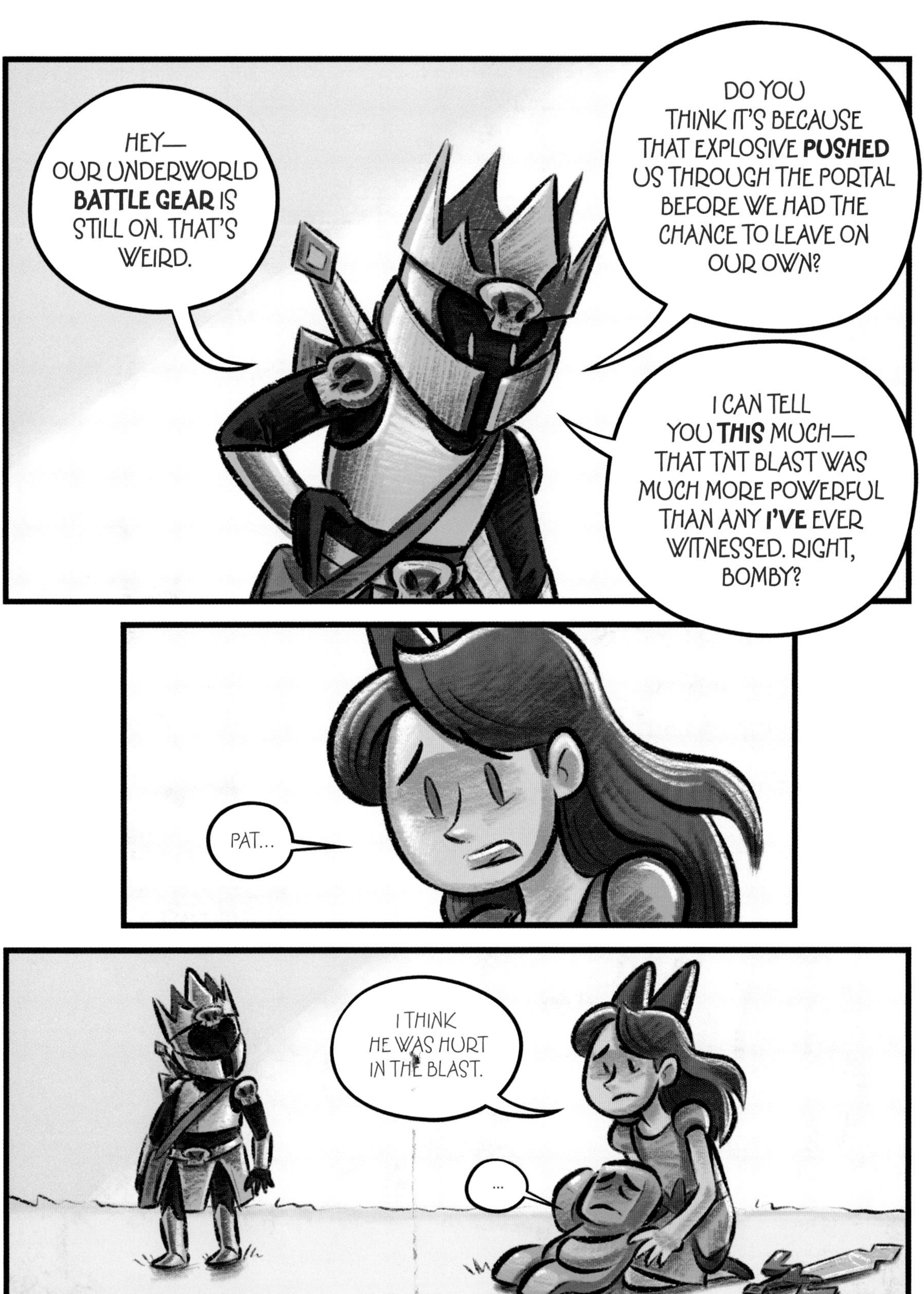
HEY— OUR UNDERWORLD **BATTLE GEAR** IS STILL ON. THAT'S WEIRD.
DO YOU THINK IT'S BECAUSE THAT EXPLOSIVE **PUSHED** US THROUGH THE PORTAL BEFORE WE HAD THE CHANCE TO LEAVE ON OUR OWN?
I CAN TELL YOU **THIS** MUCH— THAT TNT BLAST WAS MUCH MORE POWERFUL THAN ANY **I'VE** EVER WITNESSED. RIGHT, BOMBY?
PAT...
I THINK HE WAS HURT IN THE BLAST.
...

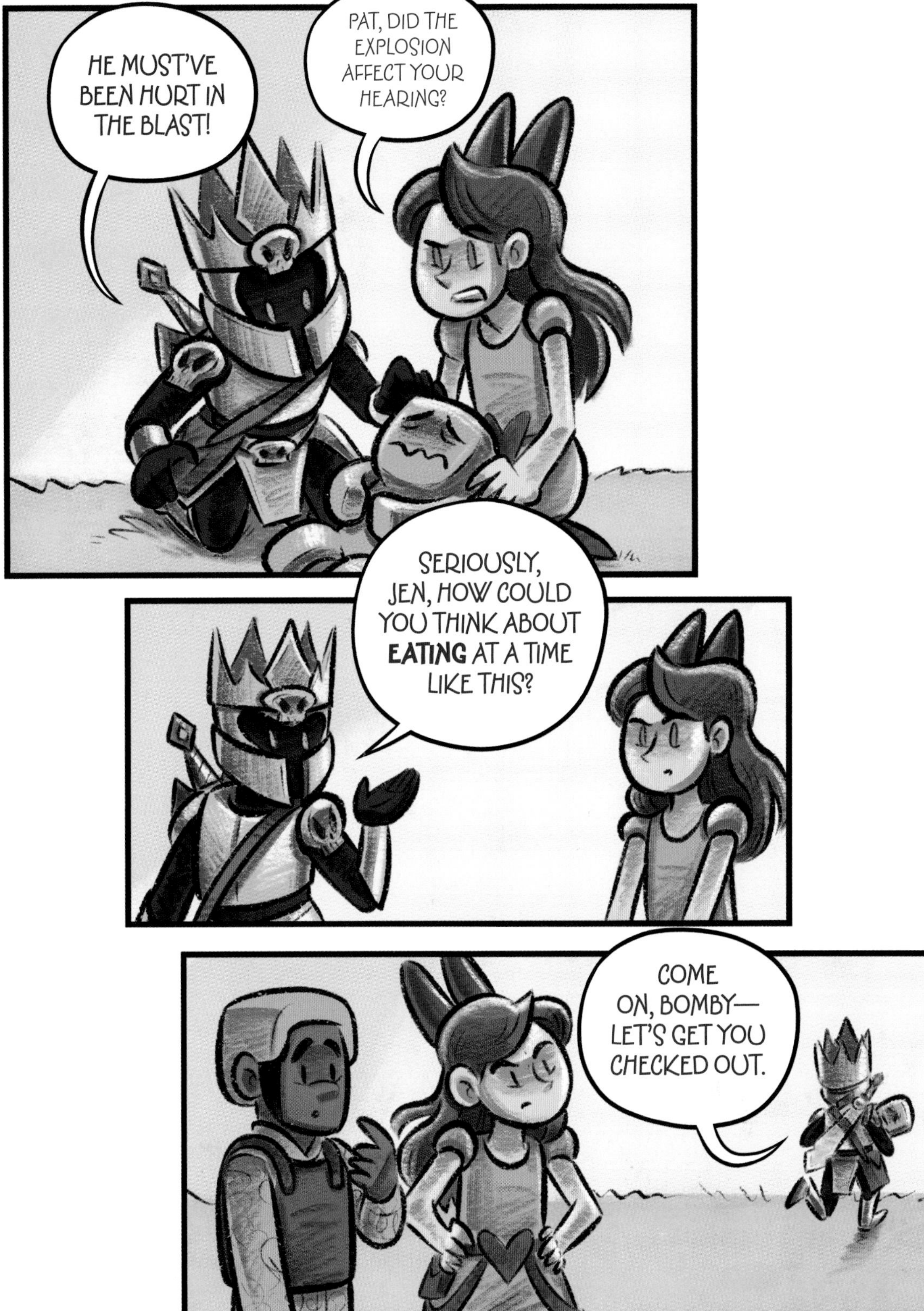
HE MUST'VE BEEN HURT IN THE BLAST!
PAT, DID THE EXPLOSION AFFECT YOUR HEARING?
SERIOUSLY, JEN, HOW COULD YOU THINK ABOUT **EATING** AT A TIME LIKE THIS?
COME ON, BOMBY— LET'S GET YOU CHECKED OUT.

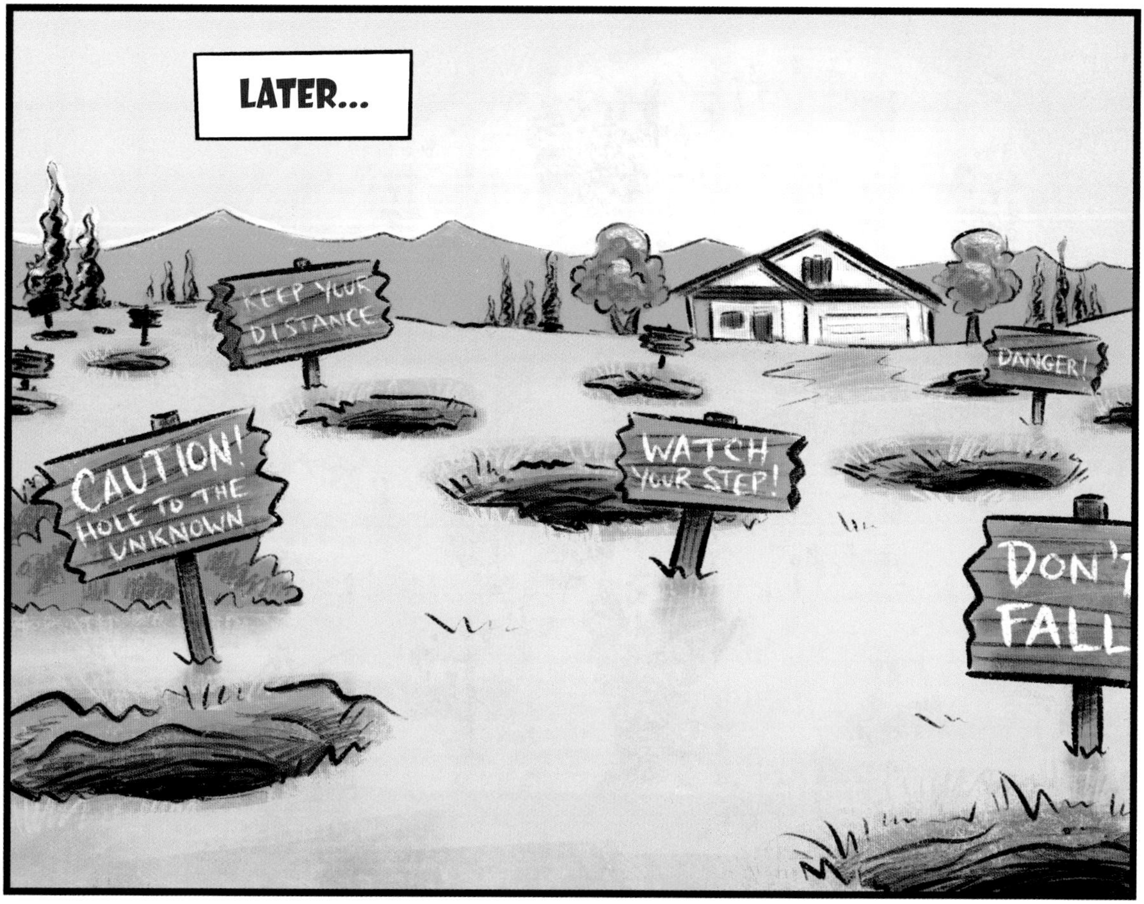
LATER...
KEEP YOUR DISTANCE
DANGER!
CAUTION! HOLE TO THE UNKNOWN
WATCH YOUR STEP!

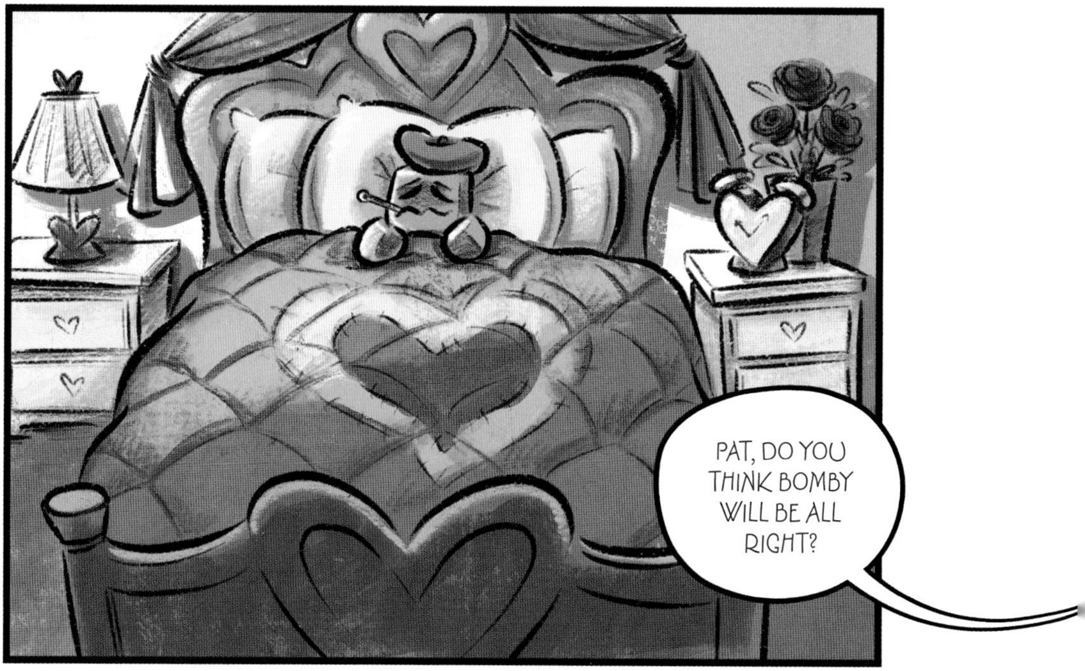
PAT, DO YOU THINK BOMBY WILL BE ALL RIGHT?

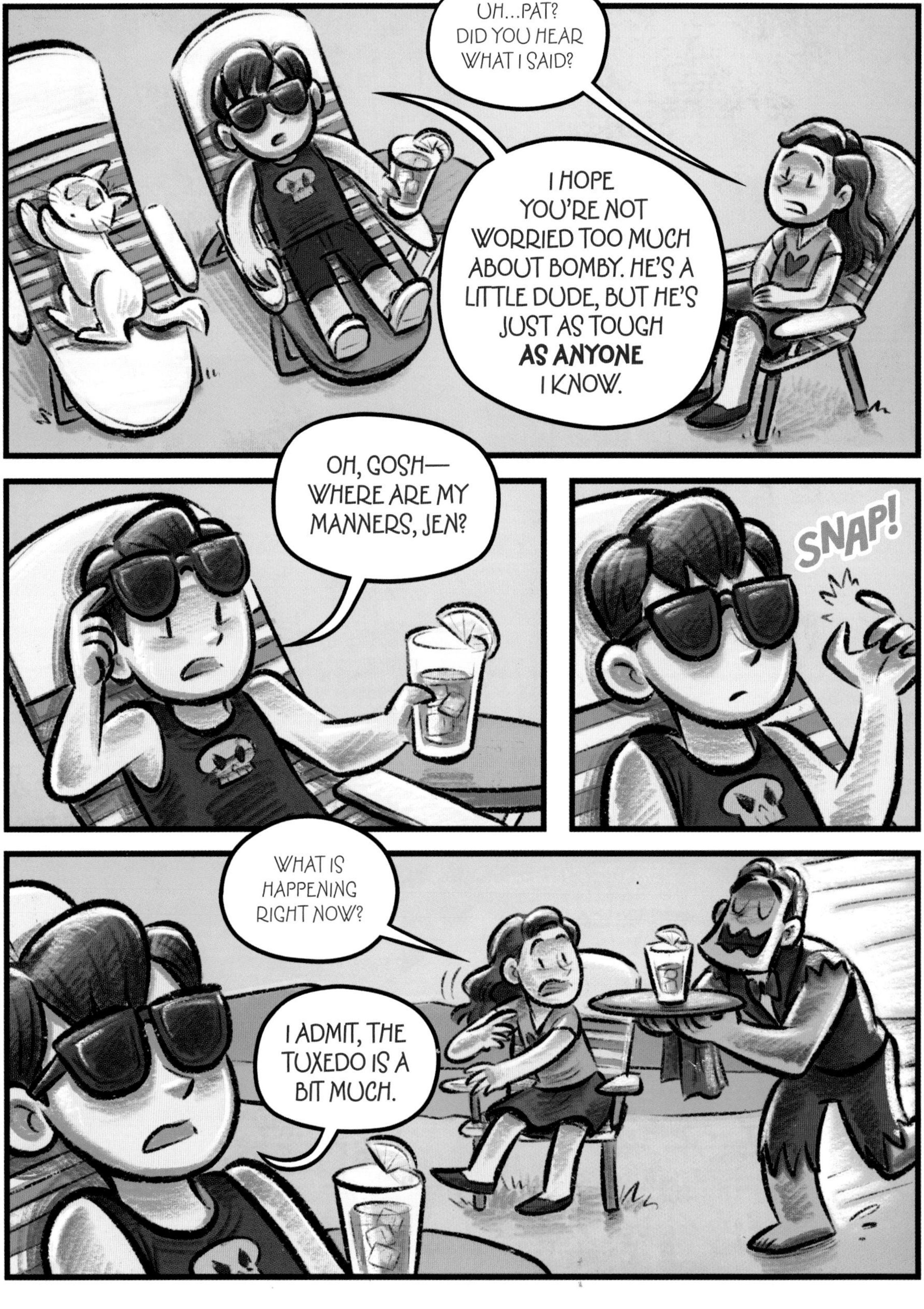
UH...PAT? DID YOU HEAR WHAT I SAID?
I HOPE YOU'RE NOT WORRIED TOO MUCH ABOUT BOMBY. HE'S A LITTLE DUDE, BUT HE'S JUST AS TOUGH **AS ANYONE** I KNOW.
OH, GOSH— WHERE ARE MY MANNERS, JEN?
SNAP!
WHAT IS HAPPENING RIGHT NOW?
I ADMIT, THE TUXEDO IS A BIT MUCH.

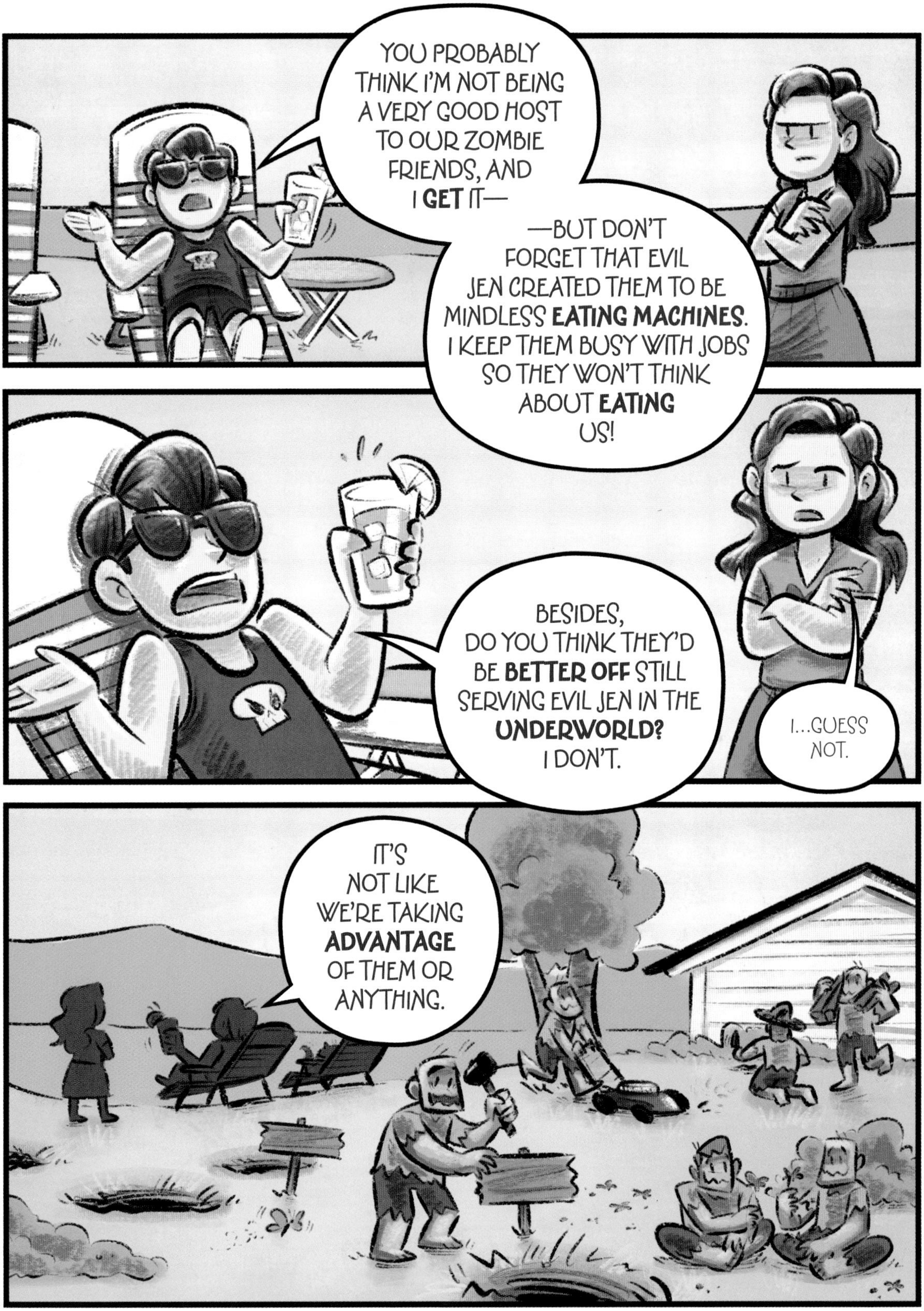
YOU PROBABLY THINK I'M NOT BEING A VERY GOOD HOST TO OUR ZOMBIE FRIENDS, AND I **GET** IT—
—BUT DON'T FORGET THAT EVIL JEN CREATED THEM TO BE MINDLESS **EATING MACHINES**. I KEEP THEM BUSY WITH JOBS SO THEY WON'T THINK ABOUT **EATING** US!
BESIDES, DO YOU THINK THEY'D BE **BETTER OFF** STILL SERVING EVIL JEN IN THE **UNDERWORLD?** I DON'T.
I...GUESS NOT.
IT'S NOT LIKE WE'RE TAKING **ADVANTAGE** OF THEM OR ANYTHING.

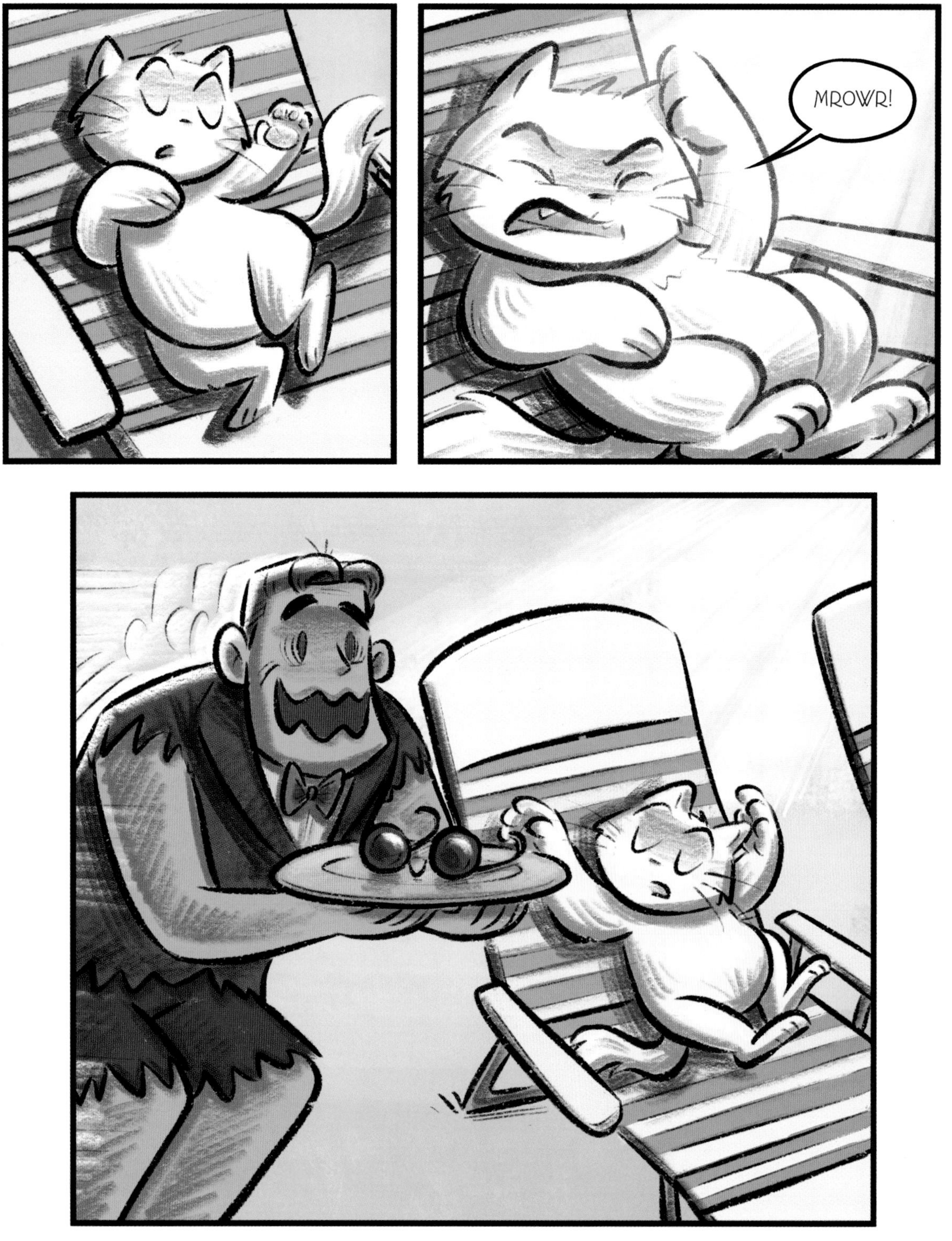
MROWR!

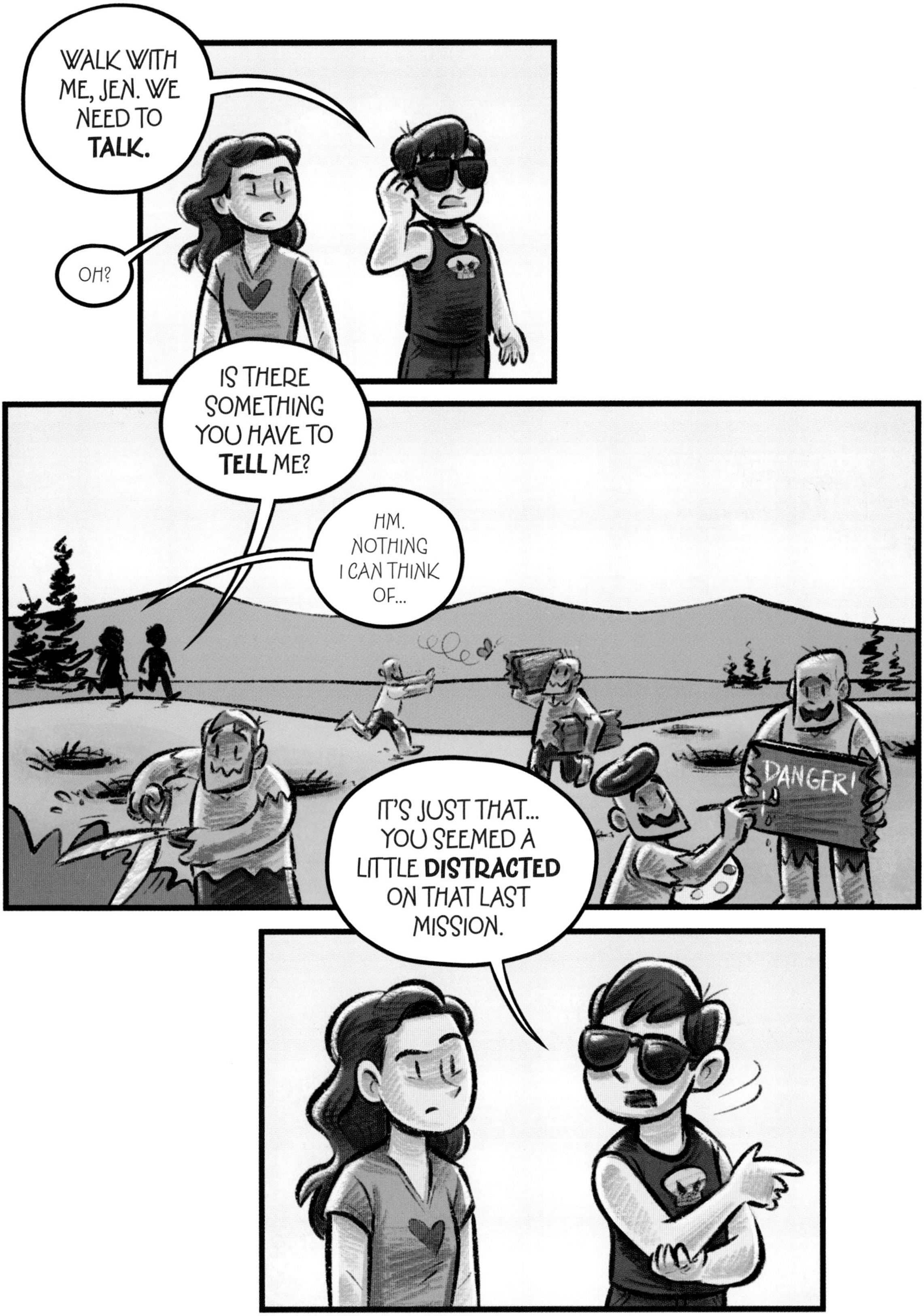
WALK WITH ME, JEN. WE NEED TO **TALK.**
OH?
IS THERE SOMETHING YOU HAVE TO **TELL** ME?
HM. NOTHING I CAN THINK OF...
DANGER!
IT'S JUST THAT... YOU SEEMED A LITTLE **DISTRACTED** ON THAT LAST MISSION.

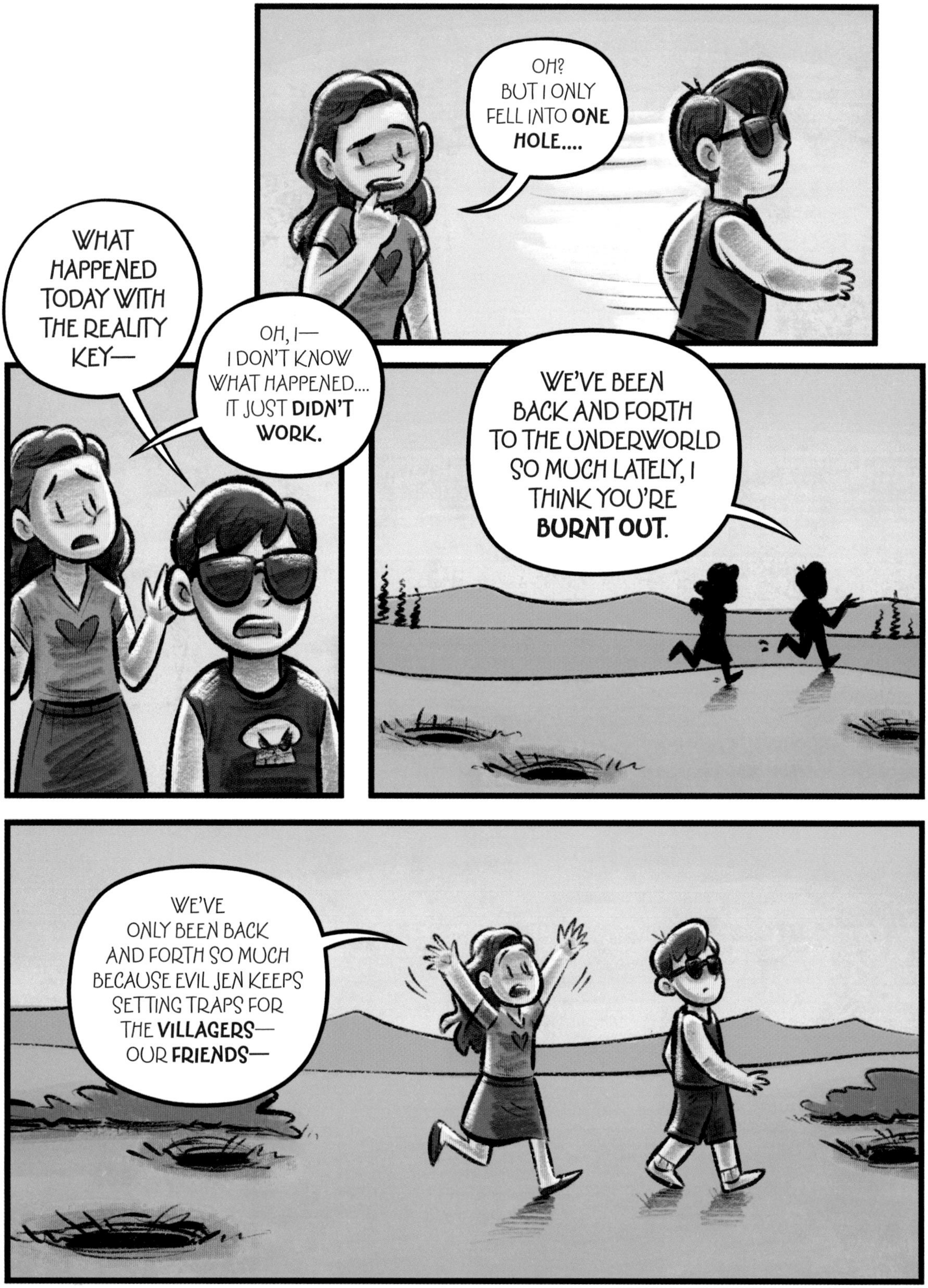

OH? BUT I ONLY FELL INTO **ONE HOLE....**
WHAT HAPPENED TODAY WITH THE REALITY KEY—
OH, I— I DON'T KNOW WHAT HAPPENED.... IT JUST **DIDN'T WORK.**
WE'VE BEEN BACK AND FORTH TO THE UNDERWORLD SO MUCH LATELY, I THINK YOU'RE **BURNT OUT.**
WE'VE ONLY BEEN BACK AND FORTH SO MUCH BECAUSE EVIL JEN KEEPS SETTING TRAPS FOR THE **VILLAGERS**— OUR **FRIENDS**—

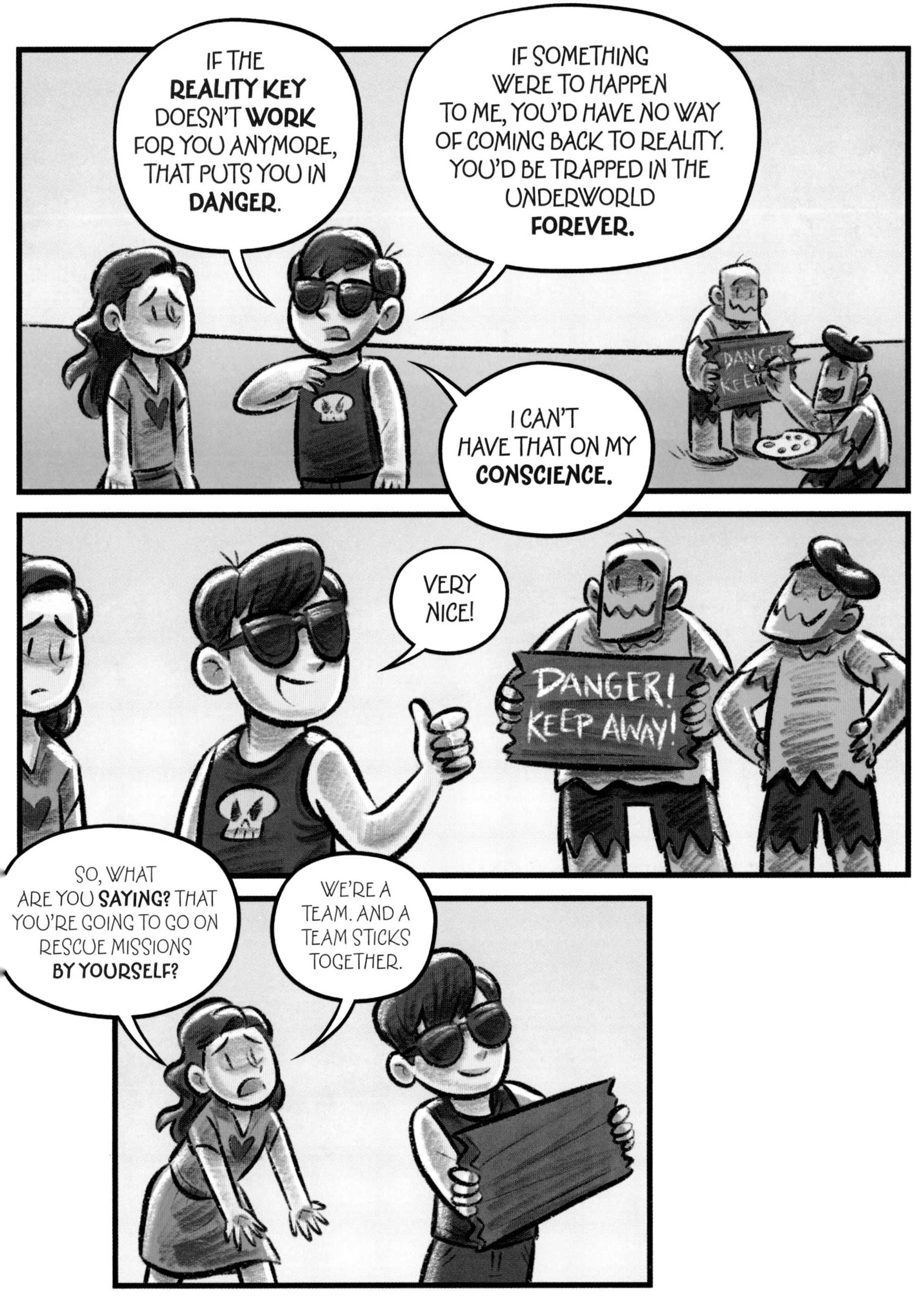
IF THE **REALITY KEY** DOESN'T **WORK** FOR YOU ANYMORE, THAT PUTS YOU IN **DANGER**.
IF SOMETHING WERE TO HAPPEN TO ME, YOU'D HAVE NO WAY OF COMING BACK TO REALITY. YOU'D BE TRAPPED IN THE UNDERWORLD **FOREVER.**
I CAN'T HAVE THAT ON MY **CONSCIENCE.**
VERY NICE!
DANGER! KEEP AWAY!
SO, WHAT ARE YOU **SAYING?** THAT YOU'RE GOING TO GO ON RESCUE MISSIONS **BY YOURSELF?**
WE'RE A TEAM. AND A TEAM STICKS TOGETHER.

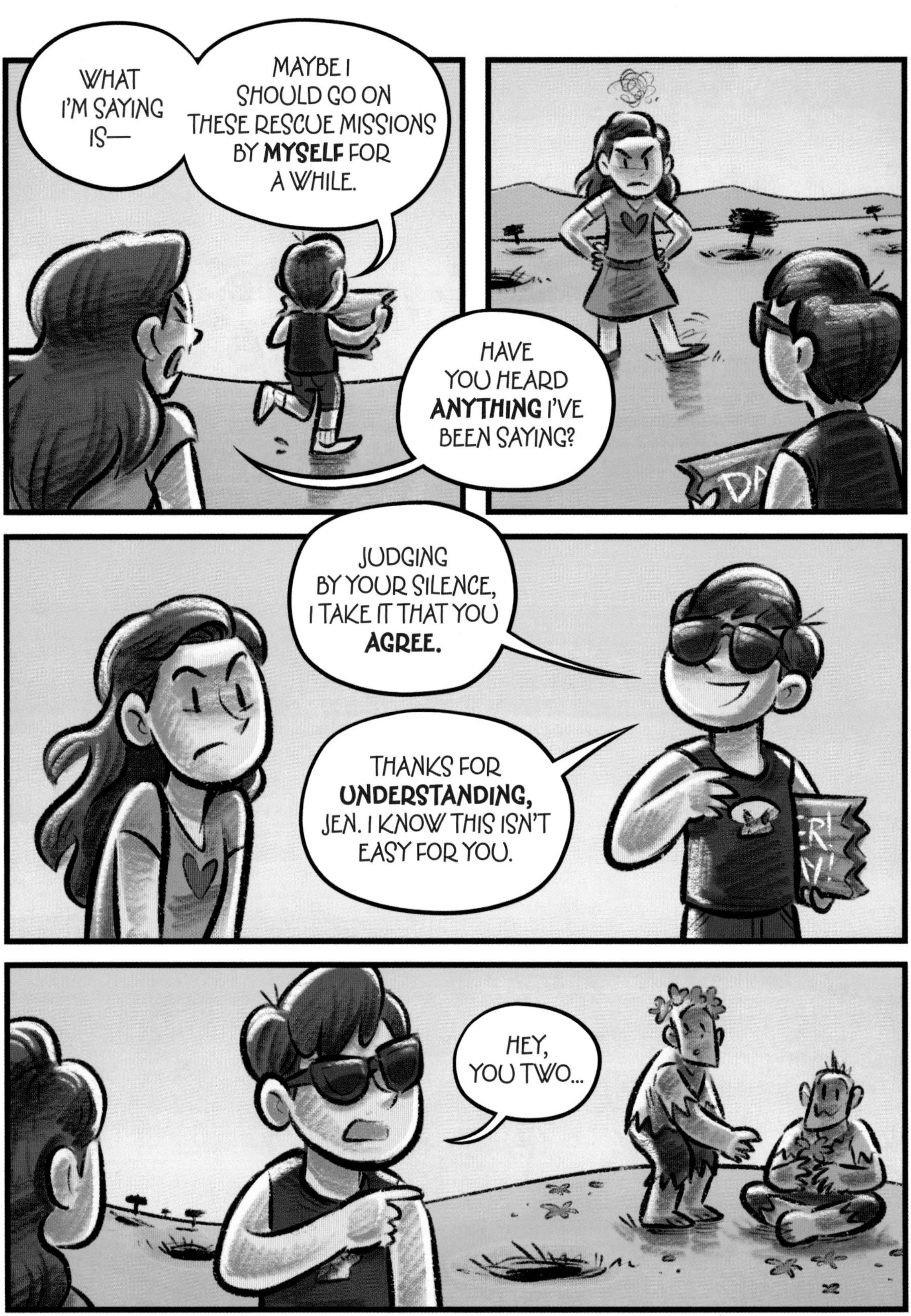
WHAT I'M SAYING IS—
MAYBE I SHOULD GO ON THESE RESCUE MISSIONS BY MYSELF FOR A WHILE.
HAVE YOU HEARD ANYTHING I'VE BEEN SAYING?
JUDGING BY YOUR SILENCE, I TAKE IT THAT YOU AGREE.
THANKS FOR UNDERSTANDING, JEN. I KNOW THIS ISN'T EASY FOR YOU.
HEY, YOU TWO...

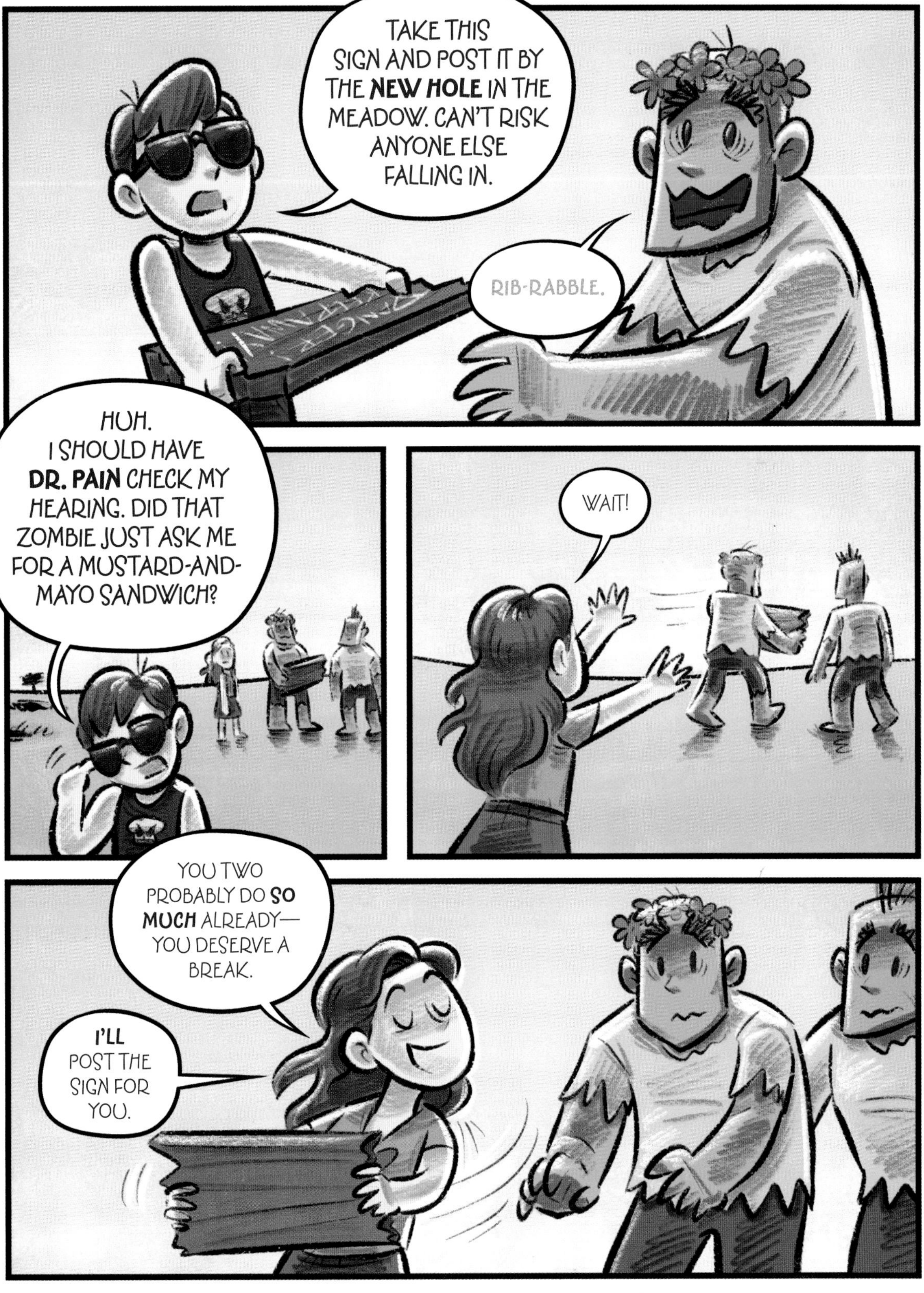
TAKE THIS SIGN AND POST IT BY THE **NEW HOLE** IN THE MEADOW. CAN'T RISK ANYONE ELSE FALLING IN.
RIB-RABBLE.
HUH. I SHOULD HAVE **DR. PAIN** CHECK MY HEARING. DID THAT ZOMBIE JUST ASK ME FOR A MUSTARD-AND-MAYO SANDWICH?
WAIT!
YOU TWO PROBABLY DO **SO MUCH** ALREADY—YOU DESERVE A BREAK.
I'LL POST THE SIGN FOR YOU.

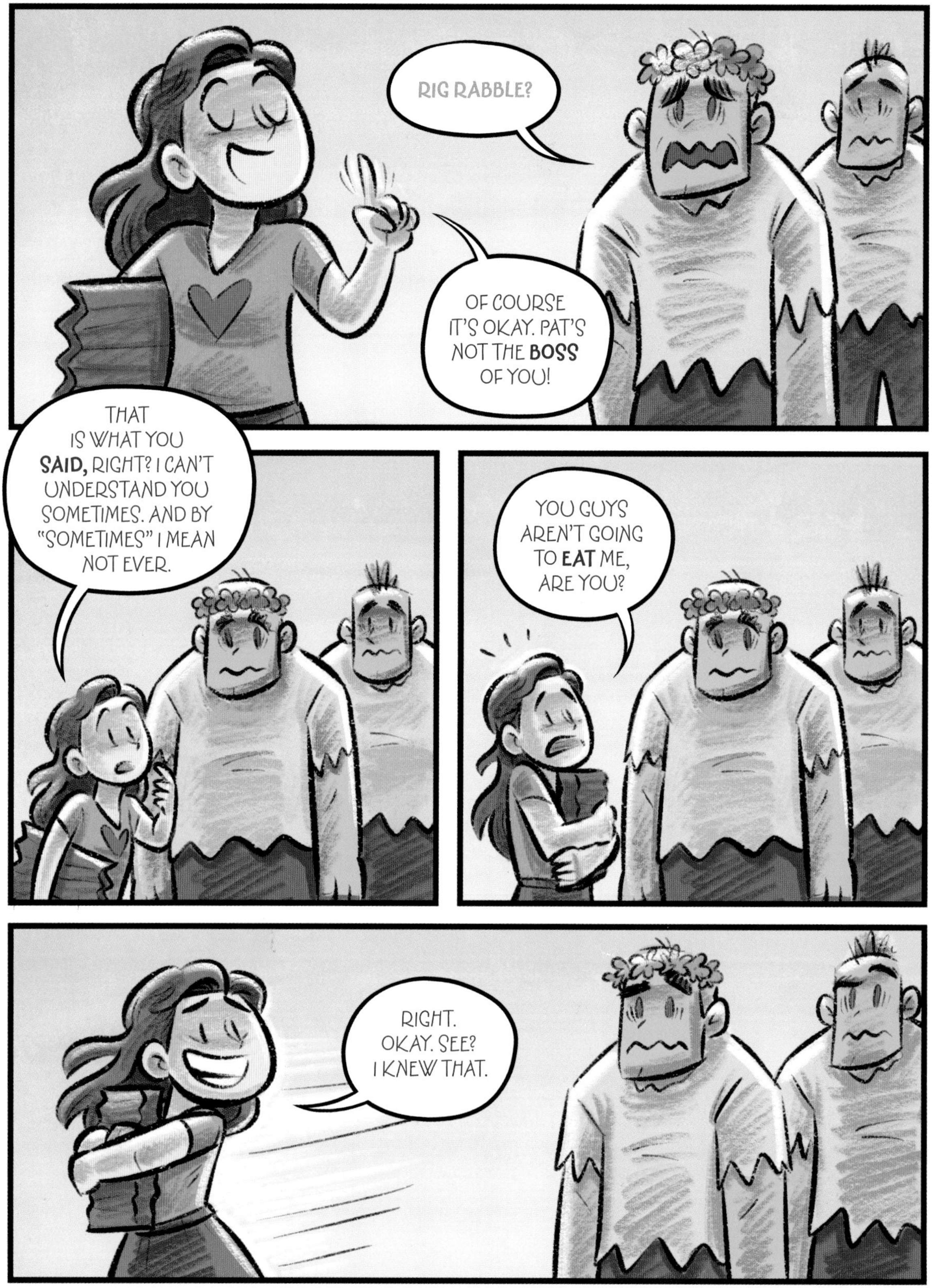
RIG RABBLE?
OF COURSE IT'S OKAY. PAT'S NOT THE **BOSS** OF YOU!
THAT IS WHAT YOU **SAID,** RIGHT? I CAN'T UNDERSTAND YOU SOMETIMES. AND BY "SOMETIMES" I MEAN NOT EVER.
YOU GUYS AREN'T GOING TO **EAT** ME, ARE YOU?
RIGHT. OKAY. SEE? I KNEW THAT.

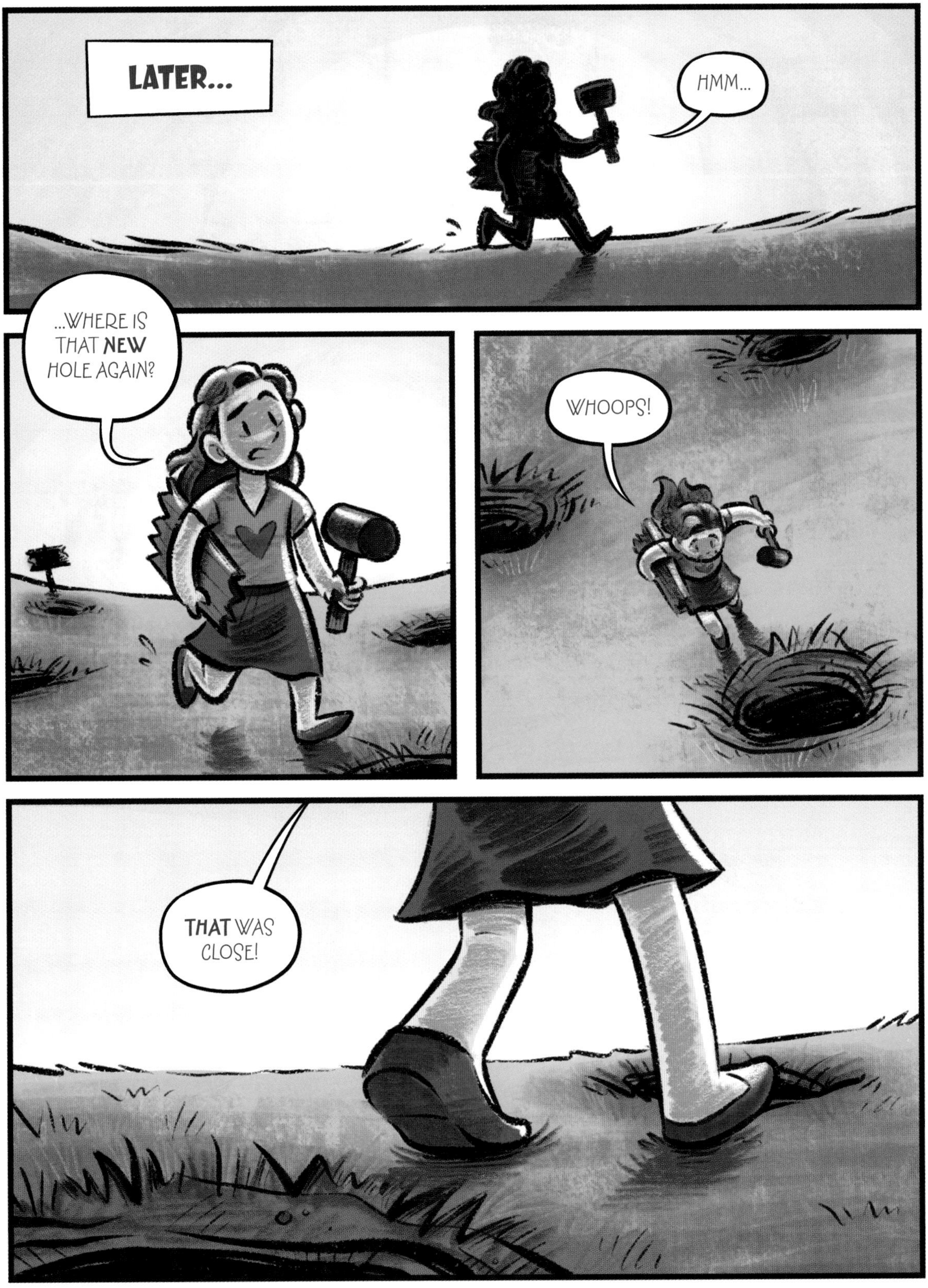
LATER...
HMM...
...WHERE IS THAT **NEW** HOLE AGAIN?
WHOOPS!
THAT WAS CLOSE!

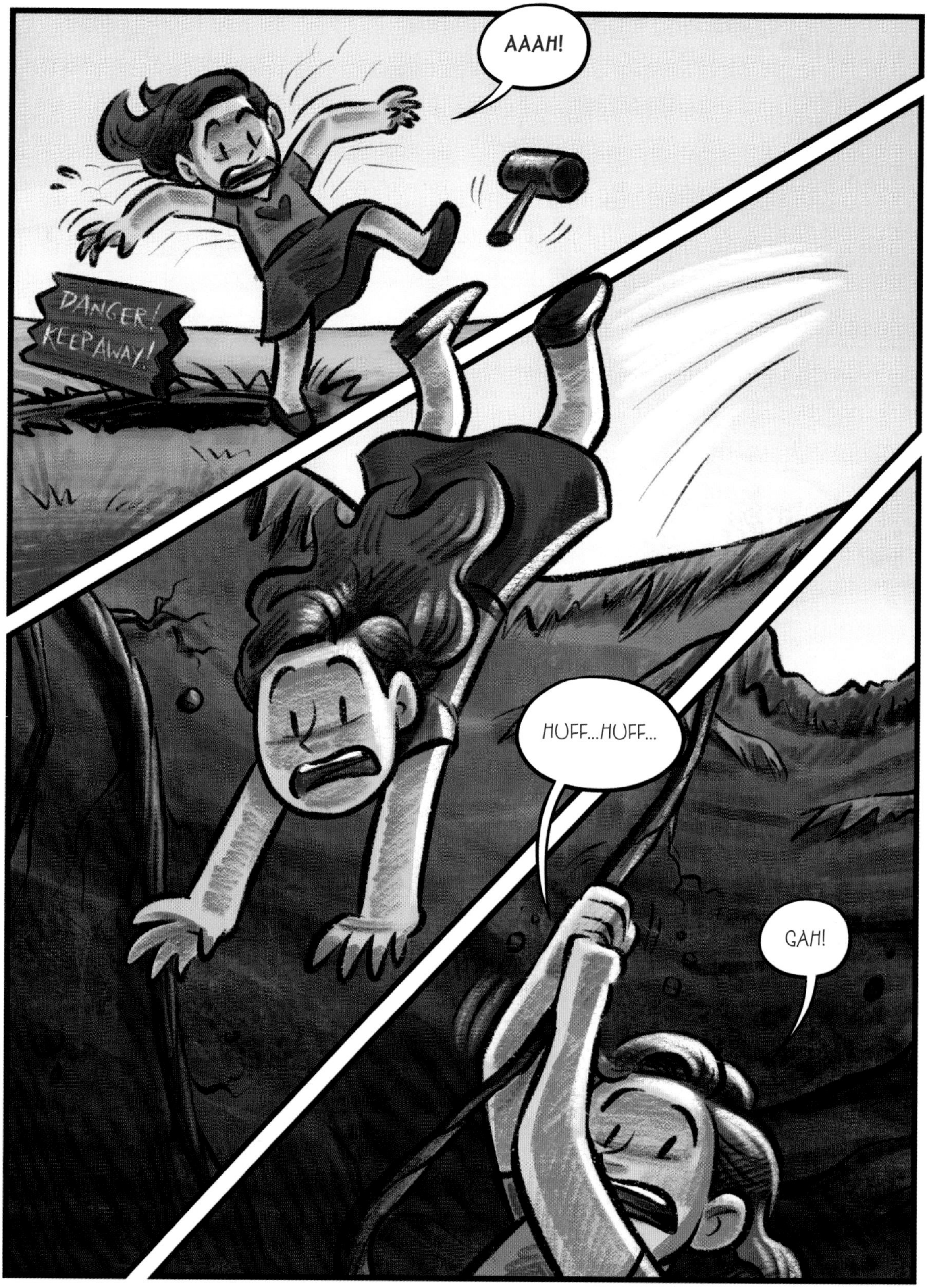
AAAH!
DANGER! KEEP AWAY!
HUFF...HUFF...
GAH!

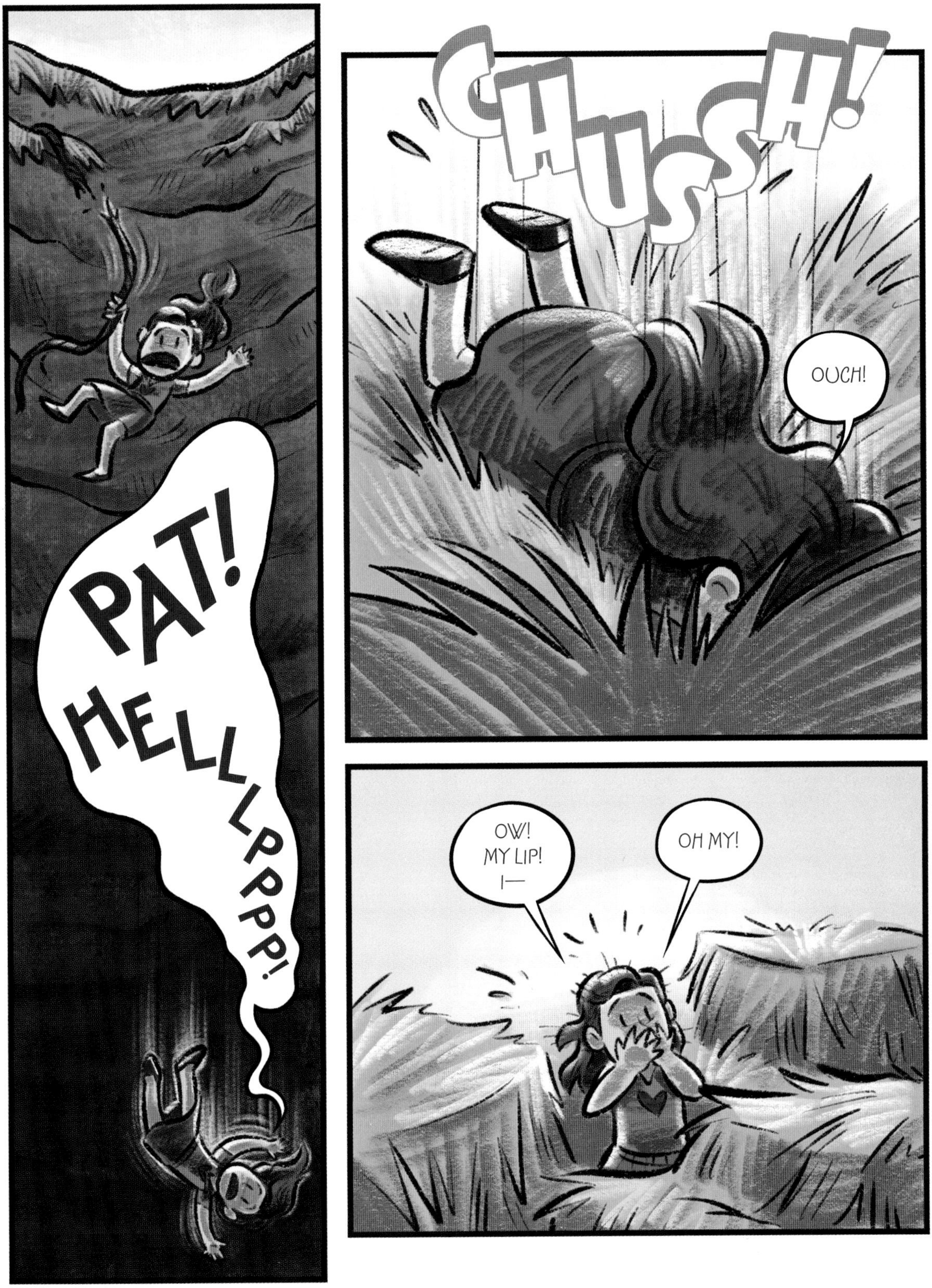
PAT! HELLLPPPP!
CHUSSH!
OUCH!
OW! MY LIP! I—
OH MY!

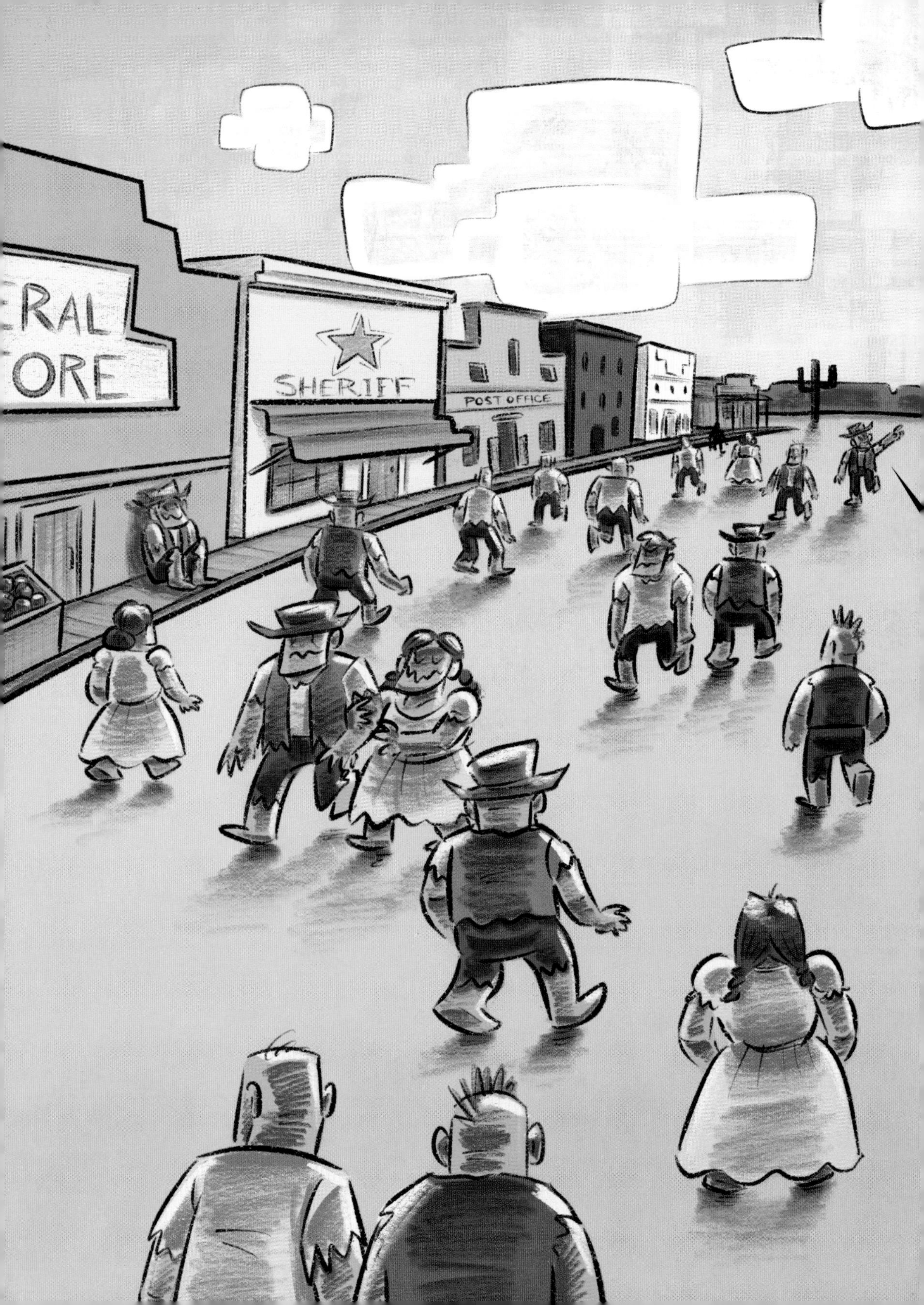

ERAL
ORE
SHERIFF
POST OFFICE

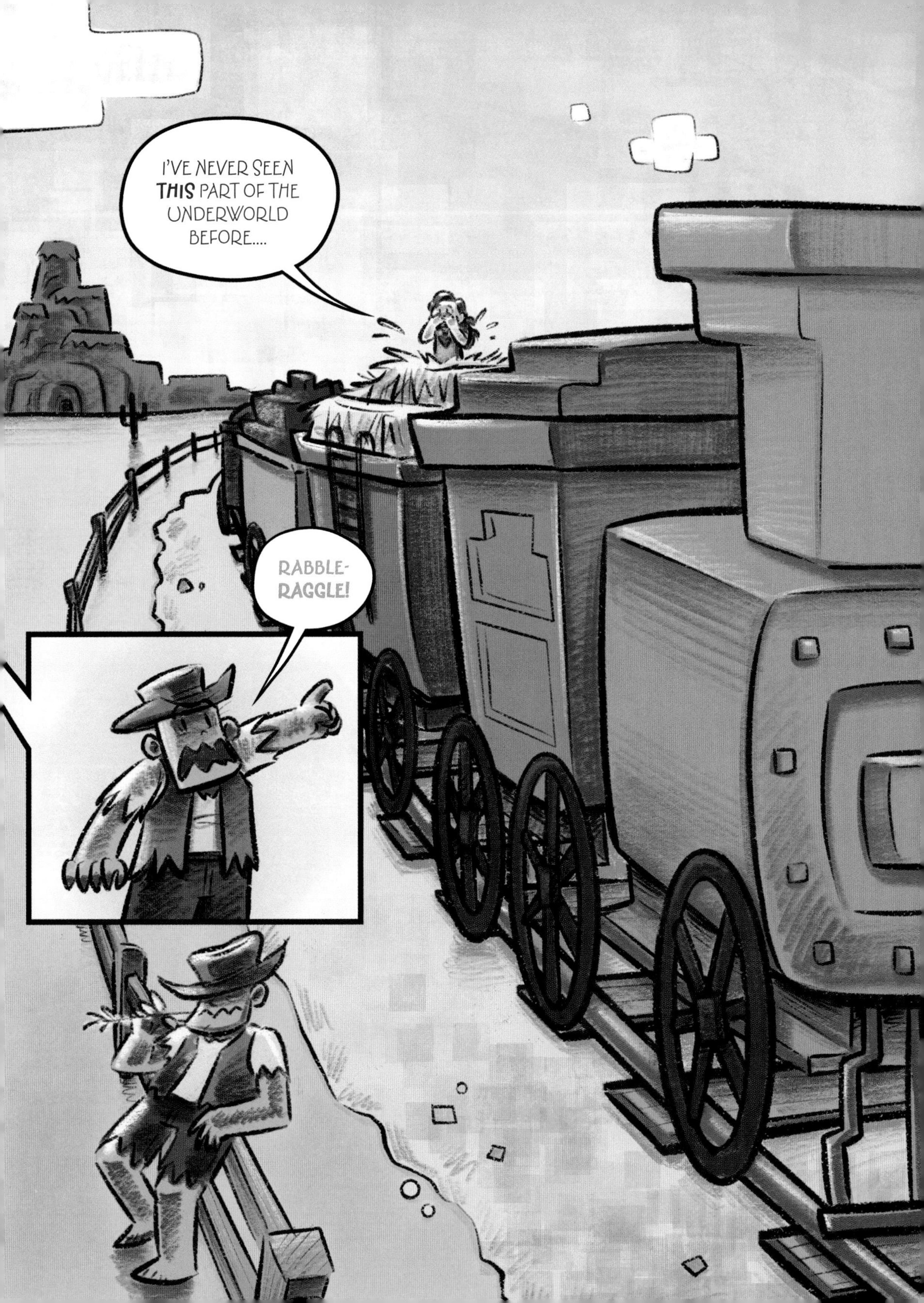
I'VE NEVER SEEN THIS PART OF THE UNDERWORLD BEFORE....
RABBLE-RAGGLE!

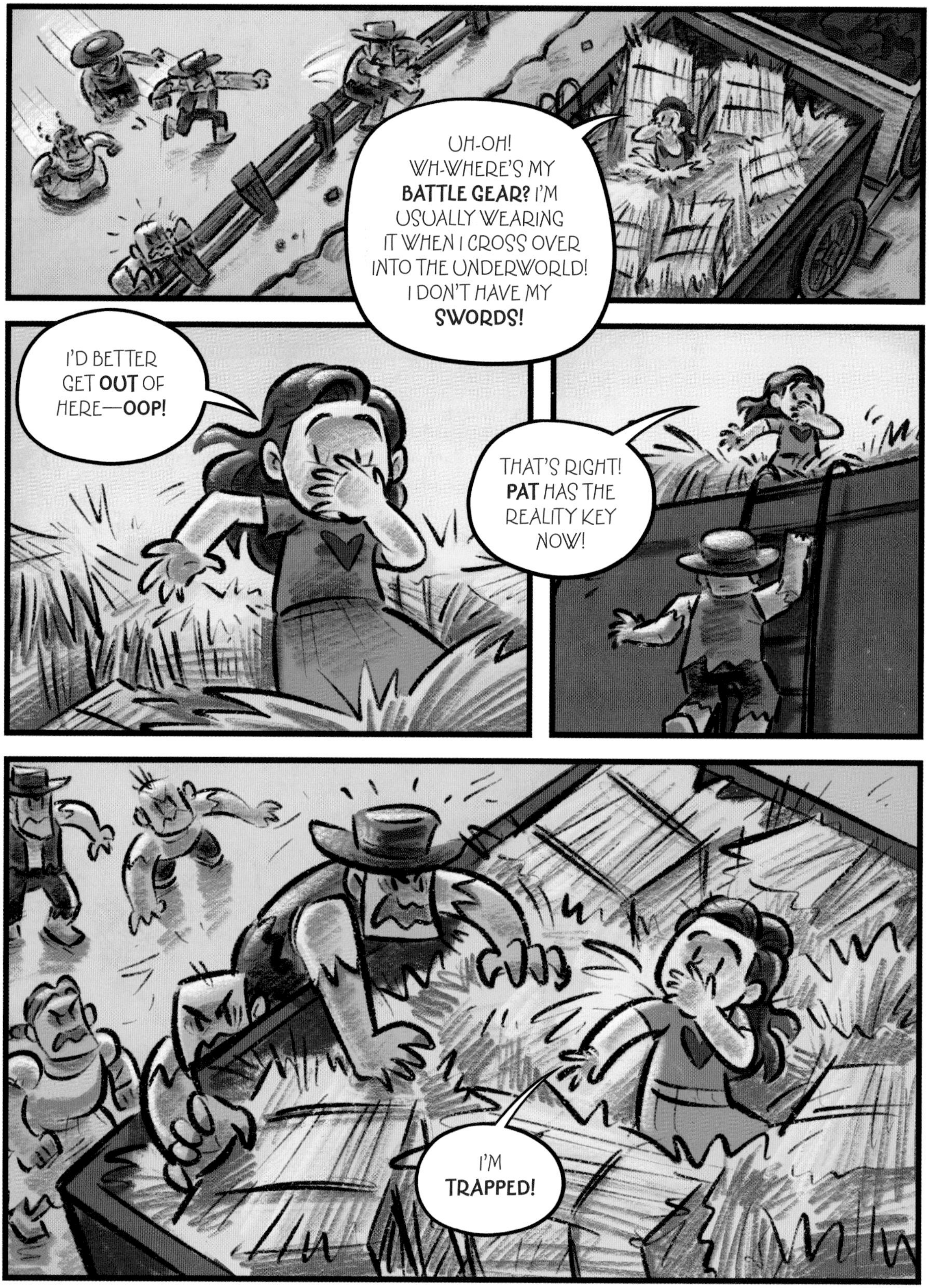
UH-OH! WH-WHERE'S MY **BATTLE GEAR?** I'M USUALLY WEARING IT WHEN I CROSS OVER INTO THE UNDERWORLD! I DON'T HAVE MY **SWORDS!**
I'D BETTER GET **OUT** OF HERE—**OOP!**
THAT'S RIGHT! **PAT** HAS THE REALITY KEY NOW!
I'M **TRAPPED!**

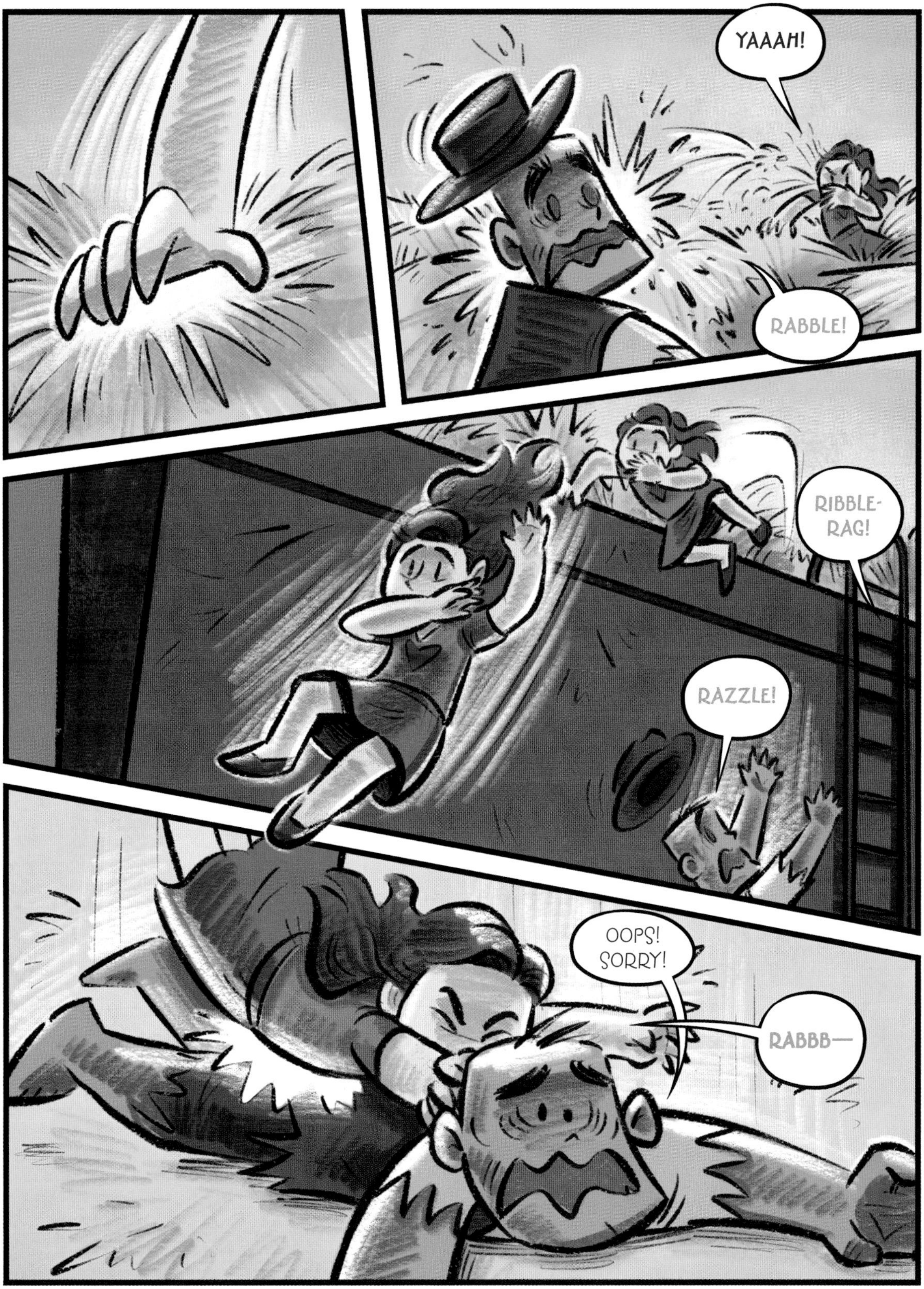
YAAAH!
RABBLE!
RIBBLE-RAG!
RAZZLE!
OOPS! SORRY!
RABBB—

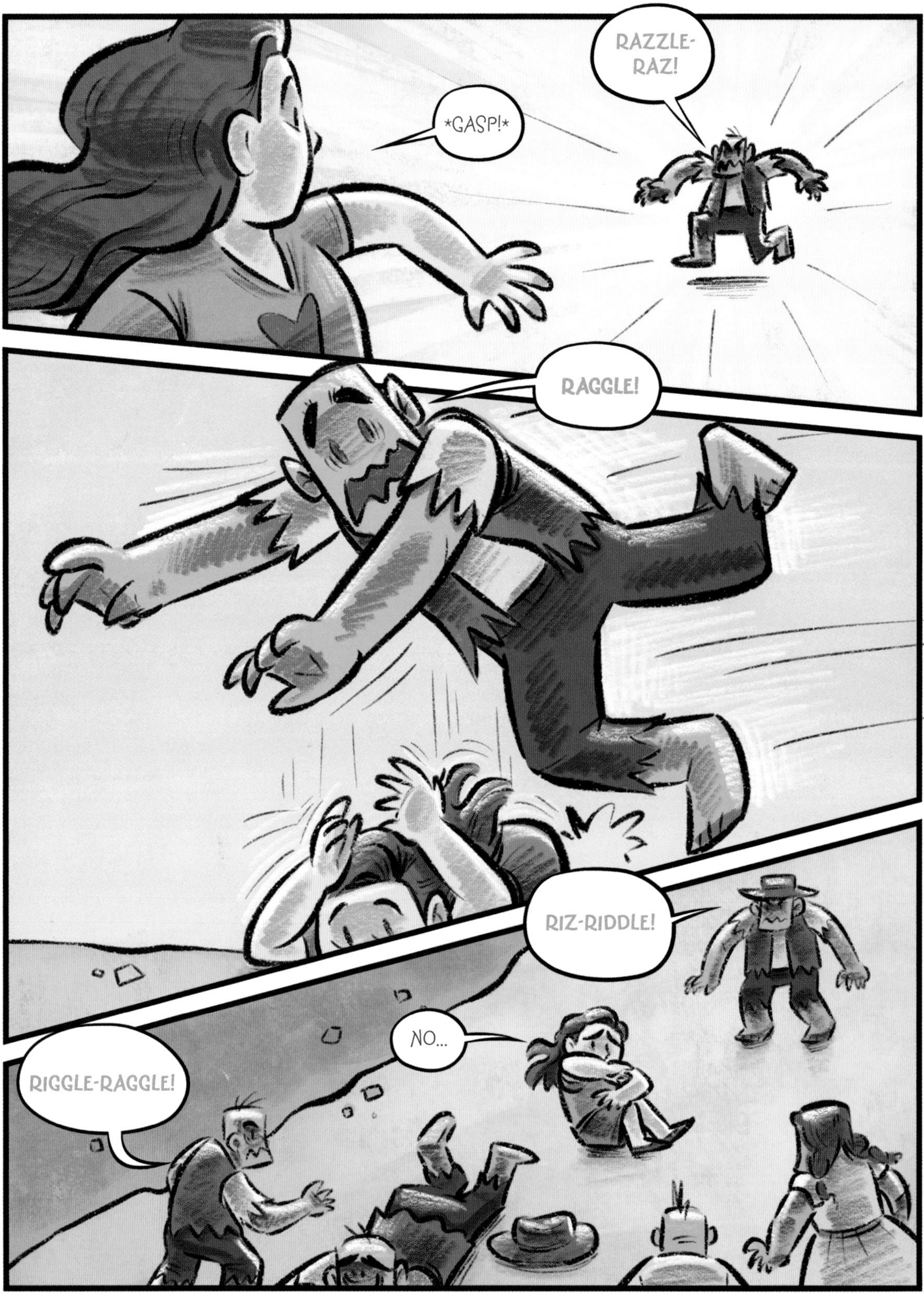

GASP!
RAZZLE-RAZZ!
RAGGLE!
RIZ-RIDDLE!
NO...
RIGGLE-RAGGLE!

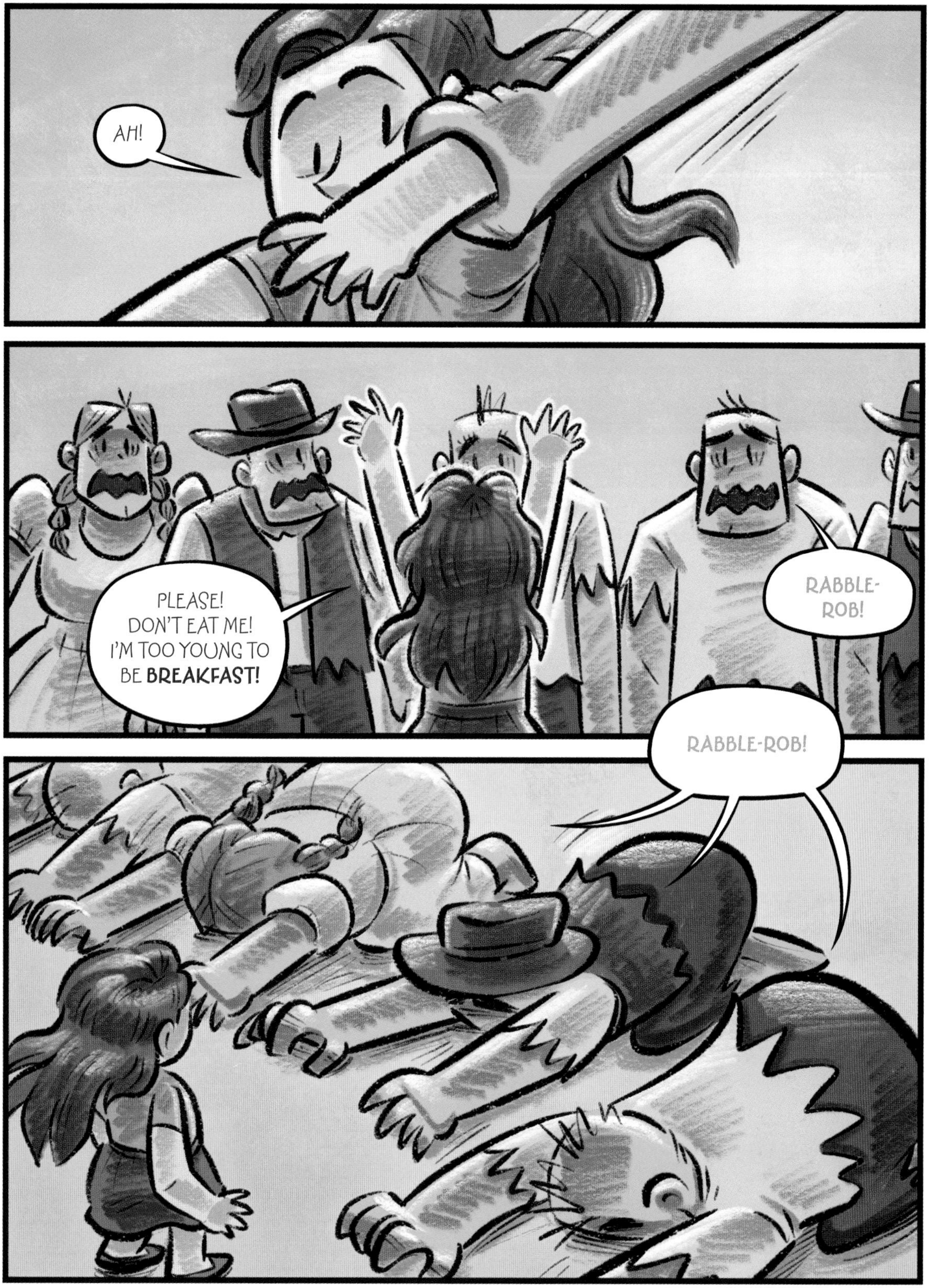
AH!
PLEASE! DON'T EAT ME! I'M TOO YOUNG TO BE **BREAKFAST!**
RABBLE-ROB!
RABBLE-ROB!

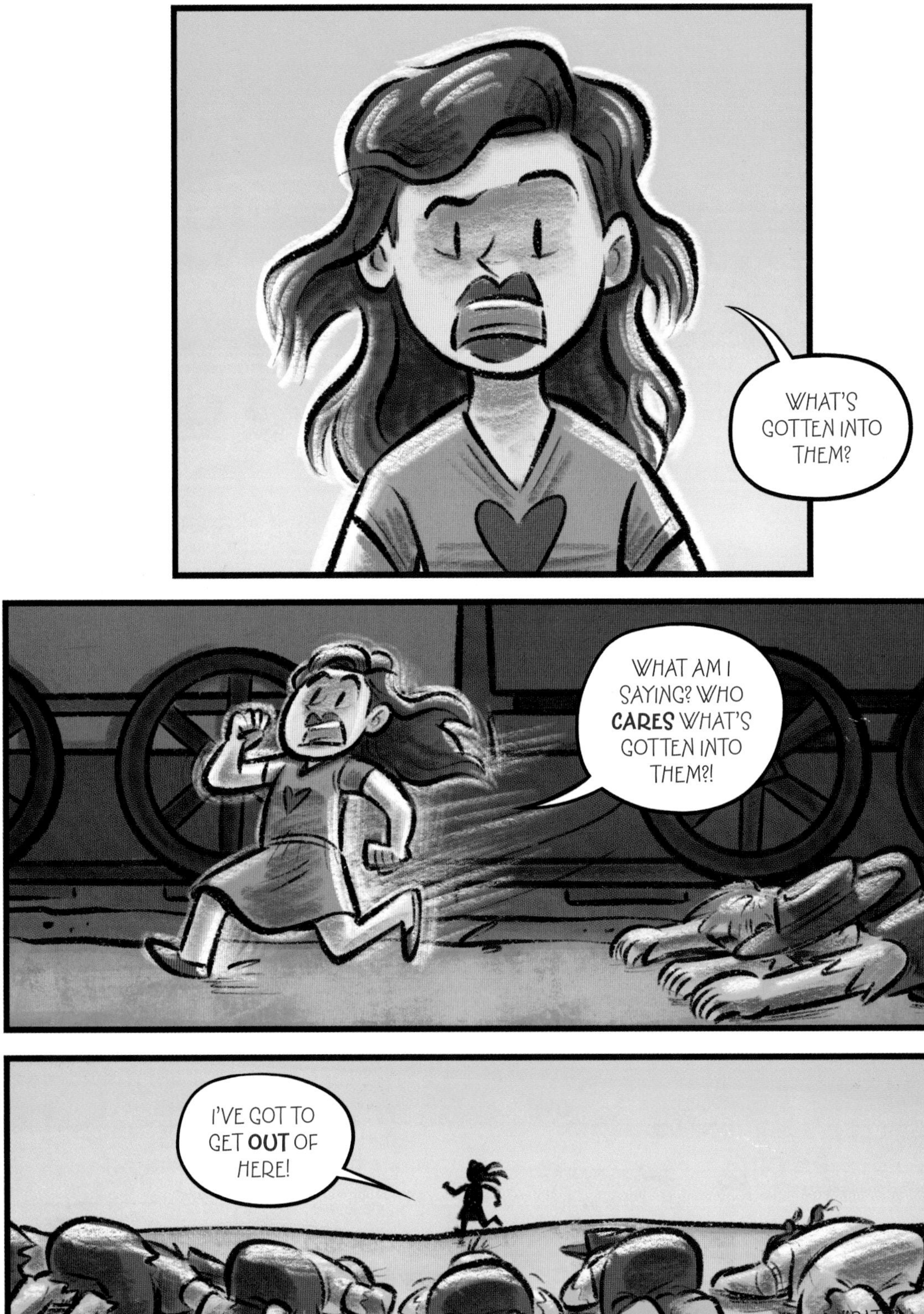
WHAT'S GOTTEN INTO THEM?
WHAT AM I SAYING? WHO **CARES** WHAT'S GOTTEN INTO THEM?!
I'VE GOT TO GET **OUT** OF HERE!

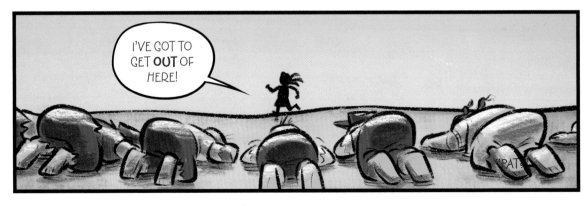

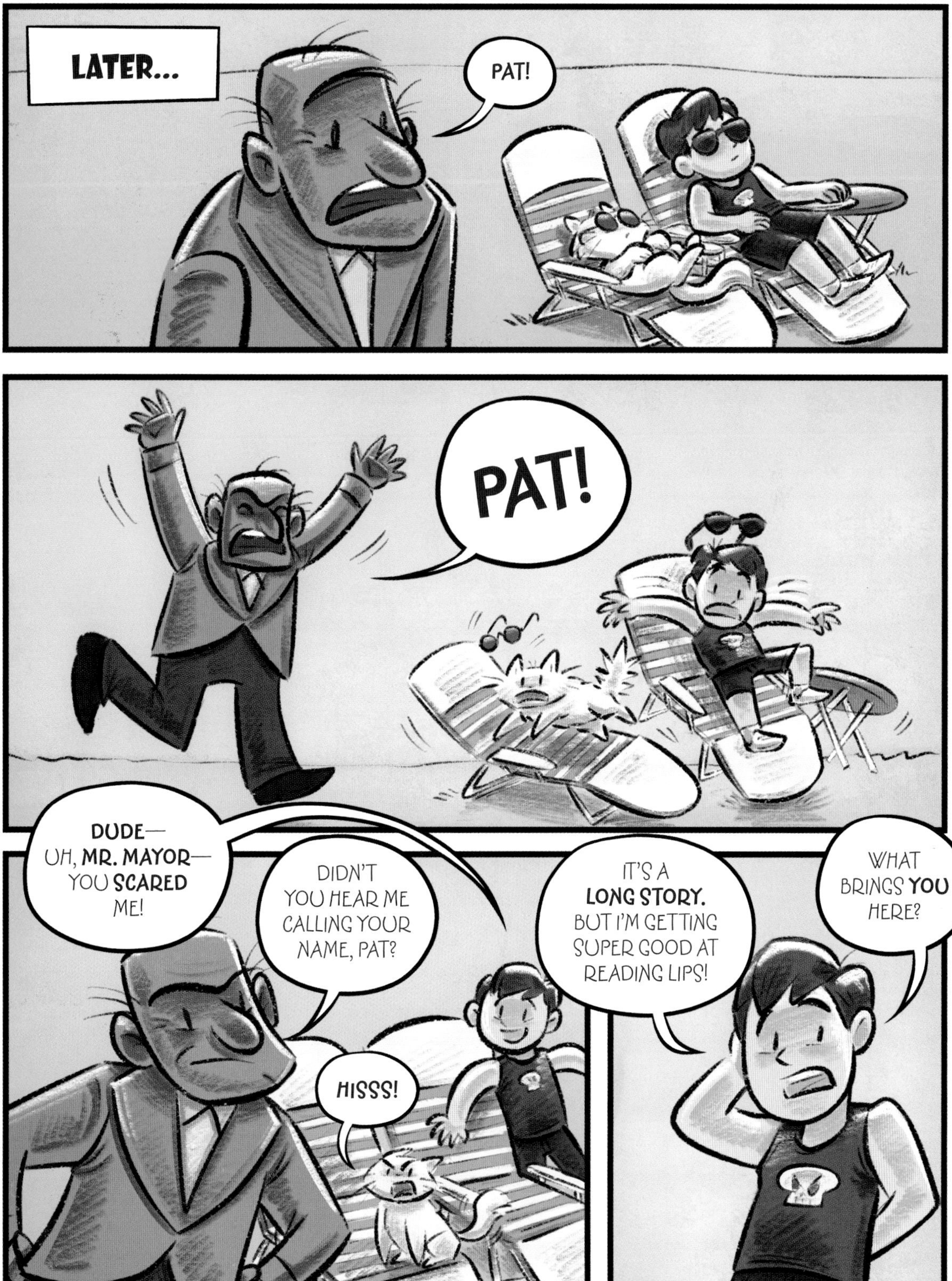
LATER...
PAT!
PAT!
DUDE— UH, MR. MAYOR— YOU SCARED ME!
DIDN'T YOU HEAR ME CALLING YOUR NAME, PAT?
HISSS!
IT'S A LONG STORY. BUT I'M GETTING SUPER GOOD AT READING LIPS!
WHAT BRINGS YOU HERE?

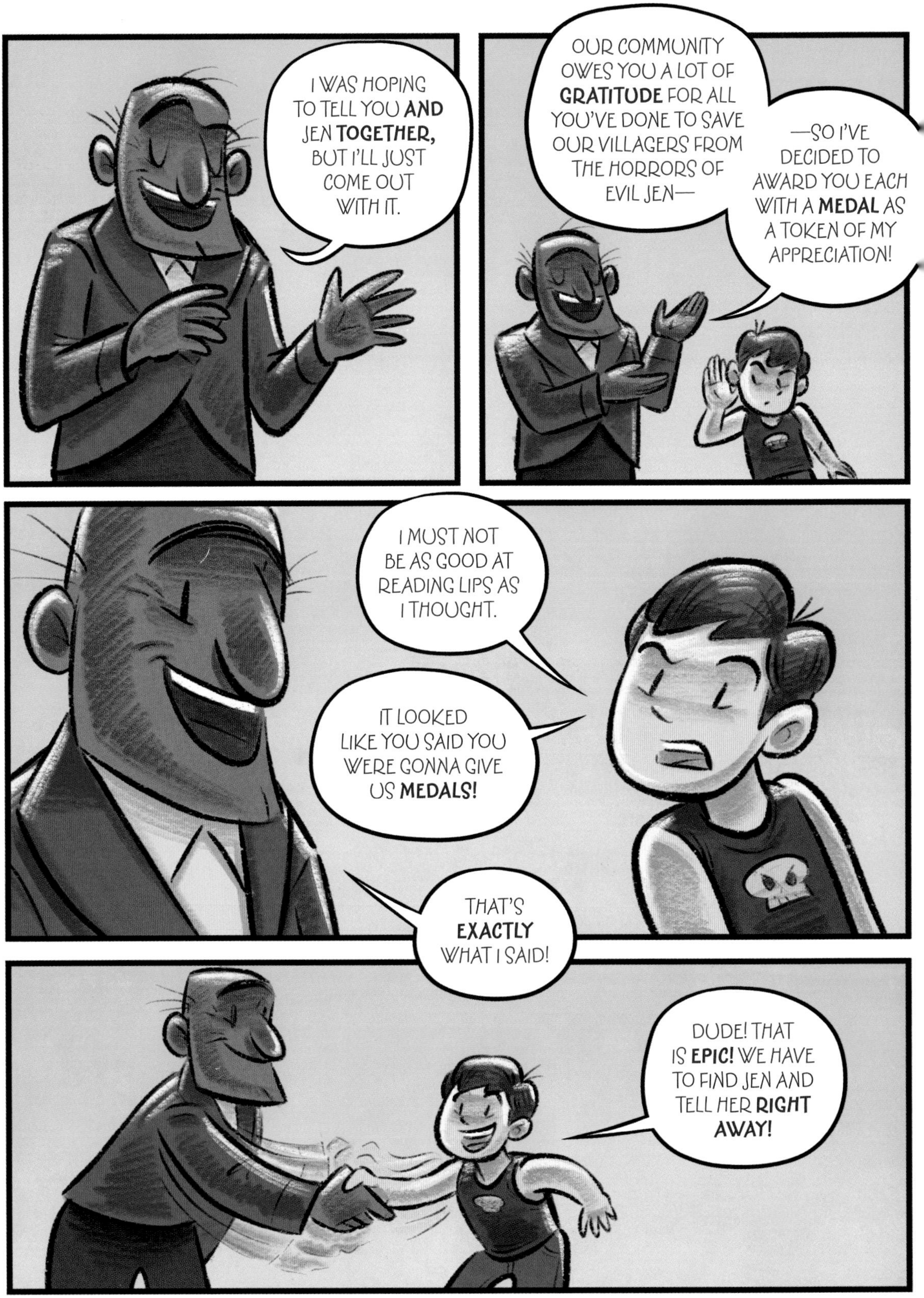
I WAS HOPING TO TELL YOU **AND** JEN **TOGETHER,** BUT I'LL JUST COME OUT WITH IT.
OUR COMMUNITY OWES YOU A LOT OF **GRATITUDE** FOR ALL YOU'VE DONE TO SAVE OUR VILLAGERS FROM THE HORRORS OF EVIL JEN—
—SO I'VE DECIDED TO AWARD YOU EACH WITH A **MEDAL** AS A TOKEN OF MY APPRECIATION!
I MUST NOT BE AS GOOD AT READING LIPS AS I THOUGHT.
IT LOOKED LIKE YOU SAID YOU WERE GONNA GIVE US **MEDALS!**
THAT'S **EXACTLY** WHAT I SAID!
DUDE! THAT IS **EPIC!** WE HAVE TO FIND JEN AND TELL HER **RIGHT AWAY!**

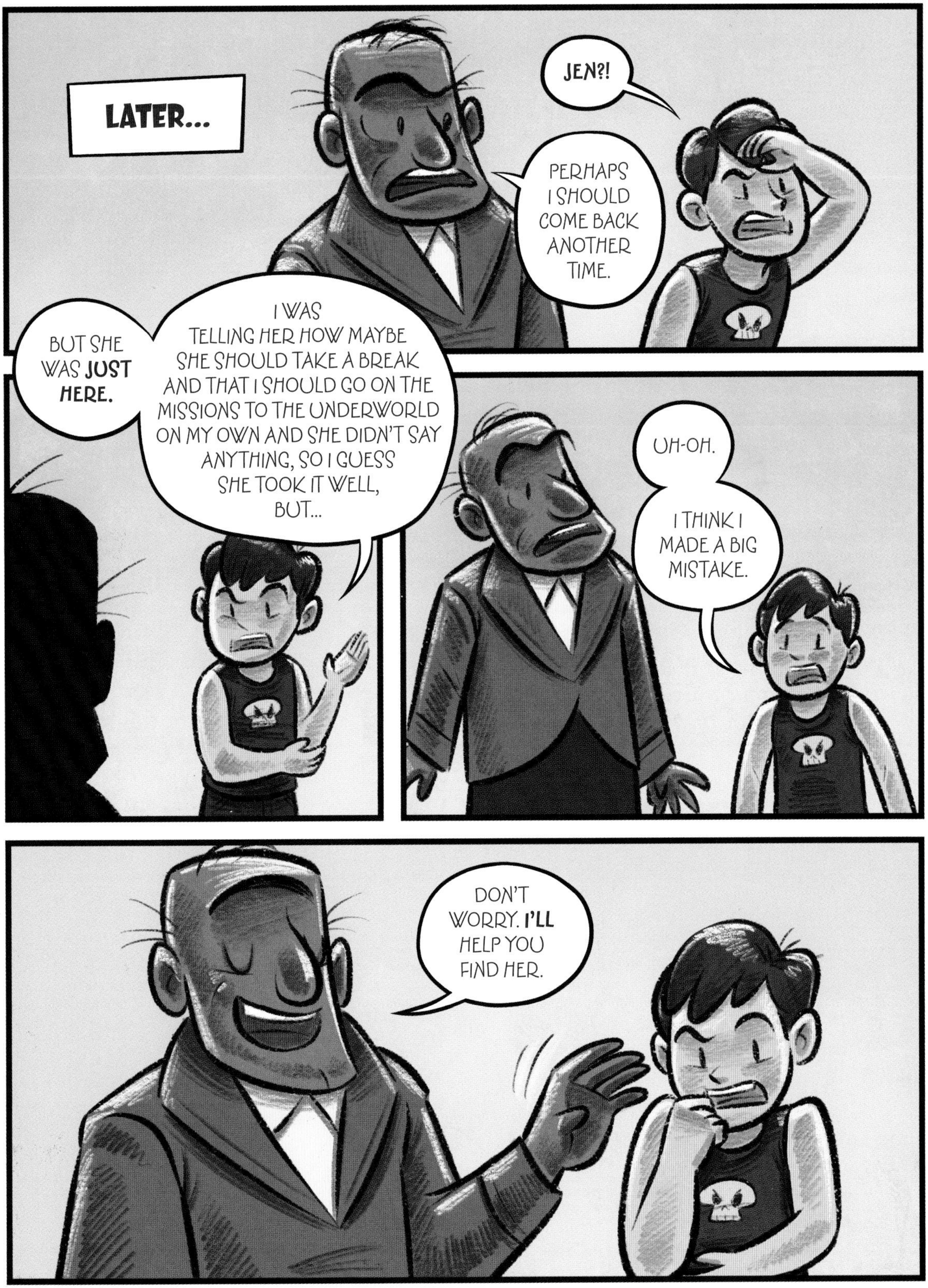
LATER...
JEN?!
PERHAPS I SHOULD COME BACK ANOTHER TIME.
BUT SHE WAS **JUST HERE.**
I WAS TELLING HER HOW MAYBE SHE SHOULD TAKE A BREAK AND THAT I SHOULD GO ON THE MISSIONS TO THE UNDERWORLD ON MY OWN AND SHE DIDN'T SAY ANYTHING, SO I GUESS SHE TOOK IT WELL, BUT...
UH-OH.
I THINK I MADE A BIG MISTAKE.
DON'T WORRY. **I'LL** HELP YOU FIND HER.

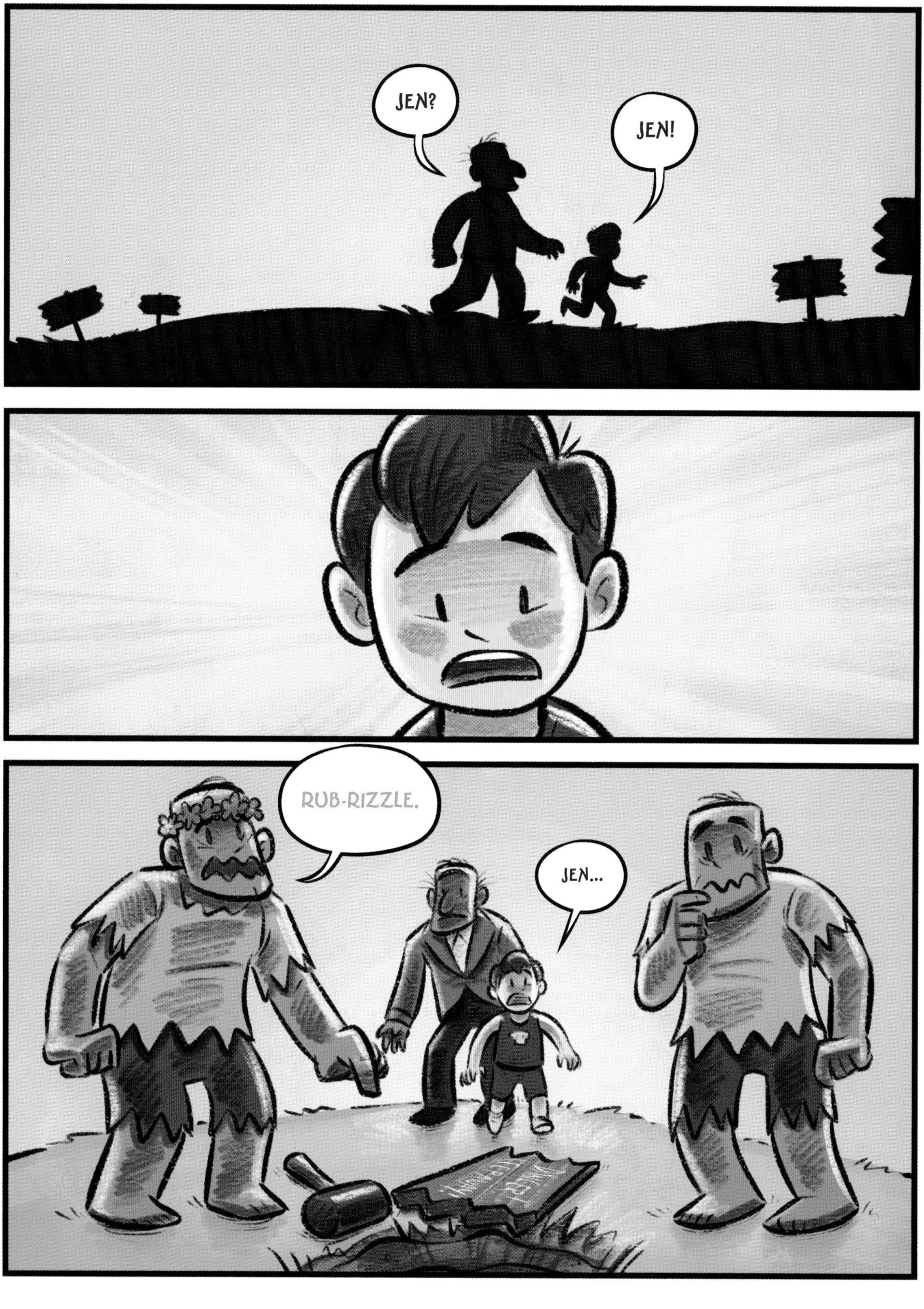
JEN?
JEN!
RUB-RIZZLE.
JEN...

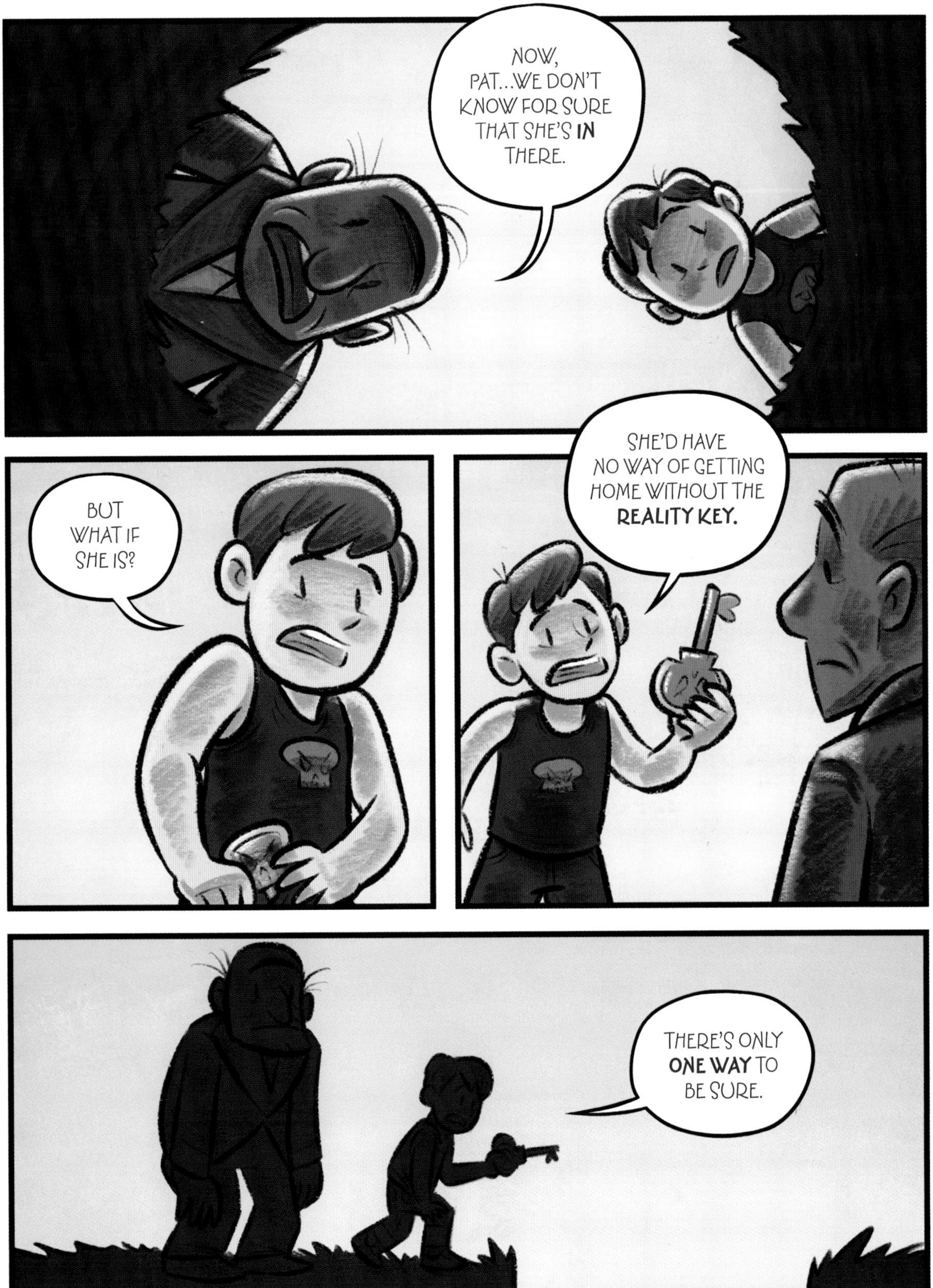
NOW, PAT...WE DON'T KNOW FOR SURE THAT SHE'S **IN** THERE.
BUT WHAT IF SHE IS?
SHE'D HAVE NO WAY OF GETTING HOME WITHOUT THE **REALITY KEY.**
THERE'S ONLY **ONE WAY** TO BE SURE.

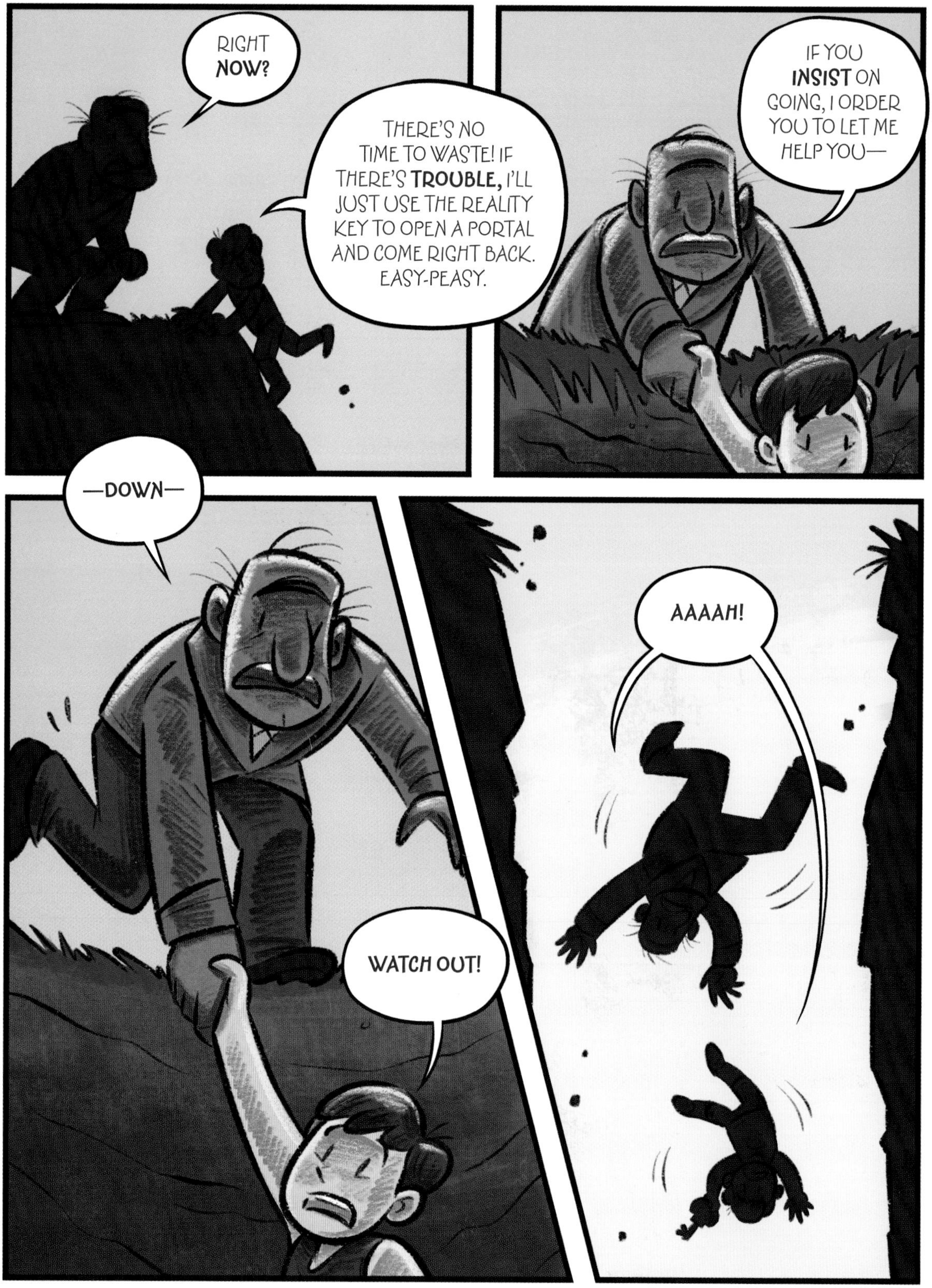
RIGHT NOW?
THERE'S NO TIME TO WASTE! IF THERE'S TROUBLE, I'LL JUST USE THE REALITY KEY TO OPEN A PORTAL AND COME RIGHT BACK. EASY-PEASY.
IF YOU INSIST ON GOING, I ORDER YOU TO LET ME HELP YOU—
—DOWN—
WATCH OUT!
AAAAH!

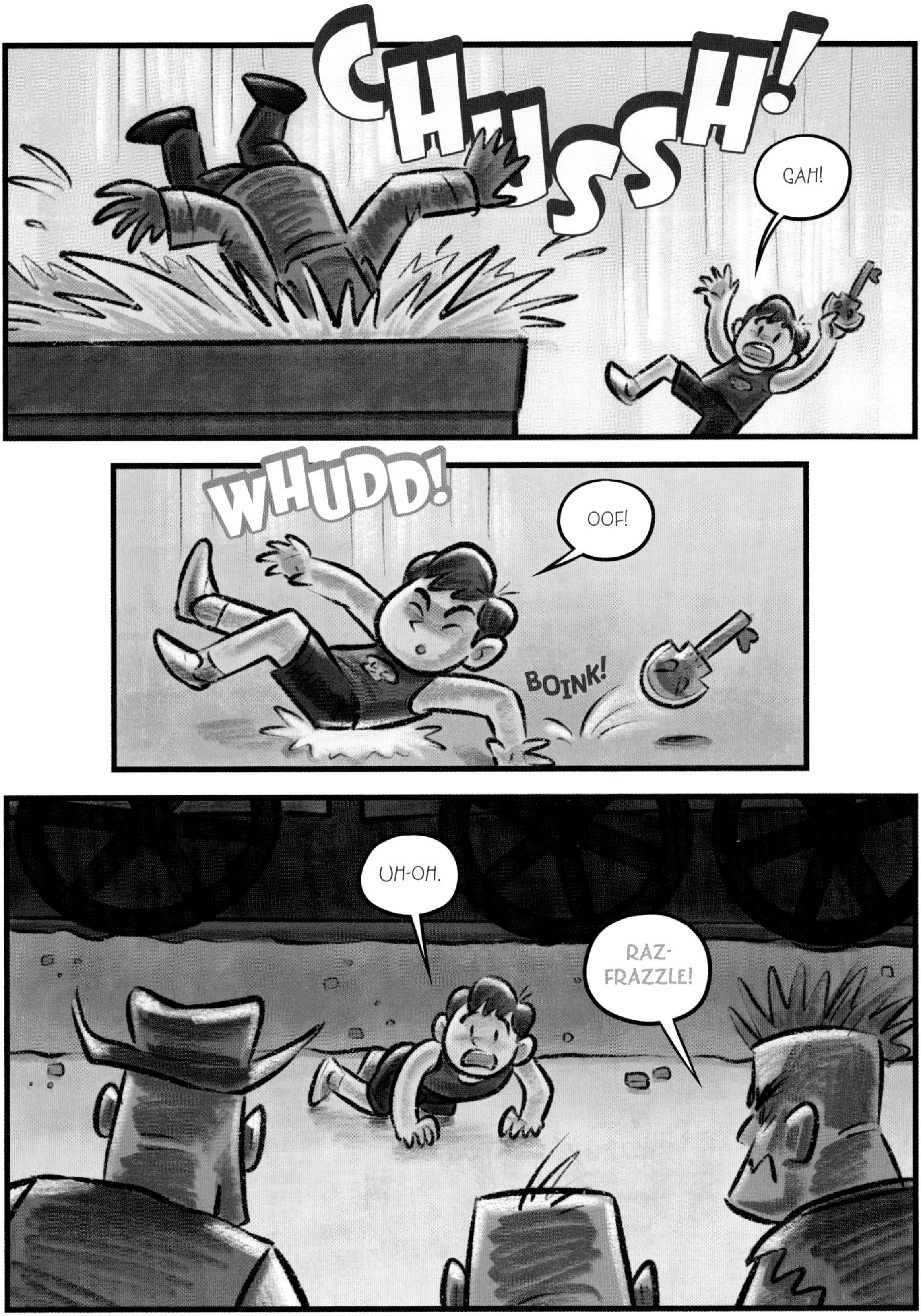
CHUSSH!
GAH!
WHUDD!
OOF!
BOINK!
UH-OH.
RAZ-
FRAZZLE!

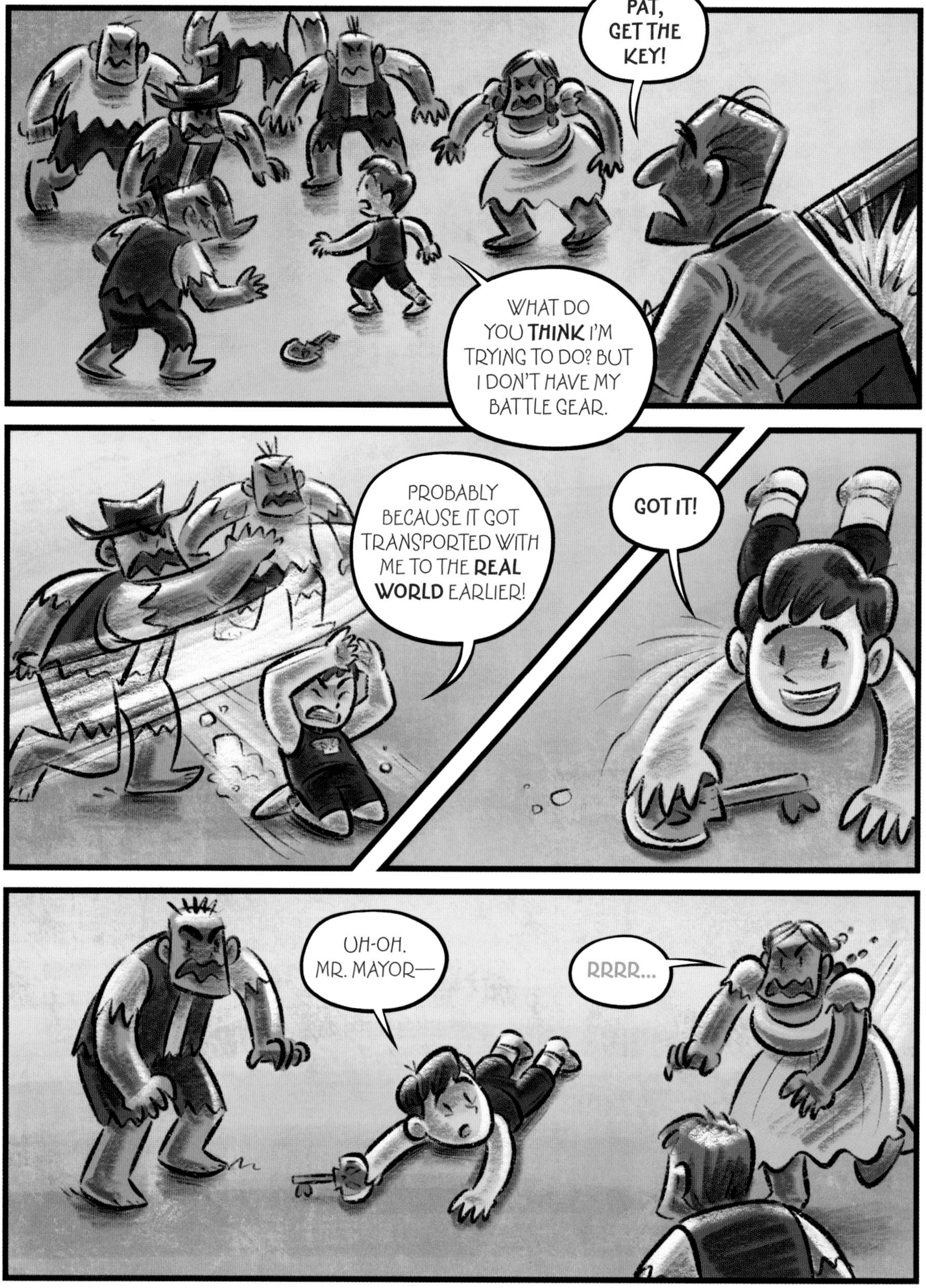
PAT, GET THE KEY!
WHAT DO YOU **THINK** I'M TRYING TO DO? BUT I DON'T HAVE MY BATTLE GEAR.
PROBABLY BECAUSE IT GOT TRANSPORTED WITH ME TO THE **REAL WORLD** EARLIER!
GOT IT!
UH-OH. MR. MAYOR—
RRRR...

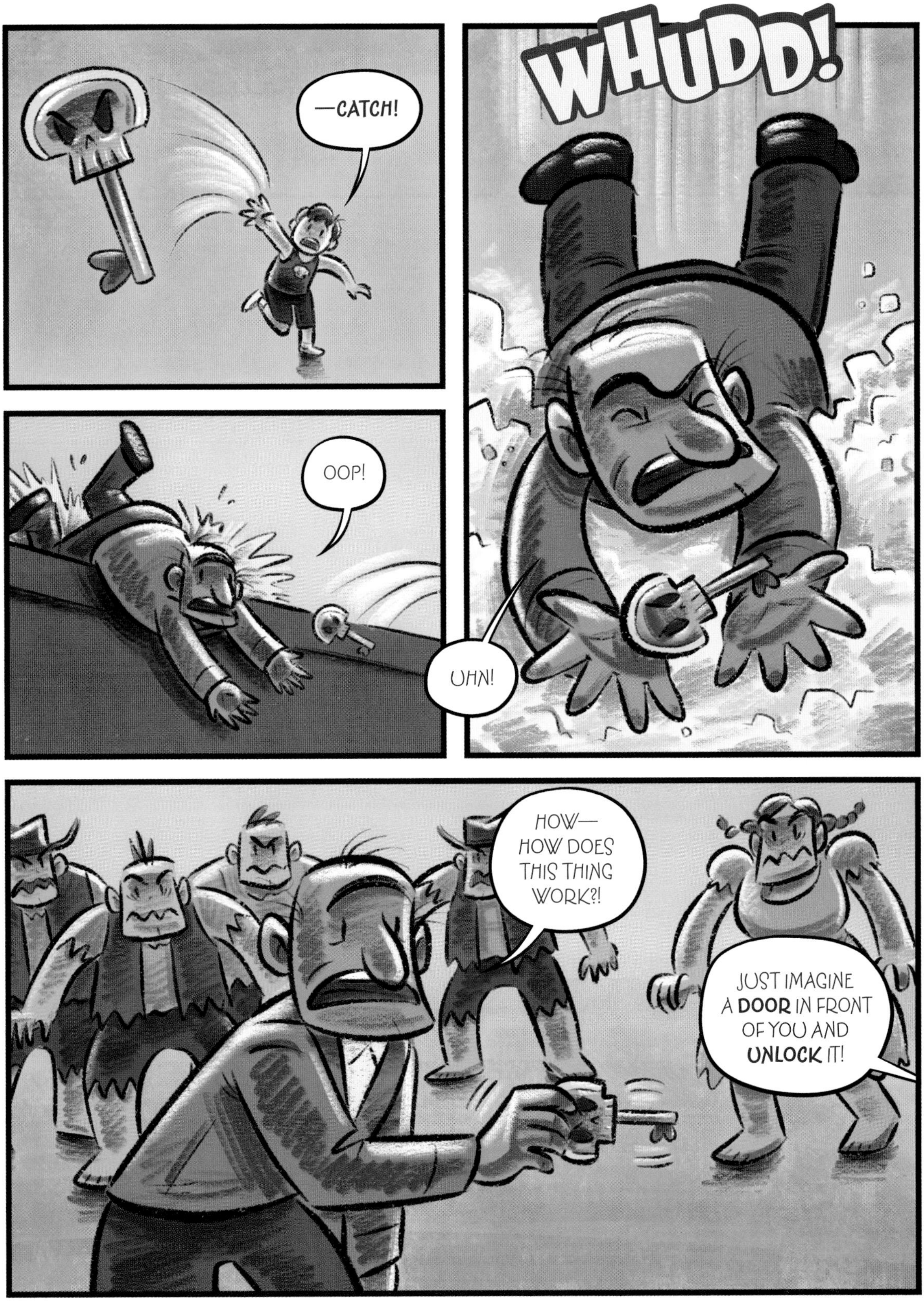
—CATCH!
WHUDD!
OOP!
UHN!
HOW— HOW DOES THIS THING WORK?!
JUST IMAGINE A **DOOR** IN FRONT OF YOU AND **UNLOCK** IT!

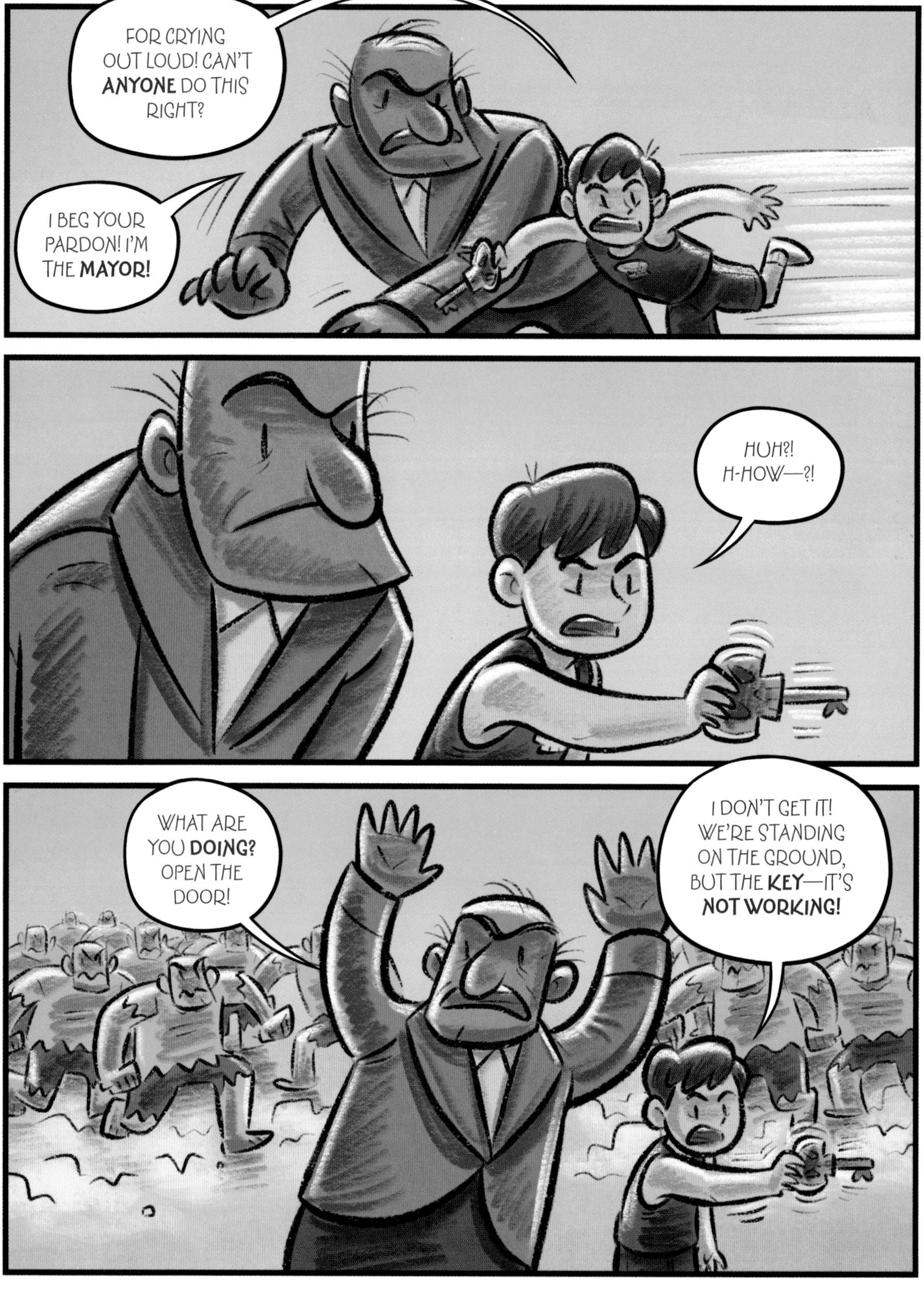

FOR CRYING OUT LOUD! CAN'T **ANYONE** DO THIS RIGHT?
I BEG YOUR PARDON! I'M THE **MAYOR!**
HUH?! H-HOW—?!
WHAT ARE YOU **DOING?** OPEN THE DOOR!
I DON'T GET IT! WE'RE STANDING ON THE GROUND, BUT THE **KEY**—IT'S **NOT WORKING!**

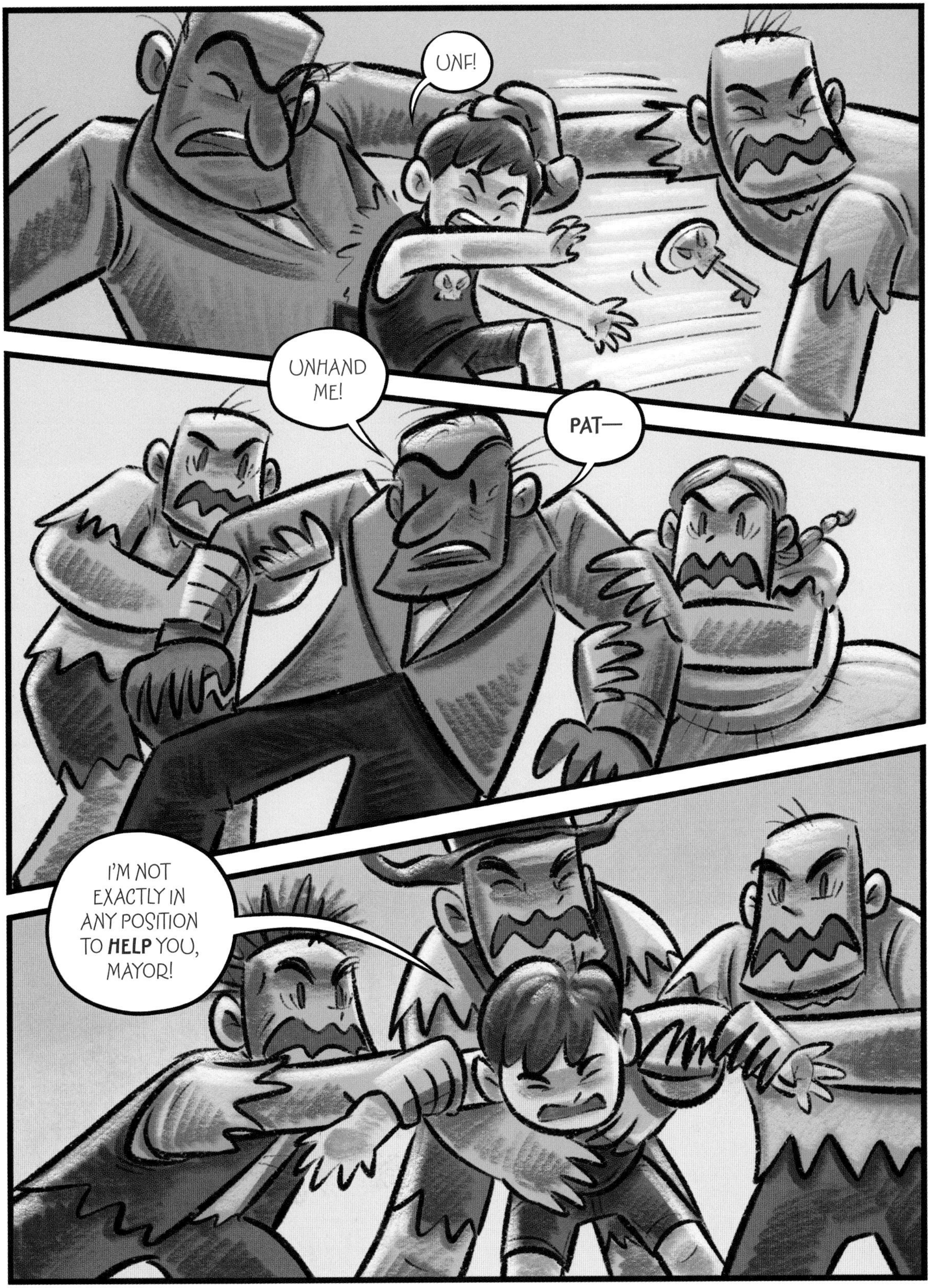
UNF!
UNHAND ME!
PAT—
I'M NOT EXACTLY IN ANY POSITION TO **HELP** YOU, MAYOR!

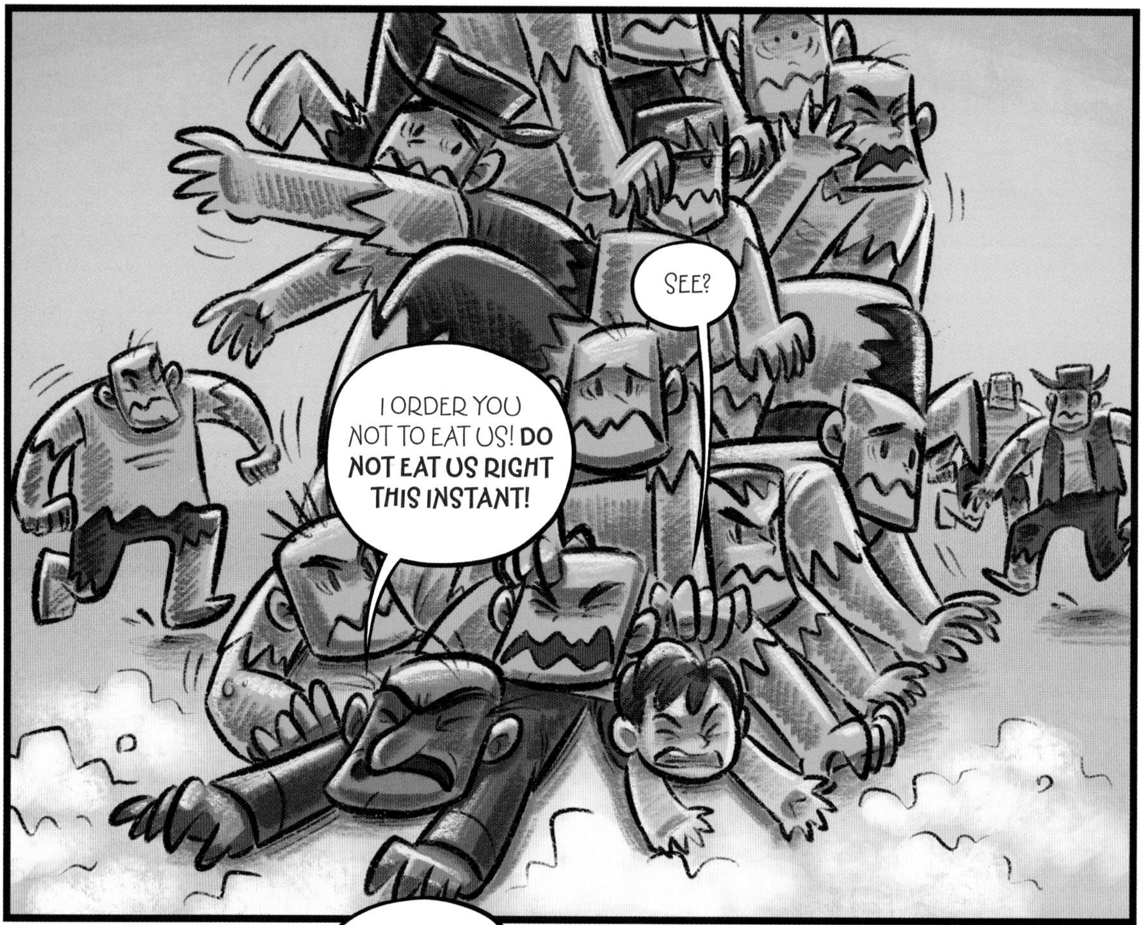
SEE?
I ORDER YOU NOT TO EAT US! **DO NOT EAT US RIGHT THIS INSTANT!**

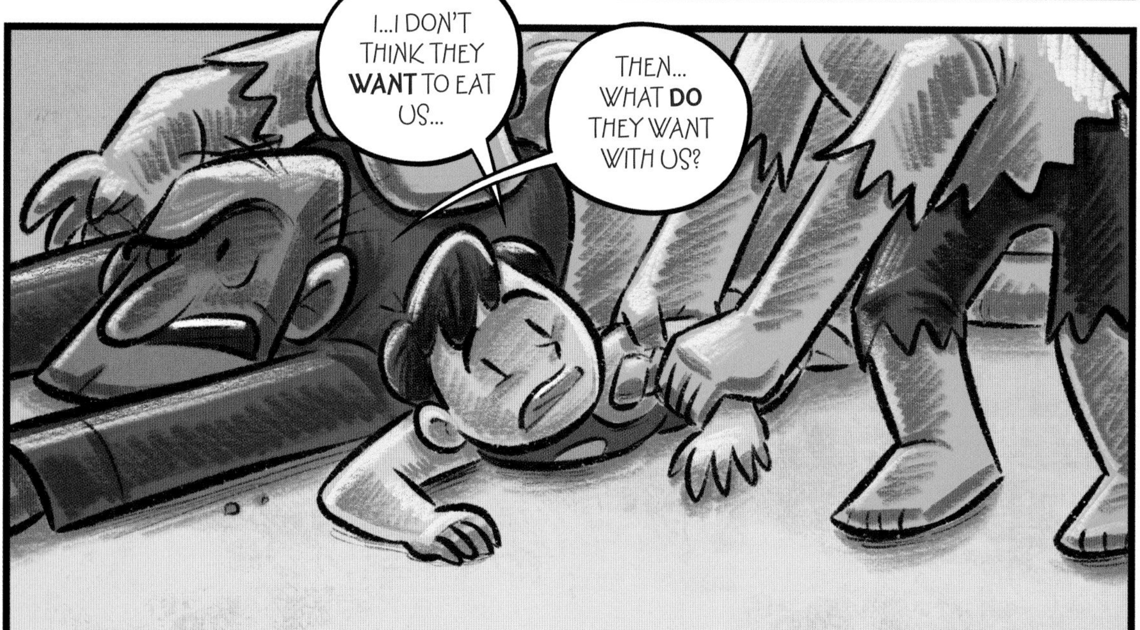
I...I DON'T THINK THEY **WANT** TO EAT US...
THEN... WHAT **DO** THEY WANT WITH US?

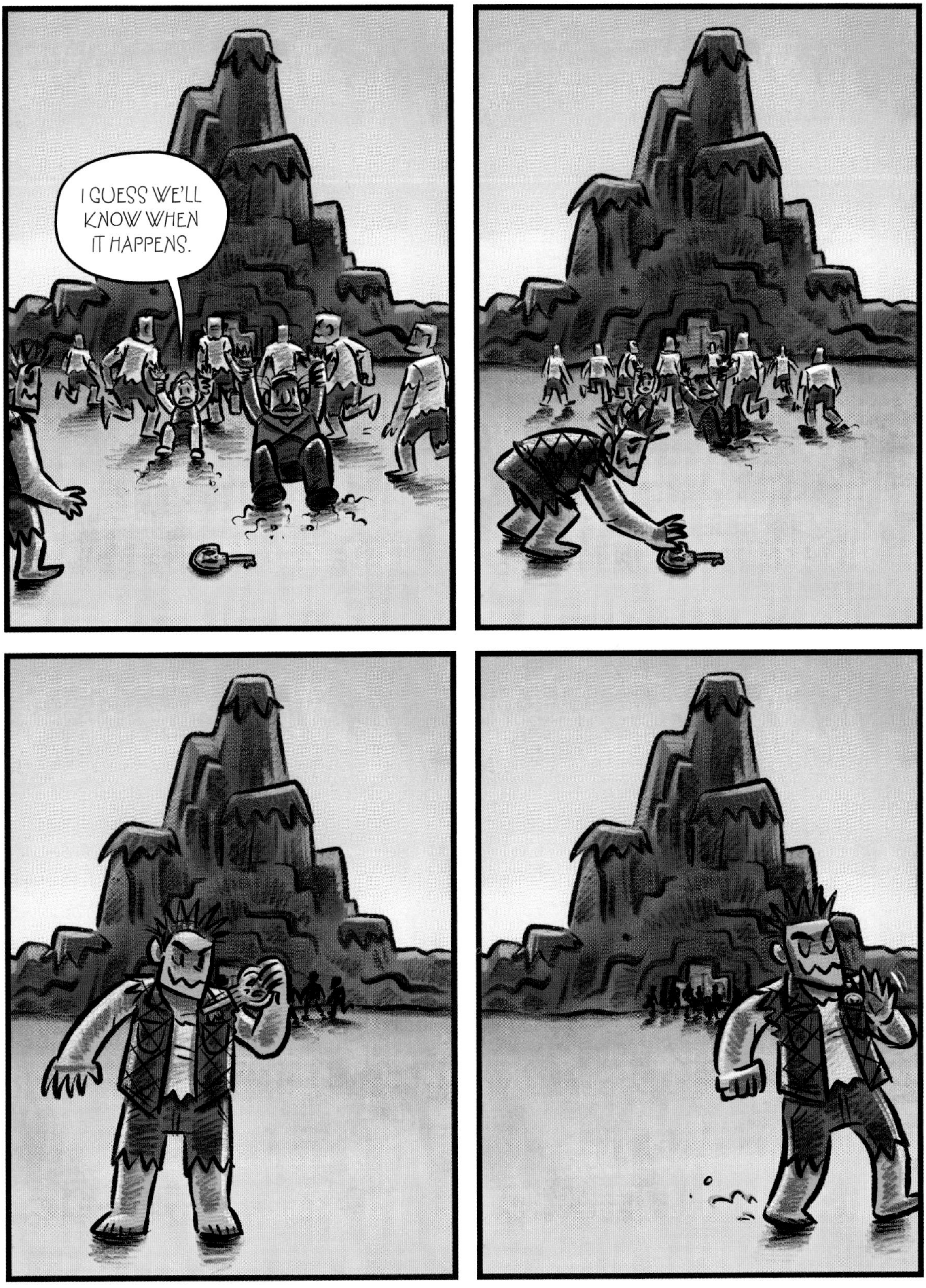
I GUESS WE'LL KNOW WHEN IT HAPPENS.

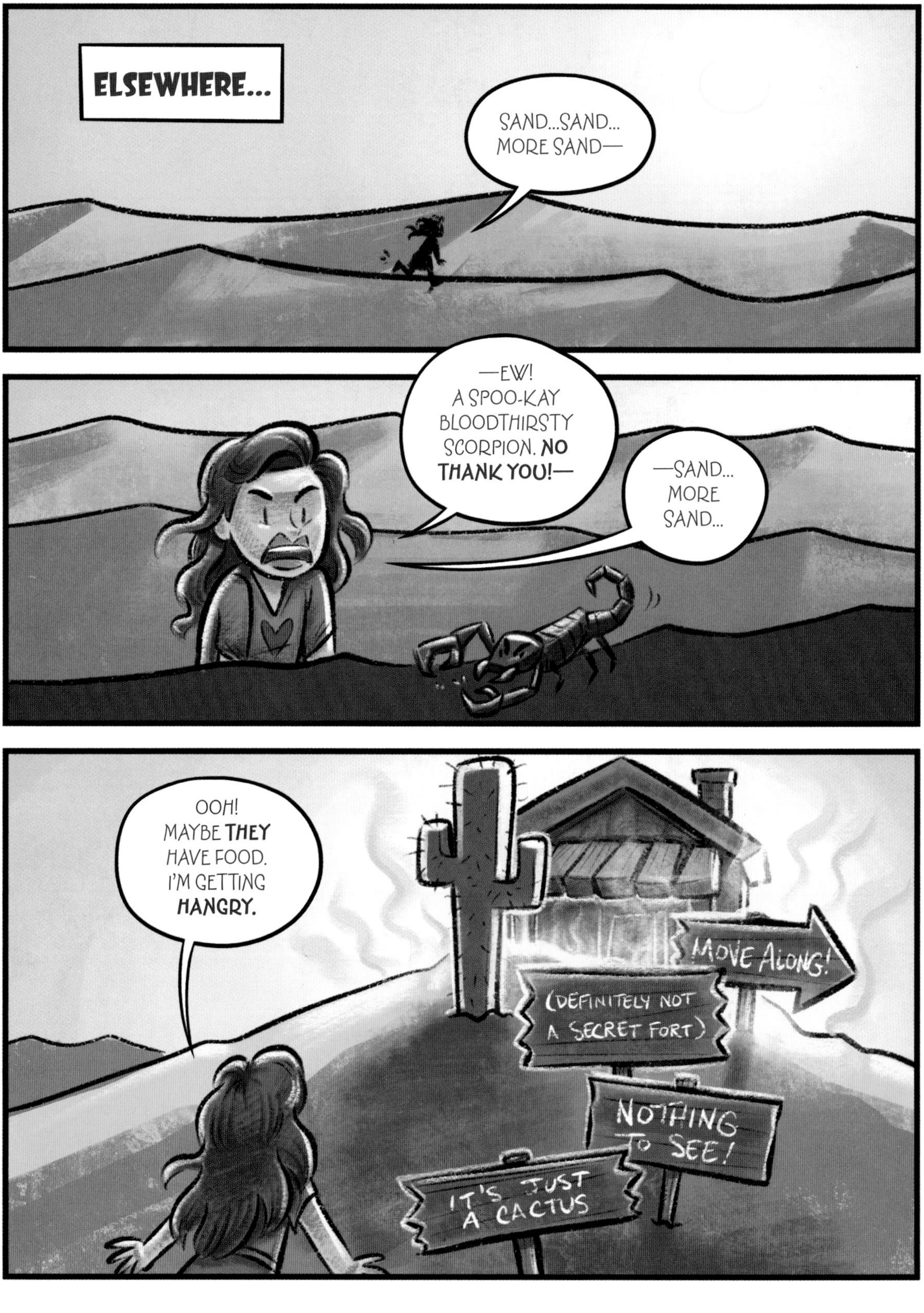
ELSEWHERE...
SAND...SAND... MORE SAND—
—EW! A SPOO-KAY BLOODTHIRSTY SCORPION. **NO THANK YOU!**—
—SAND... MORE SAND...
OOH! MAYBE **THEY** HAVE FOOD. I'M GETTING **HANGRY.**
MOVE ALONG!
(DEFINITELY NOT A SECRET FORT)
NOTHING TO SEE!
IT'S JUST A CACTUS

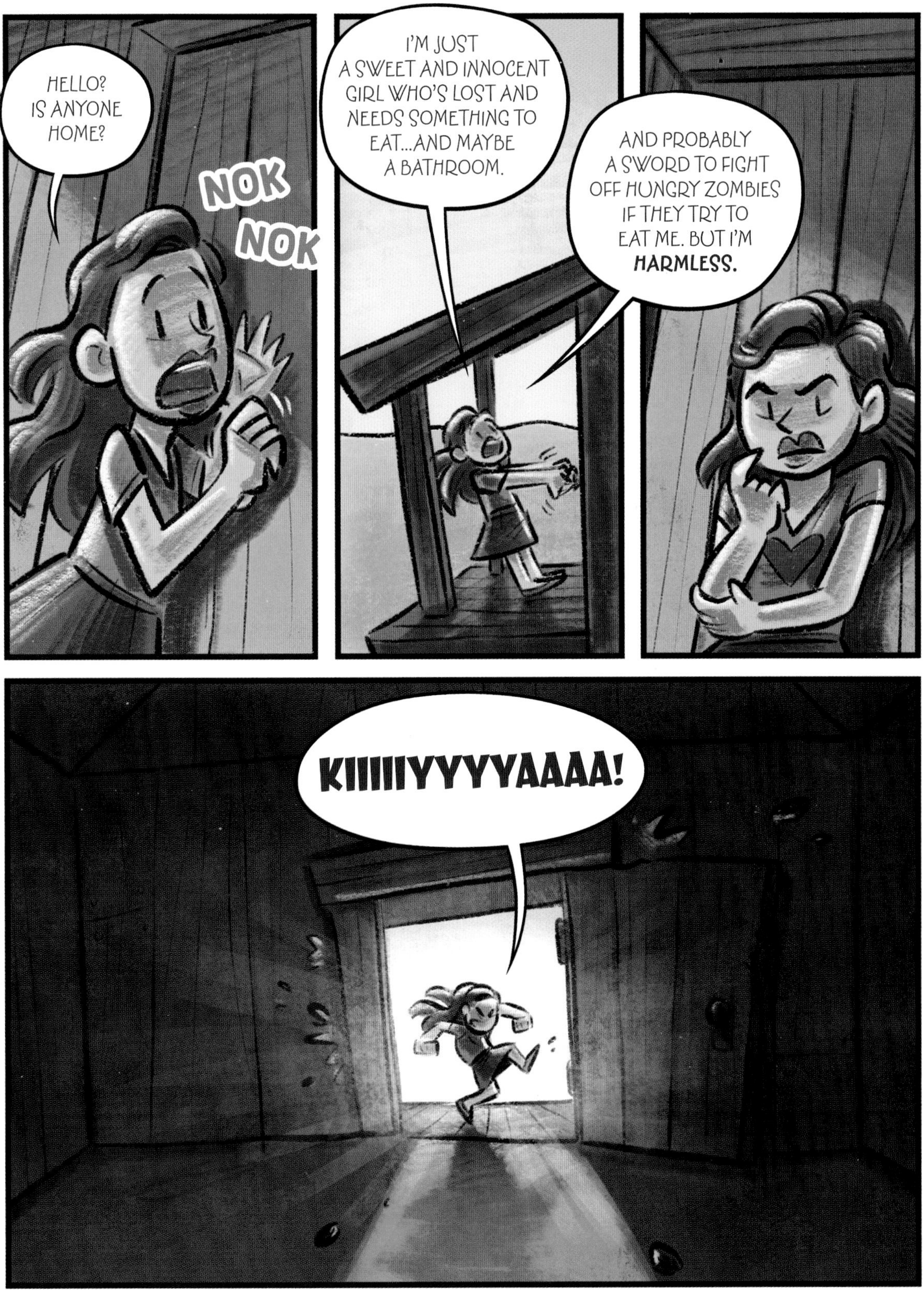
HELLO? IS ANYONE HOME?
NOK
NOK
I'M JUST A SWEET AND INNOCENT GIRL WHO'S LOST AND NEEDS SOMETHING TO EAT...AND MAYBE A BATHROOM.
AND PROBABLY A SWORD TO FIGHT OFF HUNGRY ZOMBIES IF THEY TRY TO EAT ME. BUT I'M **HARMLESS.**
KIIIIIYYYYAAAA!

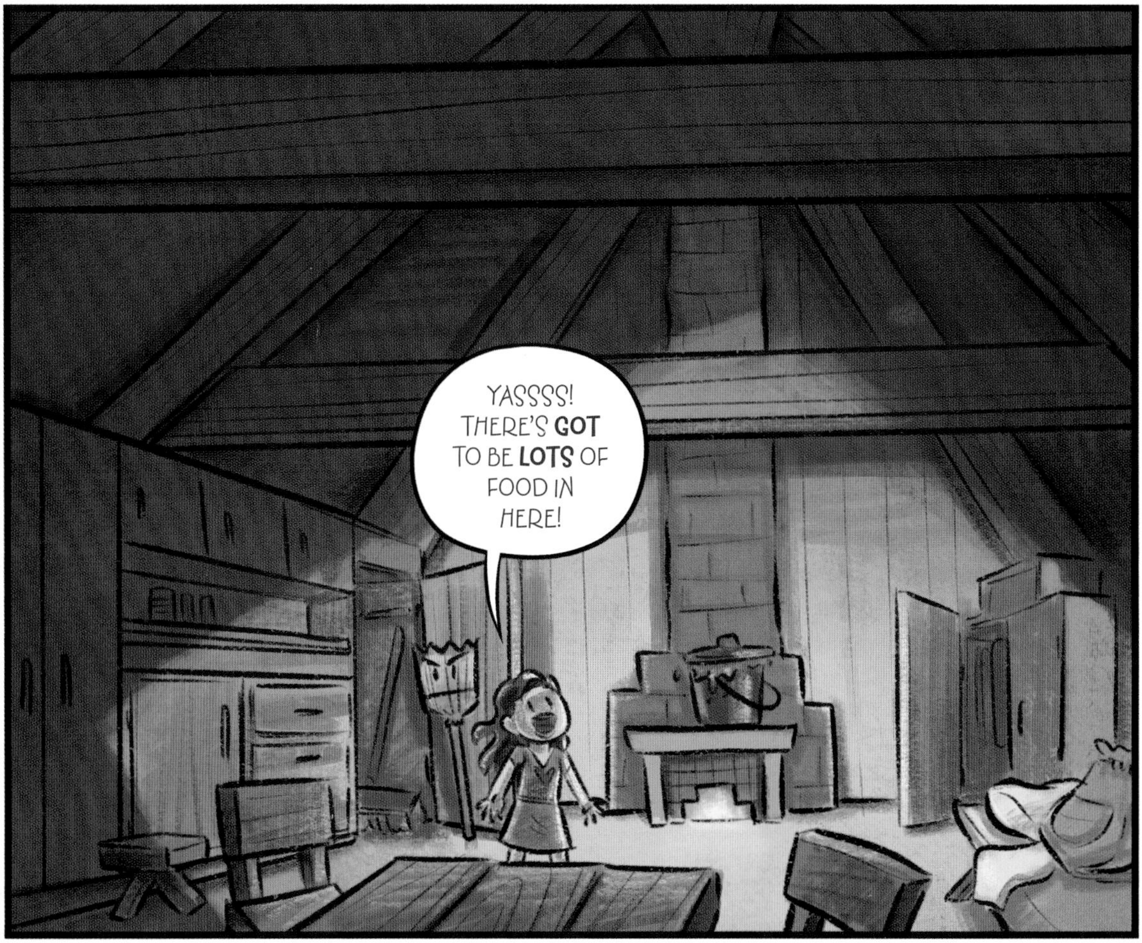
YASSSS! THERE'S **GOT** TO BE **LOTS** OF FOOD IN HERE!

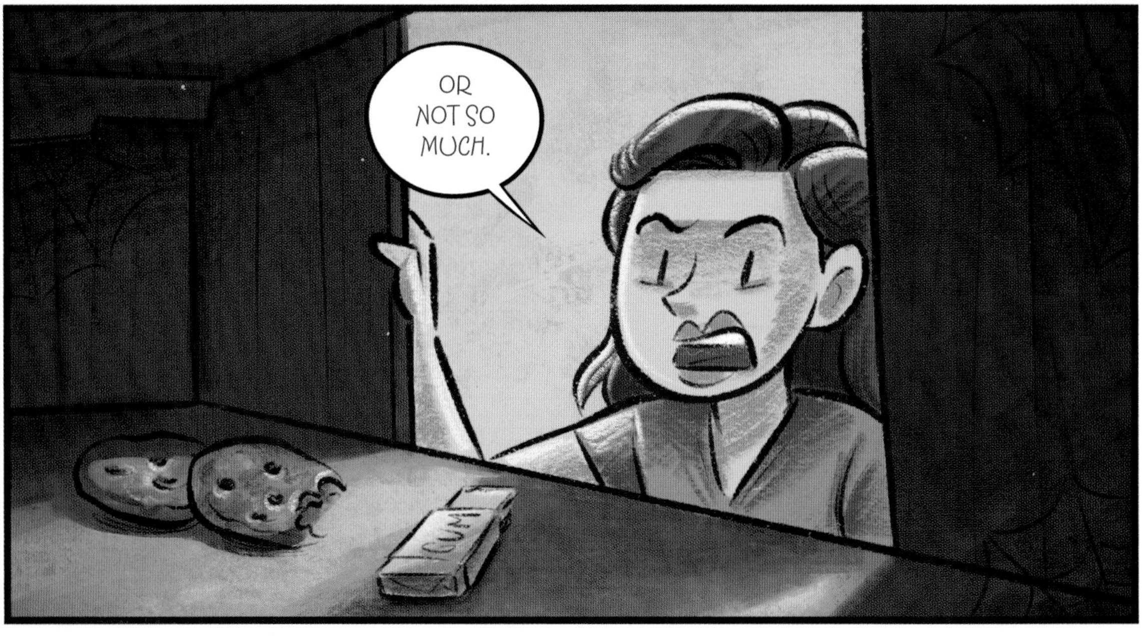
OR NOT SO MUCH.

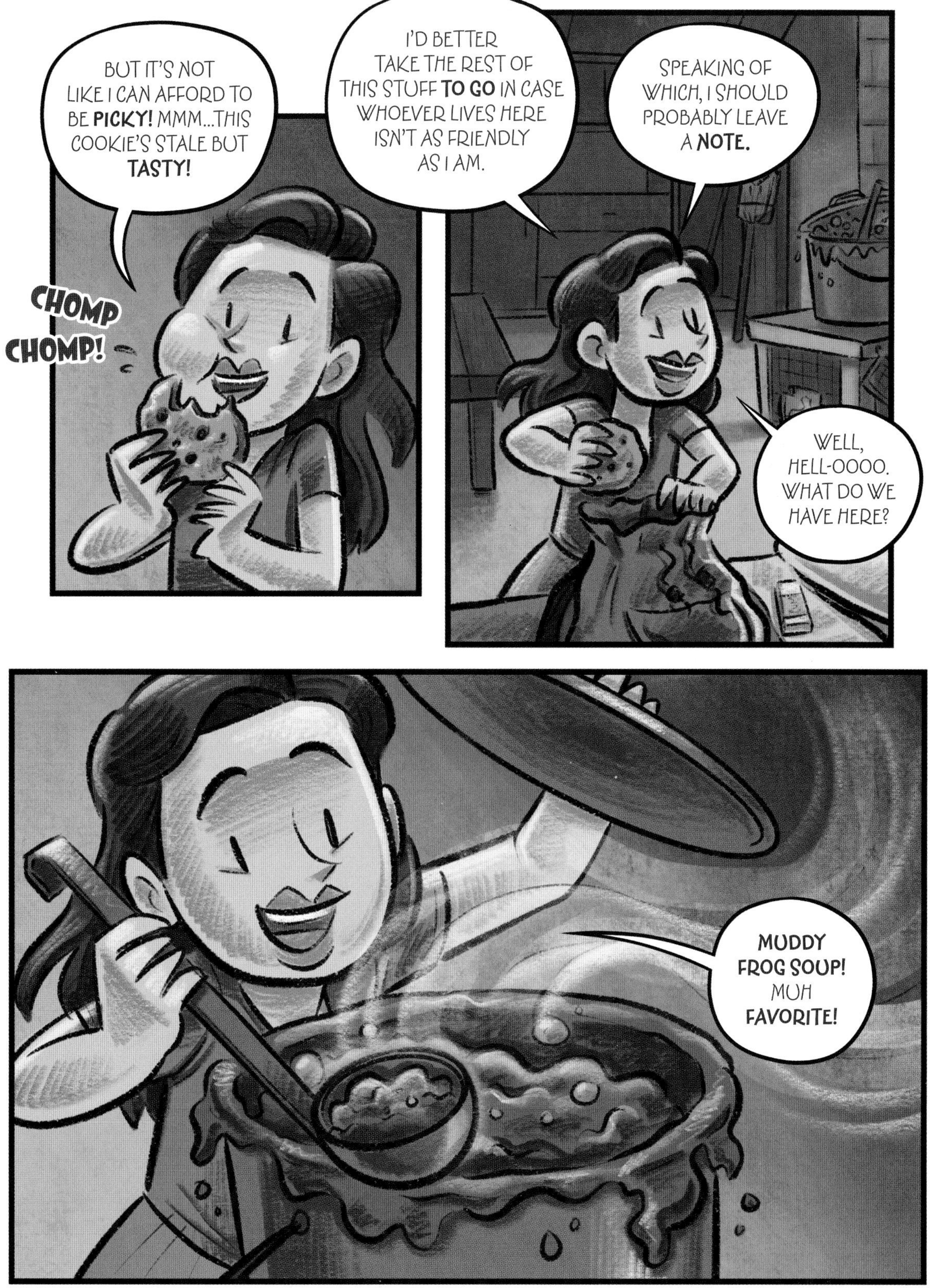

BUT IT'S NOT LIKE I CAN AFFORD TO BE **PICKY!** MMM...THIS COOKIE'S STALE BUT **TASTY!**
CHOMP CHOMP!
I'D BETTER TAKE THE REST OF THIS STUFF **TO GO** IN CASE WHOEVER LIVES HERE ISN'T AS FRIENDLY AS I AM.
SPEAKING OF WHICH, I SHOULD PROBABLY LEAVE A **NOTE.**
WELL, HELL-OOOO. WHAT DO WE HAVE HERE?
MUDDY FROG SOUP! MUH **FAVORITE!**

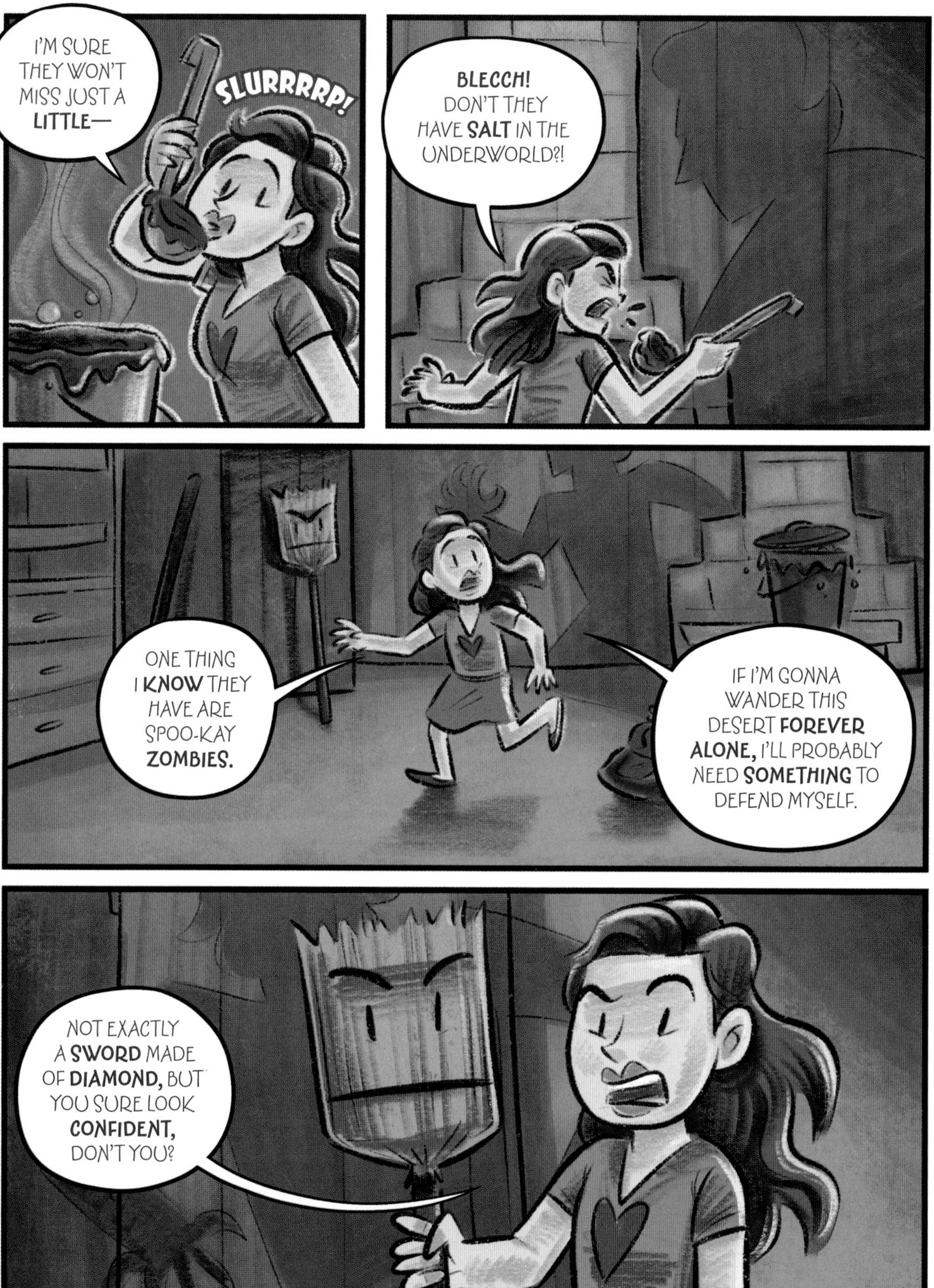
I'M SURE THEY WON'T MISS JUST A **LITTLE**—
SLURRRRP!
BLECCH! DON'T THEY HAVE **SALT** IN THE UNDERWORLD?!
ONE THING I **KNOW** THEY HAVE ARE SPOO-KAY **ZOMBIES.**
IF I'M GONNA WANDER THIS DESERT **FOREVER ALONE,** I'LL PROBABLY NEED **SOMETHING** TO DEFEND MYSELF.
NOT EXACTLY A **SWORD** MADE OF **DIAMOND,** BUT YOU SURE LOOK **CONFIDENT,** DON'T YOU?

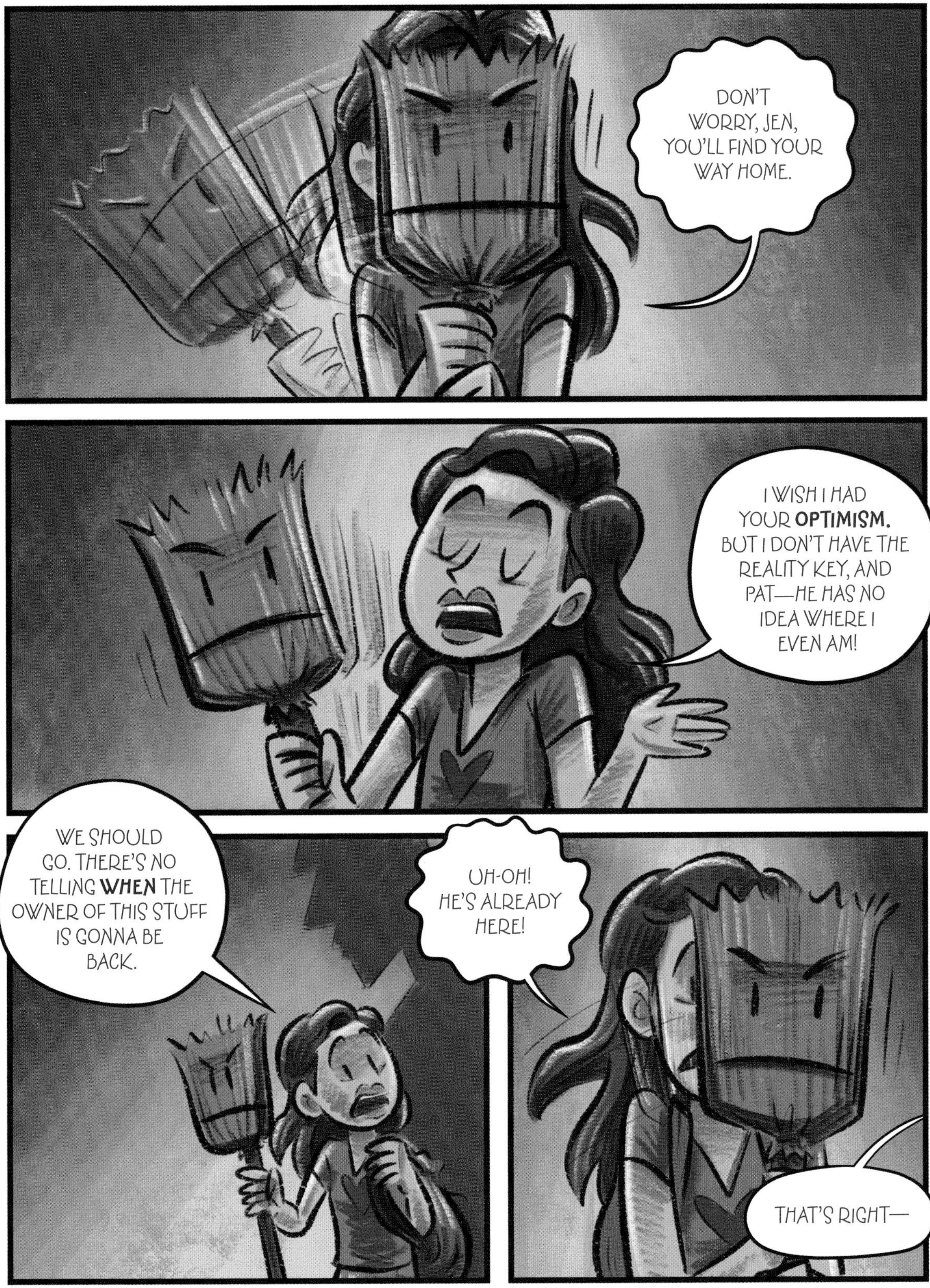
DON'T WORRY, JEN, YOU'LL FIND YOUR WAY HOME.
I WISH I HAD YOUR **OPTIMISM.** BUT I DON'T HAVE THE REALITY KEY, AND PAT—HE HAS NO IDEA WHERE I EVEN AM!
WE SHOULD GO. THERE'S NO TELLING **WHEN** THE OWNER OF THIS STUFF IS GONNA BE BACK.
UH-OH! HE'S ALREADY HERE!
THAT'S RIGHT—

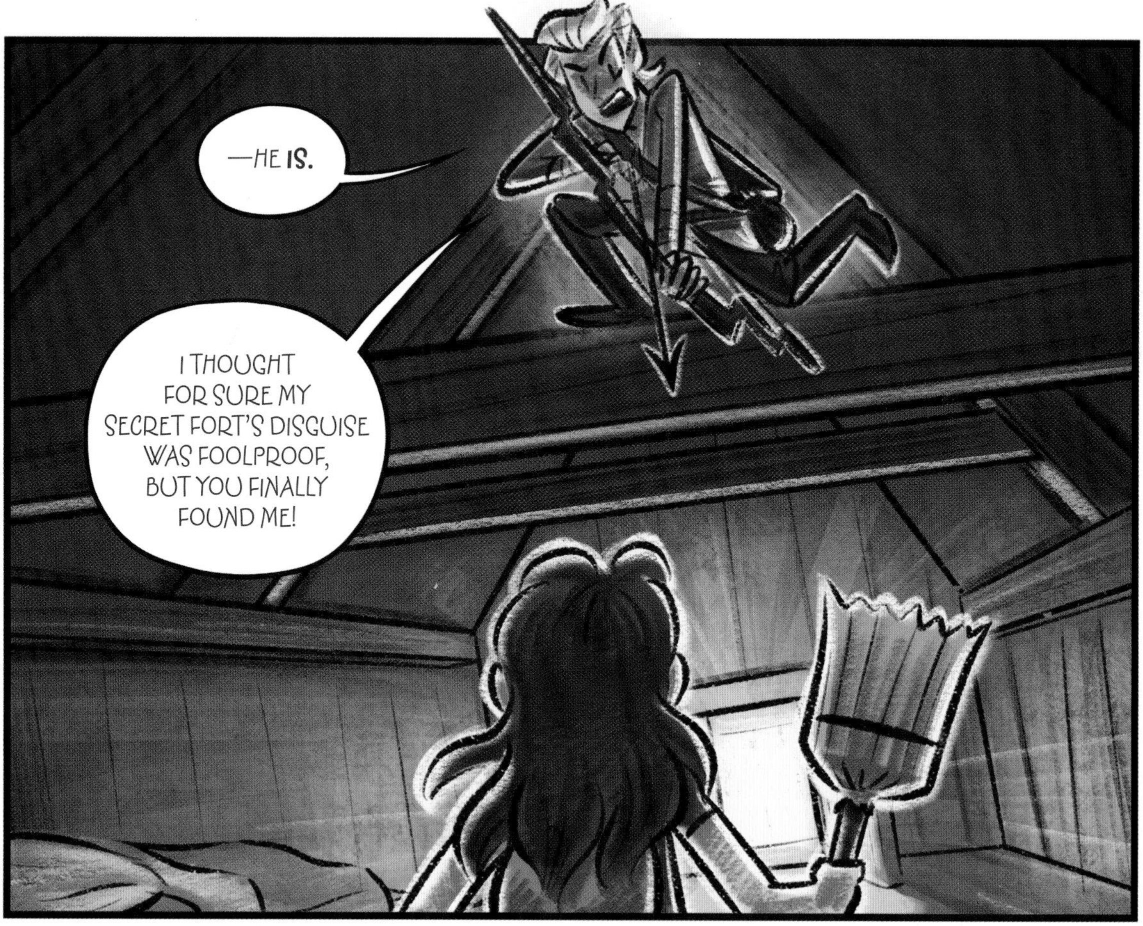
—HE IS.
I THOUGHT FOR SURE MY SECRET FORT'S DISGUISE WAS FOOLPROOF, BUT YOU FINALLY FOUND ME!

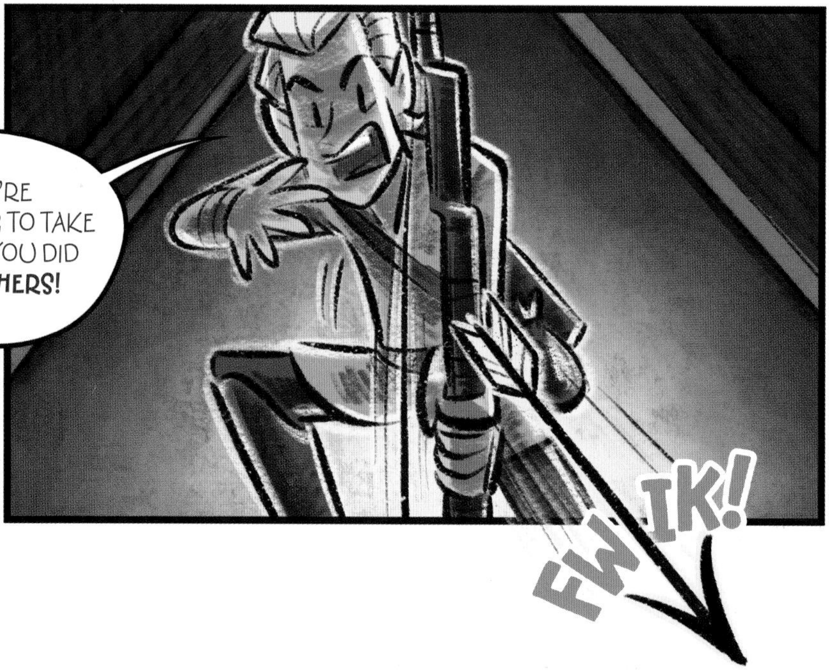
YOU'RE NOT GOING TO TAKE ME LIKE YOU DID THE **OTHERS!**
FWIK!

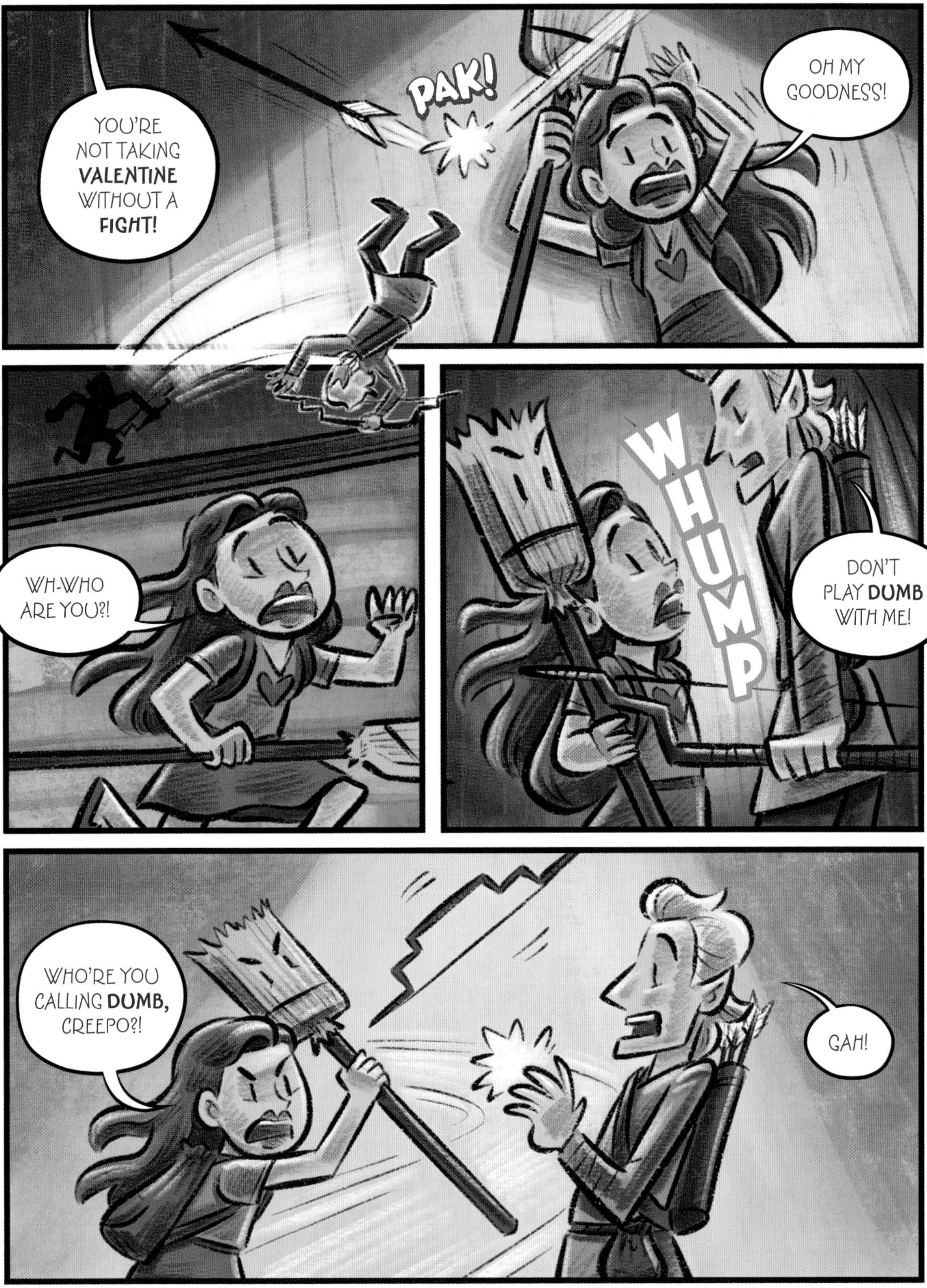
YOU'RE NOT TAKING VALENTINE WITHOUT A FIGHT!
PAK!
OH MY GOODNESS!
WH-WHO ARE YOU?!
WHUMP
DON'T PLAY DUMB WITH ME!
WHO'RE YOU CALLING DUMB, CREEPO?!
GAH!

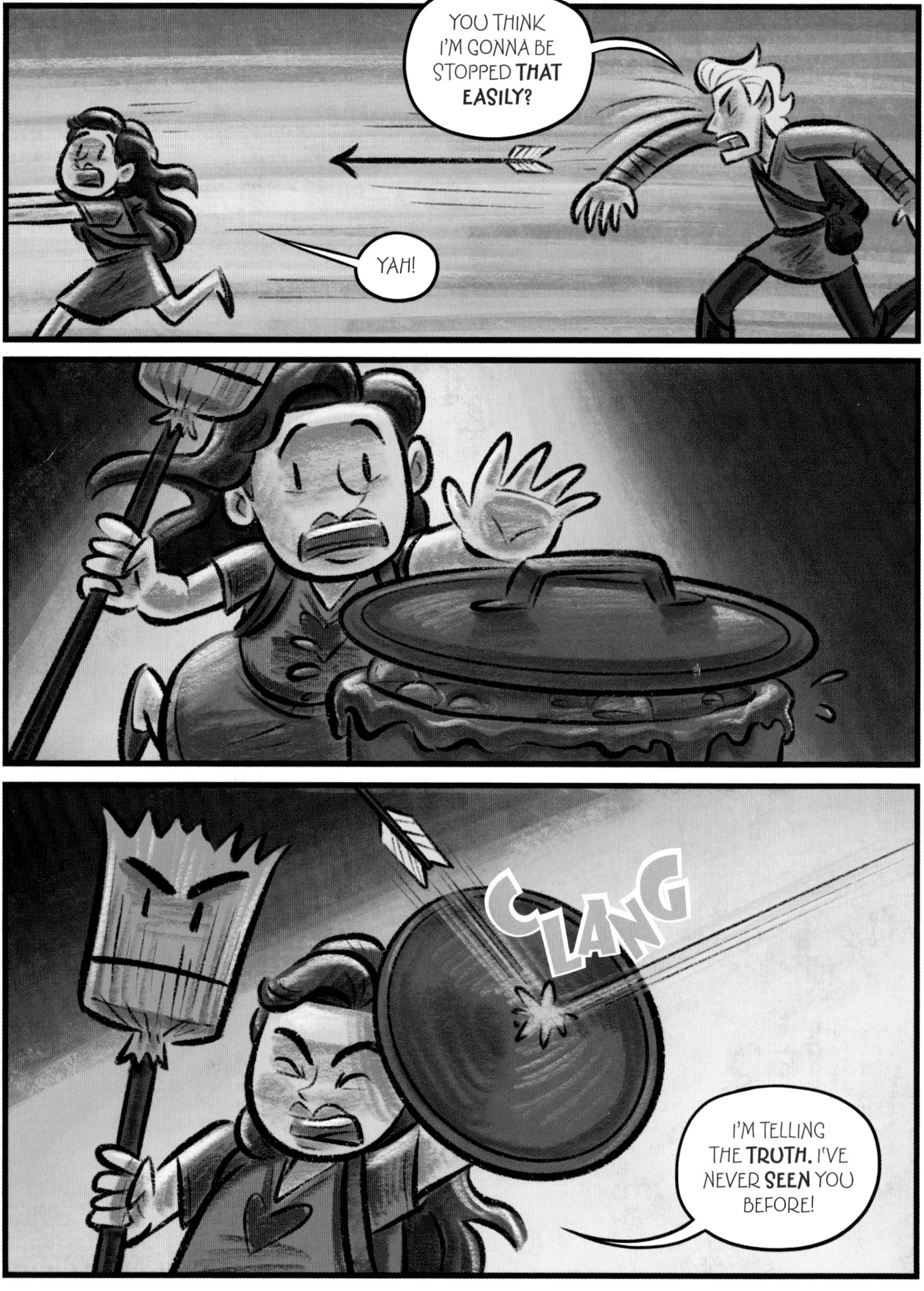
YOU THINK I'M GONNA BE STOPPED **THAT EASILY?**
YAH!
CLANG
I'M TELLING THE **TRUTH.** I'VE NEVER **SEEN** YOU BEFORE!

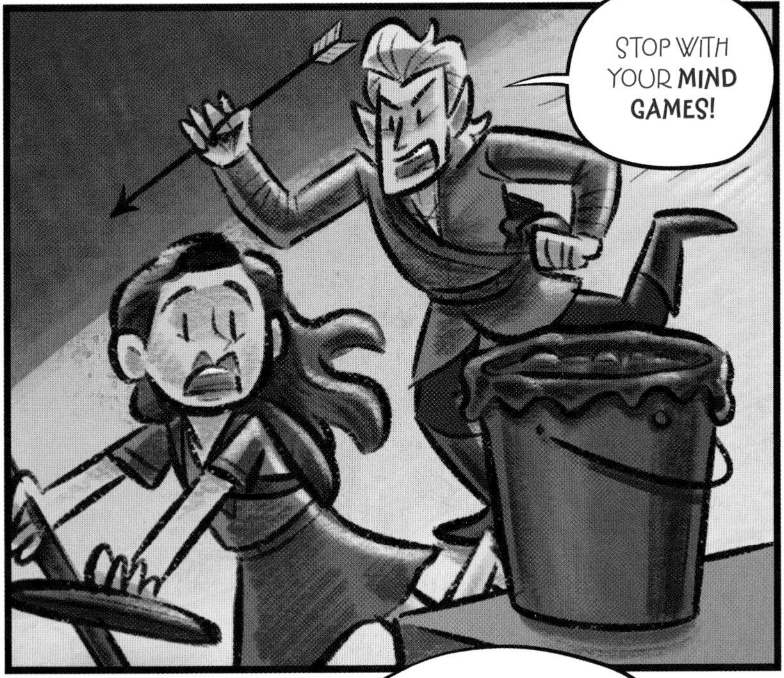
STOP WITH YOUR MIND GAMES!

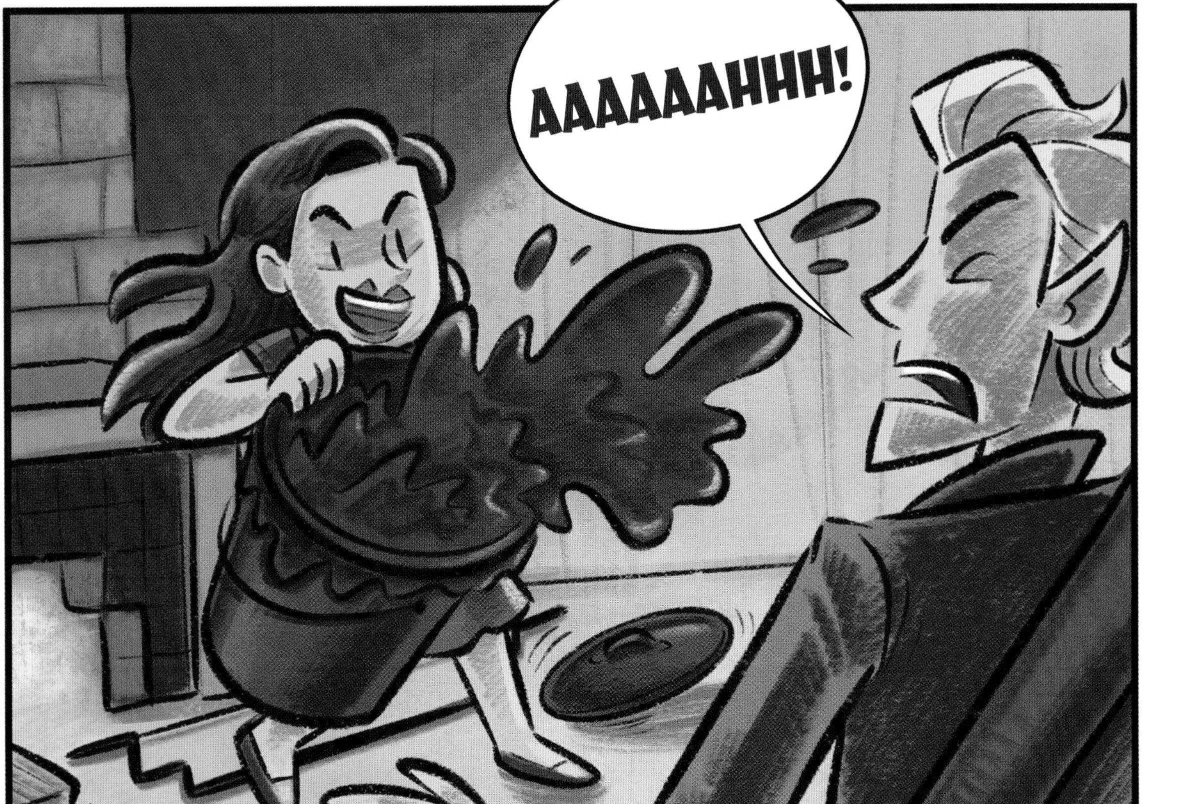
AAAAAAHHH!

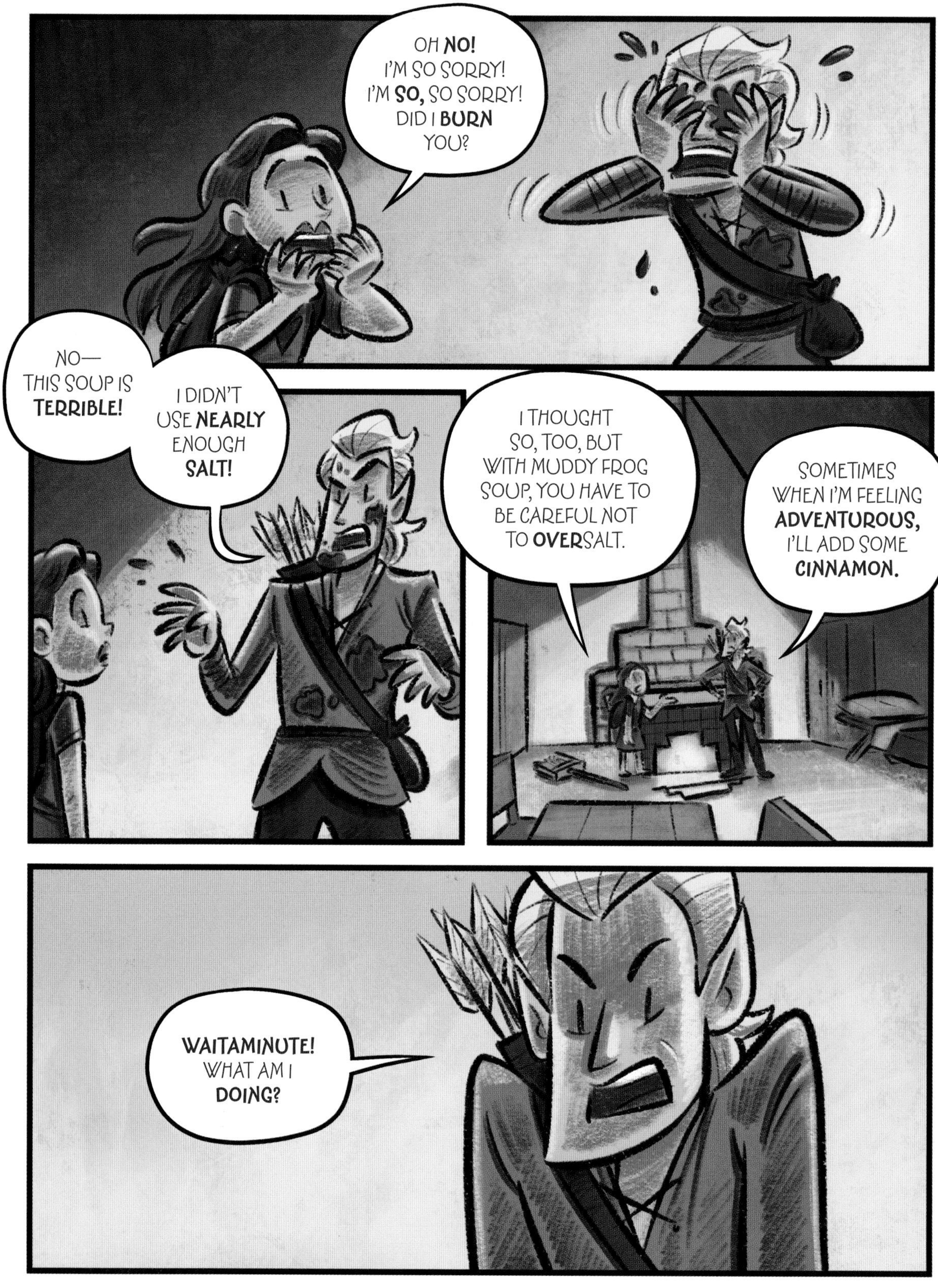
OH **NO!** I'M SO SORRY! I'M **SO,** SO SORRY! DID I **BURN** YOU?
NO— THIS SOUP IS **TERRIBLE!**
I DIDN'T USE **NEARLY** ENOUGH **SALT!**
I THOUGHT SO, TOO, BUT WITH MUDDY FROG SOUP, YOU HAVE TO BE CAREFUL NOT TO **OVER**SALT.
SOMETIMES WHEN I'M FEELING **ADVENTUROUS,** I'LL ADD SOME **CINNAMON.**
WAITAMINUTE! WHAT AM I **DOING?**

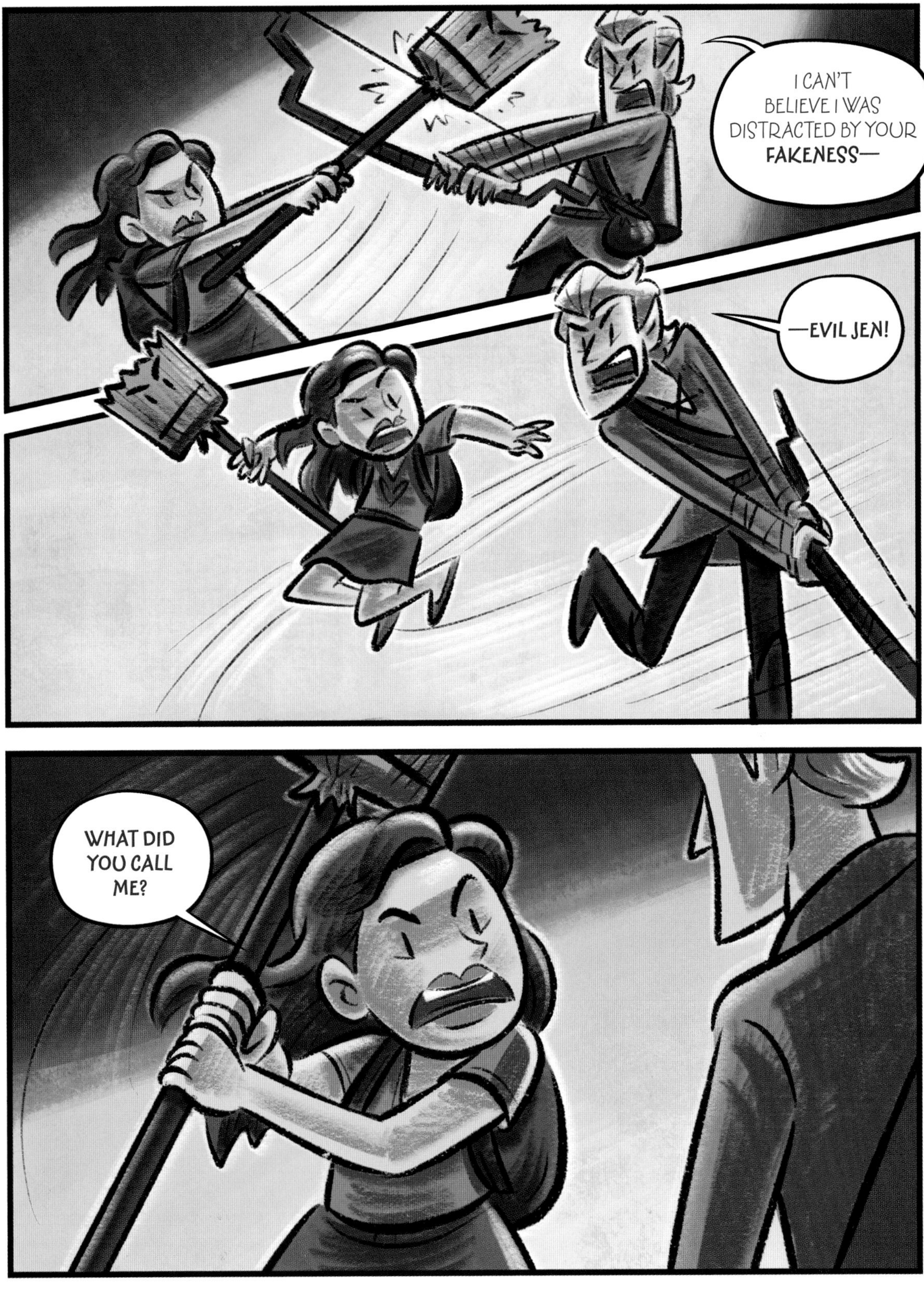
I CAN'T BELIEVE I WAS DISTRACTED BY YOUR **FAKENESS**—
—EVIL JEN!
WHAT DID YOU CALL ME?

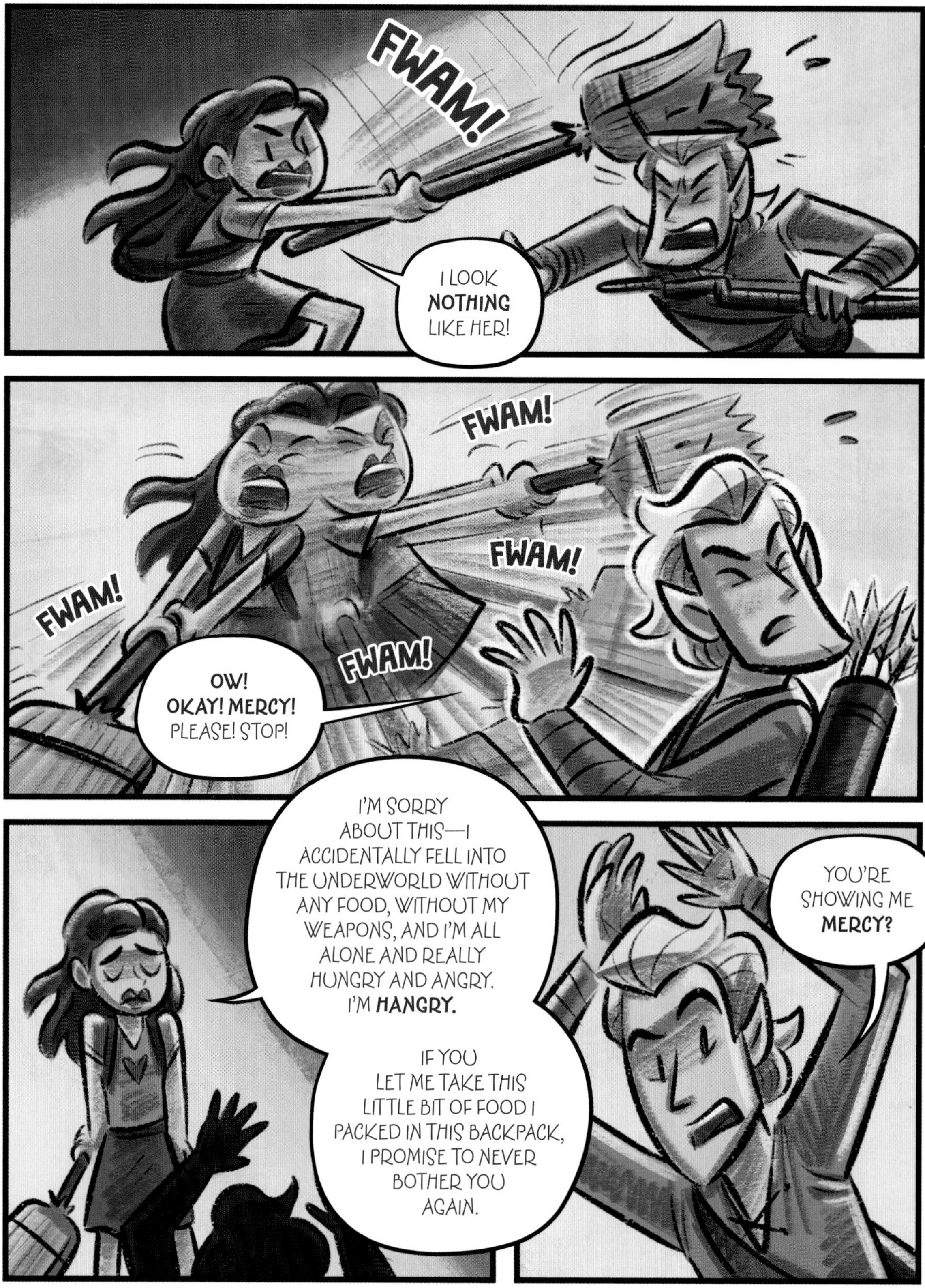
FWAM!
I LOOK **NOTHING** LIKE HER!
FWAM!
FWAM!
FWAM!
FWAM!
OW! OKAY! MERCY! PLEASE! STOP!
I'M SORRY ABOUT THIS—I ACCIDENTALLY FELL INTO THE UNDERWORLD WITHOUT ANY FOOD, WITHOUT MY WEAPONS, AND I'M ALL ALONE AND REALLY HUNGRY AND ANGRY. I'M **HANGRY.**
IF YOU LET ME TAKE THIS LITTLE BIT OF FOOD I PACKED IN THIS BACKPACK, I PROMISE TO NEVER BOTHER YOU AGAIN.
YOU'RE SHOWING ME **MERCY?**

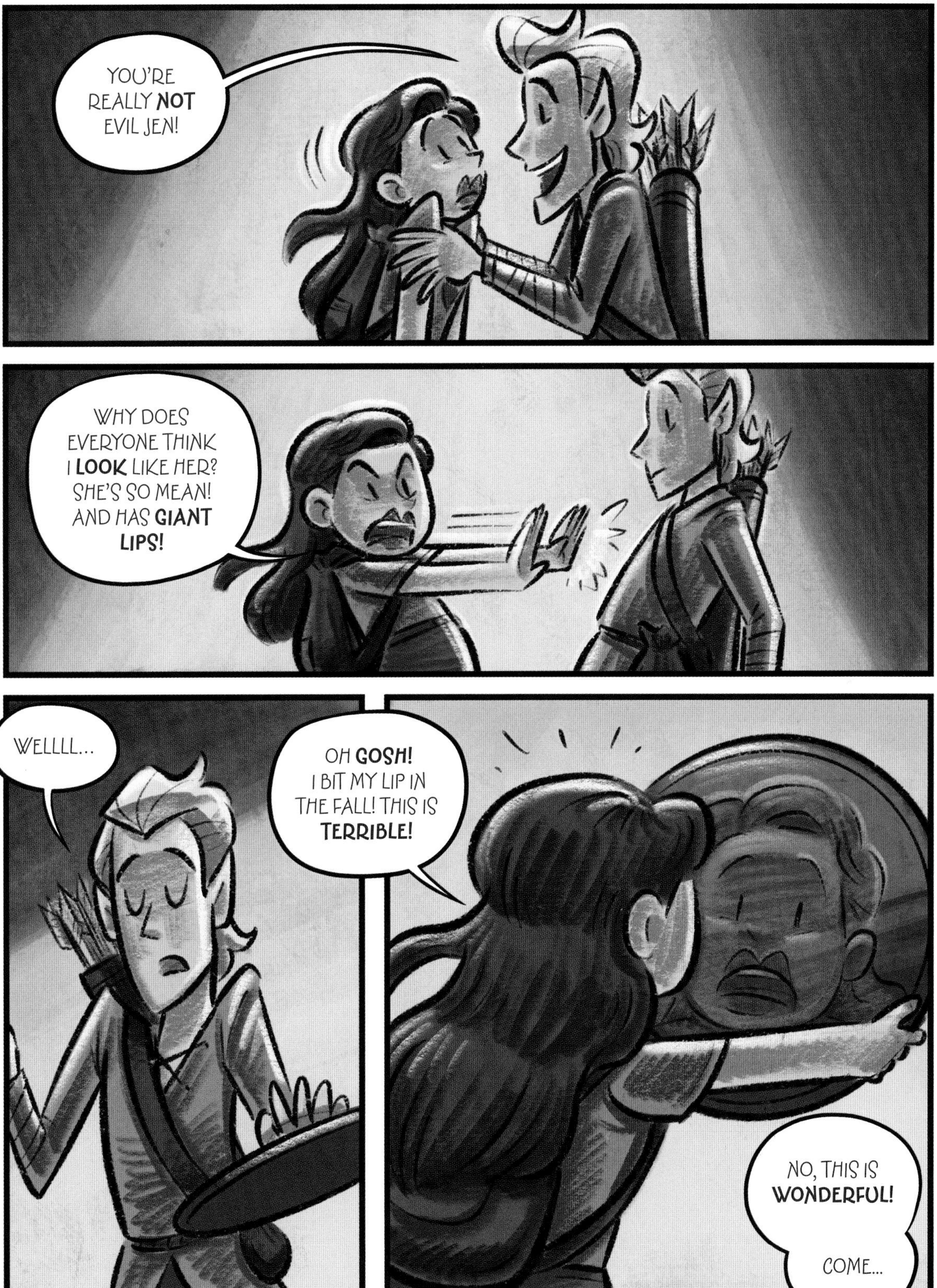
YOU'RE REALLY **NOT** EVIL JEN!
WHY DOES EVERYONE THINK I **LOOK** LIKE HER? SHE'S SO MEAN! AND HAS **GIANT LIPS!**
WELLLL...
OH **GOSH!** I BIT MY LIP IN THE FALL! THIS IS **TERRIBLE!**
NO, THIS IS **WONDERFUL!**
COME...

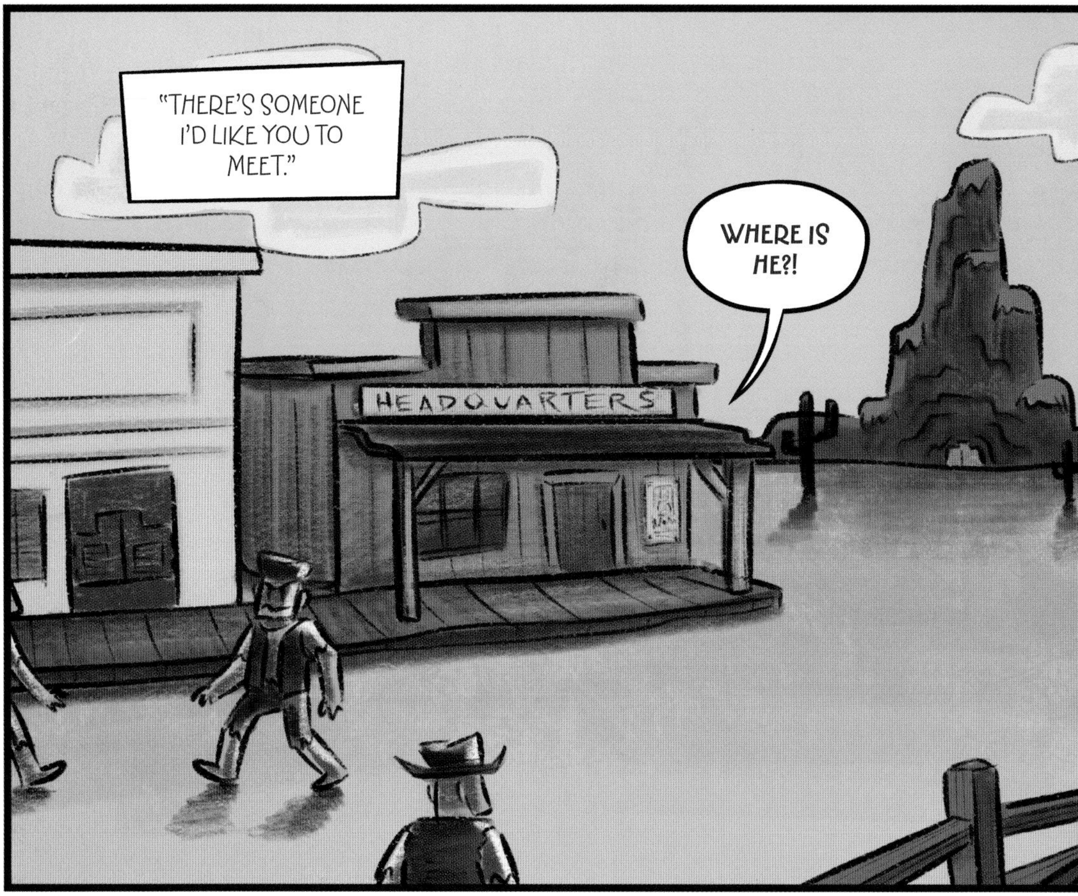
"THERE'S SOMEONE I'D LIKE YOU TO MEET."
WHERE IS HE?!
HEADQUARTERS

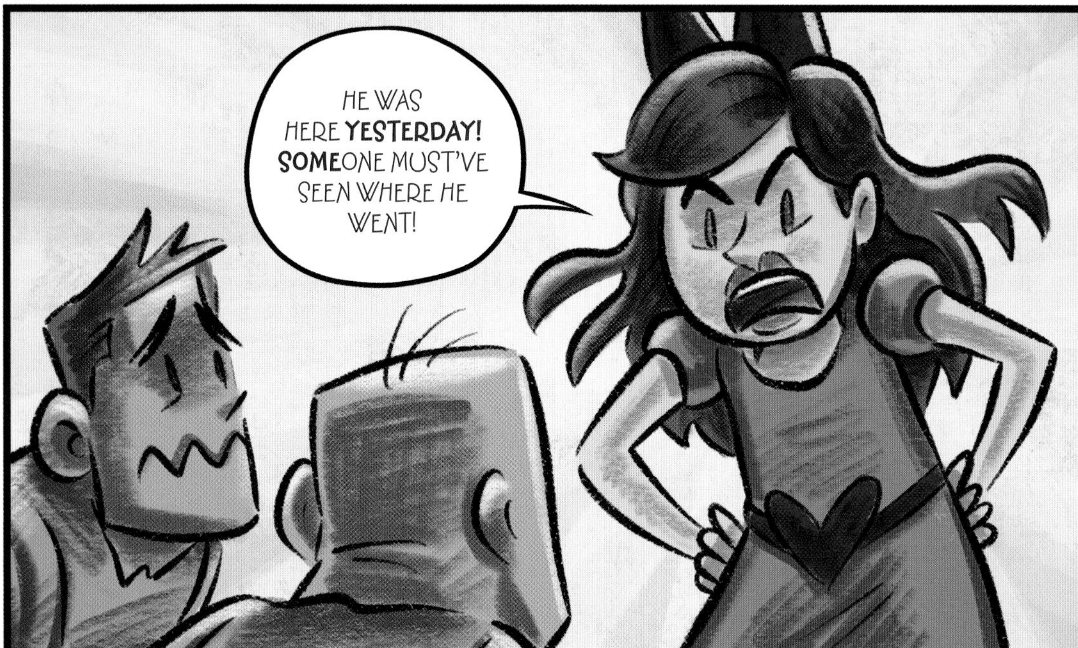
HE WAS HERE YESTERDAY! SOMEONE MUST'VE SEEN WHERE HE WENT!

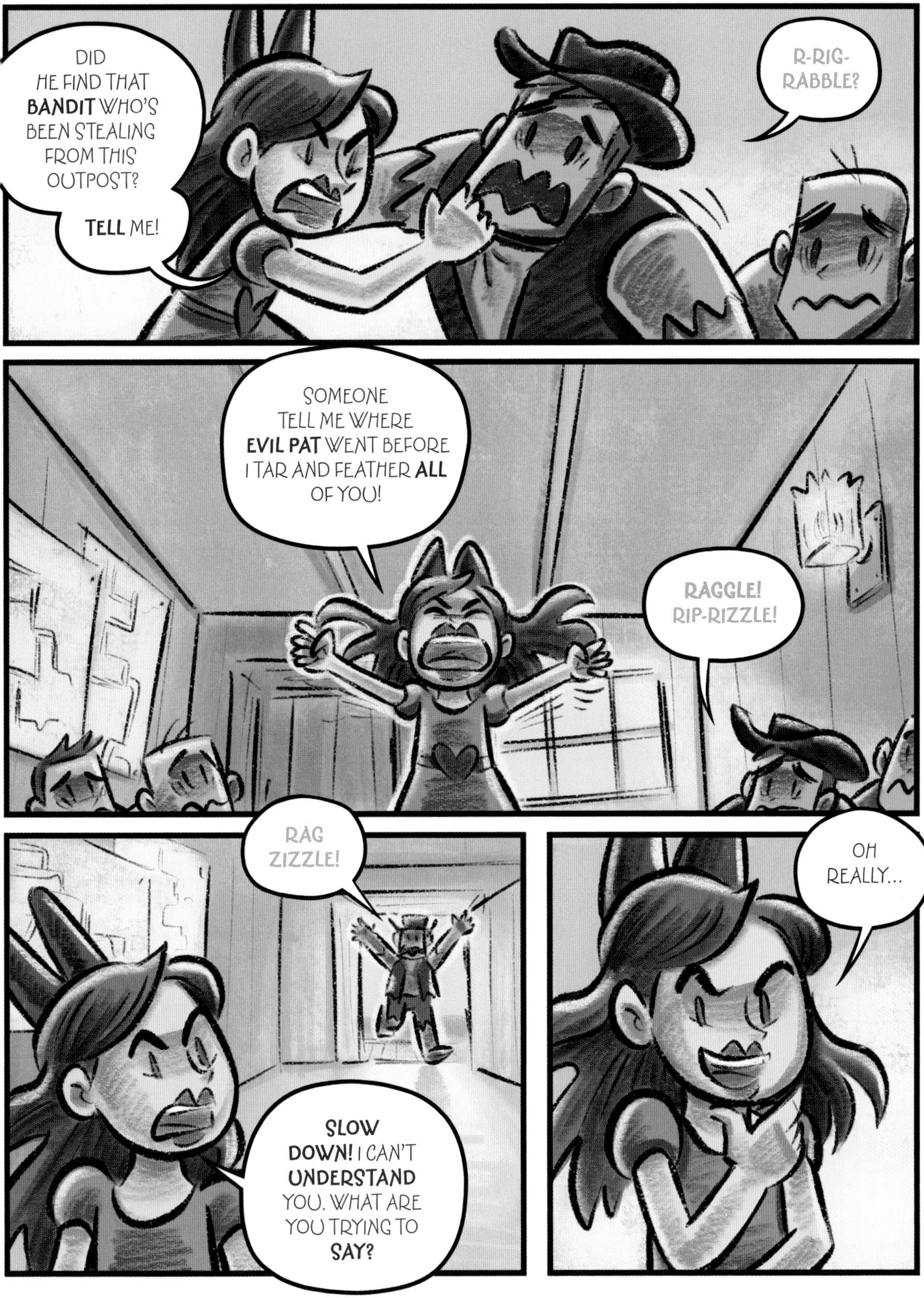
DID HE FIND THAT BANDIT WHO'S BEEN STEALING FROM THIS OUTPOST?
TELL ME!
R-RIG-RABBLE?
SOMEONE TELL ME WHERE EVIL PAT WENT BEFORE I TAR AND FEATHER ALL OF YOU!
RAGGLE! RIP-RIZZLE!
RAG ZIZZLE!
SLOW DOWN! I CAN'T UNDERSTAND YOU. WHAT ARE YOU TRYING TO SAY?
OH REALLY...

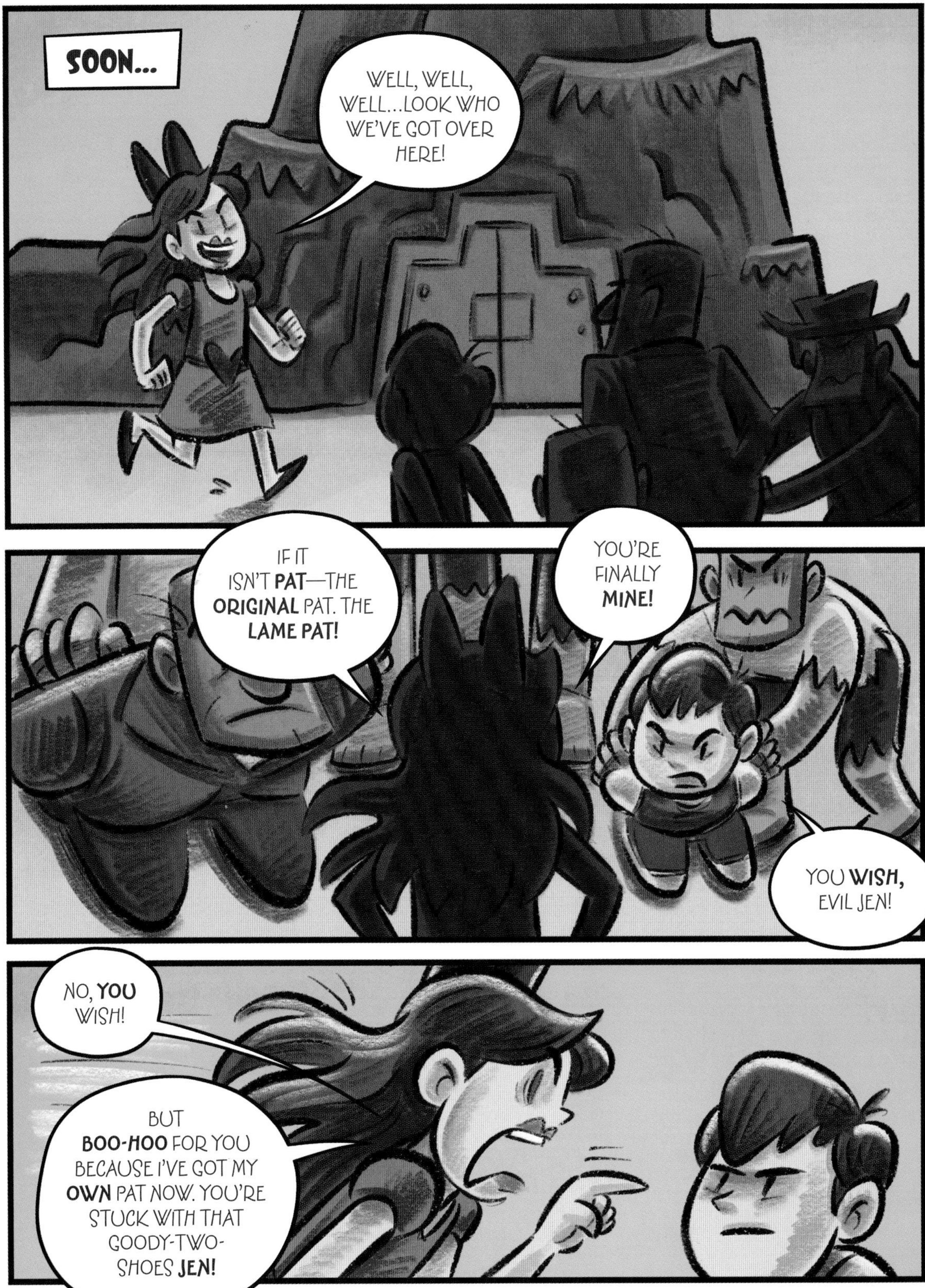
SOON...
WELL, WELL, WELL...LOOK WHO WE'VE GOT OVER HERE!
IF IT ISN'T **PAT**—THE **ORIGINAL** PAT. THE **LAME PAT!**
YOU'RE FINALLY **MINE!**
YOU **WISH,** EVIL JEN!
NO, **YOU** WISH!
BUT **BOO-HOO** FOR YOU BECAUSE I'VE GOT MY **OWN** PAT NOW. YOU'RE STUCK WITH THAT GOODY-TWO-SHOES **JEN!**

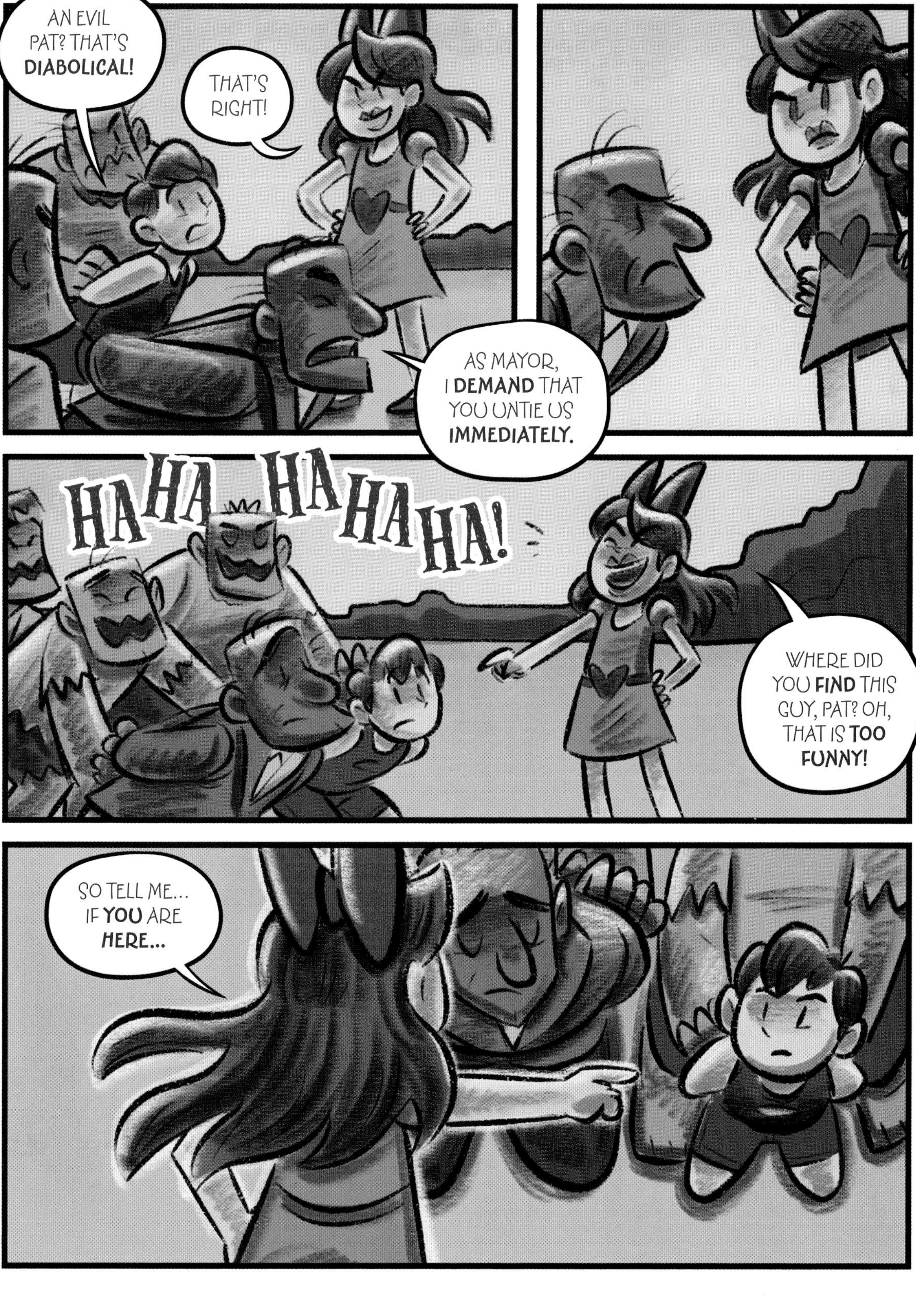

AN EVIL PAT? THAT'S **DIABOLICAL!**
THAT'S RIGHT!
AS MAYOR, I **DEMAND** THAT YOU UNTIE US **IMMEDIATELY.**
HAHA HAHAHAHA!
WHERE DID YOU **FIND** THIS GUY, PAT? OH, THAT IS **TOO FUNNY!**
SO TELL ME... IF **YOU** ARE **HERE...**

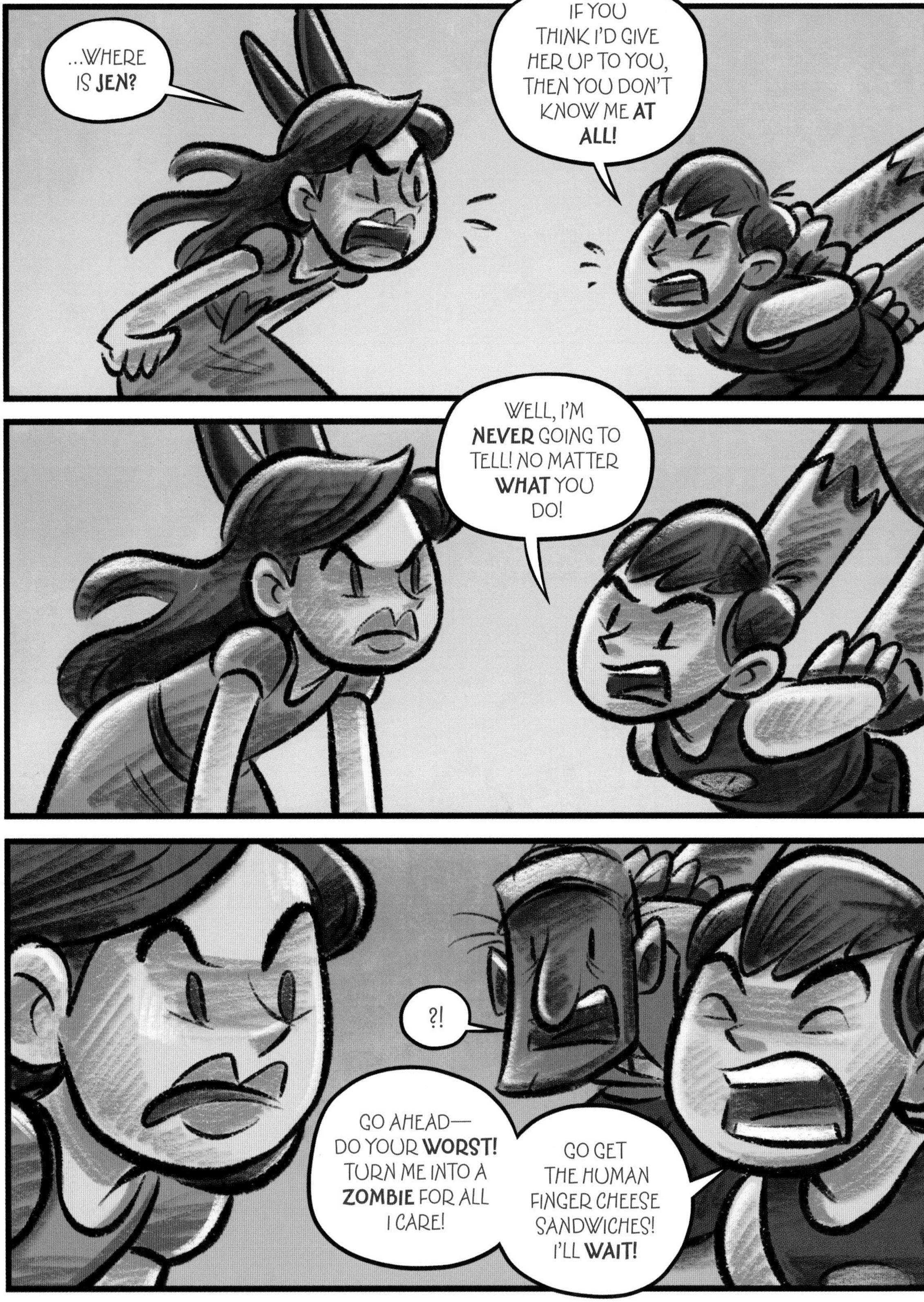

...WHERE IS **JEN?**
IF YOU THINK I'D GIVE HER UP TO YOU, THEN YOU DON'T KNOW ME **AT ALL!**
WELL, I'M **NEVER** GOING TO TELL! NO MATTER **WHAT** YOU DO!
?!
GO AHEAD— DO YOUR **WORST!** TURN ME INTO A **ZOMBIE** FOR ALL I CARE!
GO GET THE HUMAN FINGER CHEESE SANDWICHES! I'LL **WAIT!**

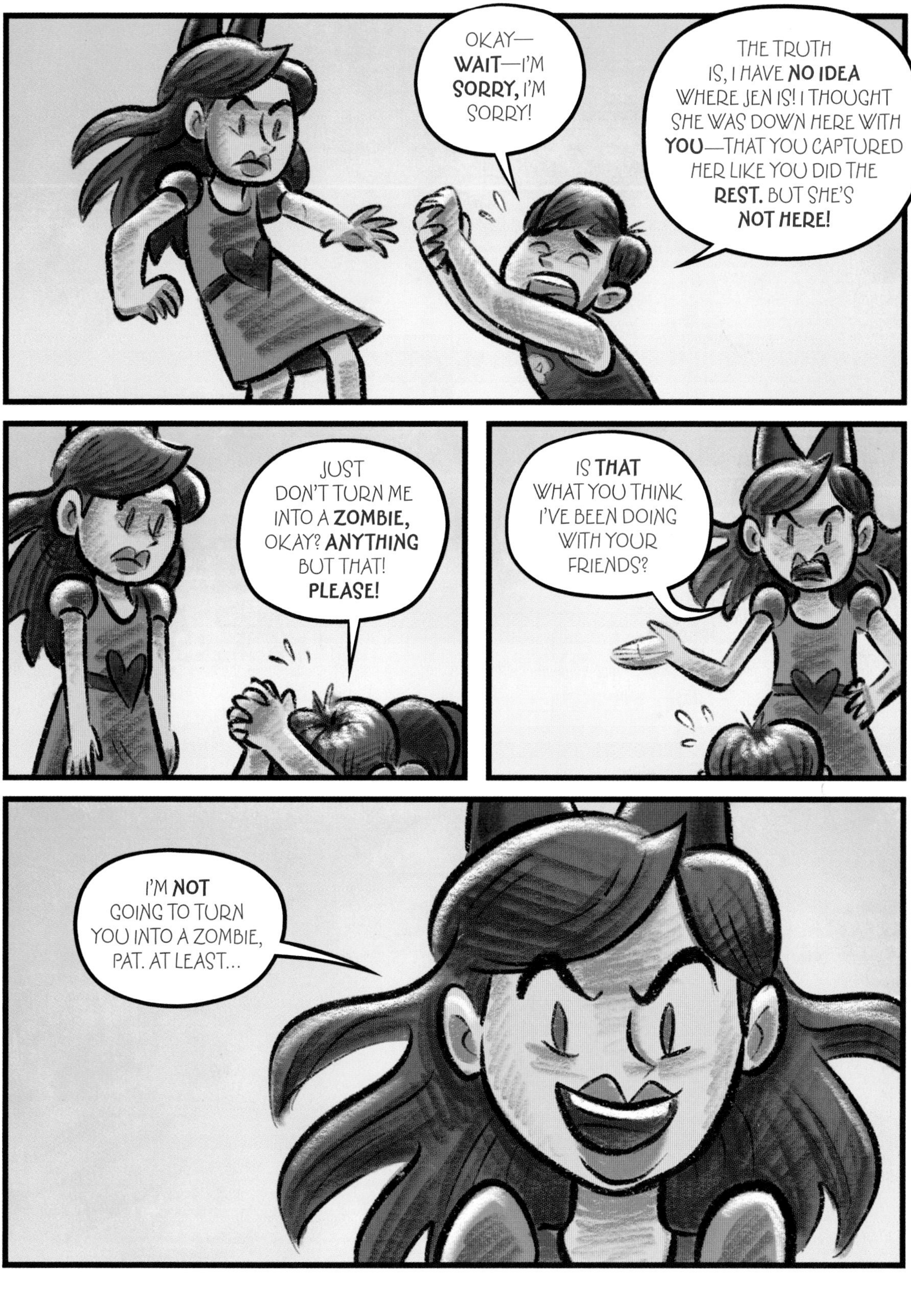
OKAY—WAIT—I'M SORRY, I'M SORRY!
THE TRUTH IS, I HAVE NO IDEA WHERE JEN IS! I THOUGHT SHE WAS DOWN HERE WITH YOU—THAT YOU CAPTURED HER LIKE YOU DID THE REST. BUT SHE'S NOT HERE!
JUST DON'T TURN ME INTO A ZOMBIE, OKAY? ANYTHING BUT THAT! PLEASE!
IS THAT WHAT YOU THINK I'VE BEEN DOING WITH YOUR FRIENDS?
I'M NOT GOING TO TURN YOU INTO A ZOMBIE, PAT. AT LEAST...

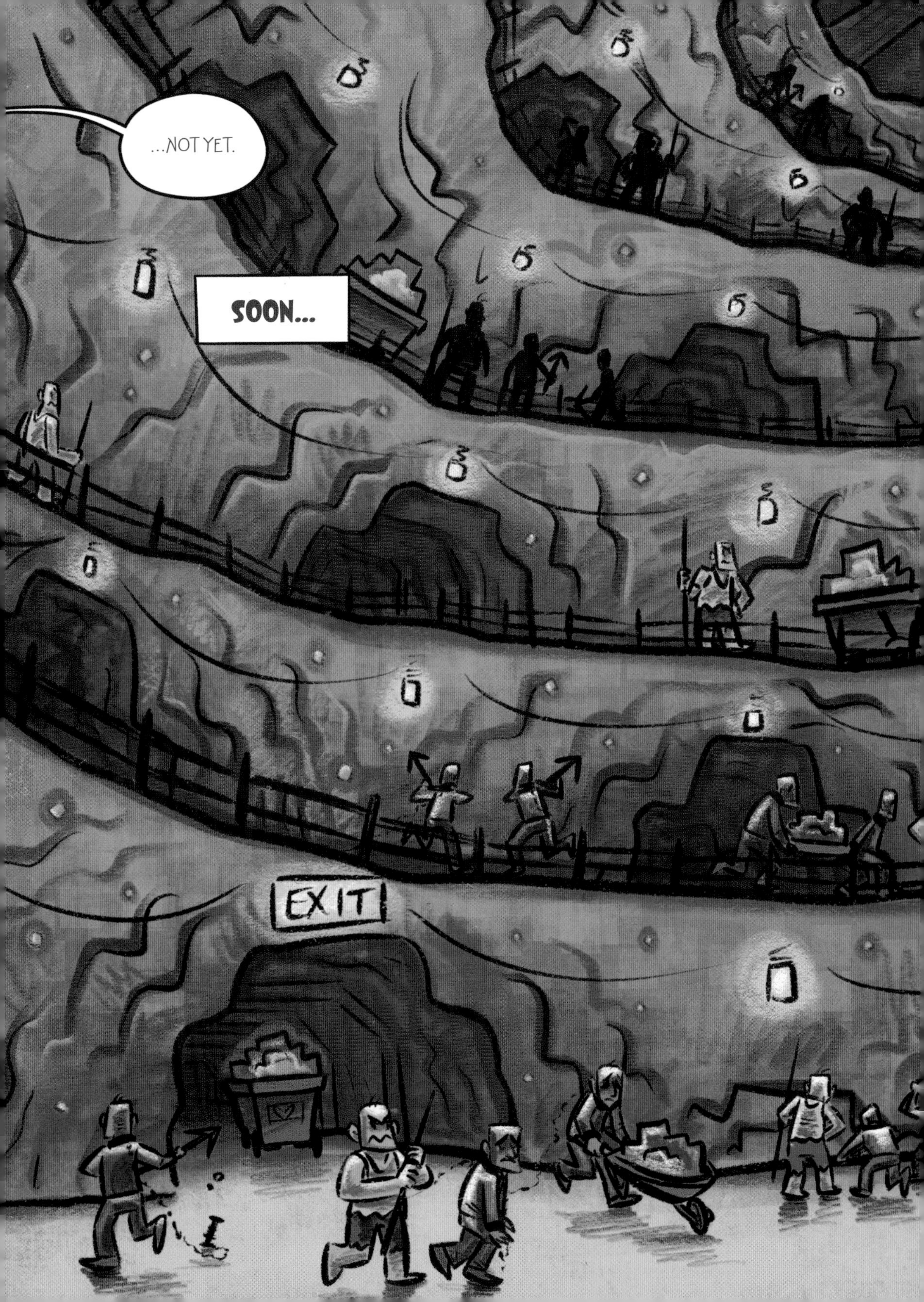

...NOT YET.
SOON...
EXIT

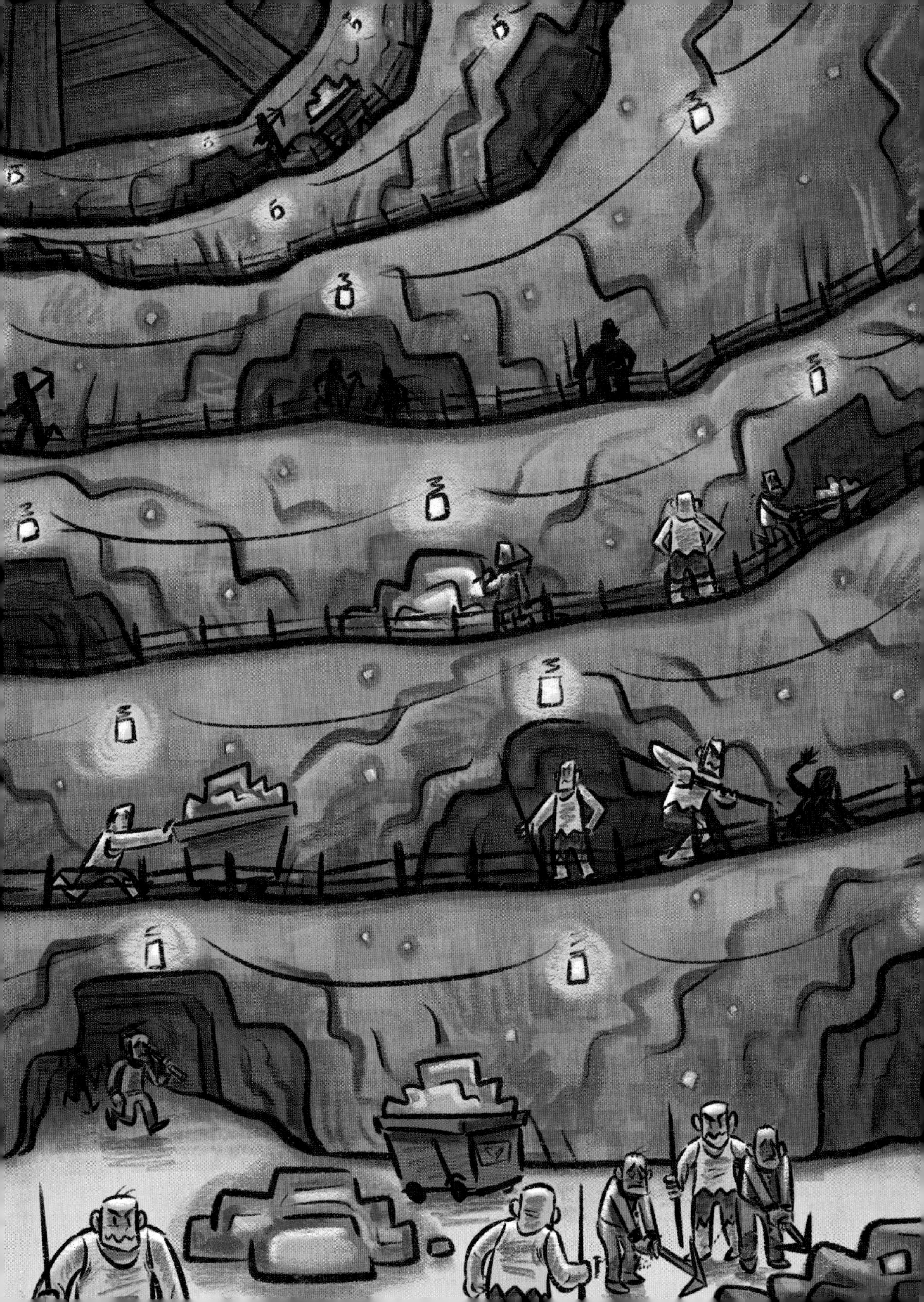

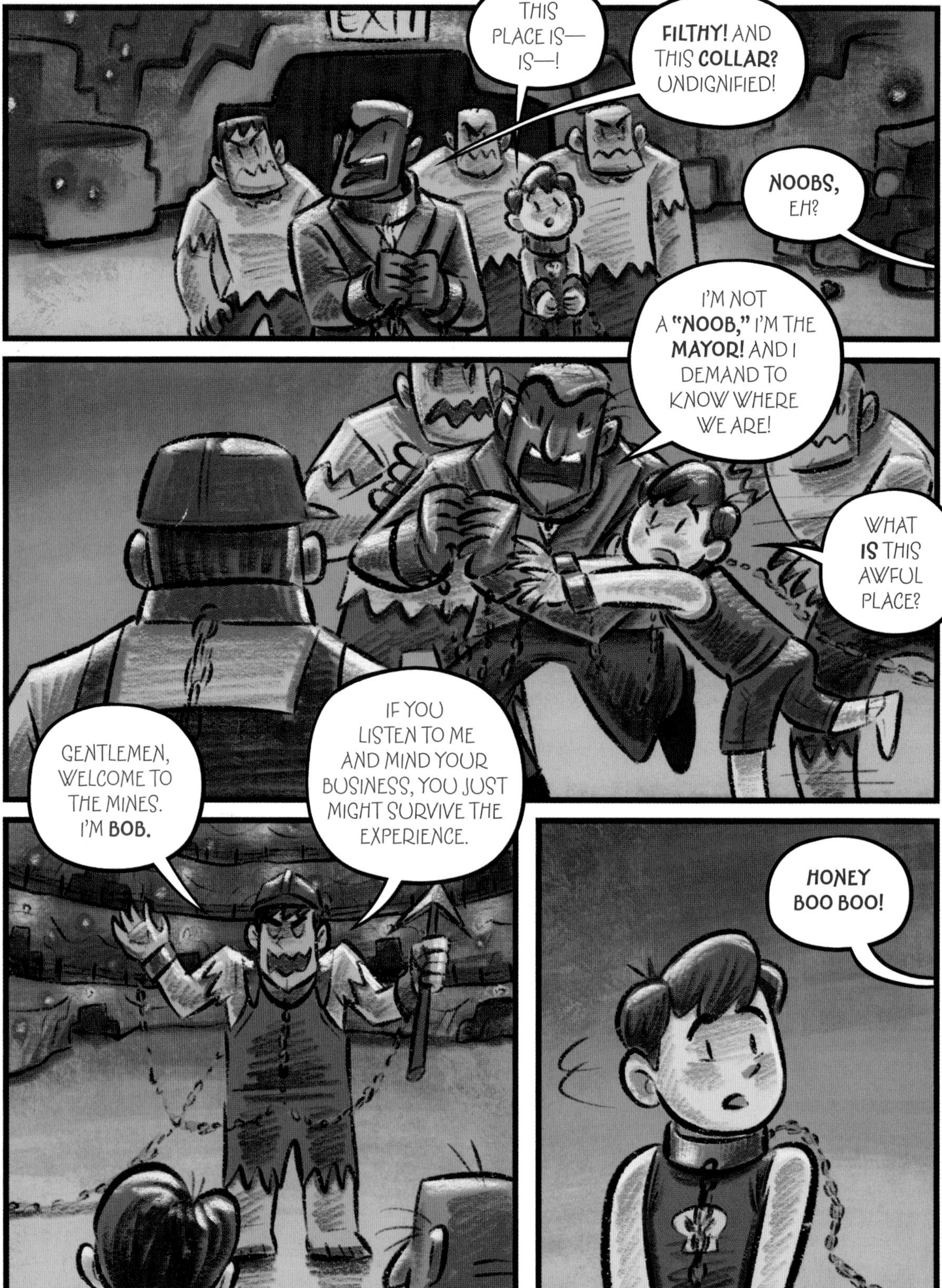
EXIT
THIS PLACE IS— IS—!
FILTHY! AND THIS COLLAR? UNDIGNIFIED!
NOOBS, EH?
I'M NOT A "NOOB," I'M THE MAYOR! AND I DEMAND TO KNOW WHERE WE ARE!
WHAT IS THIS AWFUL PLACE?
GENTLEMEN, WELCOME TO THE MINES. I'M BOB.
IF YOU LISTEN TO ME AND MIND YOUR BUSINESS, YOU JUST MIGHT SURVIVE THE EXPERIENCE.
HONEY BOO BOO!

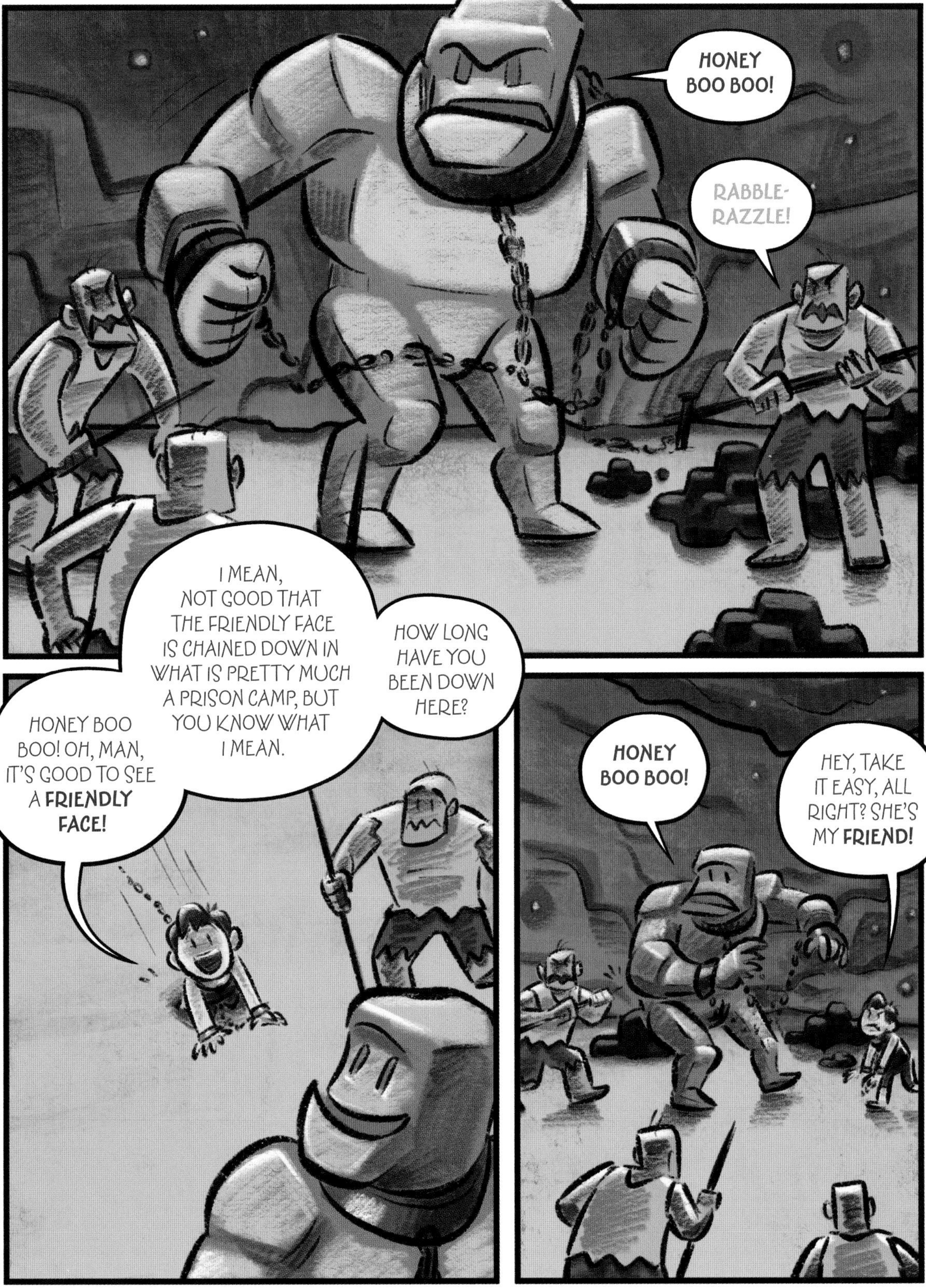
HONEY BOO BOO!
RABBLE-RAZZLE!
HONEY BOO BOO! OH, MAN, IT'S GOOD TO SEE A FRIENDLY FACE!
I MEAN, NOT GOOD THAT THE FRIENDLY FACE IS CHAINED DOWN IN WHAT IS PRETTY MUCH A PRISON CAMP, BUT YOU KNOW WHAT I MEAN.
HOW LONG HAVE YOU BEEN DOWN HERE?
HONEY BOO BOO!
HEY, TAKE IT EASY, ALL RIGHT? SHE'S MY FRIEND!

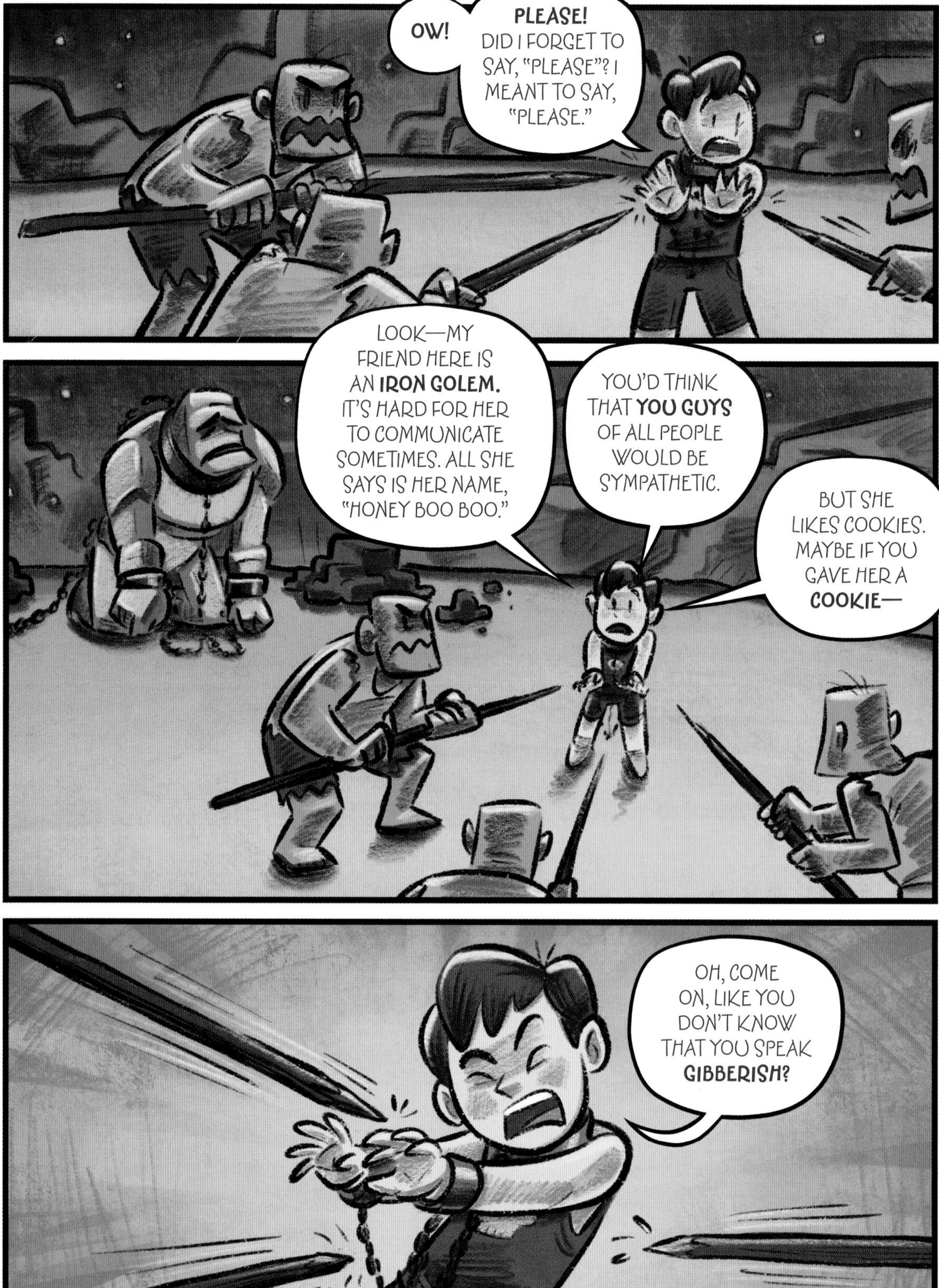
OW!
PLEASE! DID I FORGET TO SAY, "PLEASE"? I MEANT TO SAY, "PLEASE."
LOOK—MY FRIEND HERE IS AN IRON GOLEM. IT'S HARD FOR HER TO COMMUNICATE SOMETIMES. ALL SHE SAYS IS HER NAME, "HONEY BOO BOO."
YOU'D THINK THAT YOU GUYS OF ALL PEOPLE WOULD BE SYMPATHETIC.
BUT SHE LIKES COOKIES. MAYBE IF YOU GAVE HER A COOKIE—
OH, COME ON, LIKE YOU DON'T KNOW THAT YOU SPEAK GIBBERISH?

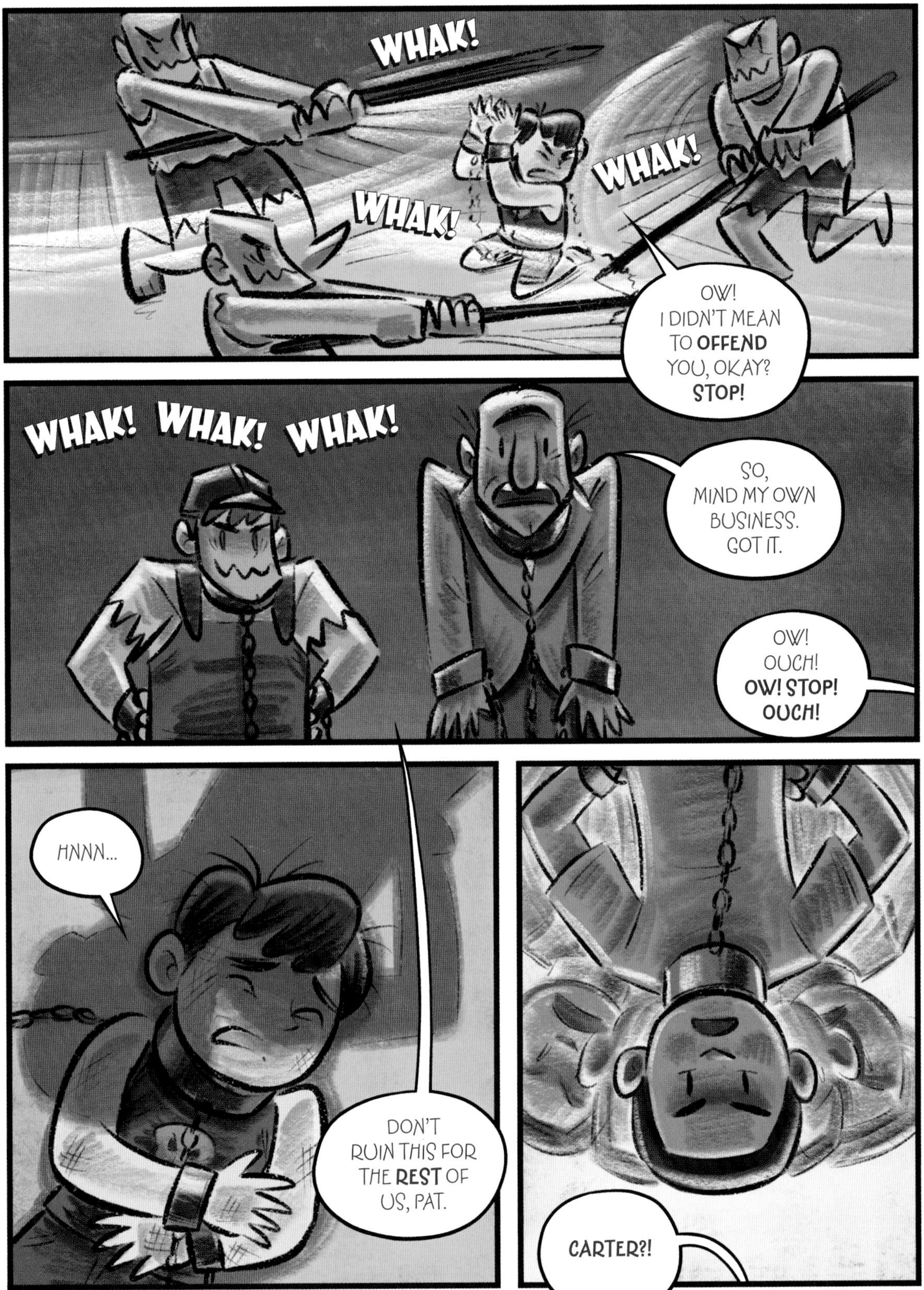
WHAK!
WHAK!
WHAK!
OW! I DIDN'T MEAN TO OFFEND YOU, OKAY? STOP!
WHAK! WHAK! WHAK!
SO, MIND MY OWN BUSINESS. GOT IT.
OW! OUCH! OW! STOP! OUCH!
HNNN...
DON'T RUIN THIS FOR THE REST OF US, PAT.
CARTER?!

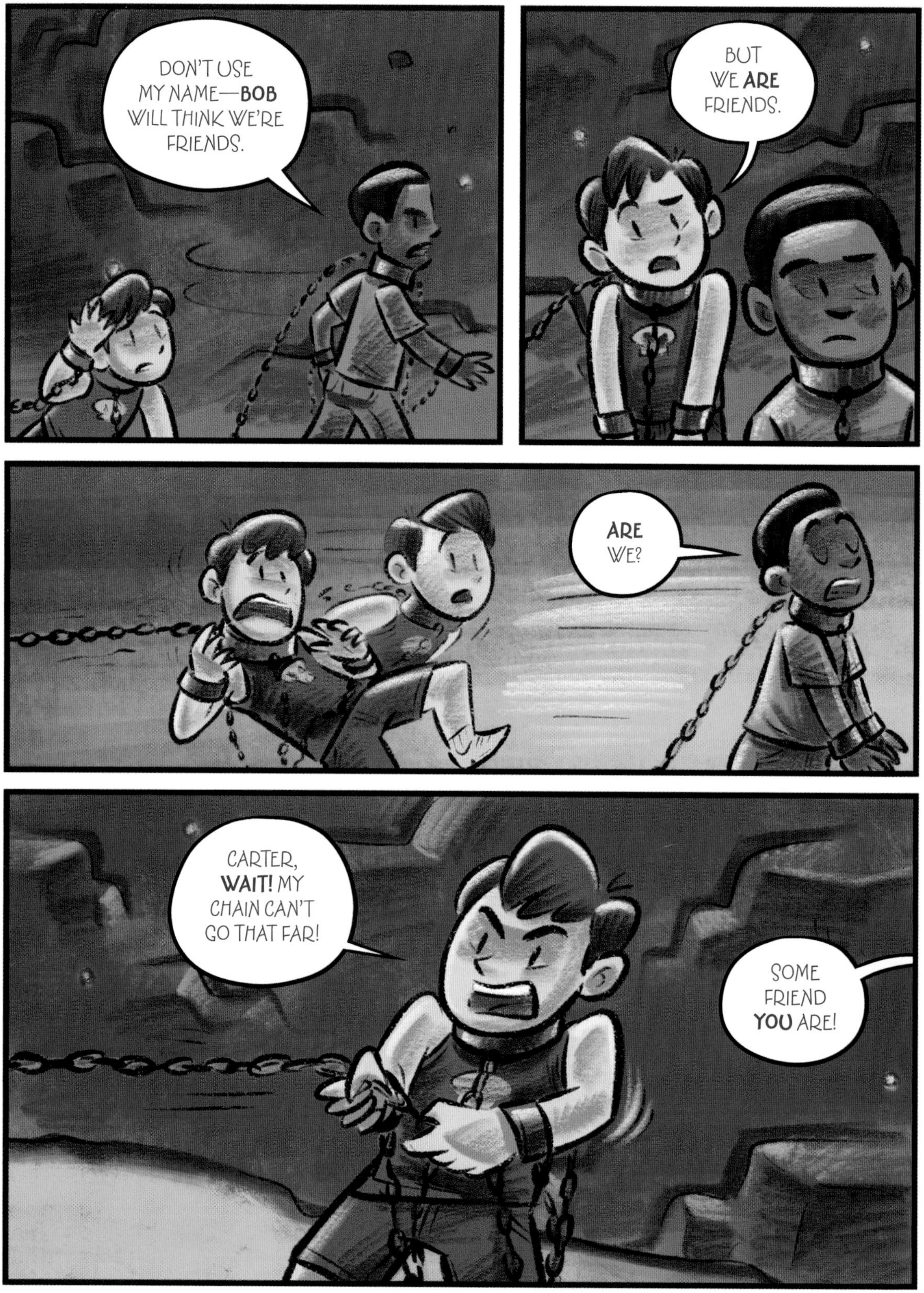
DON'T USE MY NAME—**BOB** WILL THINK WE'RE FRIENDS.
BUT WE **ARE** FRIENDS.
ARE WE?
CARTER, **WAIT!** MY CHAIN CAN'T GO THAT FAR!
SOME FRIEND **YOU** ARE!

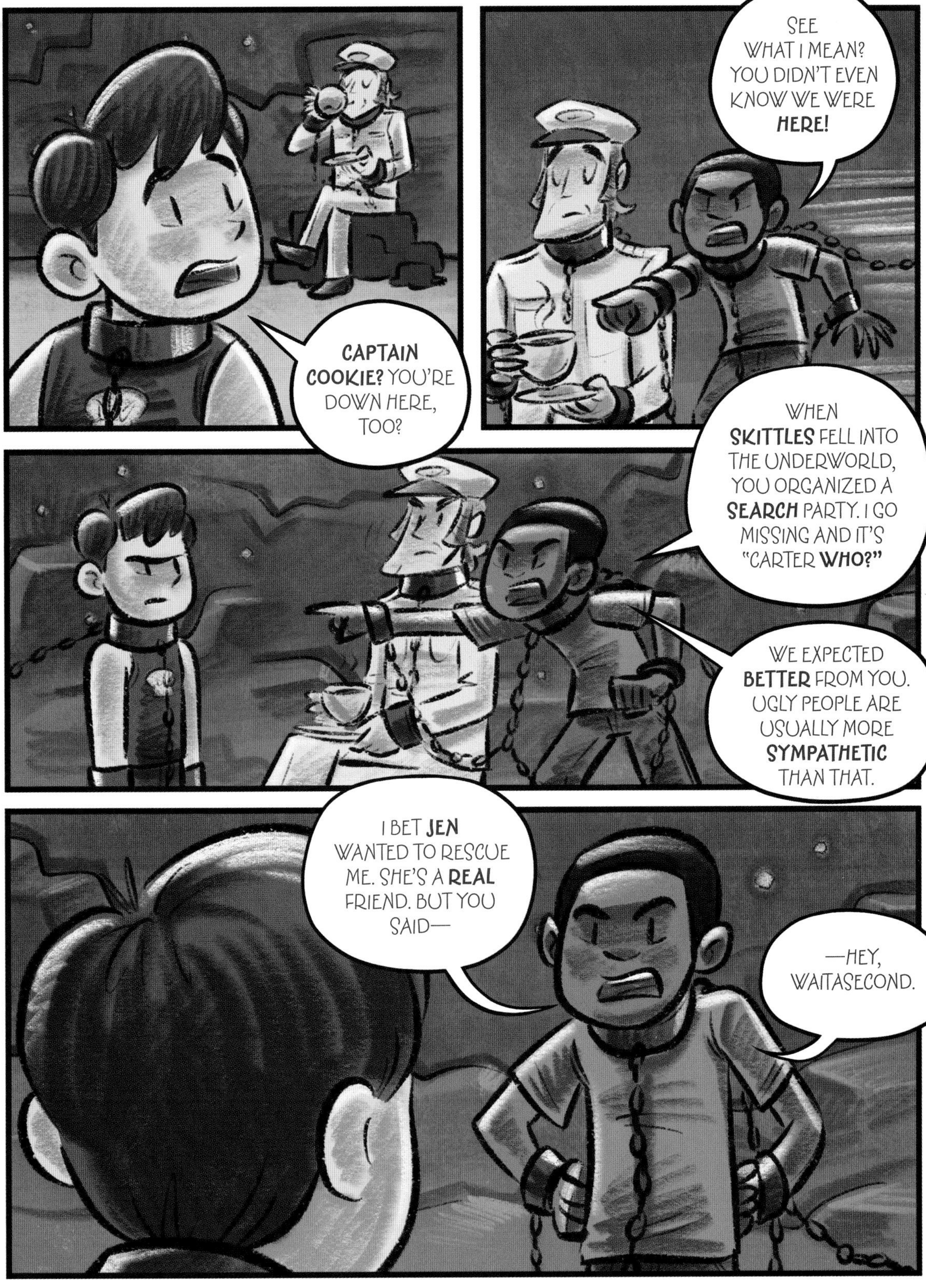
CAPTAIN COOKIE? YOU'RE DOWN HERE, TOO?
SEE WHAT I MEAN? YOU DIDN'T EVEN KNOW WE WERE HERE!
WHEN SKITTLES FELL INTO THE UNDERWORLD, YOU ORGANIZED A SEARCH PARTY. I GO MISSING AND IT'S "CARTER WHO?"
WE EXPECTED BETTER FROM YOU. UGLY PEOPLE ARE USUALLY MORE SYMPATHETIC THAN THAT.
I BET JEN WANTED TO RESCUE ME. SHE'S A REAL FRIEND. BUT YOU SAID—
—HEY, WAITASECOND.

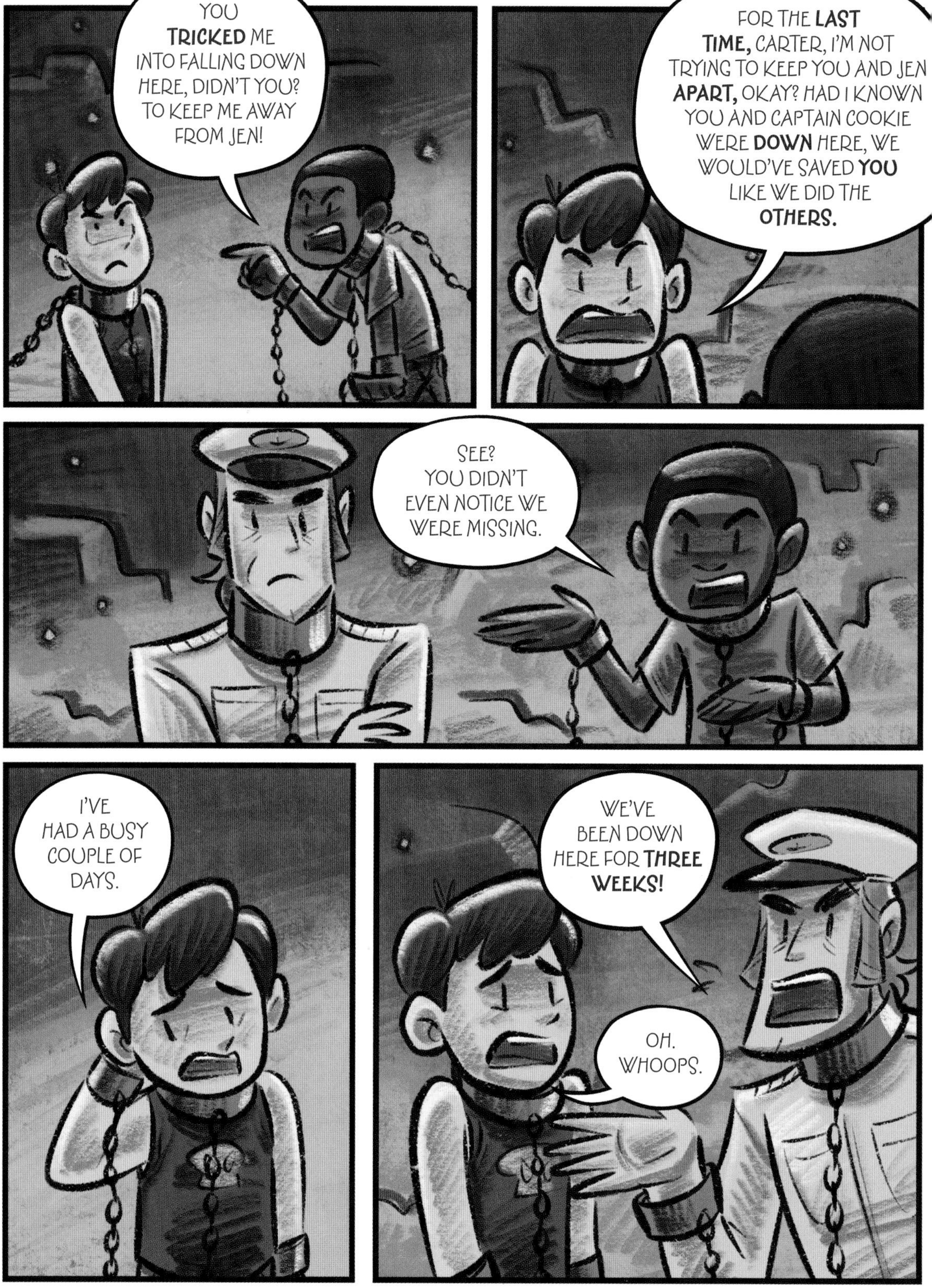
YOU TRICKED ME INTO FALLING DOWN HERE, DIDN'T YOU? TO KEEP ME AWAY FROM JEN!
FOR THE LAST TIME, CARTER, I'M NOT TRYING TO KEEP YOU AND JEN APART, OKAY? HAD I KNOWN YOU AND CAPTAIN COOKIE WERE DOWN HERE, WE WOULD'VE SAVED YOU LIKE WE DID THE OTHERS.
SEE? YOU DIDN'T EVEN NOTICE WE WERE MISSING.
I'VE HAD A BUSY COUPLE OF DAYS.
WE'VE BEEN DOWN HERE FOR THREE WEEKS!
OH. WHOOPS.

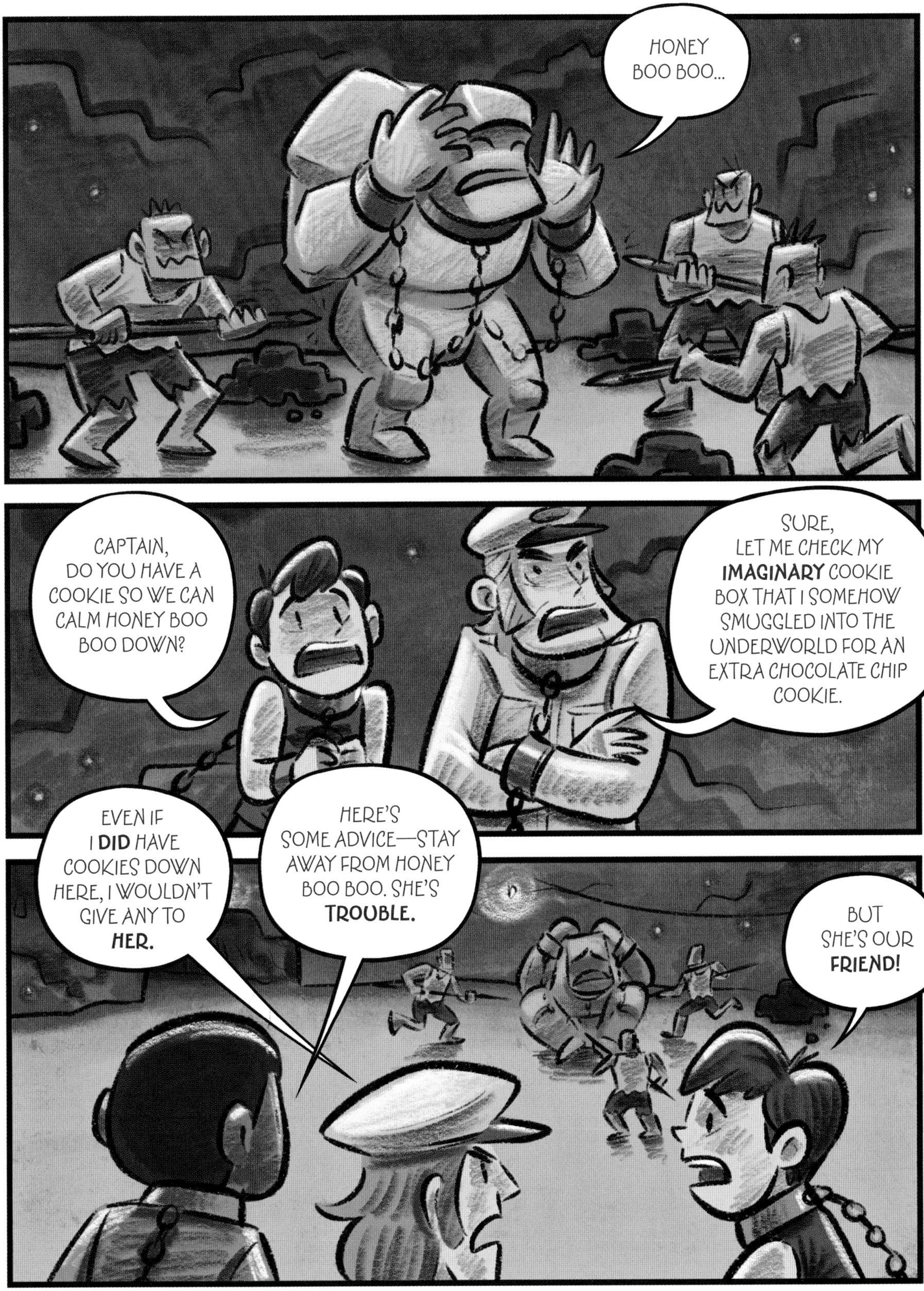
HONEY BOO BOO...
CAPTAIN, DO YOU HAVE A COOKIE SO WE CAN CALM HONEY BOO BOO DOWN?
SURE, LET ME CHECK MY **IMAGINARY** COOKIE BOX THAT I SOMEHOW SMUGGLED INTO THE UNDERWORLD FOR AN EXTRA CHOCOLATE CHIP COOKIE.
EVEN IF I **DID** HAVE COOKIES DOWN HERE, I WOULDN'T GIVE ANY TO **HER.**
HERE'S SOME ADVICE—STAY AWAY FROM HONEY BOO BOO. SHE'S **TROUBLE.**
BUT SHE'S OUR **FRIEND!**

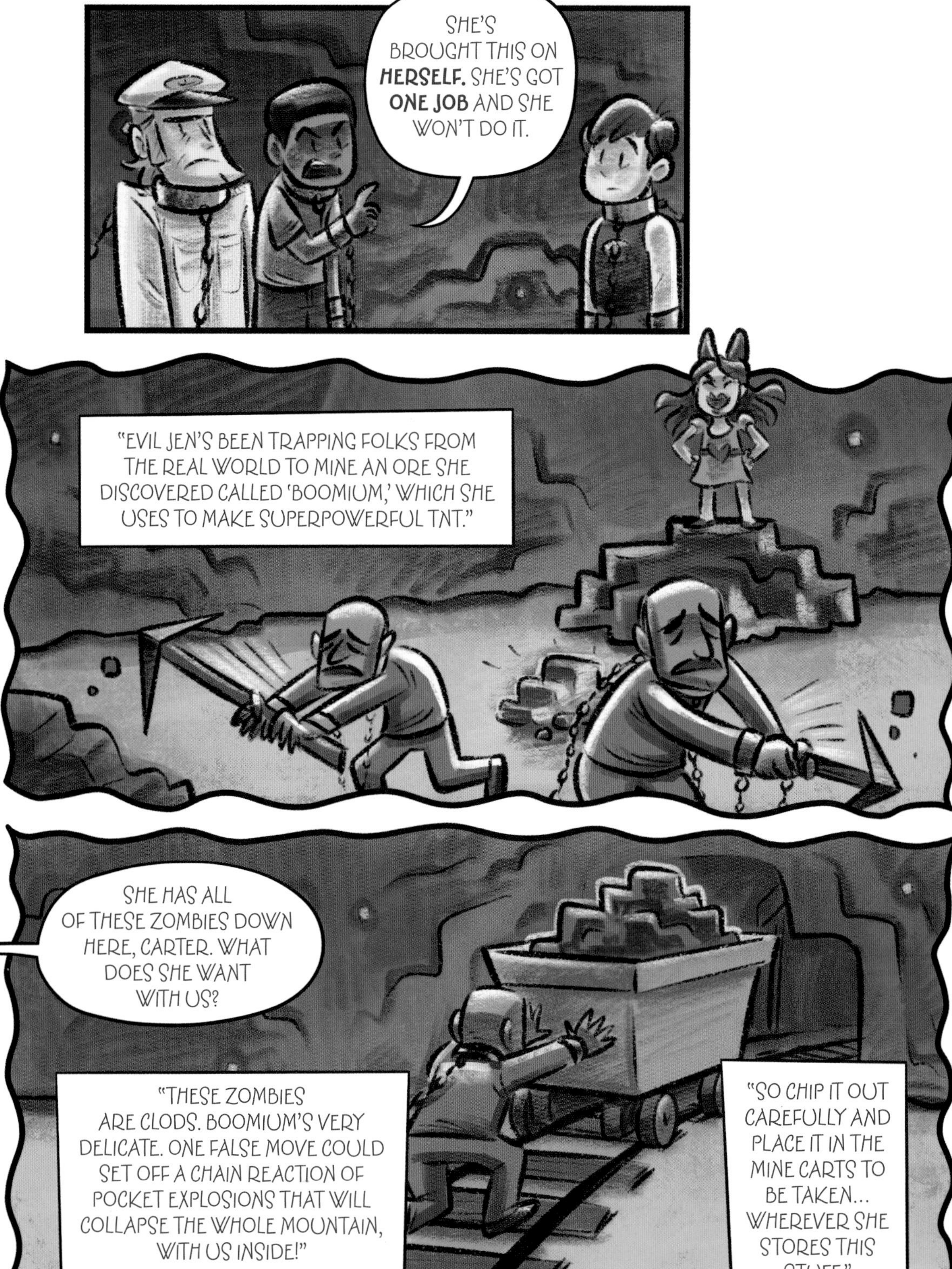
SHE'S BROUGHT THIS ON **HERSELF.** SHE'S GOT **ONE JOB** AND SHE WON'T DO IT.
"EVIL JEN'S BEEN TRAPPING FOLKS FROM THE REAL WORLD TO MINE AN ORE SHE DISCOVERED CALLED 'BOOMIUM,' WHICH SHE USES TO MAKE SUPERPOWERFUL TNT."
SHE HAS ALL OF THESE ZOMBIES DOWN HERE, CARTER. WHAT DOES SHE WANT WITH US?
"THESE ZOMBIES ARE CLODS. BOOMIUM'S VERY DELICATE. ONE FALSE MOVE COULD SET OFF A CHAIN REACTION OF POCKET EXPLOSIONS THAT WILL COLLAPSE THE WHOLE MOUNTAIN, WITH US INSIDE!"
"SO CHIP IT OUT CAREFULLY AND PLACE IT IN THE MINE CARTS TO BE TAKEN... WHEREVER SHE STORES THIS STUFF."

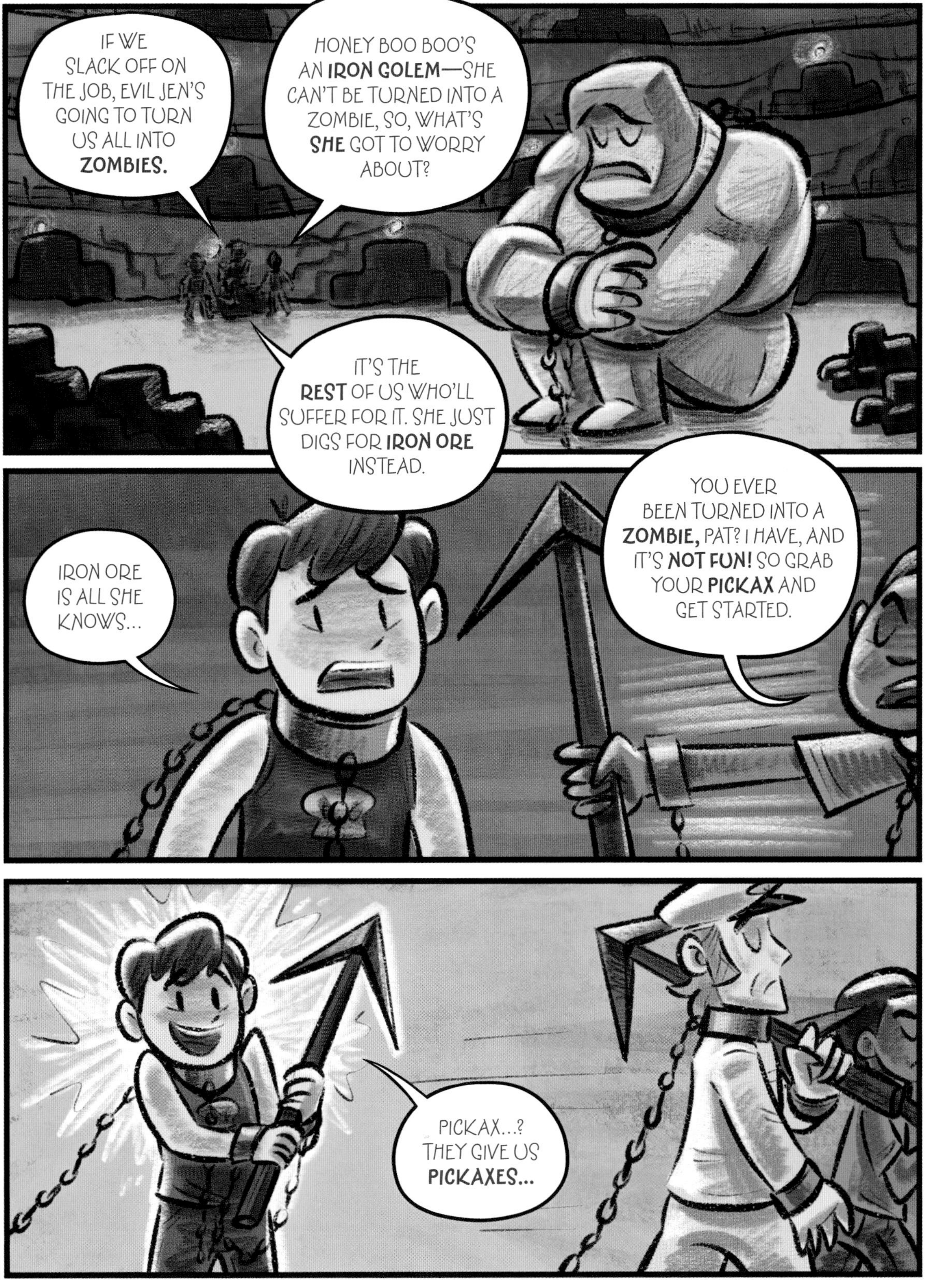

IF WE SLACK OFF ON THE JOB, EVIL JEN'S GOING TO TURN US ALL INTO **ZOMBIES.**
HONEY BOO BOO'S AN **IRON GOLEM**—SHE CAN'T BE TURNED INTO A ZOMBIE, SO, WHAT'S **SHE** GOT TO WORRY ABOUT?
IT'S THE **REST** OF US WHO'LL SUFFER FOR IT. SHE JUST DIGS FOR **IRON ORE** INSTEAD.
IRON ORE IS ALL SHE KNOWS...
YOU EVER BEEN TURNED INTO A **ZOMBIE,** PAT? I HAVE, AND IT'S **NOT FUN!** SO GRAB YOUR **PICKAX** AND GET STARTED.
PICKAX...? THEY GIVE US **PICKAXES...**

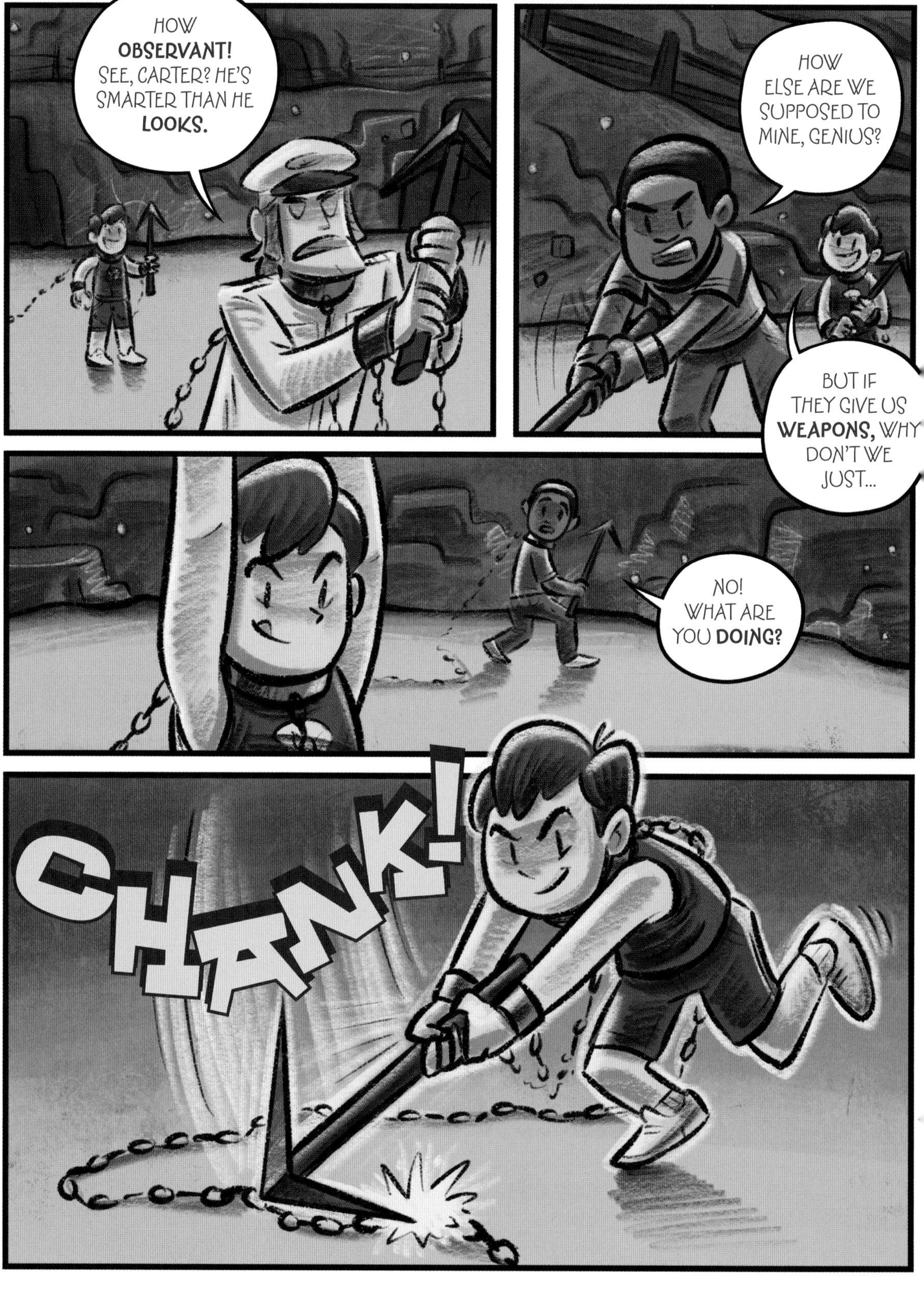
HOW **OBSERVANT!** SEE, CARTER? HE'S SMARTER THAN HE **LOOKS.**
HOW ELSE ARE WE SUPPOSED TO MINE, GENIUS?
BUT IF THEY GIVE US **WEAPONS,** WHY DON'T WE JUST...
NO! WHAT ARE YOU **DOING?**
CHANK!

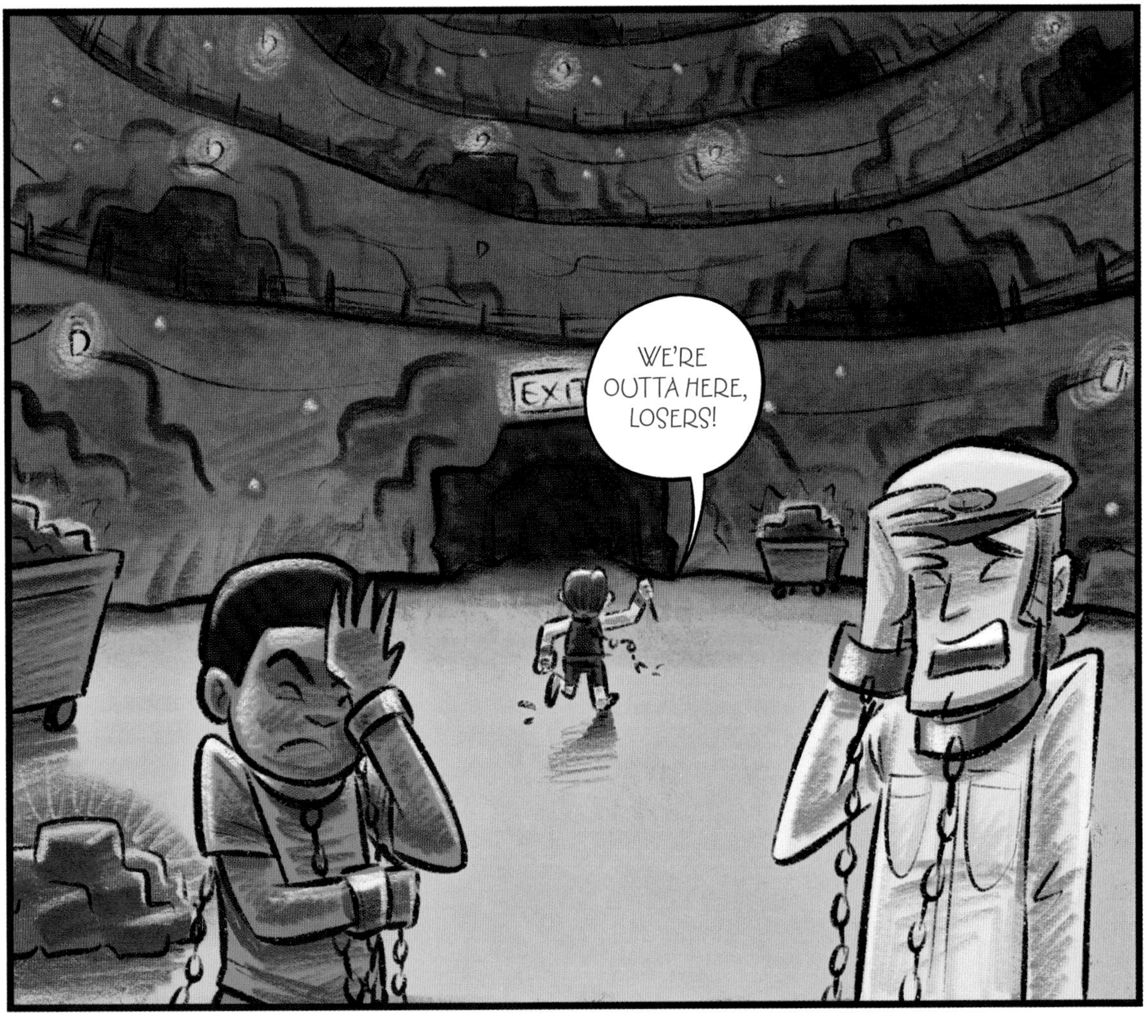
EXIT
WE'RE OUTTA HERE, LOSERS!

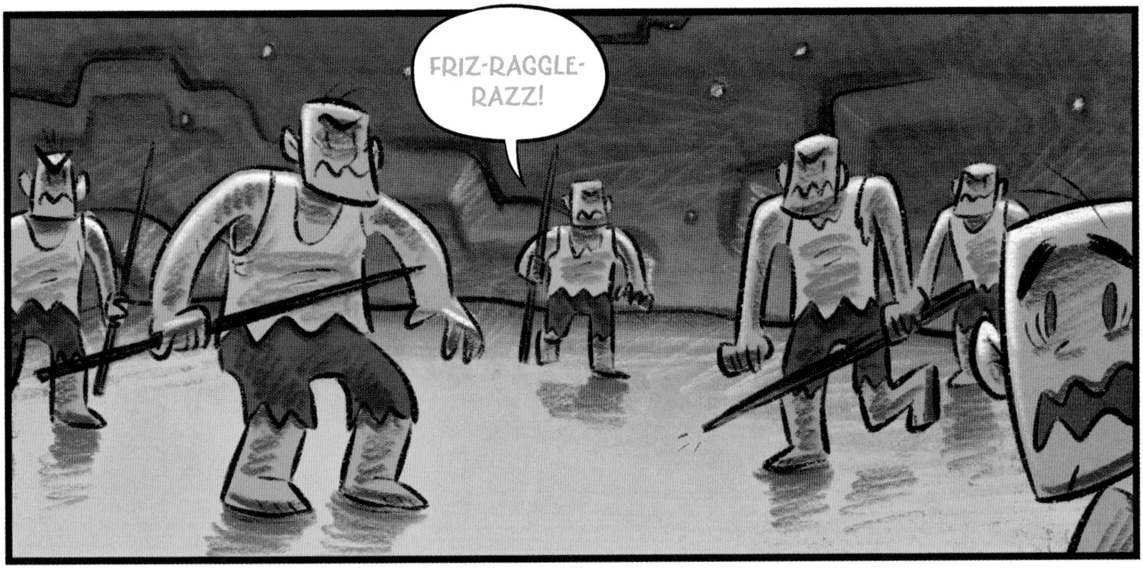
FRIZ-RAGGLE-RAZZ!

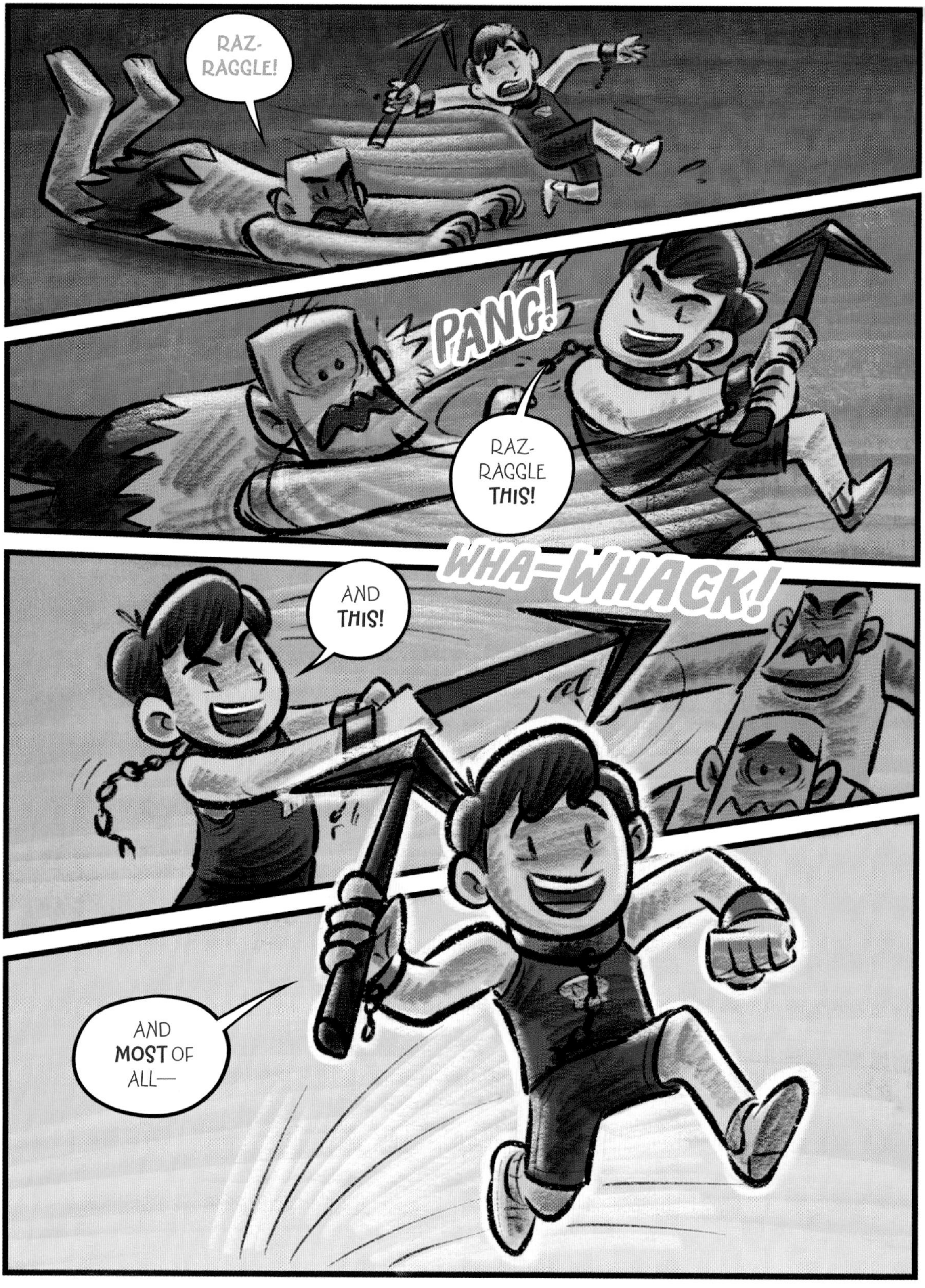
RAZ-RAGGLE!
PANG!
RAZ-RAGGLE THIS!
WHA-WHACK!
AND THIS!
AND MOST OF ALL—

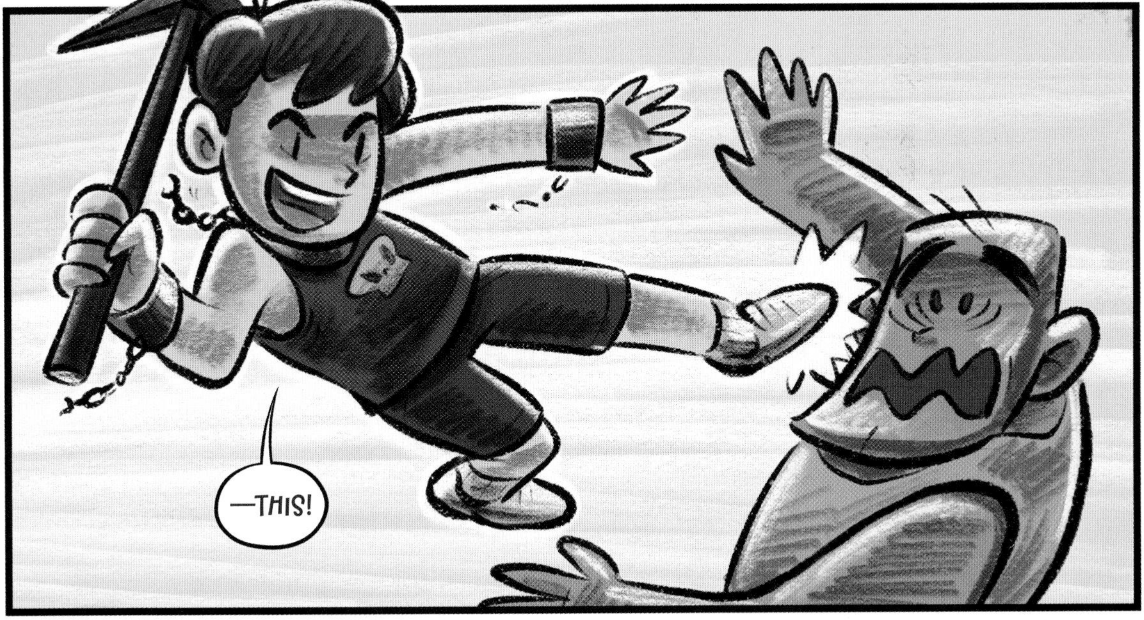
—THIS!

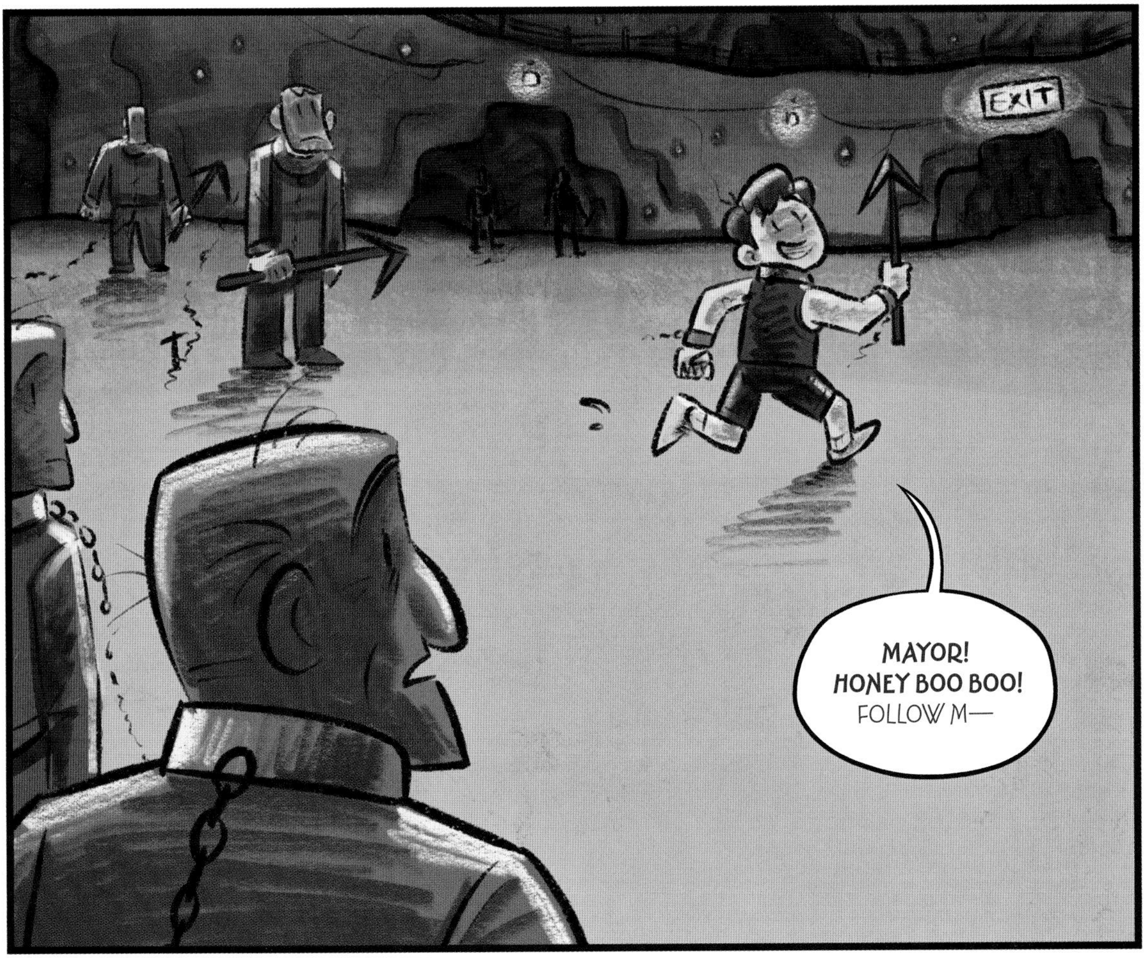
EXIT
MAYOR! HONEY BOO BOO! FOLLOW M—

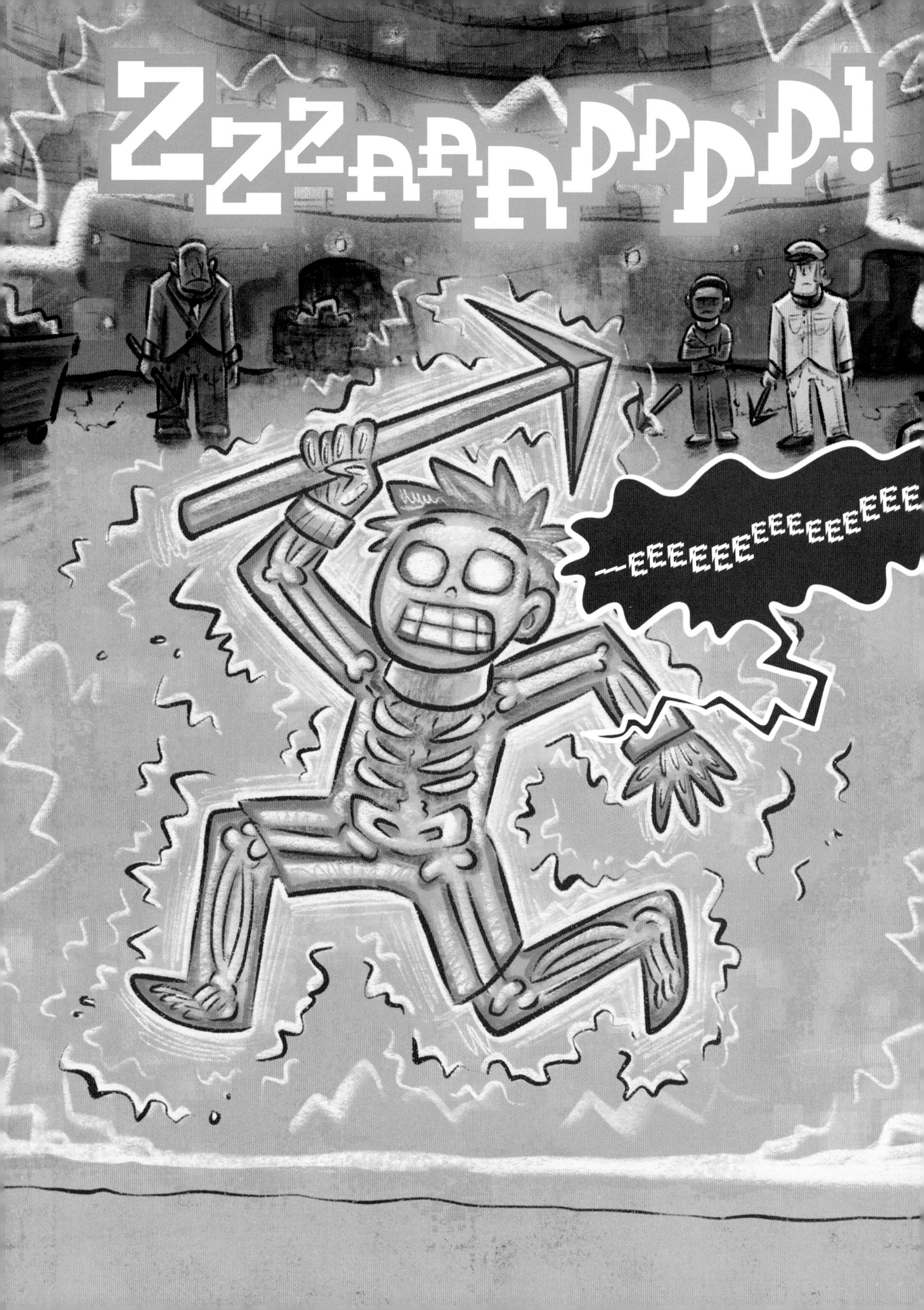
ZZZAAAPPPP!
—EEEEEEEEEEEEEEE

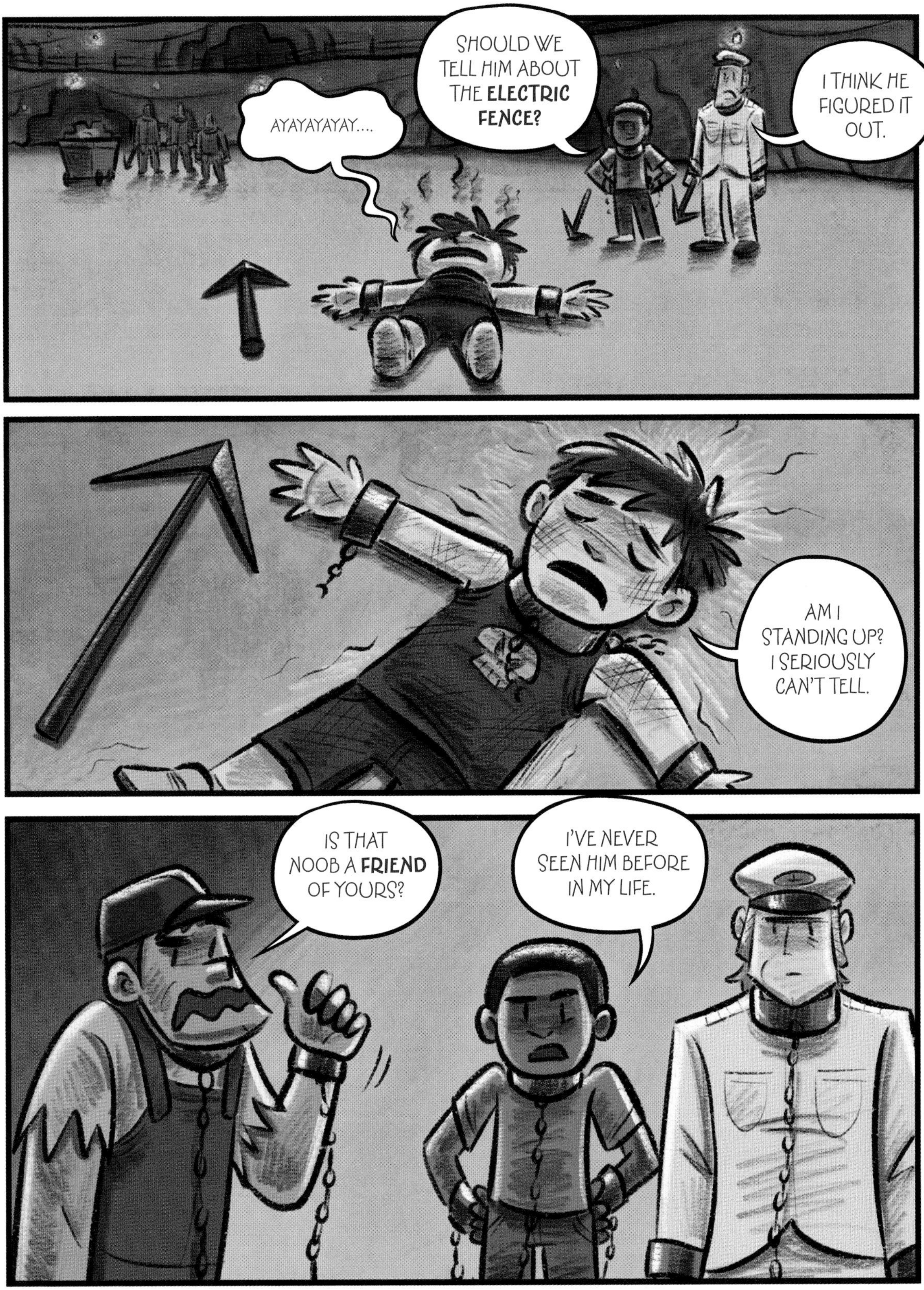
AYAYAYAYAY....
SHOULD WE TELL HIM ABOUT THE **ELECTRIC FENCE?**
I THINK HE FIGURED IT OUT.
AM I STANDING UP? I SERIOUSLY CAN'T TELL.
IS THAT NOOB A **FRIEND** OF YOURS?
I'VE NEVER SEEN HIM BEFORE IN MY LIFE.

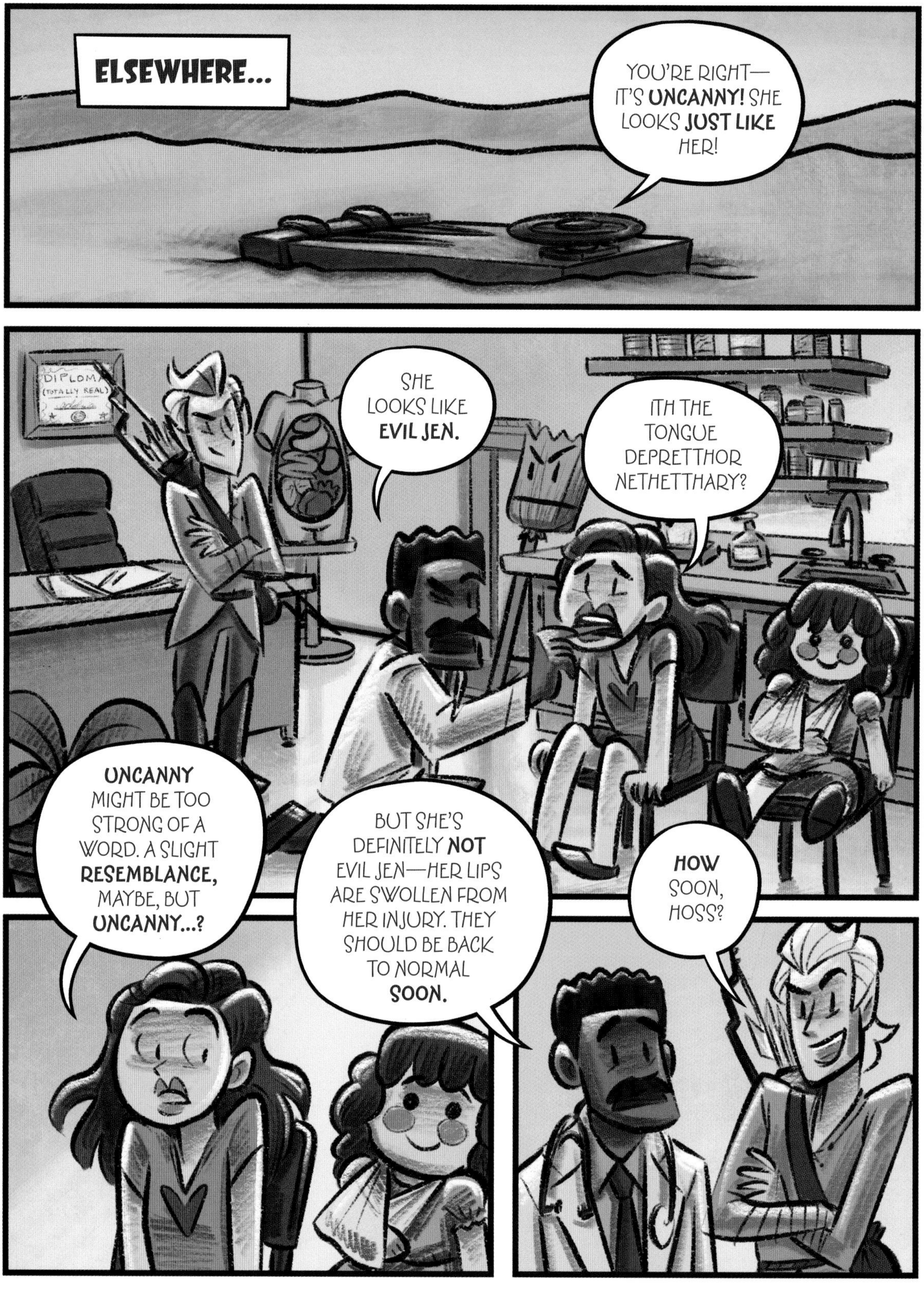
ELSEWHERE...
YOU'RE RIGHT— IT'S UNCANNY! SHE LOOKS JUST LIKE HER!
DIPLOMA (TOTALLY REAL)
SHE LOOKS LIKE EVIL JEN.
ITH THE TONGUE DEPRETTHOR NETHETTHARY?
UNCANNY MIGHT BE TOO STRONG OF A WORD. A SLIGHT RESEMBLANCE, MAYBE, BUT UNCANNY...?
BUT SHE'S DEFINITELY NOT EVIL JEN—HER LIPS ARE SWOLLEN FROM HER INJURY. THEY SHOULD BE BACK TO NORMAL SOON.
HOW SOON, HOSS?

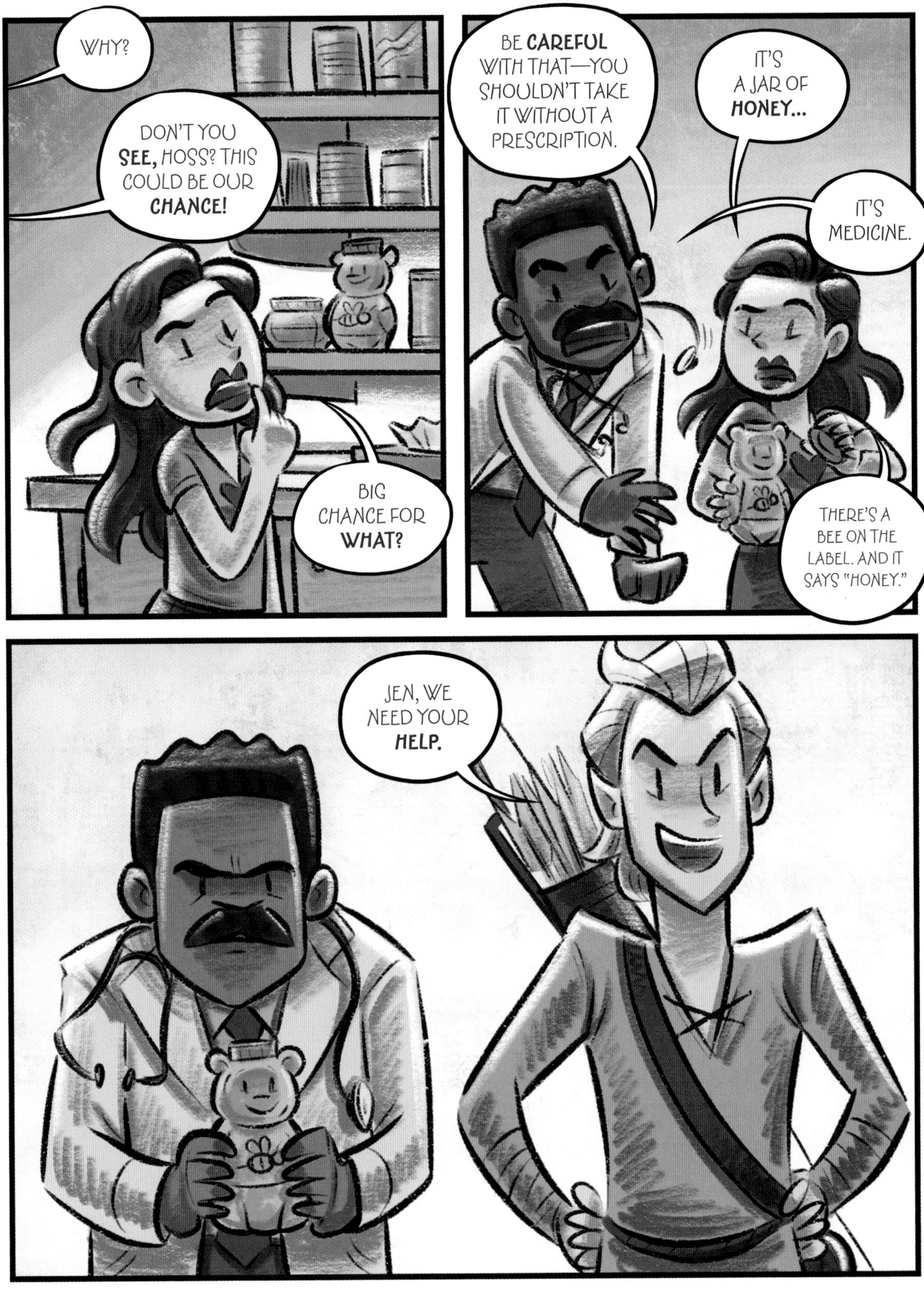
WHY?
DON'T YOU SEE, HOSS? THIS COULD BE OUR CHANCE!
BIG CHANCE FOR WHAT?
BE CAREFUL WITH THAT—YOU SHOULDN'T TAKE IT WITHOUT A PRESCRIPTION.
IT'S A JAR OF HONEY...
IT'S MEDICINE.
THERE'S A BEE ON THE LABEL. AND IT SAYS "HONEY."
JEN, WE NEED YOUR HELP.

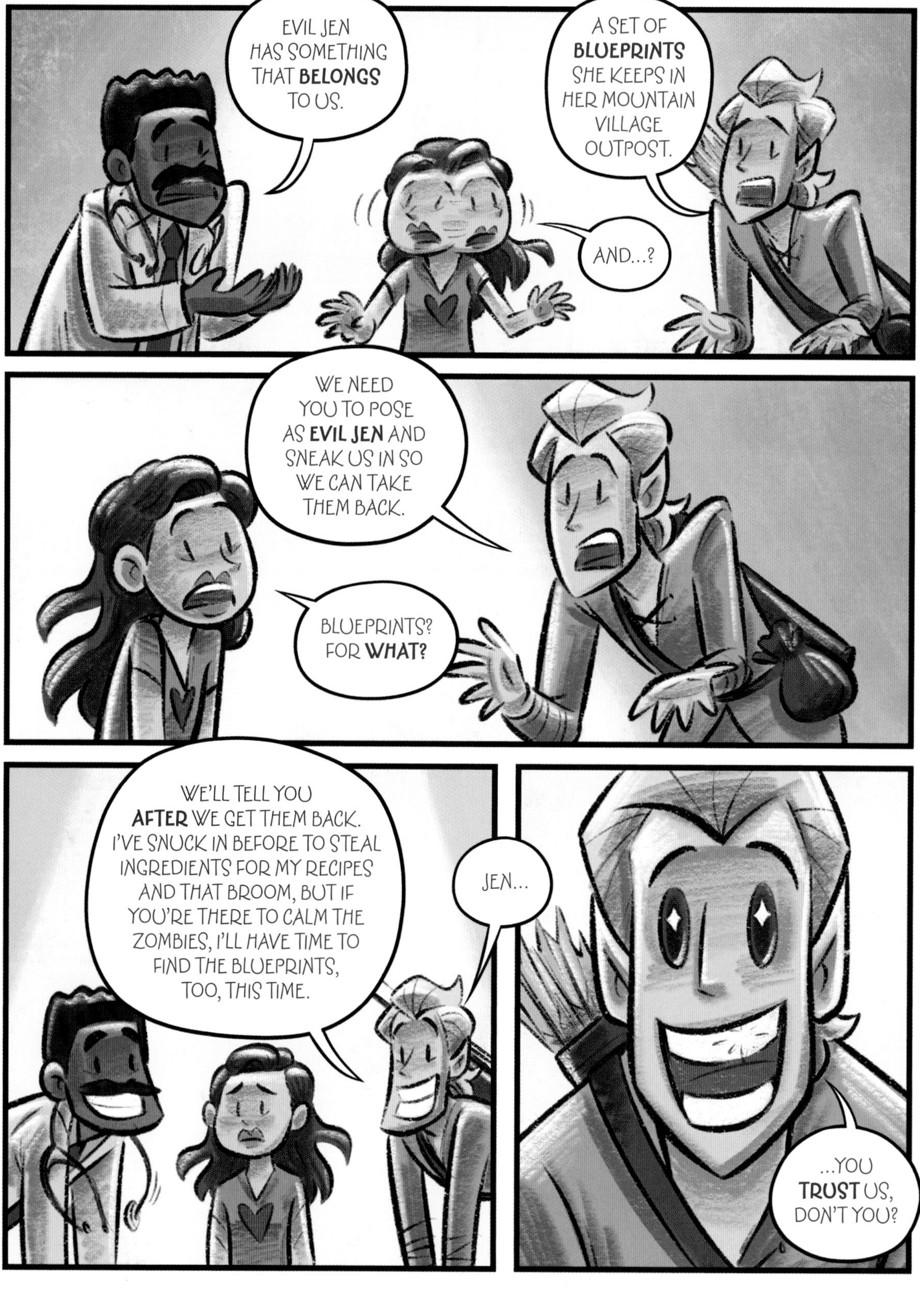
EVIL JEN HAS SOMETHING THAT **BELONGS** TO US.
A SET OF **BLUEPRINTS** SHE KEEPS IN HER MOUNTAIN VILLAGE OUTPOST.
AND...?
WE NEED YOU TO POSE AS **EVIL JEN** AND SNEAK US IN SO WE CAN TAKE THEM BACK.
BLUEPRINTS? FOR **WHAT?**
WE'LL TELL YOU **AFTER** WE GET THEM BACK. I'VE SNUCK IN BEFORE TO STEAL INGREDIENTS FOR MY RECIPES AND THAT BROOM, BUT IF YOU'RE THERE TO CALM THE ZOMBIES, I'LL HAVE TIME TO FIND THE BLUEPRINTS, TOO, THIS TIME.
JEN...
...YOU **TRUST** US, DON'T YOU?

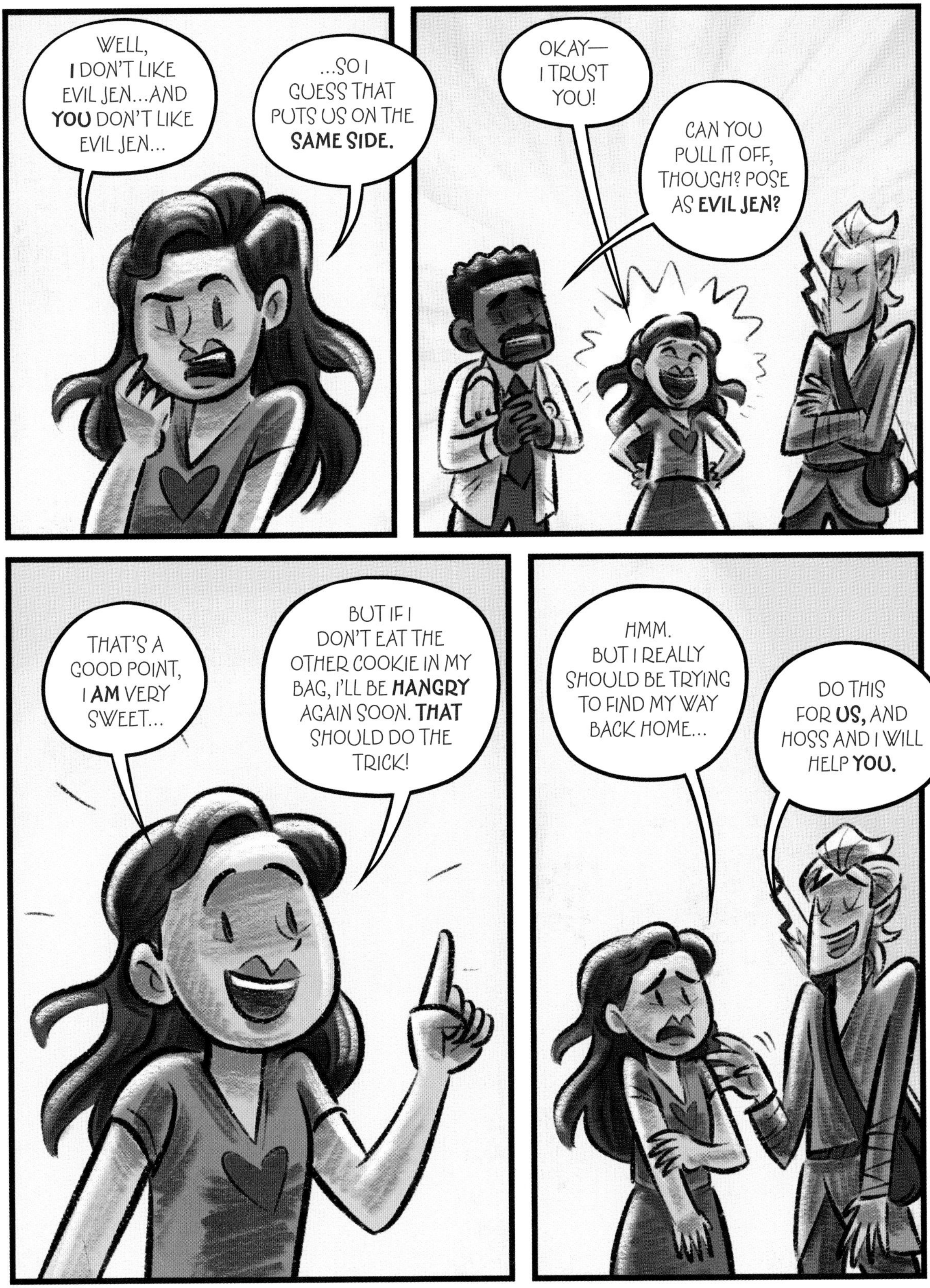
WELL, I DON'T LIKE EVIL JEN...AND YOU DON'T LIKE EVIL JEN...
...SO I GUESS THAT PUTS US ON THE SAME SIDE.
OKAY— I TRUST YOU!
CAN YOU PULL IT OFF, THOUGH? POSE AS EVIL JEN?
THAT'S A GOOD POINT, I AM VERY SWEET...
BUT IF I DON'T EAT THE OTHER COOKIE IN MY BAG, I'LL BE HANGRY AGAIN SOON. THAT SHOULD DO THE TRICK!
HMM. BUT I REALLY SHOULD BE TRYING TO FIND MY WAY BACK HOME...
DO THIS FOR US, AND HOSS AND I WILL HELP YOU.

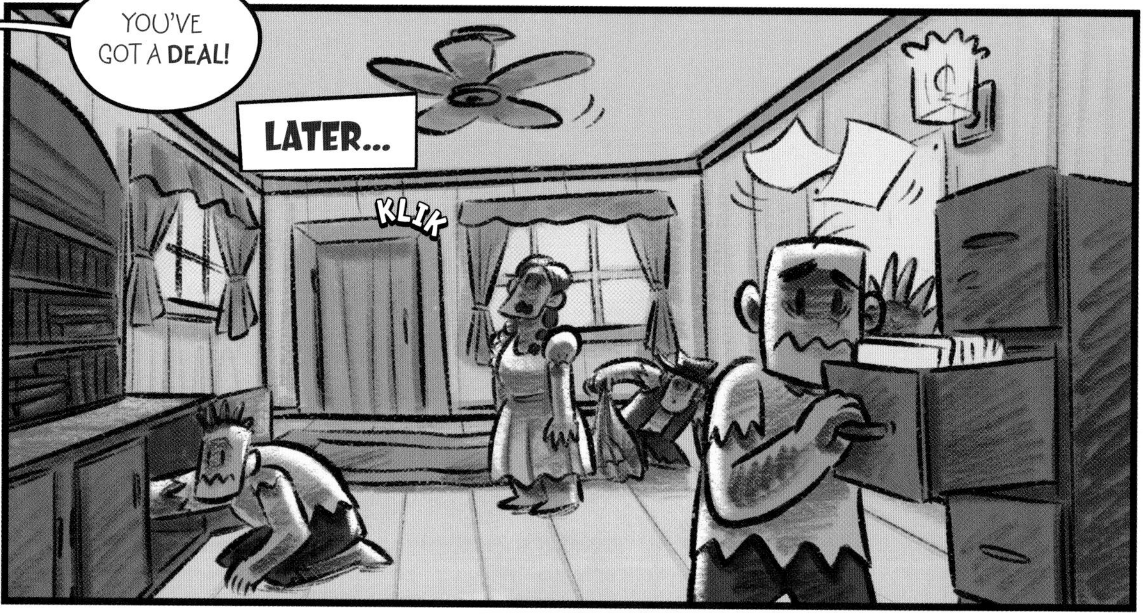
YOU'VE GOT A **DEAL!**
LATER...
KLIK

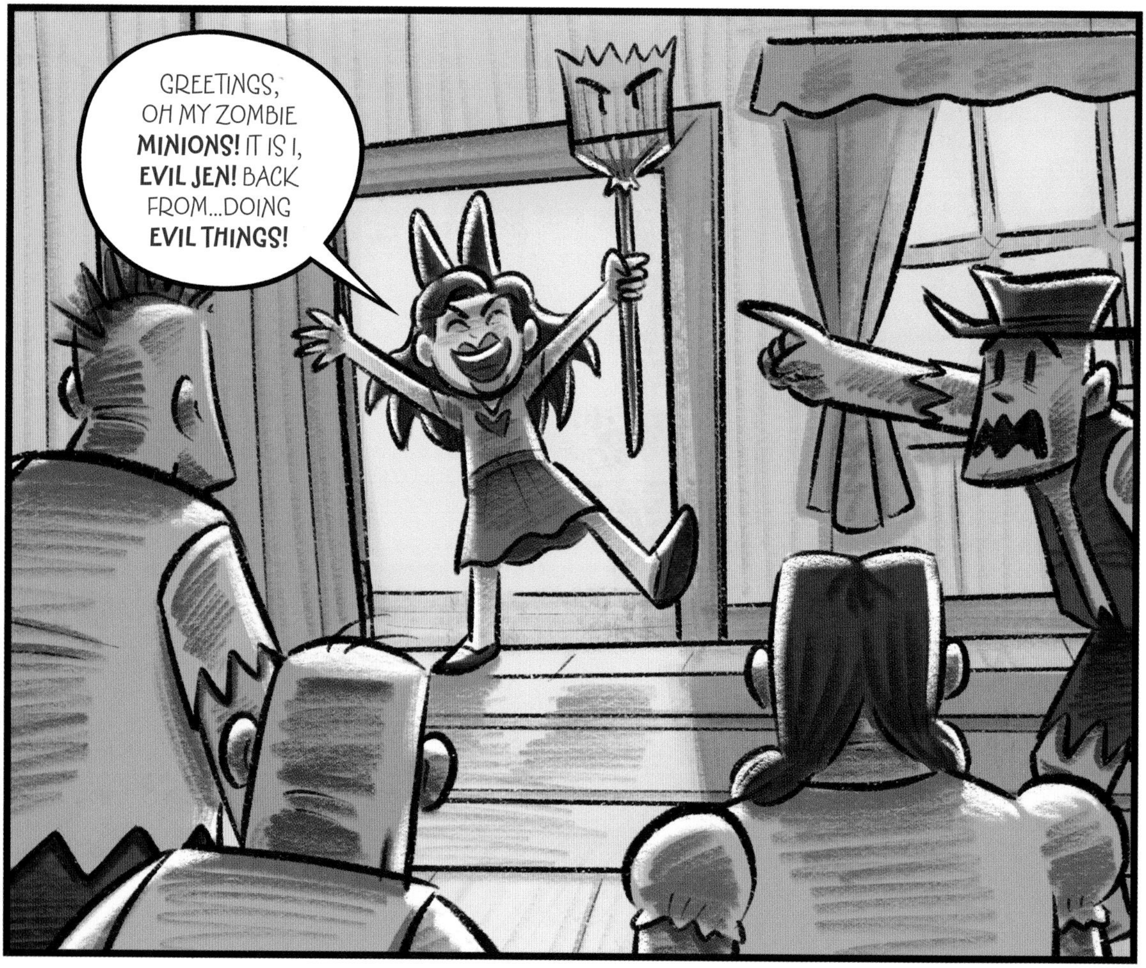
GREETINGS, OH MY ZOMBIE **MINIONS!** IT IS I, **EVIL JEN!** BACK FROM...DOING **EVIL THINGS!**

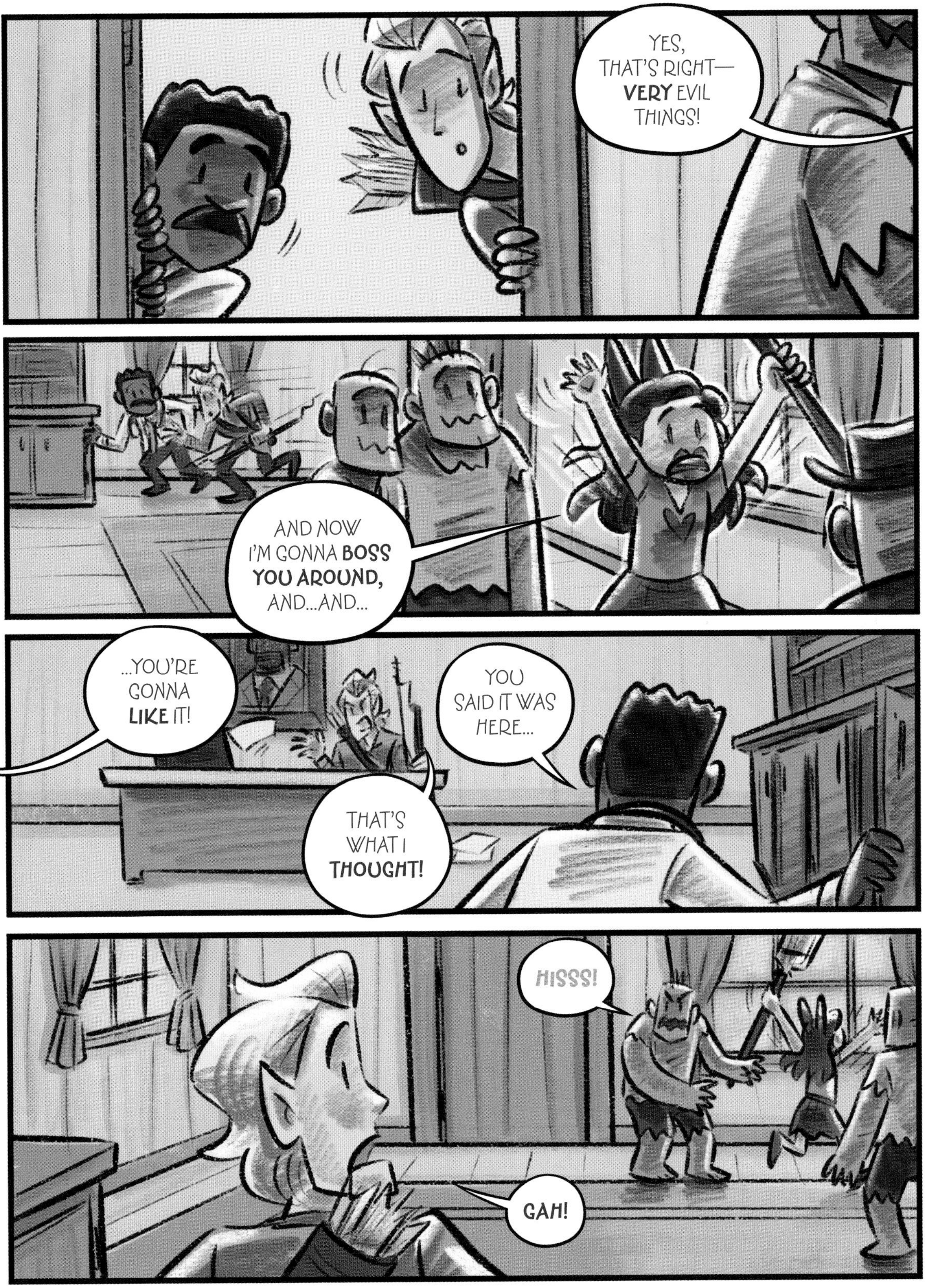
YES, THAT'S RIGHT— VERY EVIL THINGS!
AND NOW I'M GONNA BOSS YOU AROUND, AND...AND...
...YOU'RE GONNA LIKE IT!
YOU SAID IT WAS HERE...
THAT'S WHAT I THOUGHT!
HISSS!
GAH!

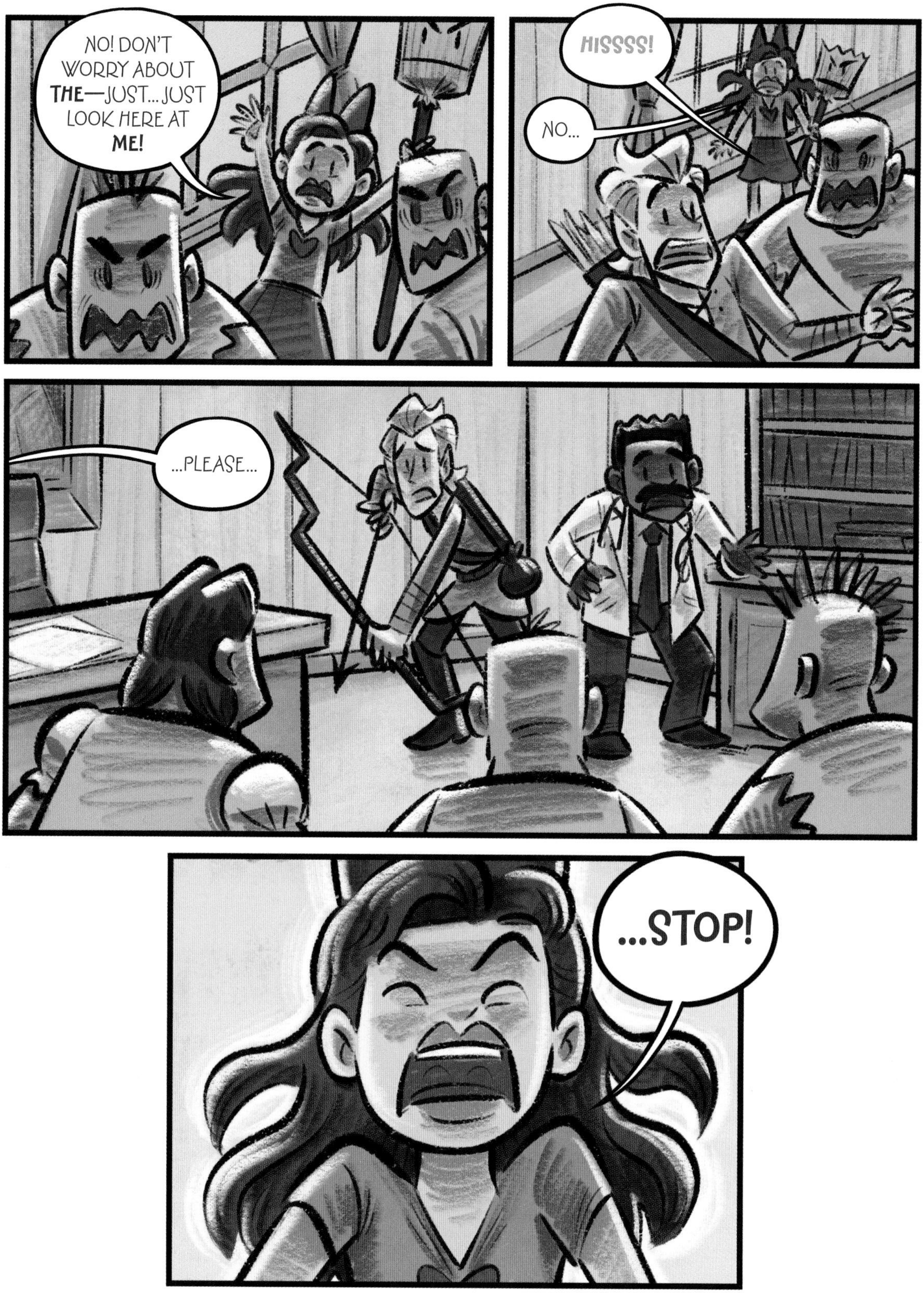
NO! DON'T WORRY ABOUT THE—JUST...JUST LOOK HERE AT ME!
HISSSS!
NO...
...PLEASE...
...STOP!

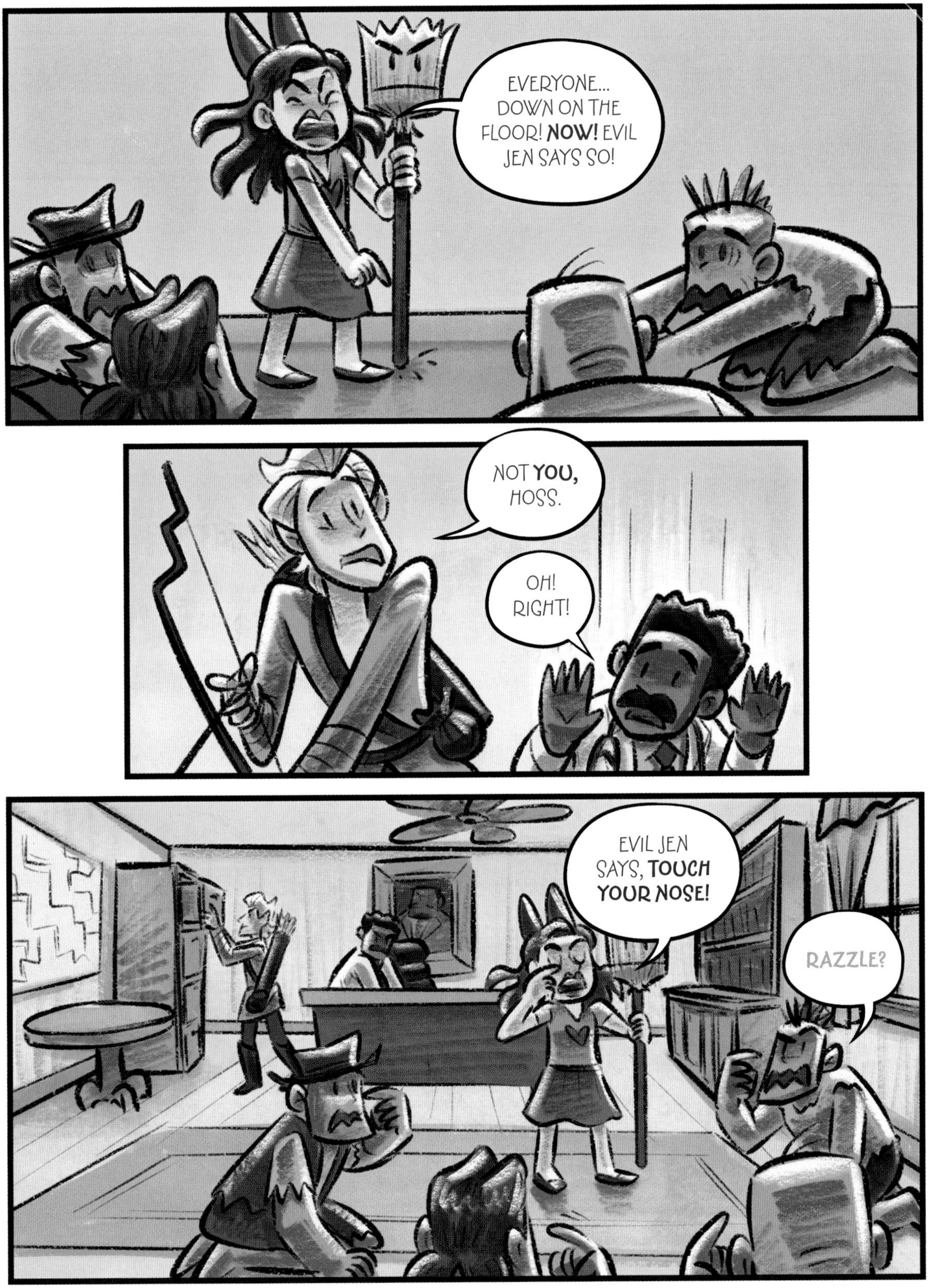
EVERYONE... DOWN ON THE FLOOR! **NOW!** EVIL JEN SAYS SO!
NOT **YOU,** HOSS.
OH! RIGHT!
EVIL JEN SAYS, **TOUCH YOUR NOSE!**
RAZZLE?

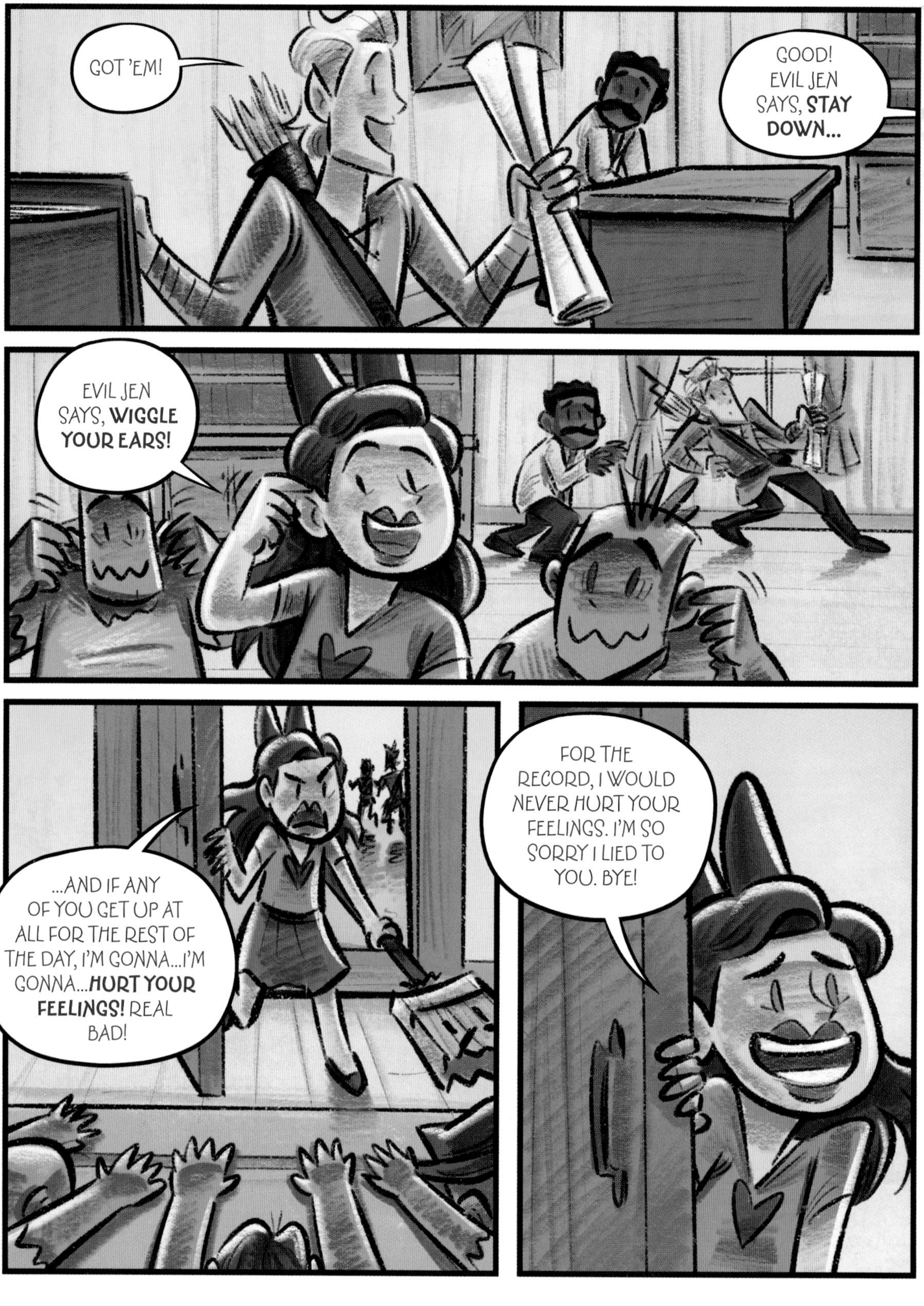
GOT 'EM!
GOOD! EVIL JEN SAYS, **STAY DOWN...**
EVIL JEN SAYS, **WIGGLE YOUR EARS!**
...AND IF ANY OF YOU GET UP AT ALL FOR THE REST OF THE DAY, I'M GONNA...I'M GONNA...**HURT YOUR FEELINGS!** REAL BAD!
FOR THE RECORD, I WOULD NEVER HURT YOUR FEELINGS. I'M SO SORRY I LIED TO YOU. BYE!

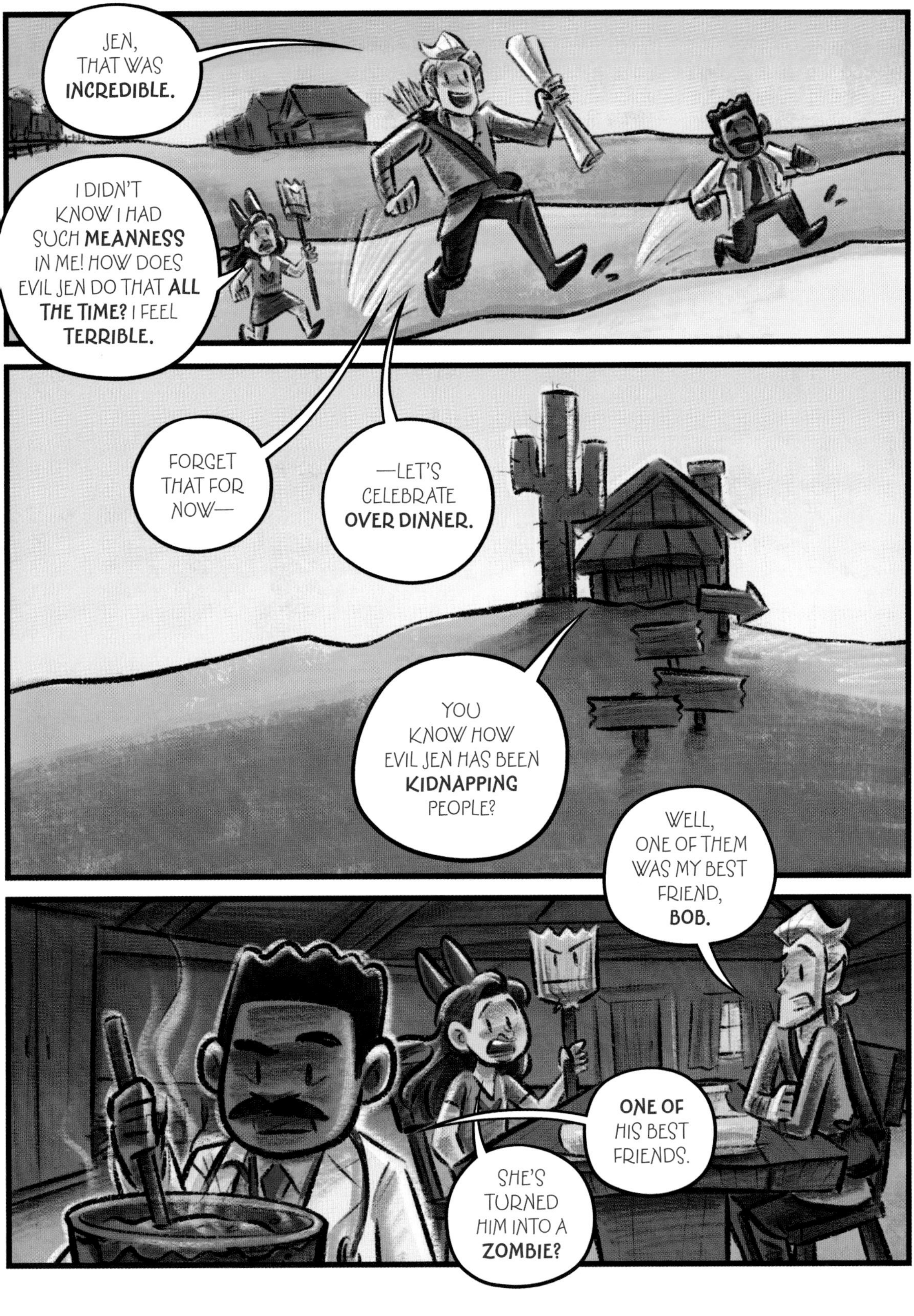
JEN, THAT WAS **INCREDIBLE.**
I DIDN'T KNOW I HAD SUCH **MEANNESS** IN ME! HOW DOES EVIL JEN DO THAT **ALL THE TIME?** I FEEL **TERRIBLE.**
FORGET THAT FOR NOW—
—LET'S CELEBRATE **OVER DINNER.**
YOU KNOW HOW EVIL JEN HAS BEEN **KIDNAPPING** PEOPLE?
WELL, ONE OF THEM WAS MY BEST FRIEND, **BOB.**
ONE OF HIS BEST FRIENDS.
SHE'S TURNED HIM INTO A **ZOMBIE?**

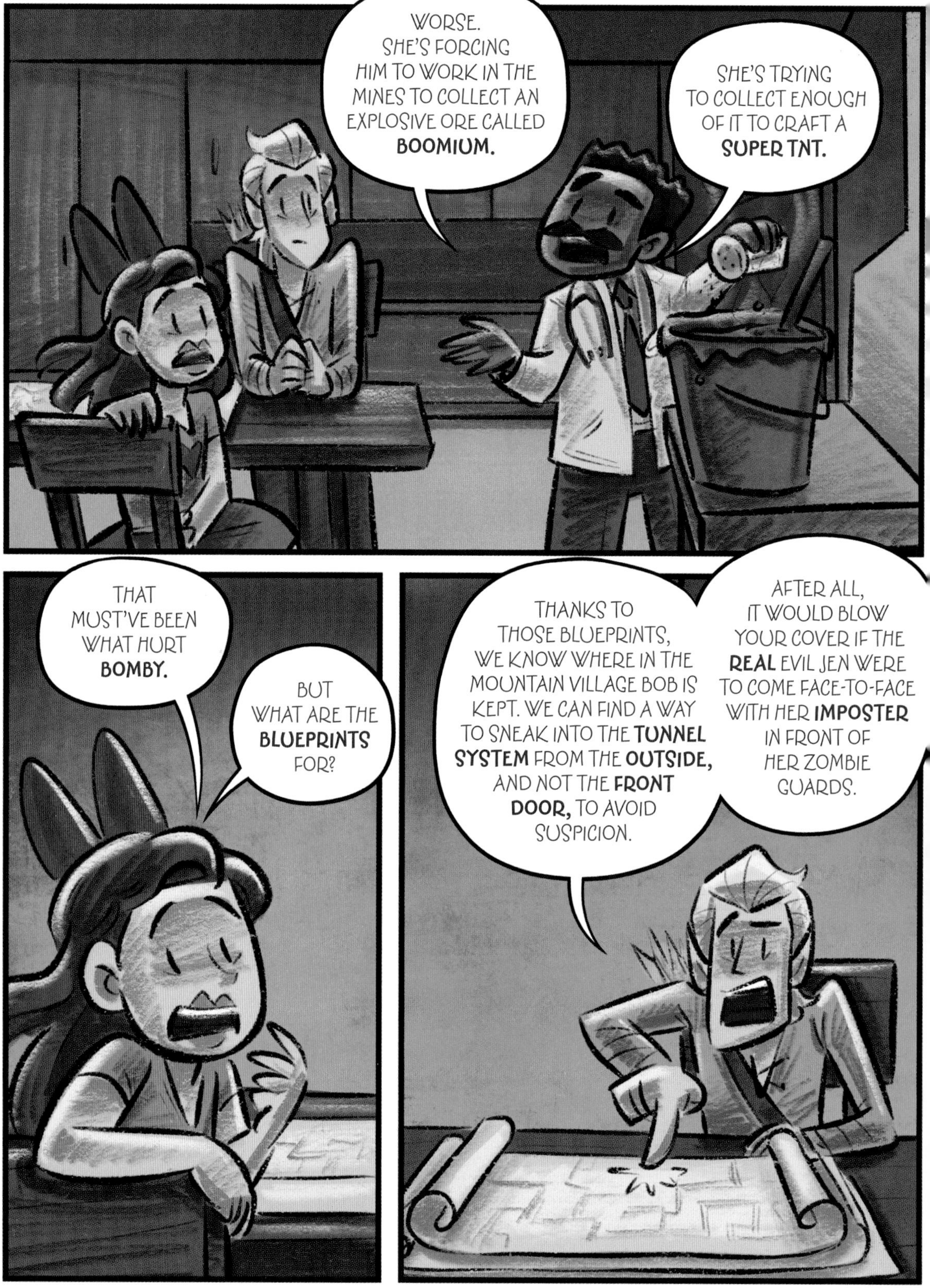
WORSE. SHE'S FORCING HIM TO WORK IN THE MINES TO COLLECT AN EXPLOSIVE ORE CALLED **BOOMIUM.**
SHE'S TRYING TO COLLECT ENOUGH OF IT TO CRAFT A **SUPER TNT.**
THAT MUST'VE BEEN WHAT HURT **BOMBY.**
BUT WHAT ARE THE **BLUEPRINTS** FOR?
THANKS TO THOSE BLUEPRINTS, WE KNOW WHERE IN THE MOUNTAIN VILLAGE BOB IS KEPT. WE CAN FIND A WAY TO SNEAK INTO THE **TUNNEL SYSTEM** FROM THE **OUTSIDE,** AND NOT THE **FRONT DOOR,** TO AVOID SUSPICION.
AFTER ALL, IT WOULD BLOW YOUR COVER IF THE **REAL** EVIL JEN WERE TO COME FACE-TO-FACE WITH HER **IMPOSTER** IN FRONT OF HER ZOMBIE GUARDS.

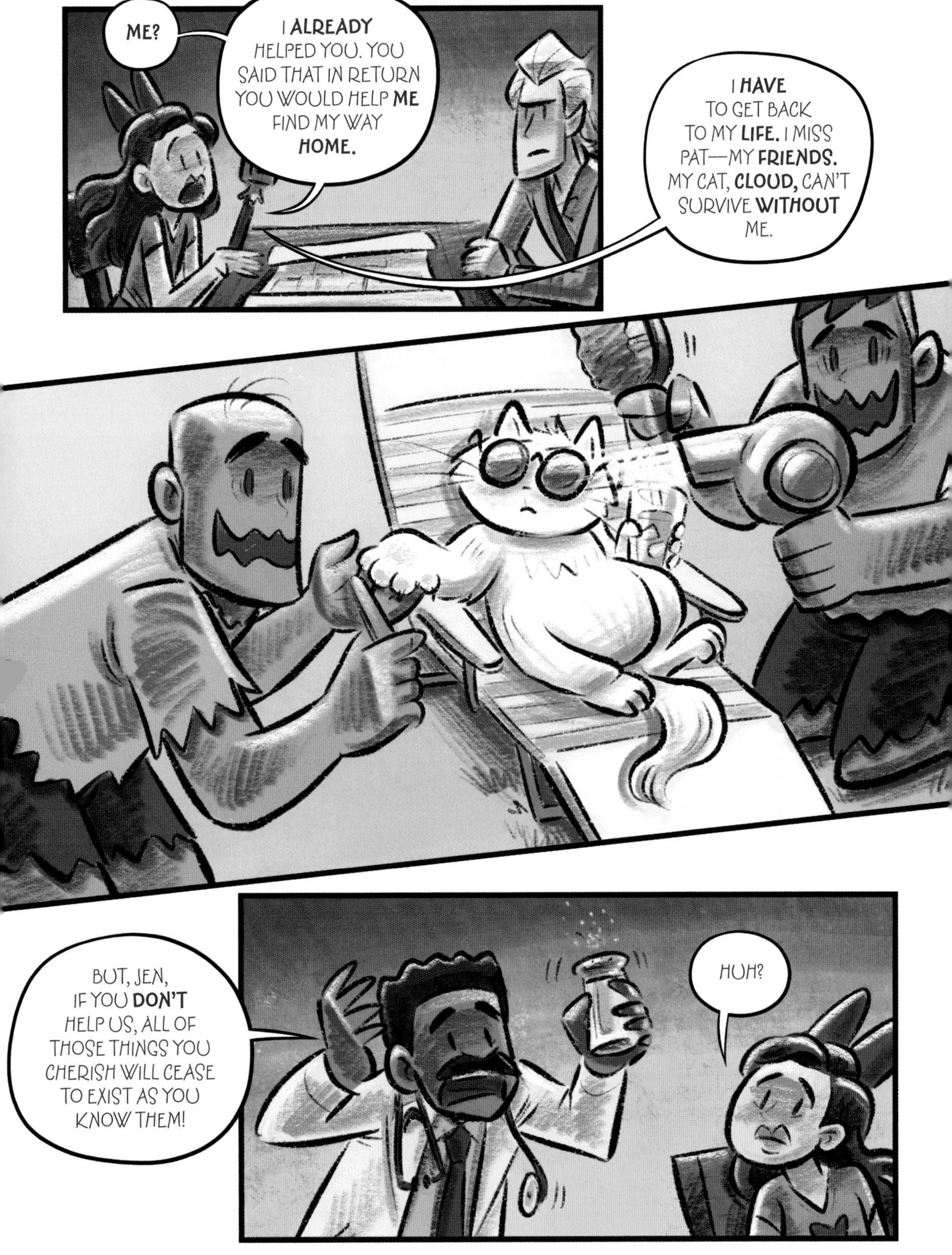
ME?
I **ALREADY** HELPED YOU. YOU SAID THAT IN RETURN YOU WOULD HELP **ME** FIND MY WAY **HOME.**
I **HAVE** TO GET BACK TO MY **LIFE.** I MISS PAT—MY **FRIENDS.** MY CAT, **CLOUD,** CAN'T SURVIVE **WITHOUT** ME.
BUT, JEN, IF YOU **DON'T** HELP US, ALL OF THOSE THINGS YOU CHERISH WILL CEASE TO EXIST AS YOU KNOW THEM!
HUH?

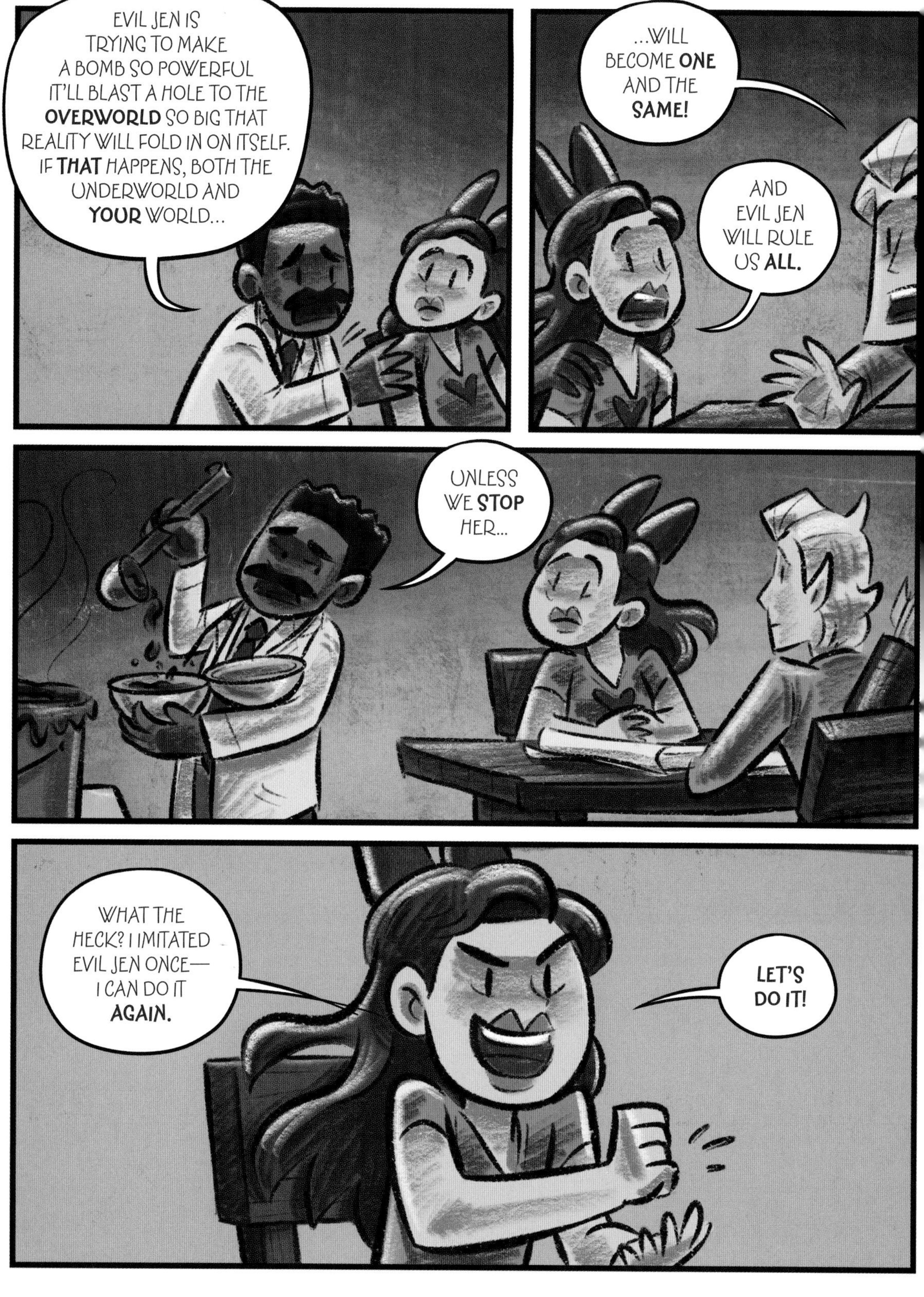
EVIL JEN IS TRYING TO MAKE A BOMB SO POWERFUL IT'LL BLAST A HOLE TO THE **OVERWORLD** SO BIG THAT REALITY WILL FOLD IN ON ITSELF. IF **THAT** HAPPENS, BOTH THE UNDERWORLD AND **YOUR** WORLD...
...WILL BECOME **ONE** AND THE **SAME!**
AND EVIL JEN WILL RULE US **ALL.**
UNLESS WE **STOP** HER...
WHAT THE HECK? I IMITATED EVIL JEN ONCE— I CAN DO IT **AGAIN.**
LET'S DO IT!

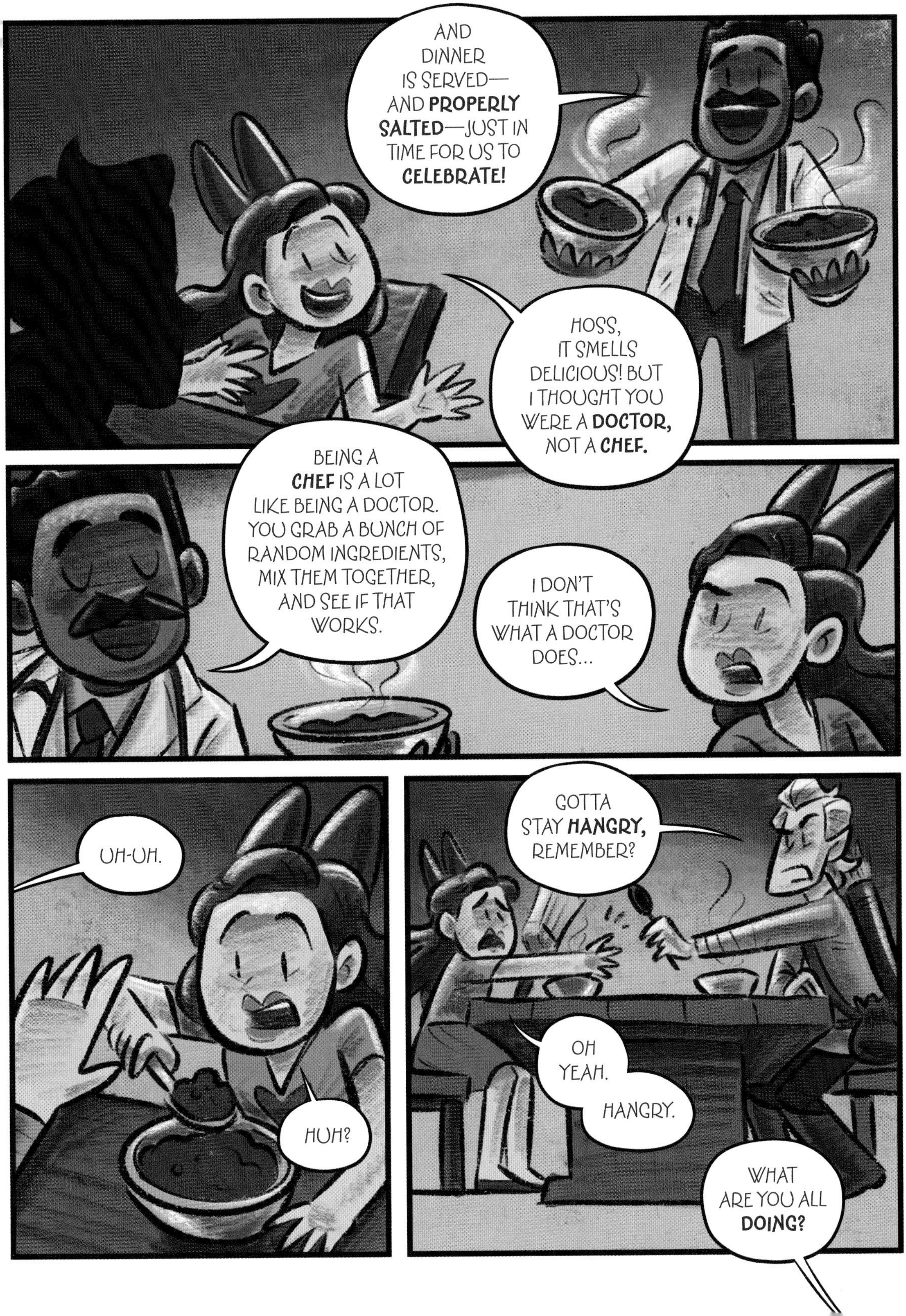
AND DINNER IS SERVED—AND PROPERLY SALTED—JUST IN TIME FOR US TO CELEBRATE!
HOSS, IT SMELLS DELICIOUS! BUT I THOUGHT YOU WERE A DOCTOR, NOT A CHEF.
BEING A CHEF IS A LOT LIKE BEING A DOCTOR. YOU GRAB A BUNCH OF RANDOM INGREDIENTS, MIX THEM TOGETHER, AND SEE IF THAT WORKS.
I DON'T THINK THAT'S WHAT A DOCTOR DOES...
UH-UH.
HUH?
GOTTA STAY HANGRY, REMEMBER?
OH YEAH.
HANGRY.
WHAT ARE YOU ALL DOING?

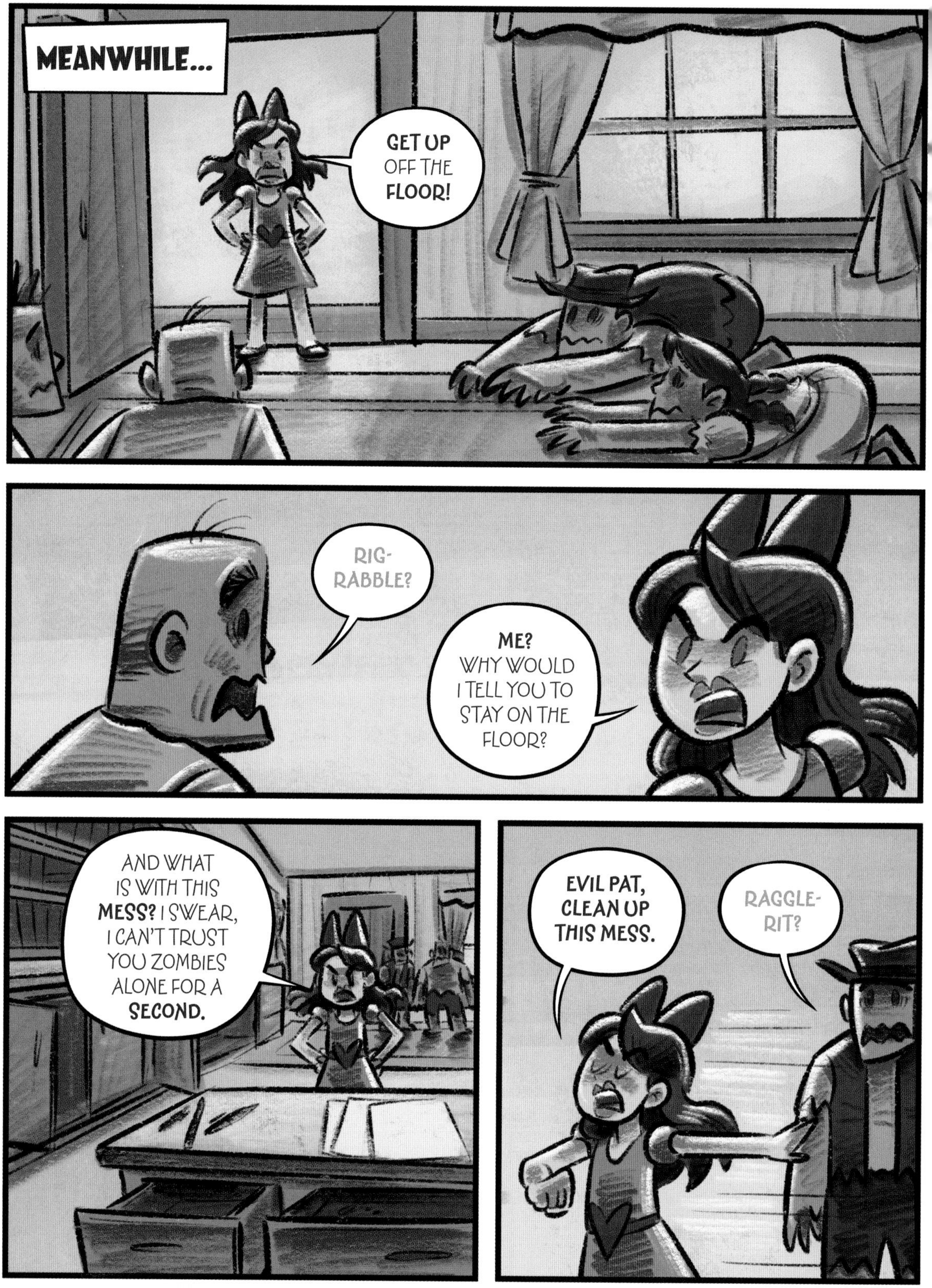
MEANWHILE...
GET UP OFF THE FLOOR!
RIG-RABBLE?
ME? WHY WOULD I TELL YOU TO STAY ON THE FLOOR?
AND WHAT IS WITH THIS MESS? I SWEAR, I CAN'T TRUST YOU ZOMBIES ALONE FOR A SECOND.
EVIL PAT, CLEAN UP THIS MESS.
RAGGLE-RIT?

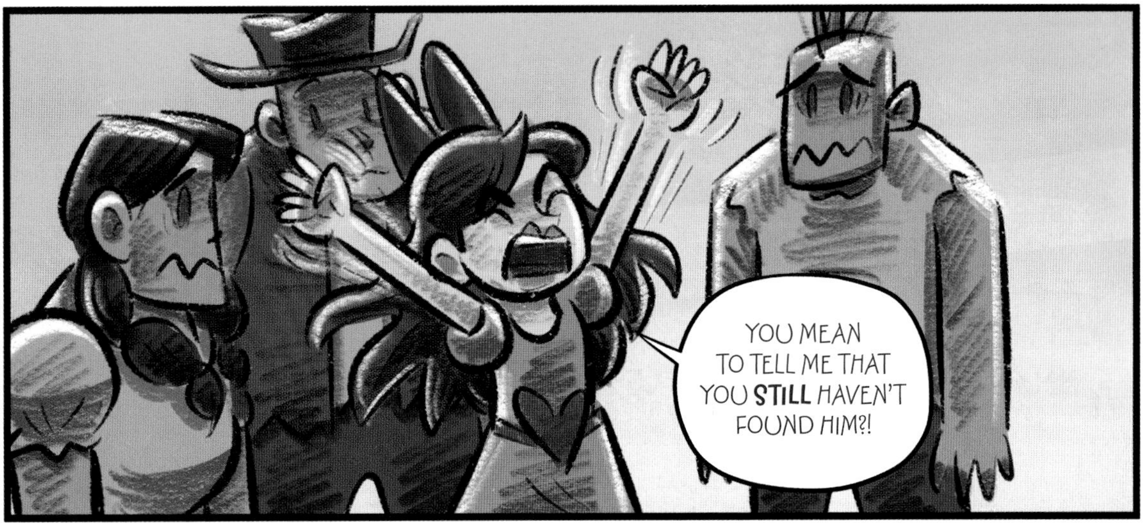
YOU MEAN TO TELL ME THAT YOU **STILL** HAVEN'T FOUND HIM?!

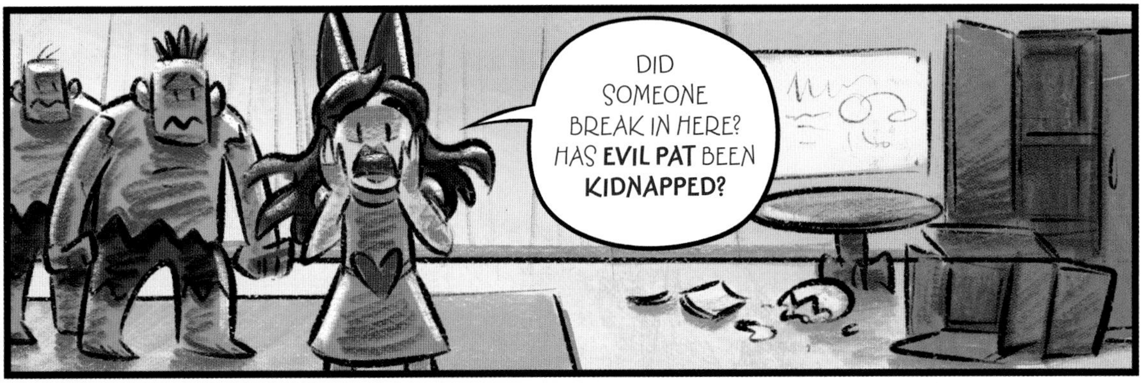
DID SOMEONE BREAK IN HERE? HAS **EVIL PAT** BEEN **KIDNAPPED?**

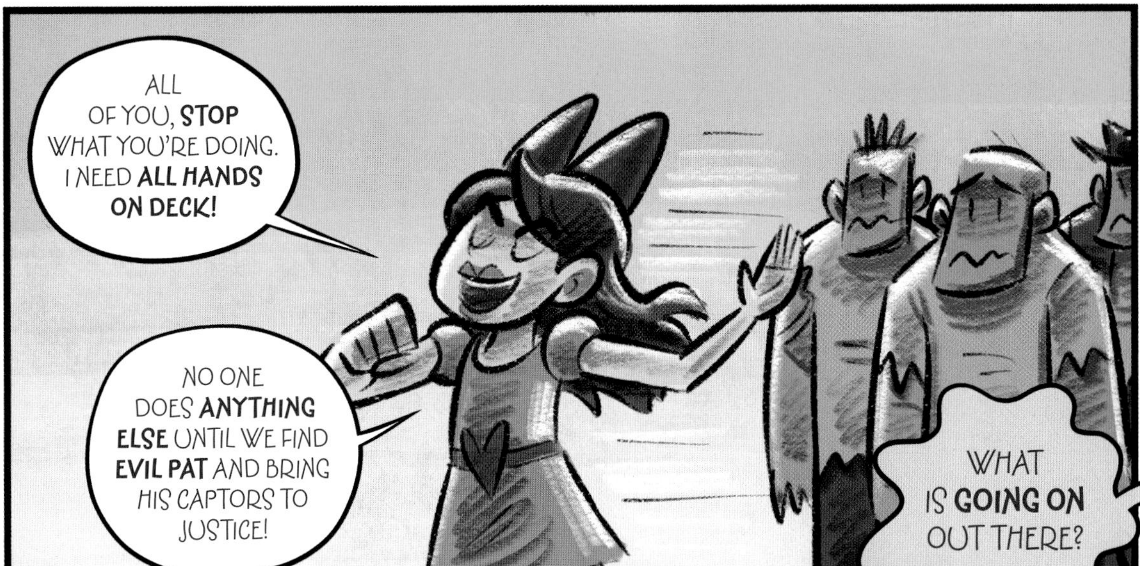
ALL OF YOU, **STOP** WHAT YOU'RE DOING. I NEED **ALL HANDS ON DECK!**
NO ONE DOES **ANYTHING ELSE** UNTIL WE FIND **EVIL PAT** AND BRING HIS CAPTORS TO JUSTICE!
WHAT IS **GOING ON** OUT THERE?

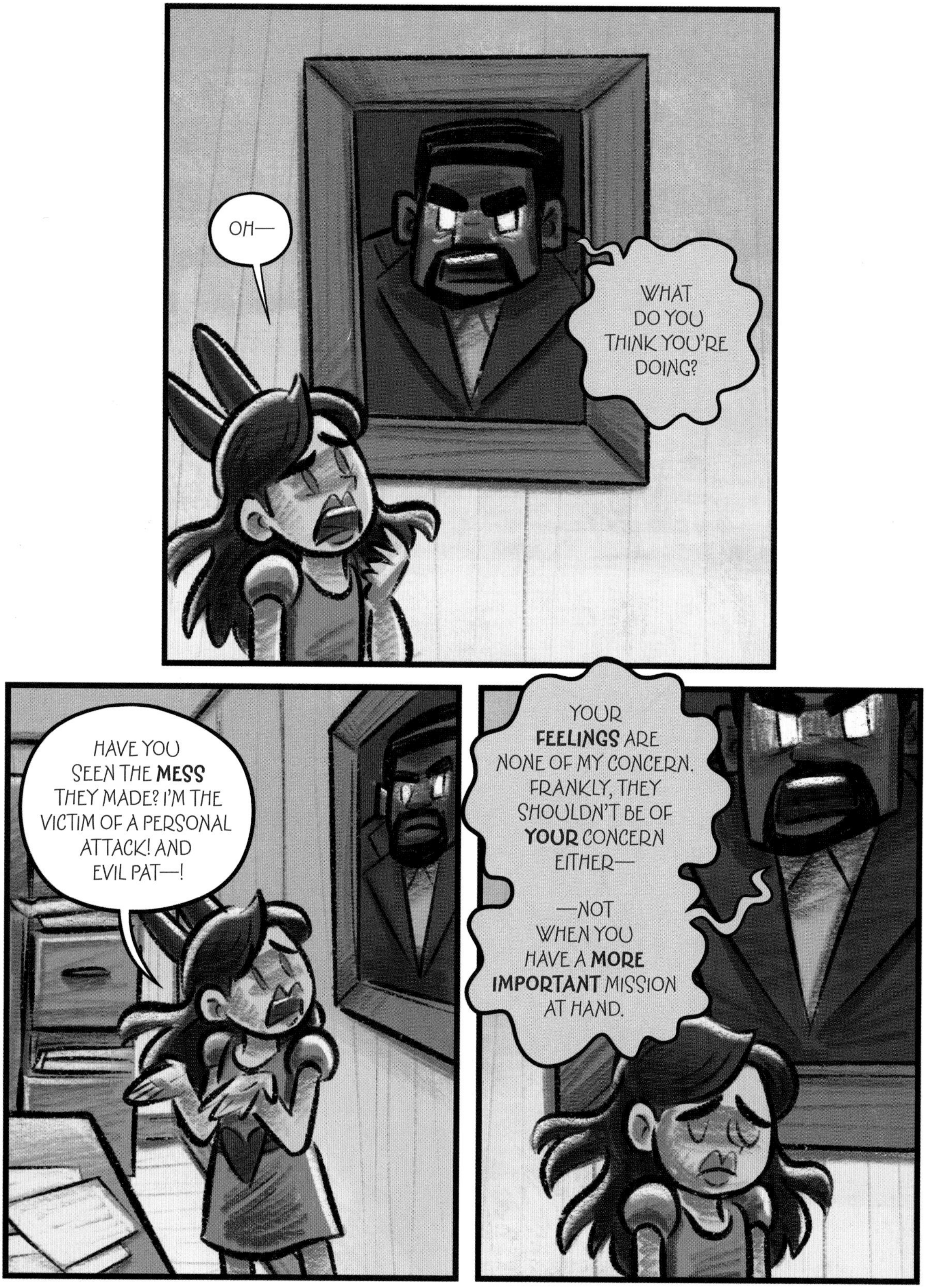
OH—
WHAT DO YOU THINK YOU'RE DOING?
HAVE YOU SEEN THE **MESS** THEY MADE? I'M THE VICTIM OF A PERSONAL ATTACK! AND EVIL PAT—!
YOUR **FEELINGS** ARE NONE OF MY CONCERN. FRANKLY, THEY SHOULDN'T BE OF **YOUR** CONCERN EITHER—
—NOT WHEN YOU HAVE A **MORE IMPORTANT** MISSION AT HAND.

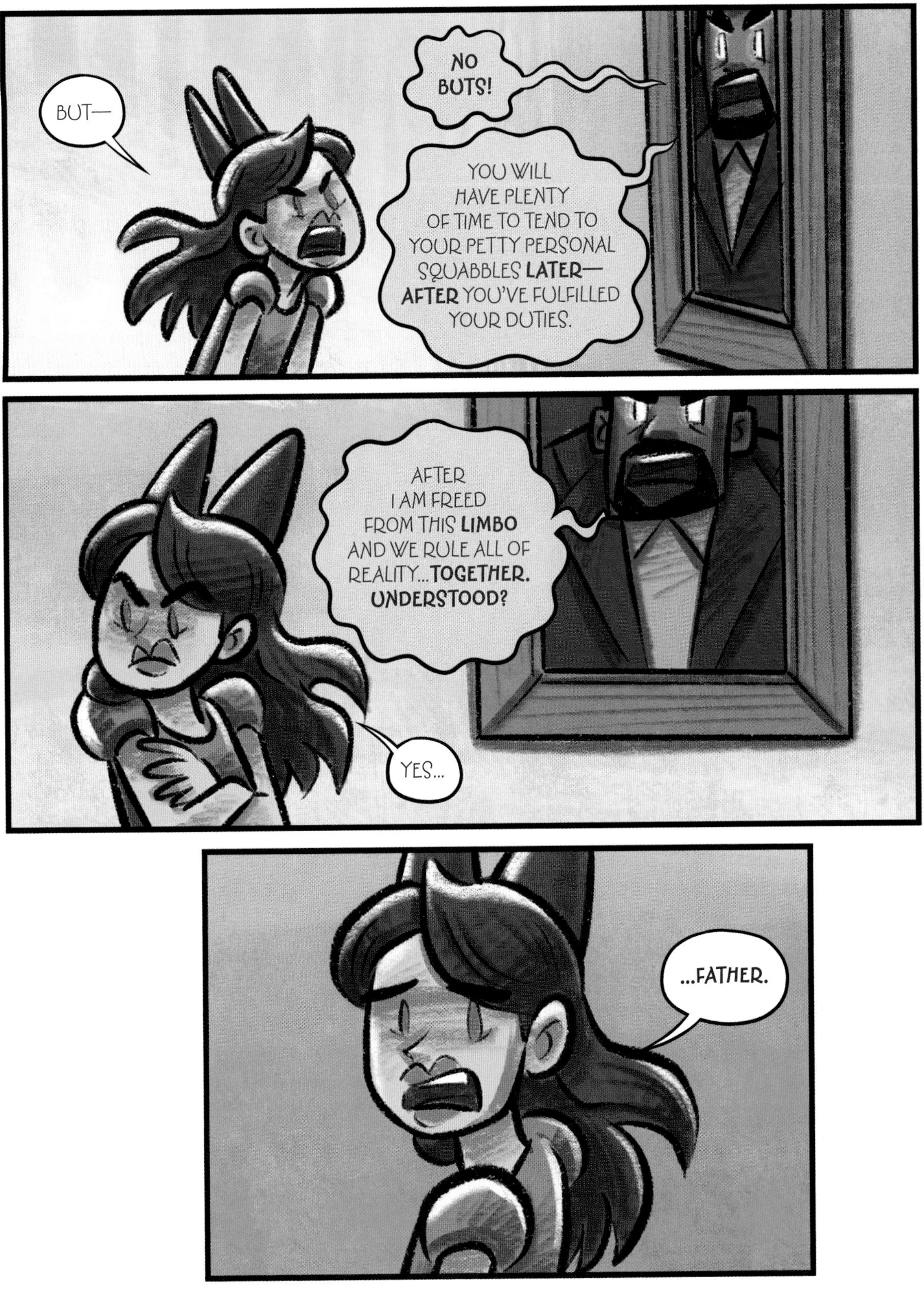
BUT—
NO BUTS!
YOU WILL HAVE PLENTY OF TIME TO TEND TO YOUR PETTY PERSONAL SQUABBLES **LATER**— **AFTER** YOU'VE FULFILLED YOUR DUTIES.
AFTER I AM FREED FROM THIS **LIMBO** AND WE RULE ALL OF REALITY... **TOGETHER. UNDERSTOOD?**
YES...
...FATHER.

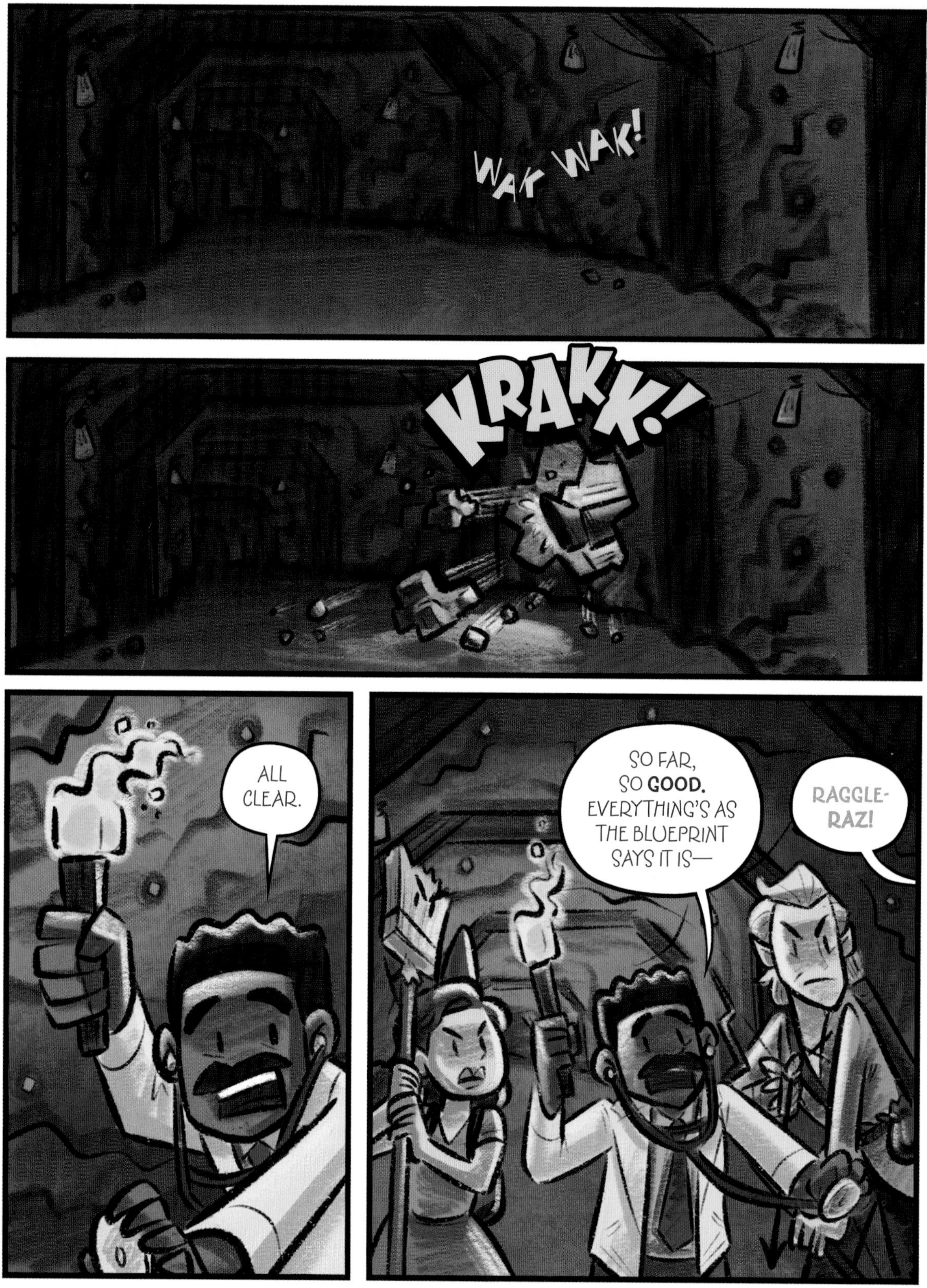
WAK WAK!
KRAKK!
ALL CLEAR.
SO FAR, SO **GOOD.** EVERYTHING'S AS THE BLUEPRINT SAYS IT IS—
RAGGLE-RAZ!

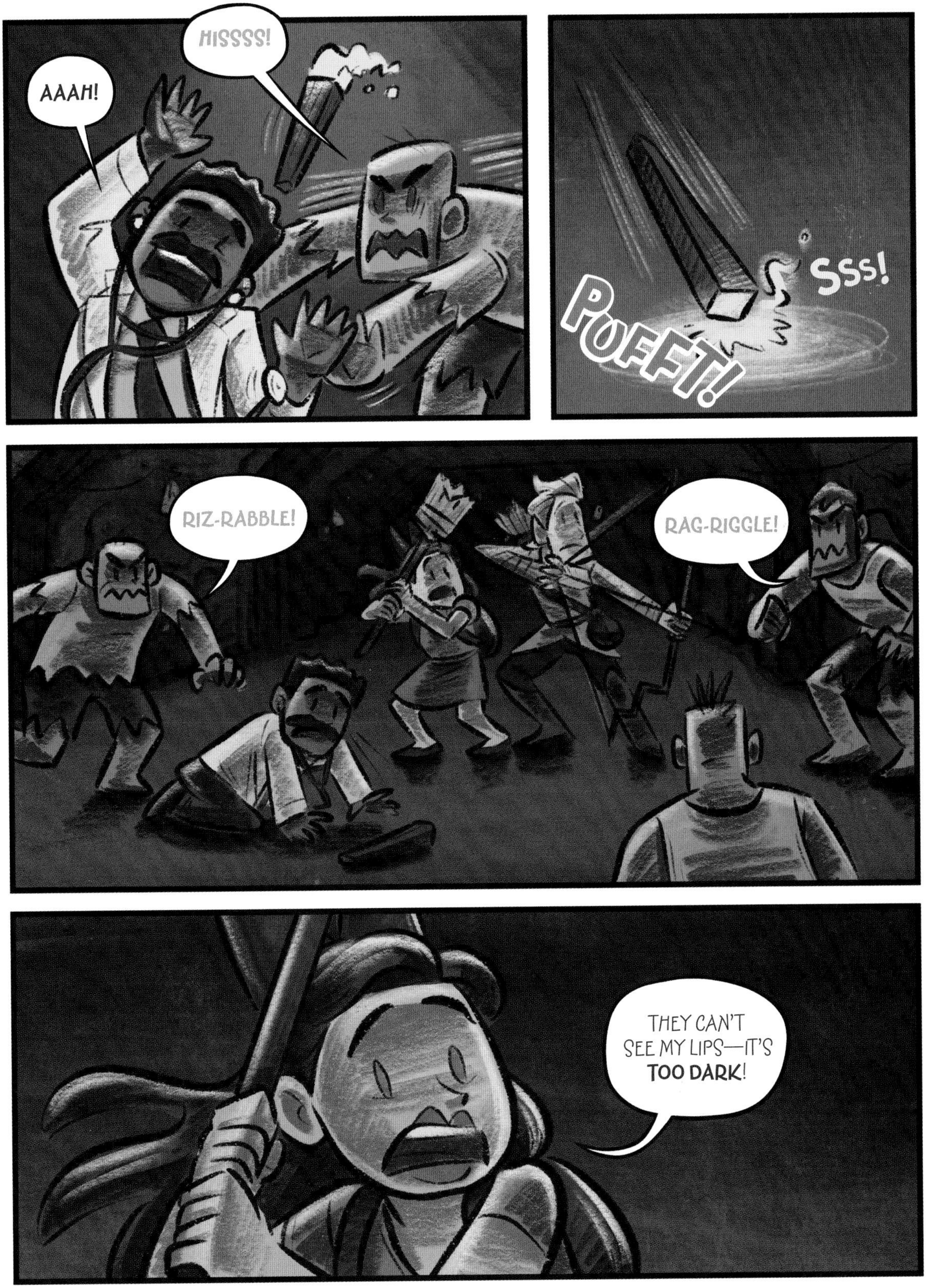
AAAH!
HISSSS!
Sss!
POFFT!
RIZ-RABBLE!
RAG-RIGGLE!
THEY CAN'T SEE MY LIPS—IT'S **TOO DARK**!

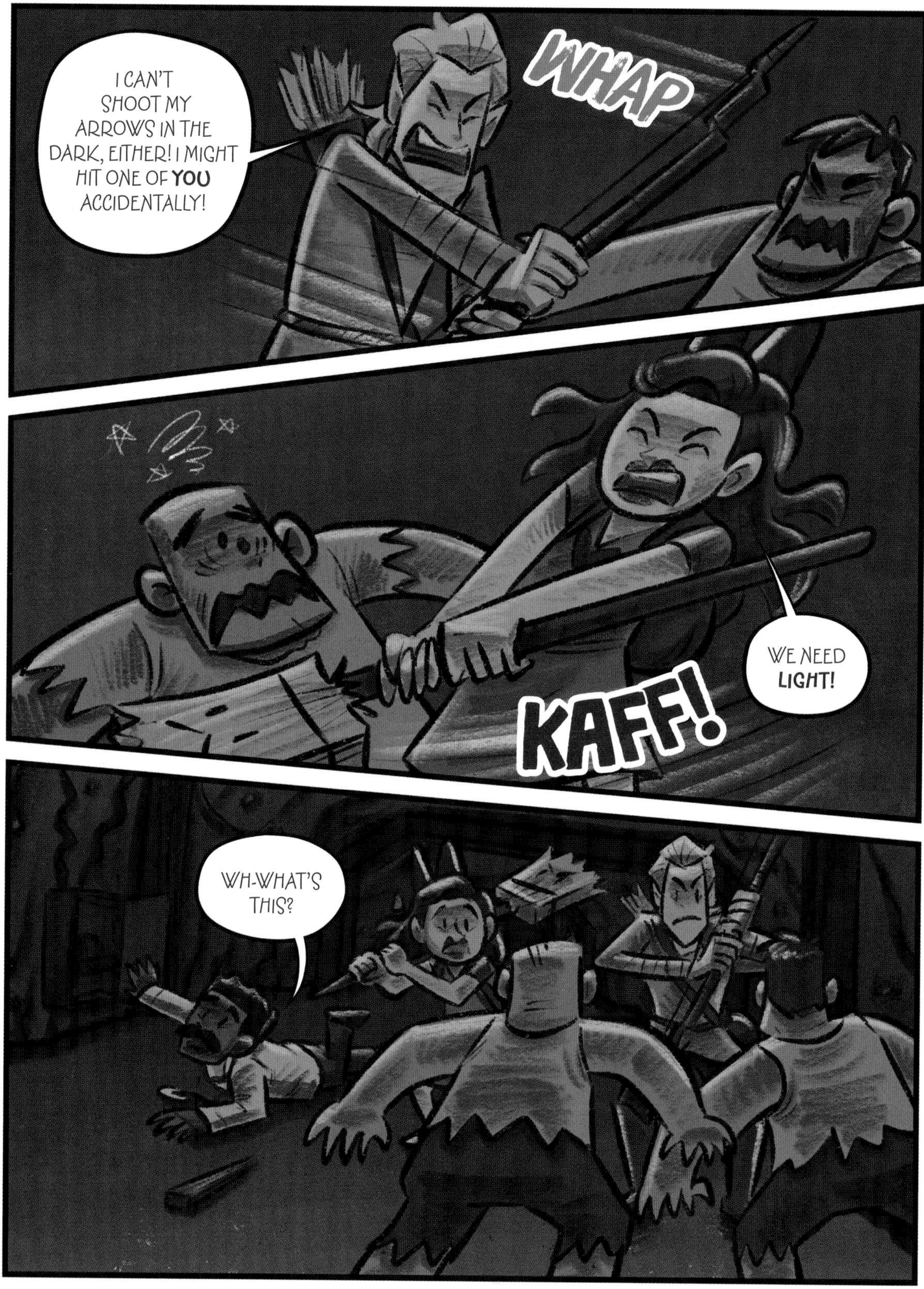
I CAN'T SHOOT MY ARROWS IN THE DARK, EITHER! I MIGHT HIT ONE OF **YOU** ACCIDENTALLY!
WHAP
WE NEED **LIGHT!**
KAFF!
WH-WHAT'S THIS?

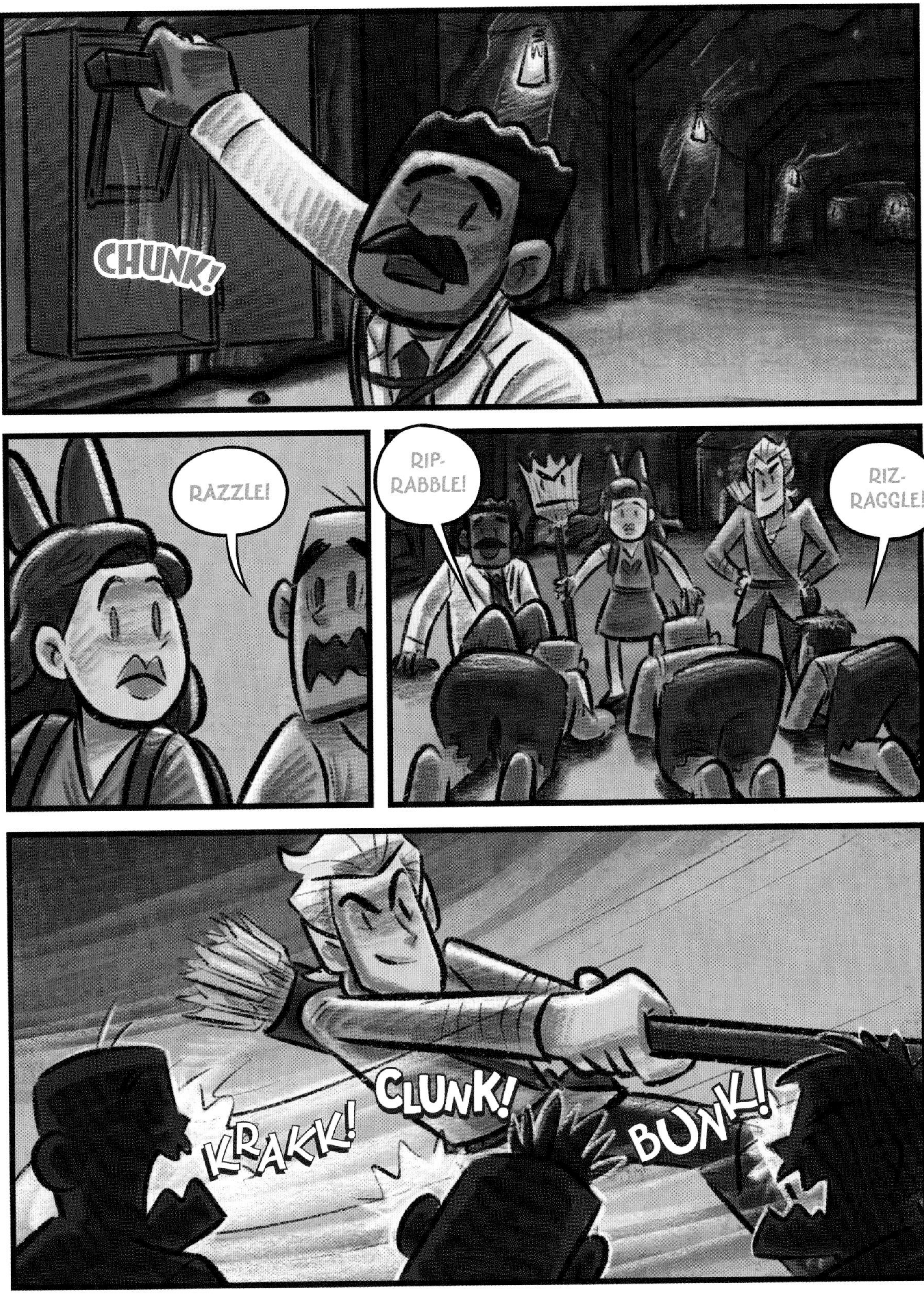
CHUNK!
RAZZLE!
RIP-
RABBLE!
RIZ-
RAGGLE!
KRAKK!
CLUNK!
BUNK!

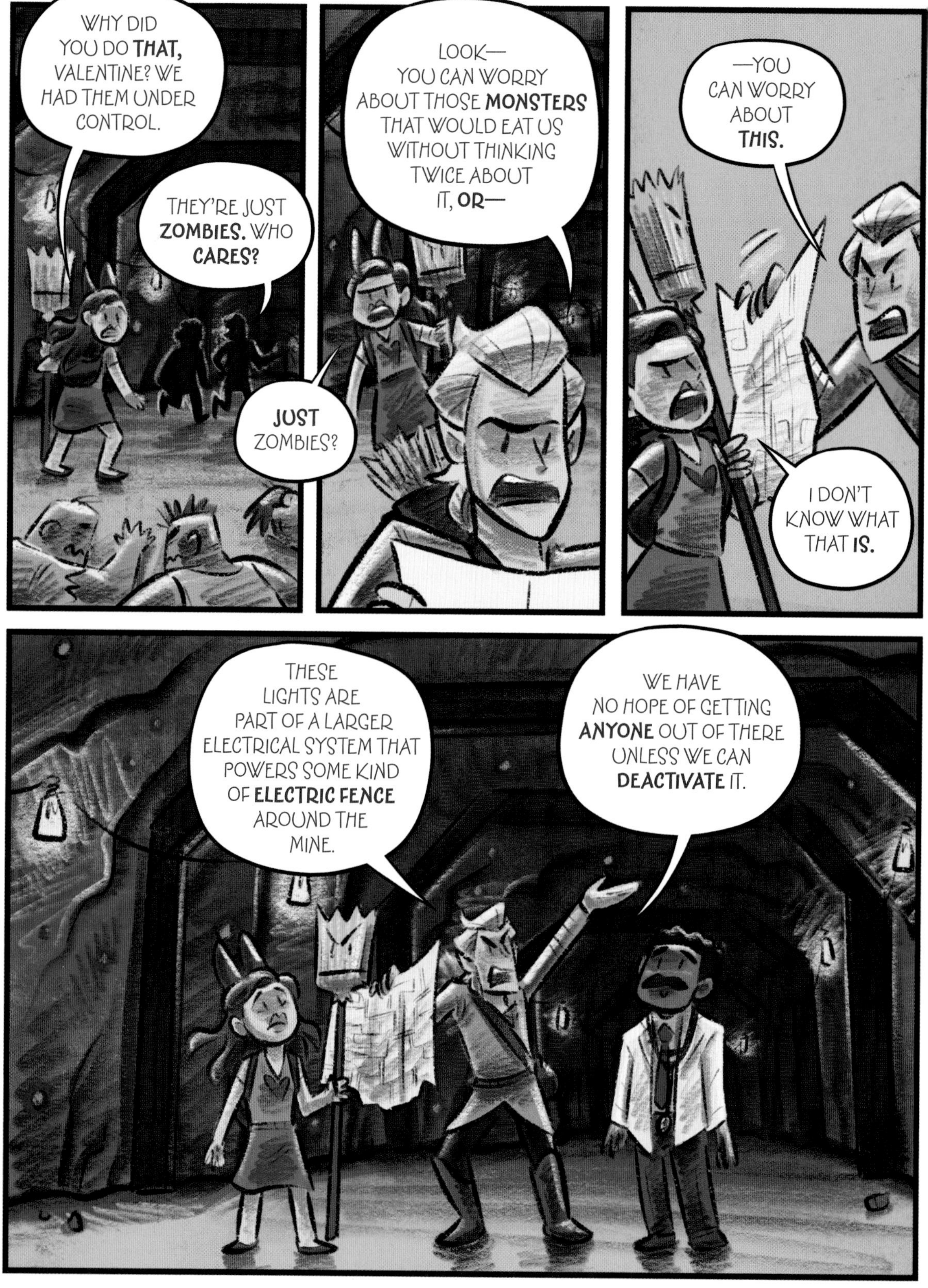
WHY DID YOU DO **THAT,** VALENTINE? WE HAD THEM UNDER CONTROL.
THEY'RE JUST **ZOMBIES.** WHO **CARES?**
JUST ZOMBIES?
LOOK— YOU CAN WORRY ABOUT THOSE **MONSTERS** THAT WOULD EAT US WITHOUT THINKING TWICE ABOUT IT, **OR—**
—YOU CAN WORRY ABOUT **THIS.**
I DON'T KNOW WHAT THAT **IS.**
THESE LIGHTS ARE PART OF A LARGER ELECTRICAL SYSTEM THAT POWERS SOME KIND OF **ELECTRIC FENCE** AROUND THE MINE.
WE HAVE NO HOPE OF GETTING **ANYONE** OUT OF THERE UNLESS WE CAN **DEACTIVATE** IT.

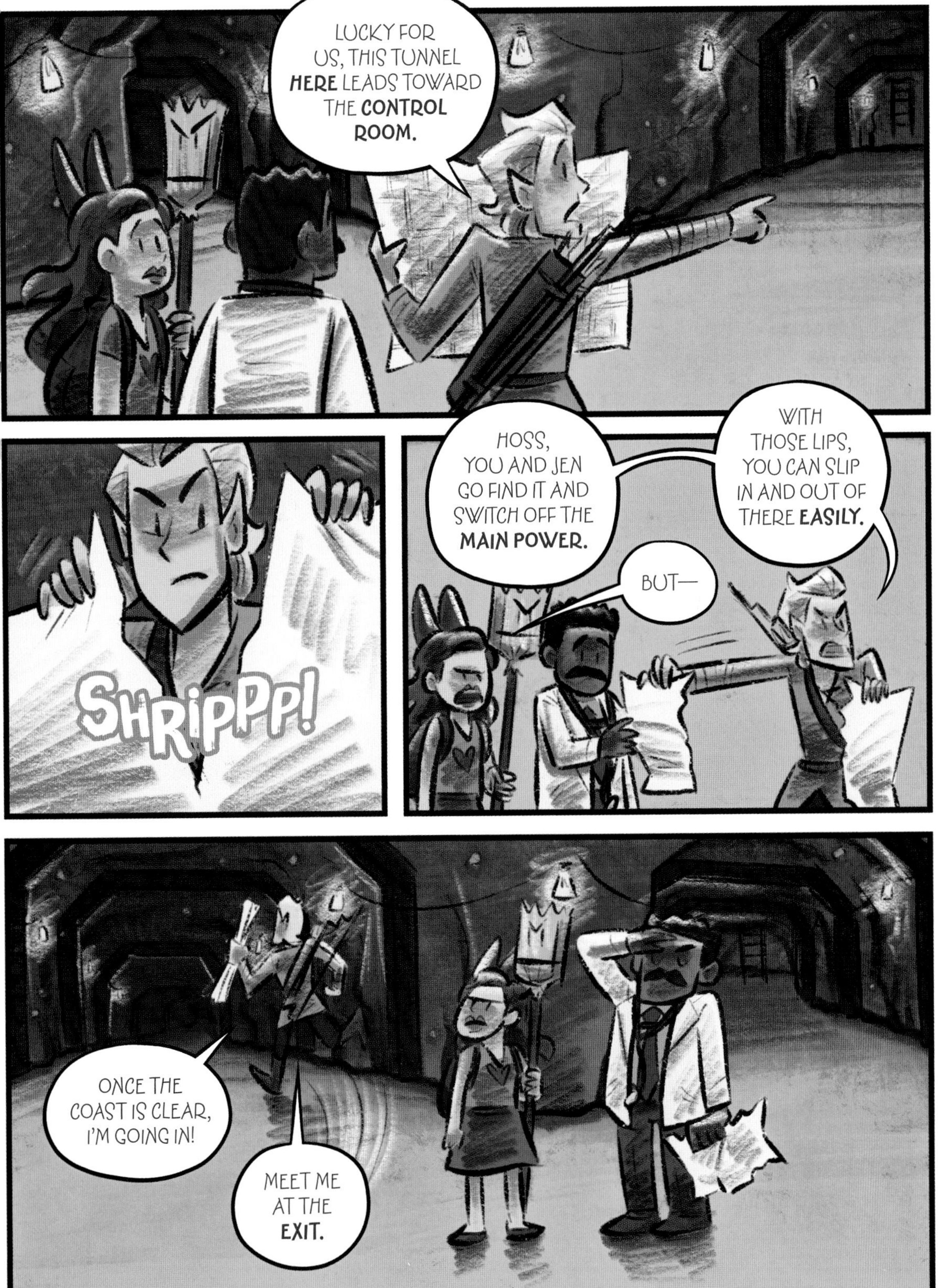
LUCKY FOR US, THIS TUNNEL **HERE** LEADS TOWARD THE **CONTROL ROOM.**
SHRIPPP!
HOSS, YOU AND JEN GO FIND IT AND SWITCH OFF THE **MAIN POWER.**
WITH THOSE LIPS, YOU CAN SLIP IN AND OUT OF THERE **EASILY.**
BUT—
ONCE THE COAST IS CLEAR, I'M GOING IN!
MEET ME AT THE **EXIT.**

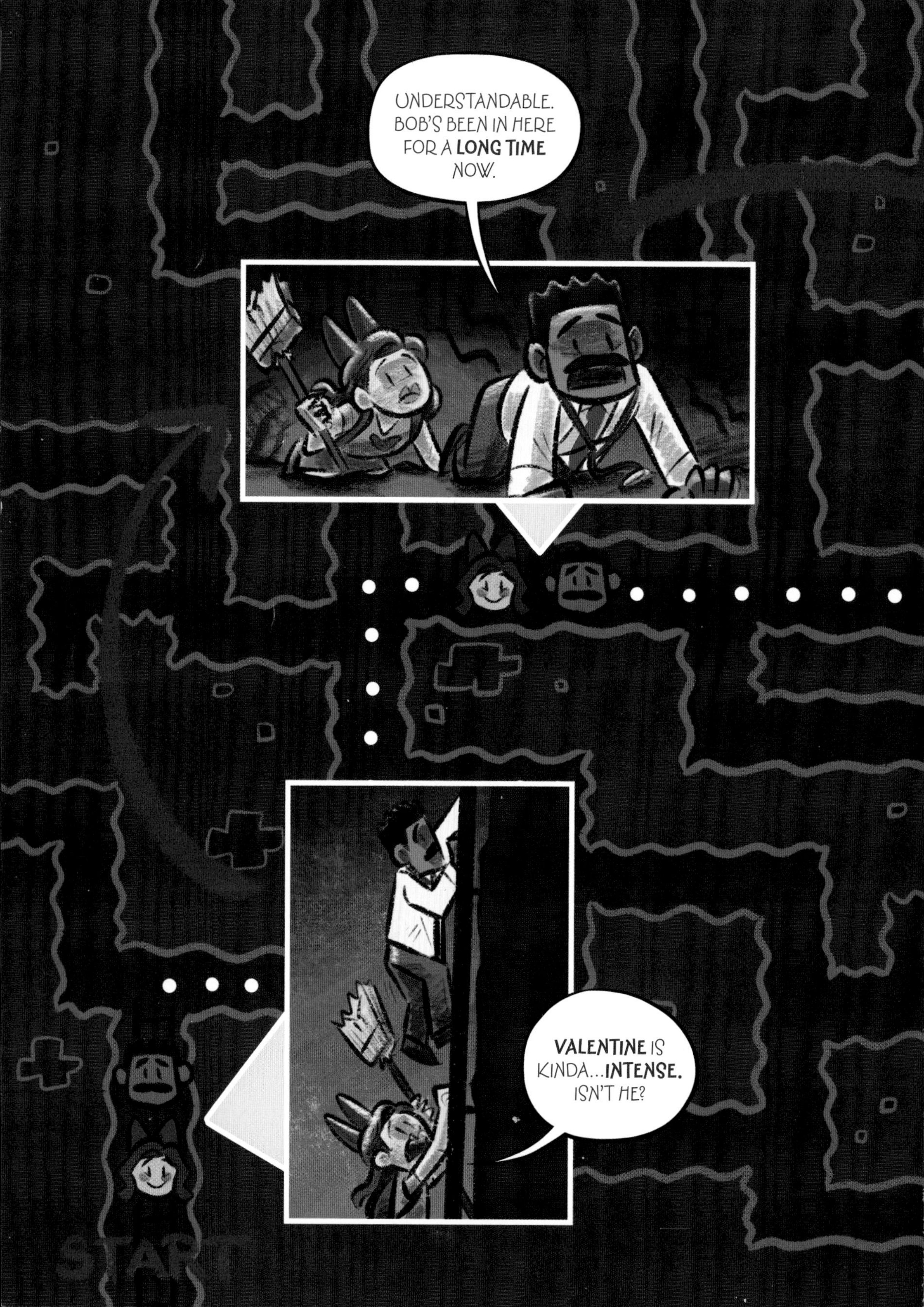
UNDERSTANDABLE. BOB'S BEEN IN HERE FOR A **LONG TIME** NOW.
VALENTINE IS KINDA...**INTENSE.** ISN'T HE?
START

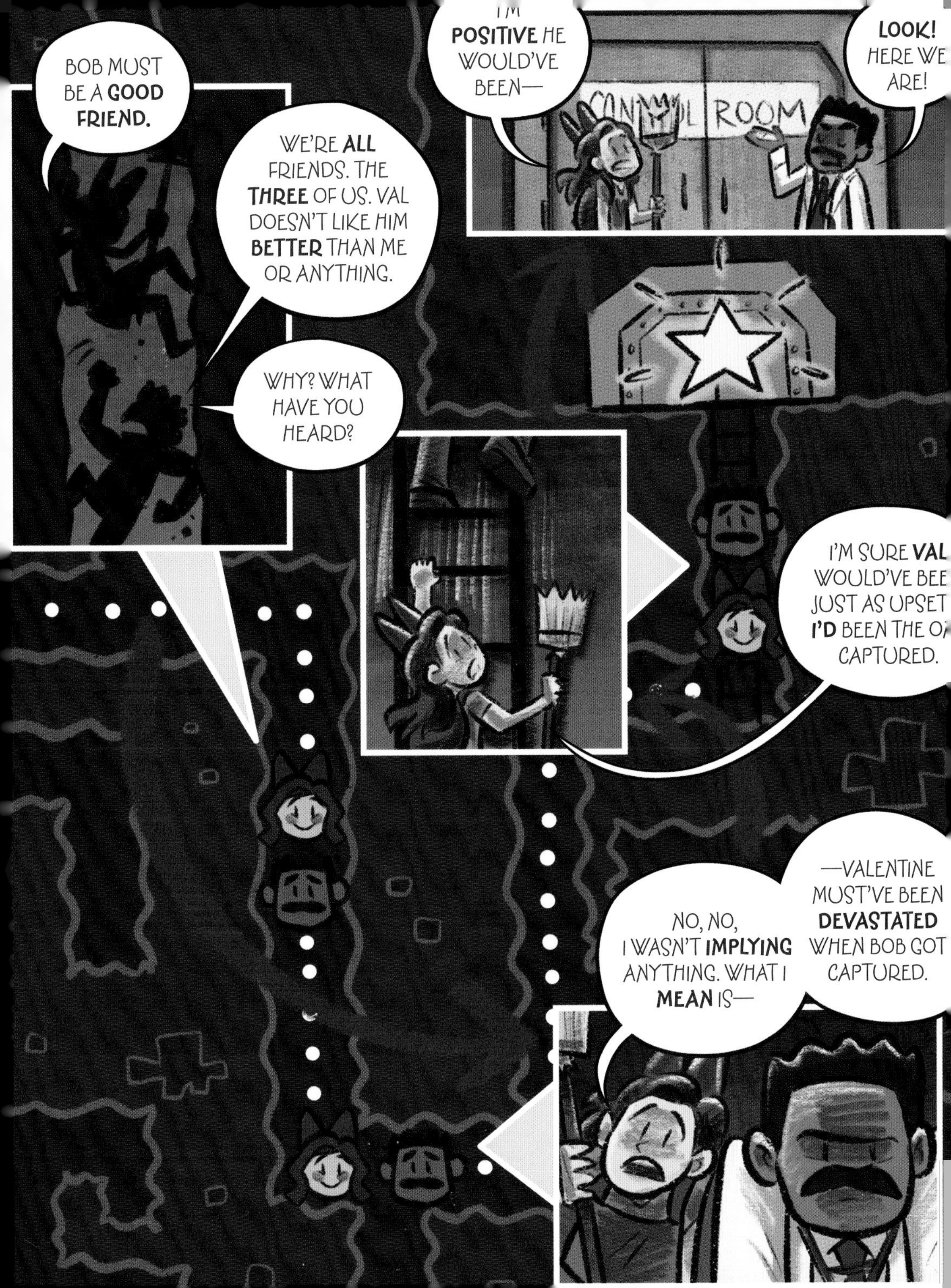
BOB MUST BE A **GOOD FRIEND.**
WE'RE **ALL** FRIENDS. THE **THREE** OF US. VAL DOESN'T LIKE HIM **BETTER** THAN ME OR ANYTHING.
WHY? WHAT HAVE YOU HEARD?
NO, NO, I WASN'T **IMPLYING** ANYTHING. WHAT I **MEAN** IS—
—VALENTINE MUST'VE BEEN **DEVASTATED** WHEN BOB GOT CAPTURED.
I'M SURE **VAL** WOULD'VE BEE JUST AS UPSET **I'D** BEEN THE O CAPTURED.
I'M **POSITIVE** HE WOULD'VE BEEN—
LOOK! HERE WE ARE!

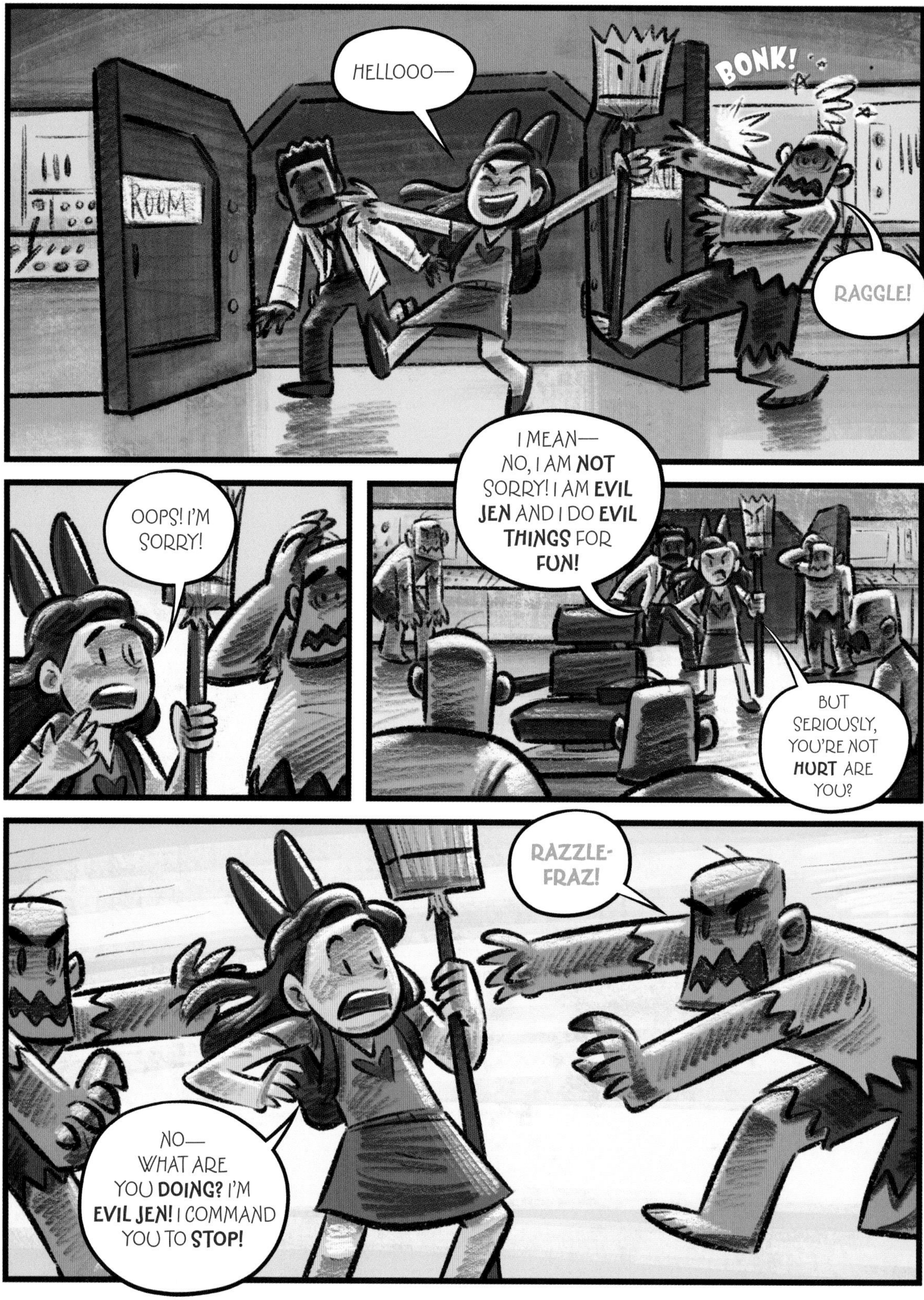

HELLOOO—
BONK!
RAGGLE!
OOPS! I'M SORRY!
I MEAN— NO, I AM NOT SORRY! I AM EVIL JEN AND I DO EVIL THINGS FOR FUN!
BUT SERIOUSLY, YOU'RE NOT HURT ARE YOU?
RAZZLE-FRAZ!
NO— WHAT ARE YOU DOING? I'M EVIL JEN! I COMMAND YOU TO STOP!

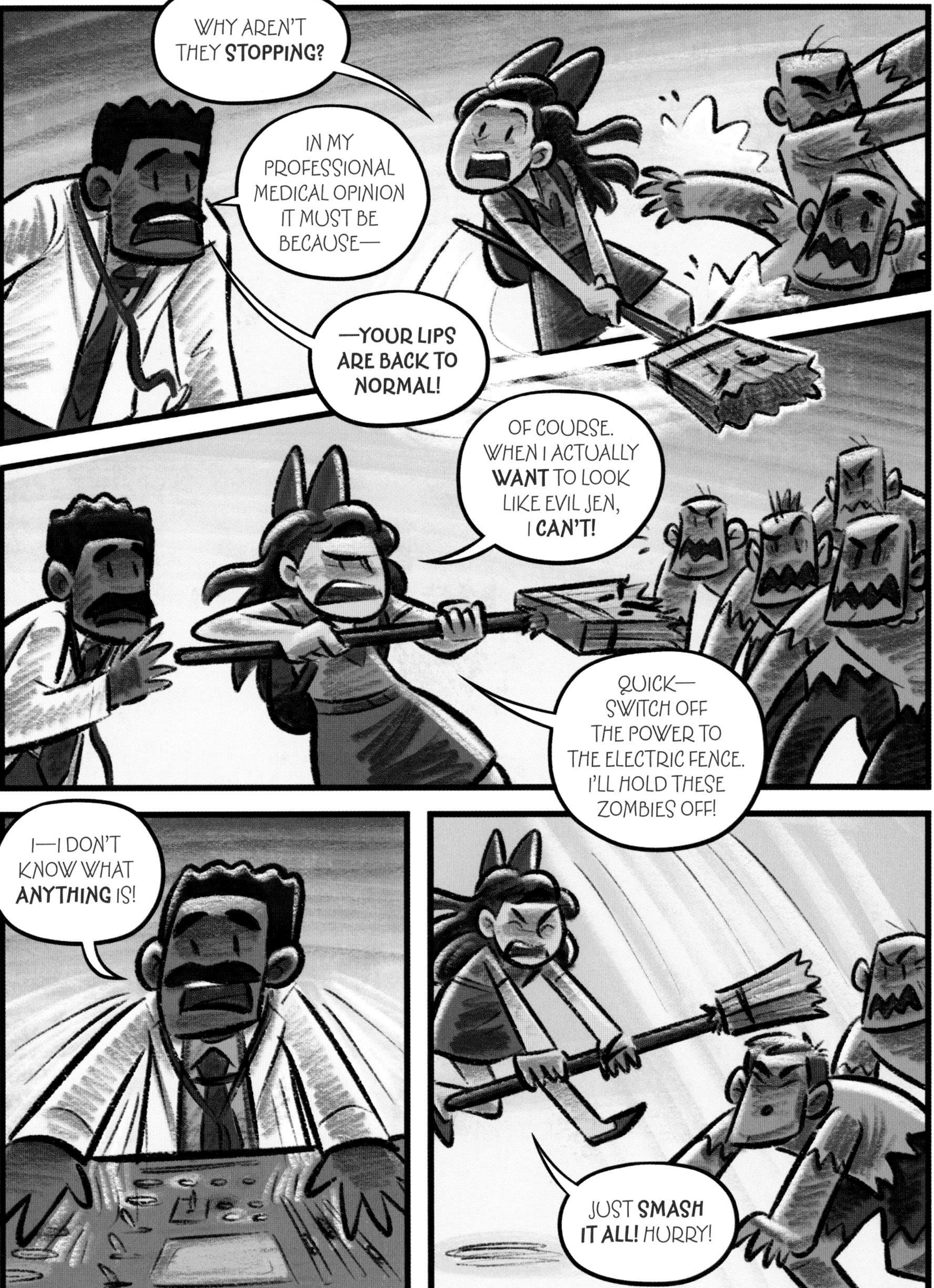
WHY AREN'T THEY **STOPPING?**
IN MY PROFESSIONAL MEDICAL OPINION IT MUST BE BECAUSE—
—YOUR LIPS ARE BACK TO NORMAL!
OF COURSE. WHEN I ACTUALLY **WANT** TO LOOK LIKE EVIL JEN, I **CAN'T!**
QUICK— SWITCH OFF THE POWER TO THE ELECTRIC FENCE. I'LL HOLD THESE ZOMBIES OFF!
I—I DON'T KNOW WHAT **ANYTHING** IS!
JUST **SMASH IT ALL!** HURRY!

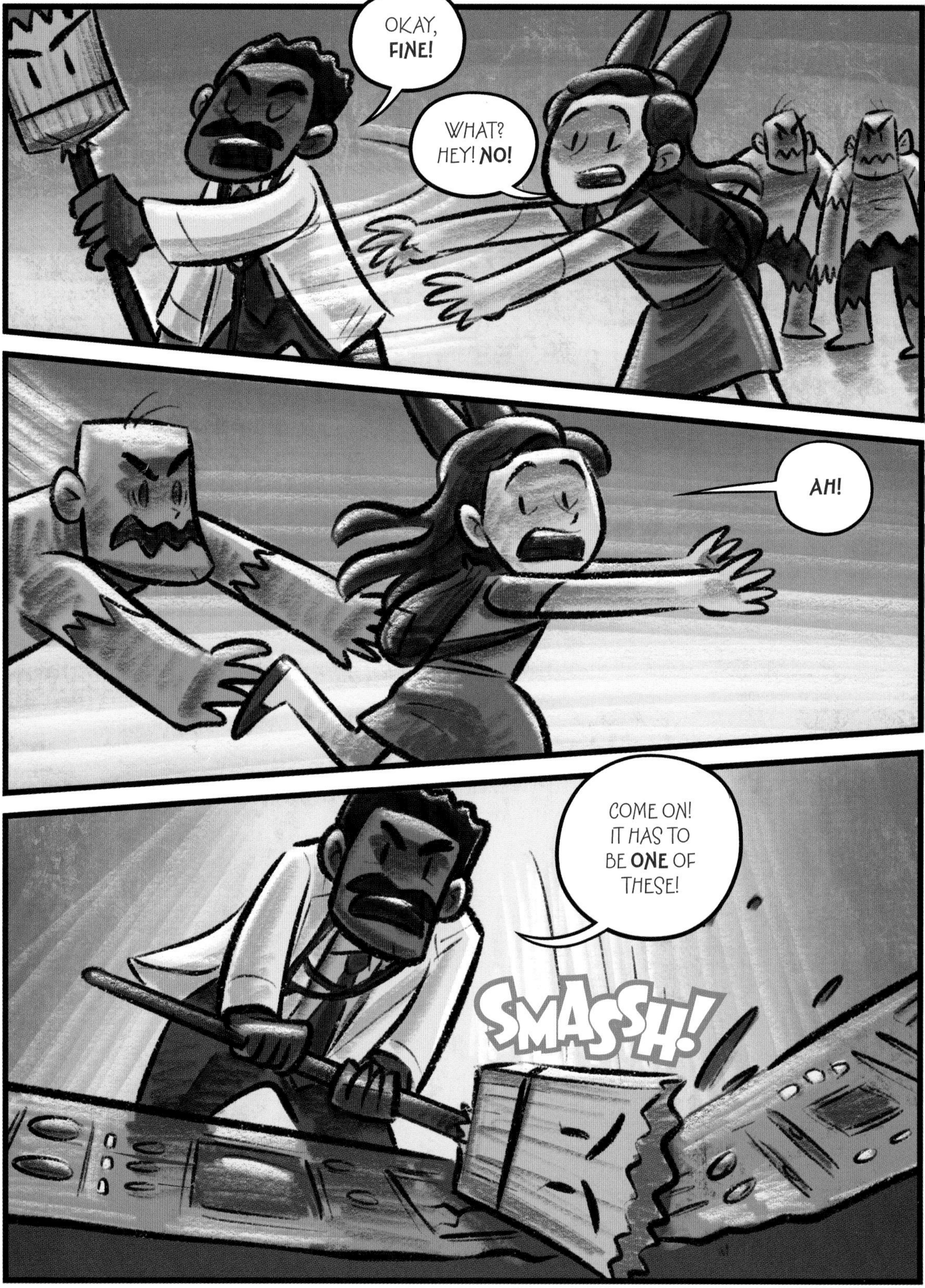
OKAY, **FINE!**
WHAT? HEY! **NO!**
AH!
COME ON! IT HAS TO BE **ONE** OF THESE!
SMASSH!

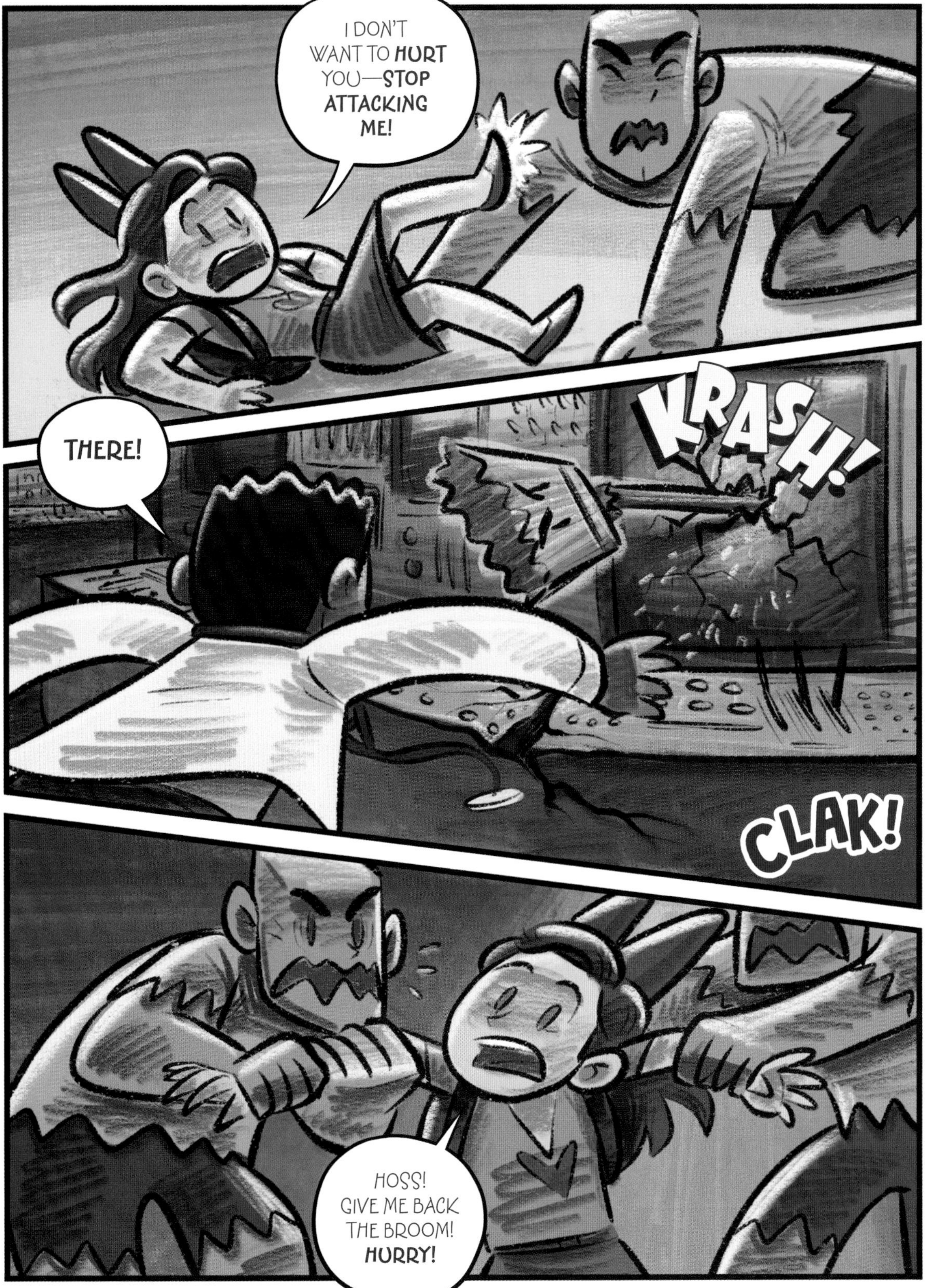

I DON'T WANT TO HURT YOU—STOP ATTACKING ME!
THERE!
KRASH!
CLAK!
HOSS! GIVE ME BACK THE BROOM! HURRY!

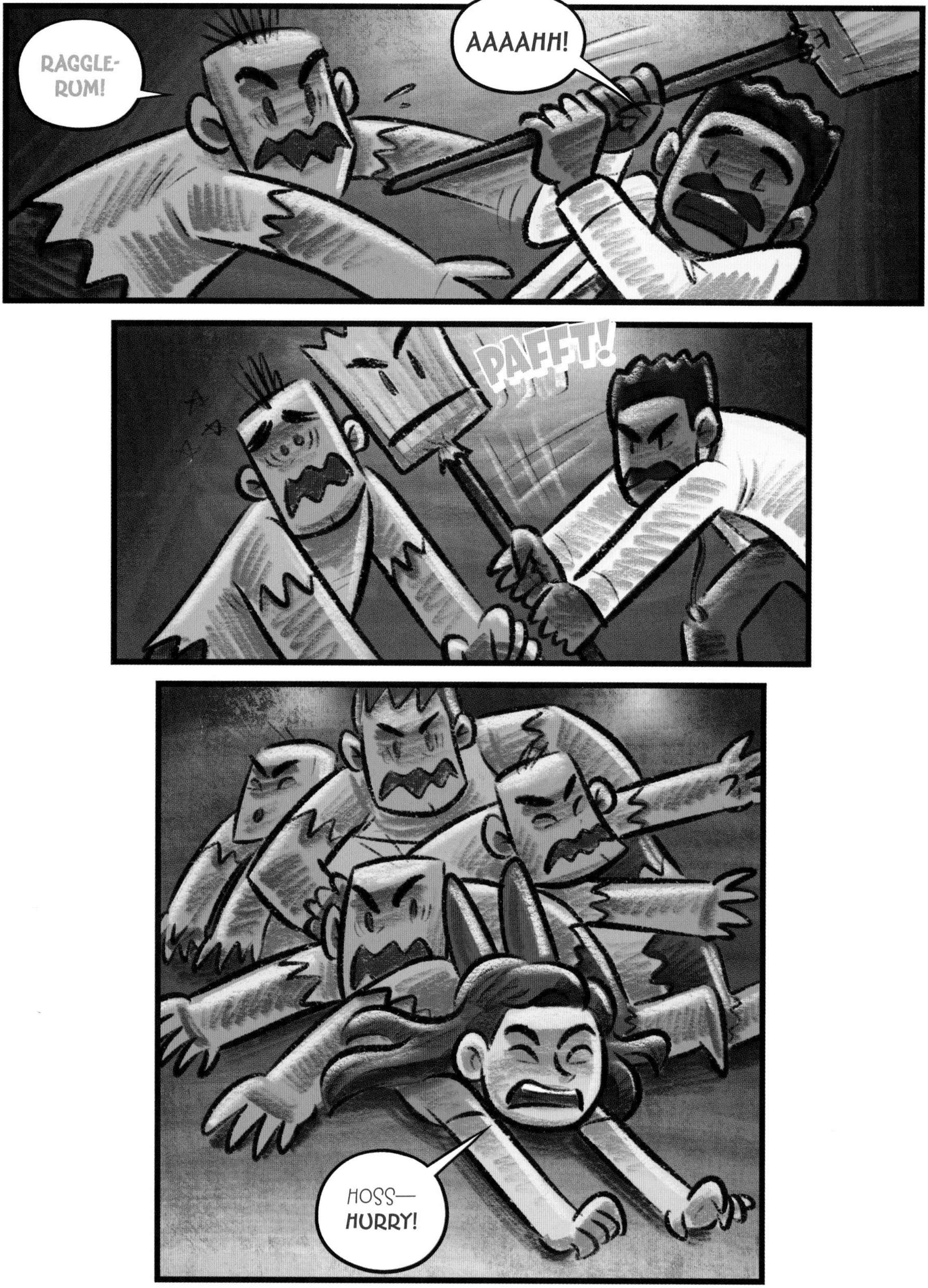
RAGGLE-
RUM!
AAAAHH!
PAFFT!
HOSS—
HURRY!

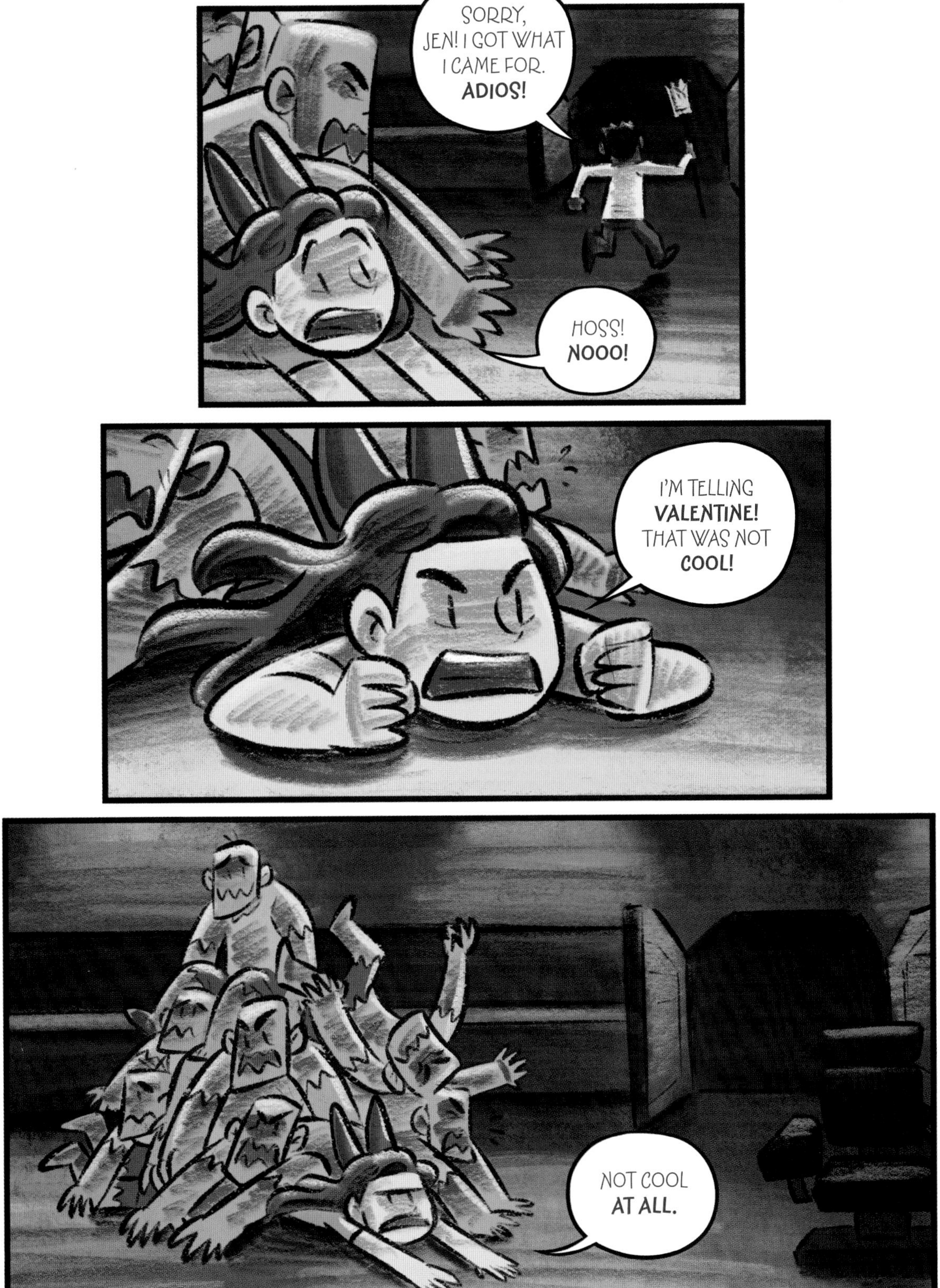
SORRY, JEN! I GOT WHAT I CAME FOR. ADIOS!
HOSS! NOOO!
I'M TELLING VALENTINE! THAT WAS NOT COOL!
NOT COOL AT ALL.

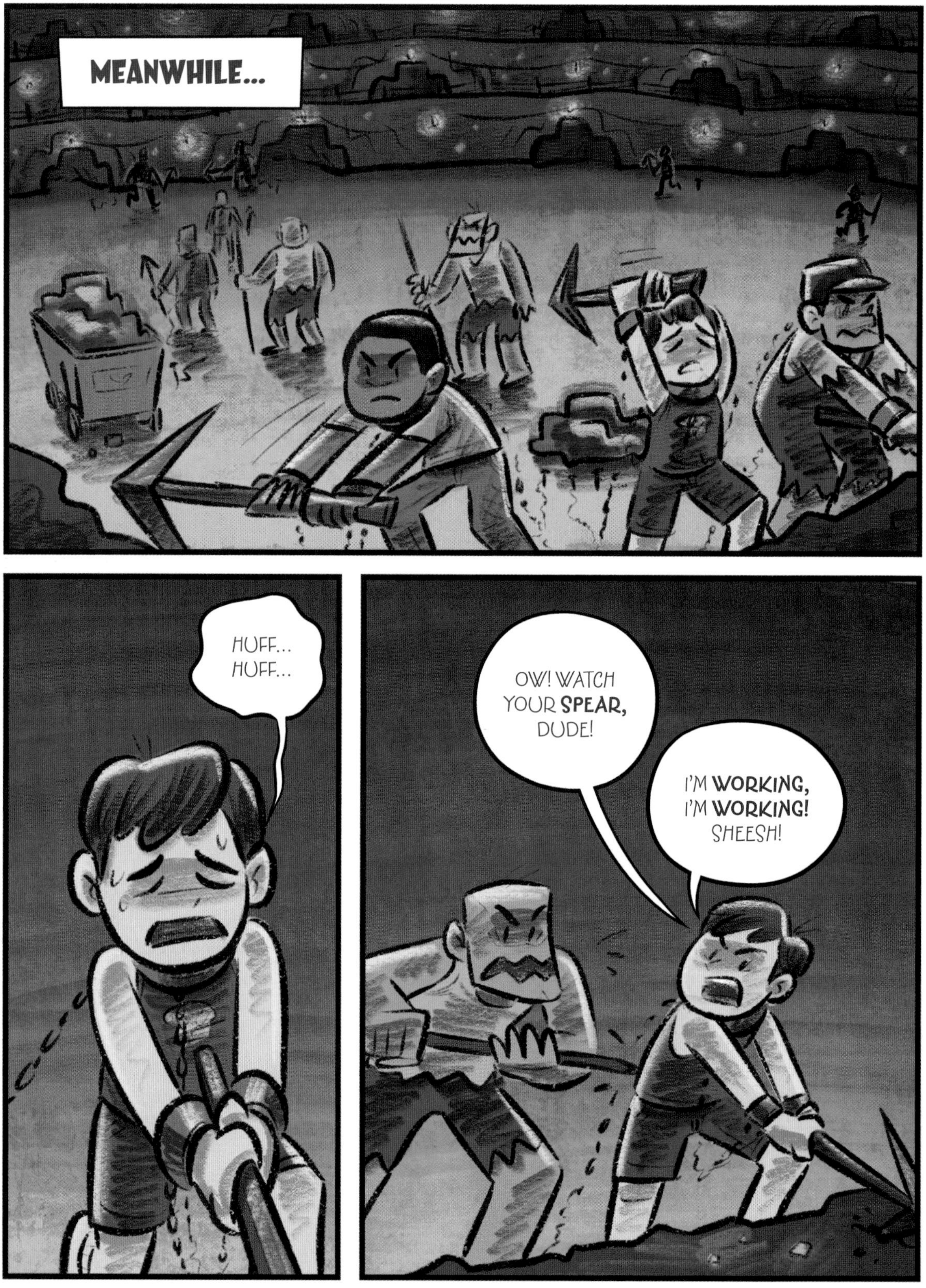
MEANWHILE...
HUFF...
HUFF...
OW! WATCH YOUR SPEAR, DUDE!
I'M WORKING, I'M WORKING! SHEESH!

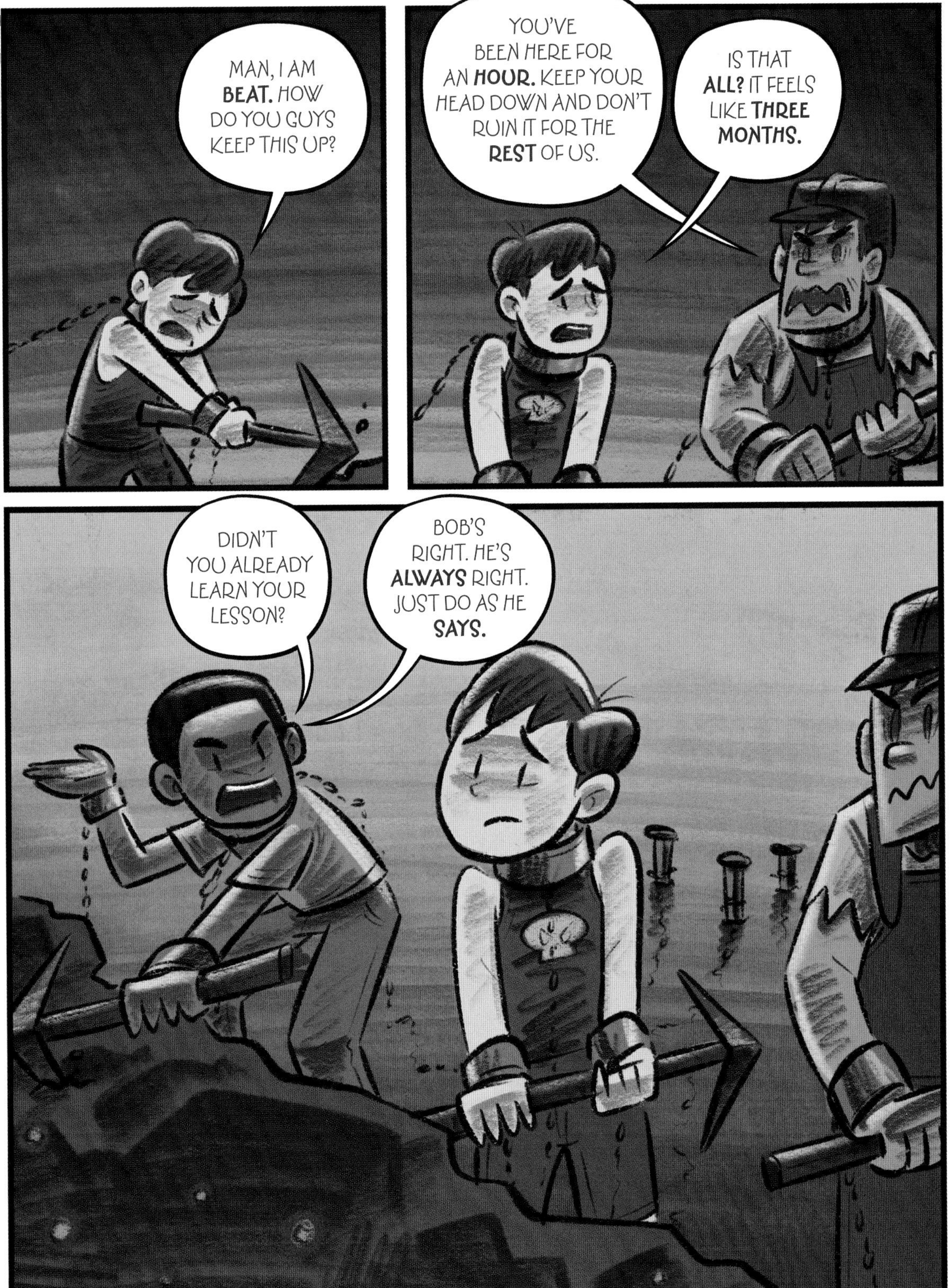
MAN, I AM BEAT. HOW DO YOU GUYS KEEP THIS UP?
YOU'VE BEEN HERE FOR AN HOUR. KEEP YOUR HEAD DOWN AND DON'T RUIN IT FOR THE REST OF US.
IS THAT ALL? IT FEELS LIKE THREE MONTHS.
DIDN'T YOU ALREADY LEARN YOUR LESSON?
BOB'S RIGHT. HE'S ALWAYS RIGHT. JUST DO AS HE SAYS.

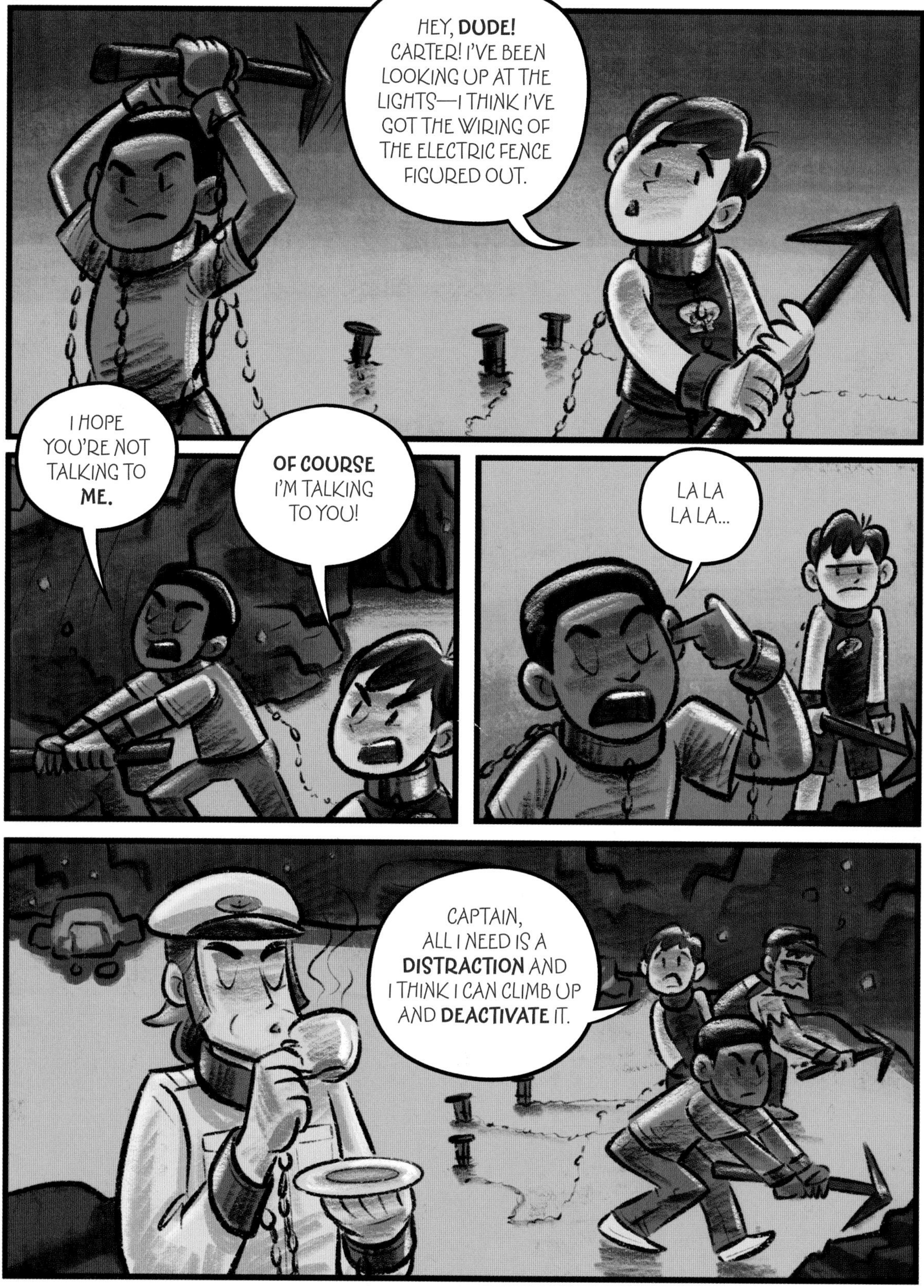
HEY, **DUDE!** CARTER! I'VE BEEN LOOKING UP AT THE LIGHTS—I THINK I'VE GOT THE WIRING OF THE ELECTRIC FENCE FIGURED OUT.
I HOPE YOU'RE NOT TALKING TO **ME.**
OF COURSE I'M TALKING TO YOU!
LA LA LA LA...
CAPTAIN, ALL I NEED IS A **DISTRACTION** AND I THINK I CAN CLIMB UP AND **DEACTIVATE** IT.

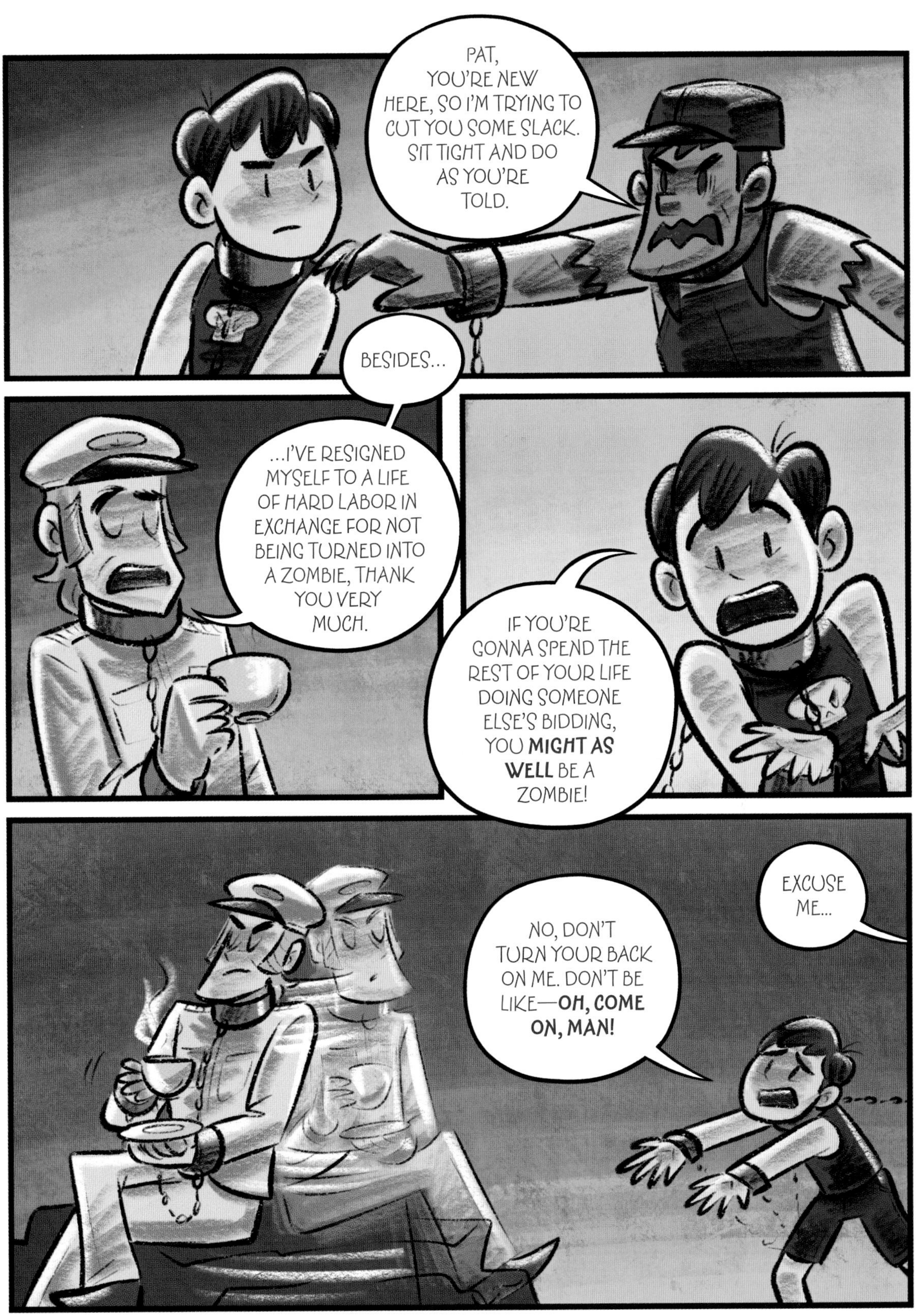
PAT, YOU'RE NEW HERE, SO I'M TRYING TO CUT YOU SOME SLACK. SIT TIGHT AND DO AS YOU'RE TOLD.
BESIDES...
...I'VE RESIGNED MYSELF TO A LIFE OF HARD LABOR IN EXCHANGE FOR NOT BEING TURNED INTO A ZOMBIE, THANK YOU VERY MUCH.
IF YOU'RE GONNA SPEND THE REST OF YOUR LIFE DOING SOMEONE ELSE'S BIDDING, YOU **MIGHT AS WELL** BE A ZOMBIE!
EXCUSE ME...
NO, DON'T TURN YOUR BACK ON ME. DON'T BE LIKE—**OH, COME ON, MAN!**

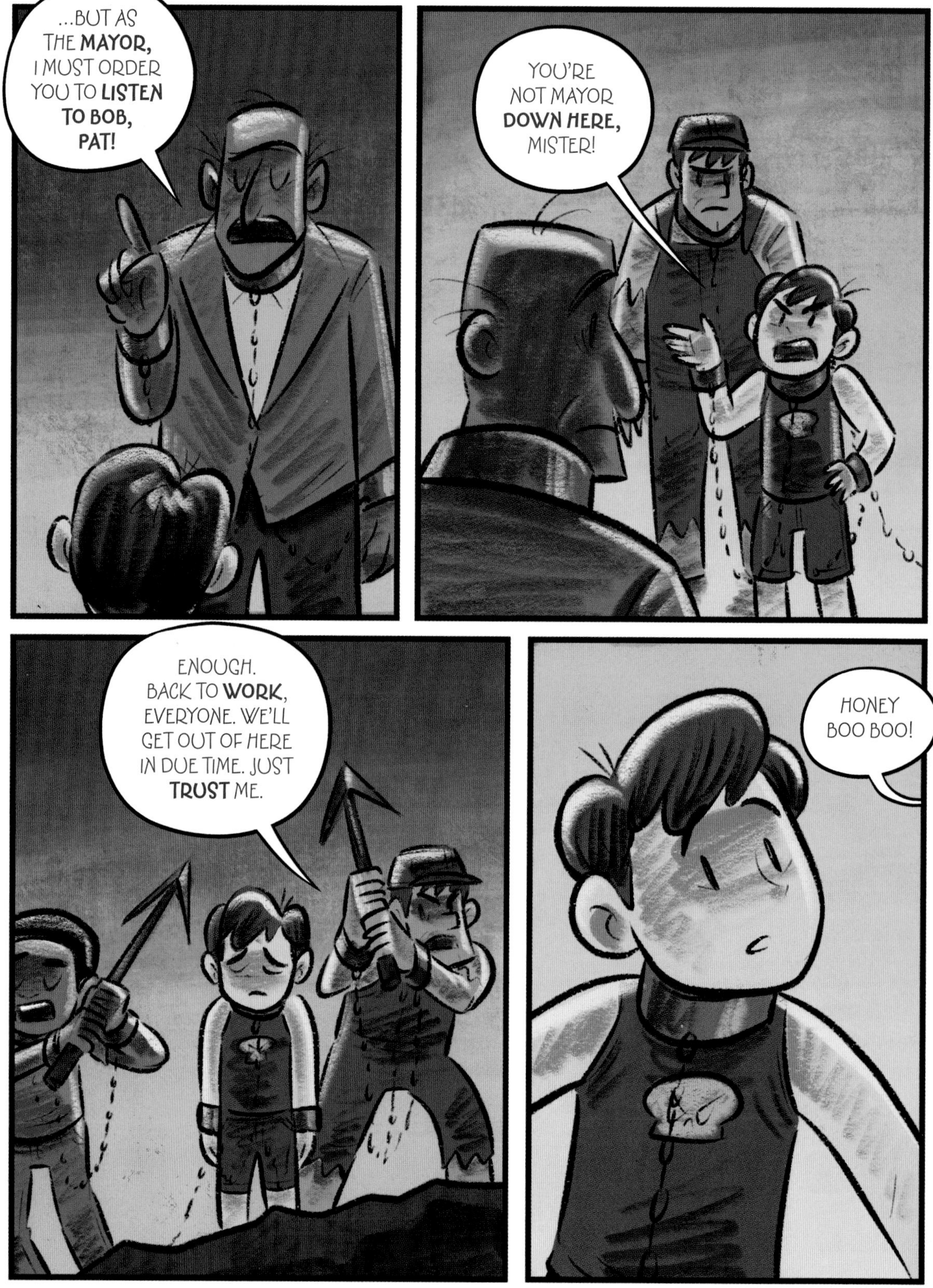
...BUT AS THE MAYOR, I MUST ORDER YOU TO LISTEN TO BOB, PAT!
YOU'RE NOT MAYOR DOWN HERE, MISTER!
ENOUGH. BACK TO WORK, EVERYONE. WE'LL GET OUT OF HERE IN DUE TIME. JUST TRUST ME.
HONEY BOO BOO!

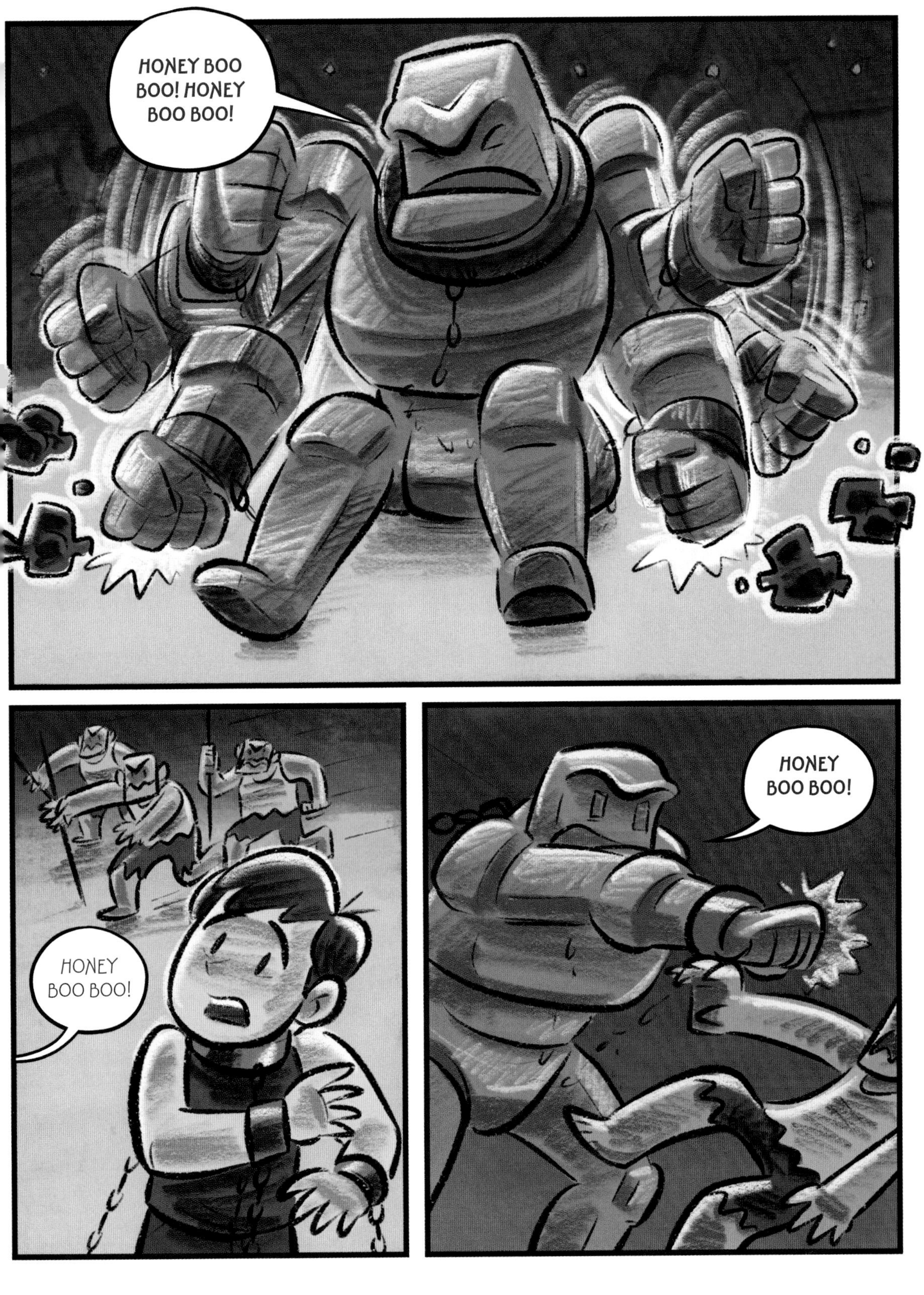
HONEY BOO BOO! HONEY BOO BOO!
HONEY BOO BOO!
HONEY BOO BOO!

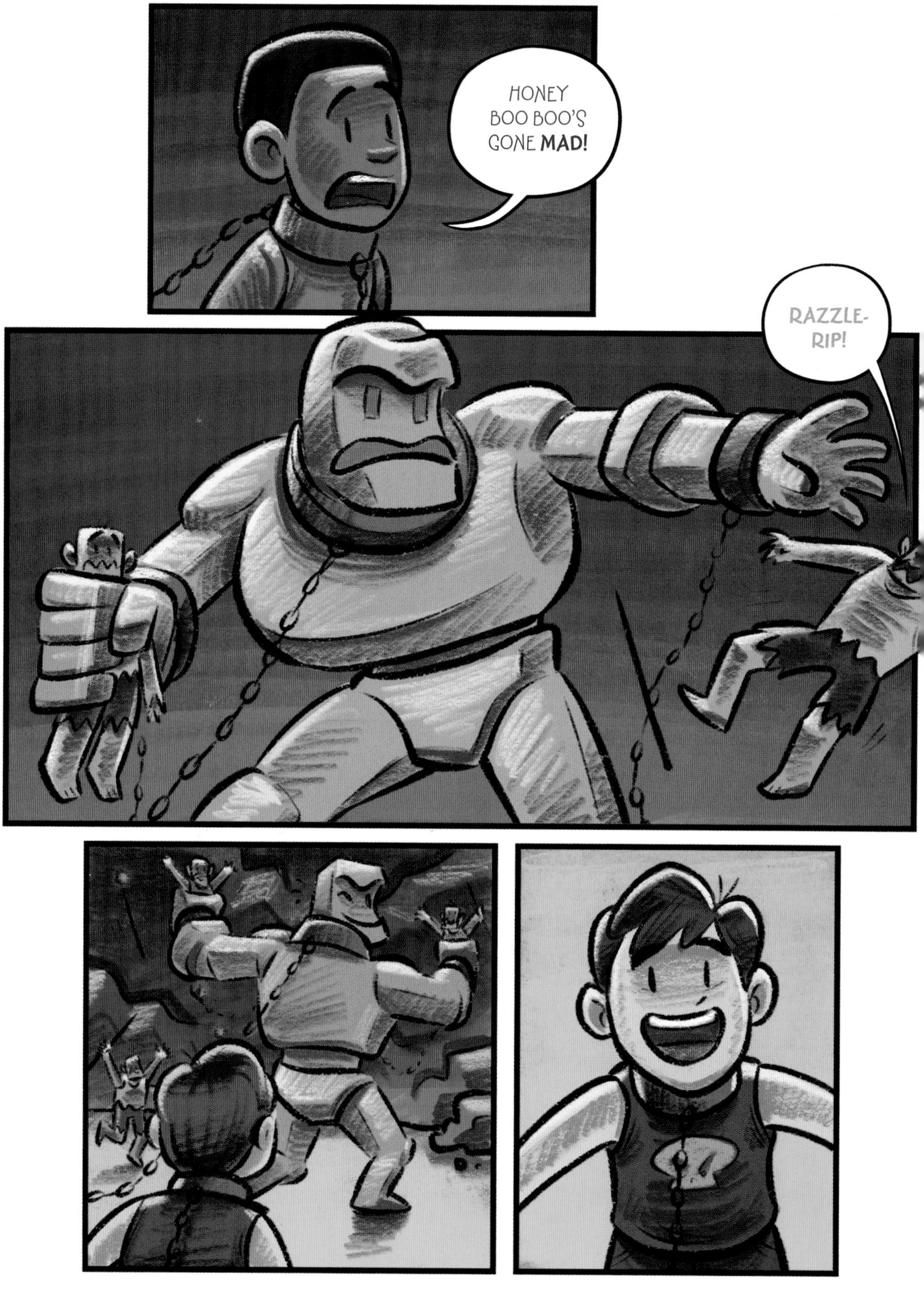
HONEY BOO BOO'S GONE **MAD!**
RAZZLE-RIP!

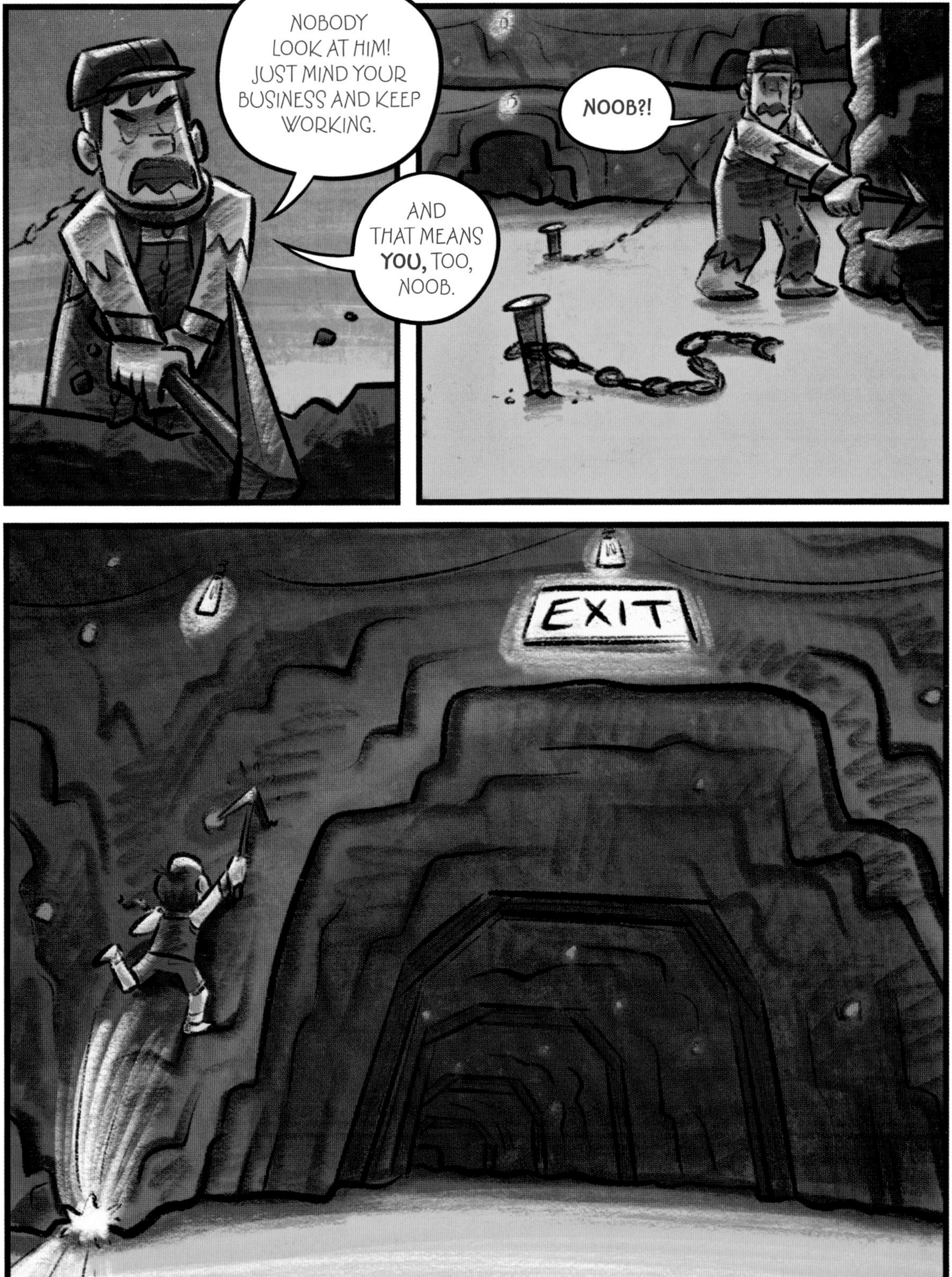
NOBODY LOOK AT HIM! JUST MIND YOUR BUSINESS AND KEEP WORKING.
AND THAT MEANS **YOU,** TOO, NOOB.
NOOB?!
EXIT

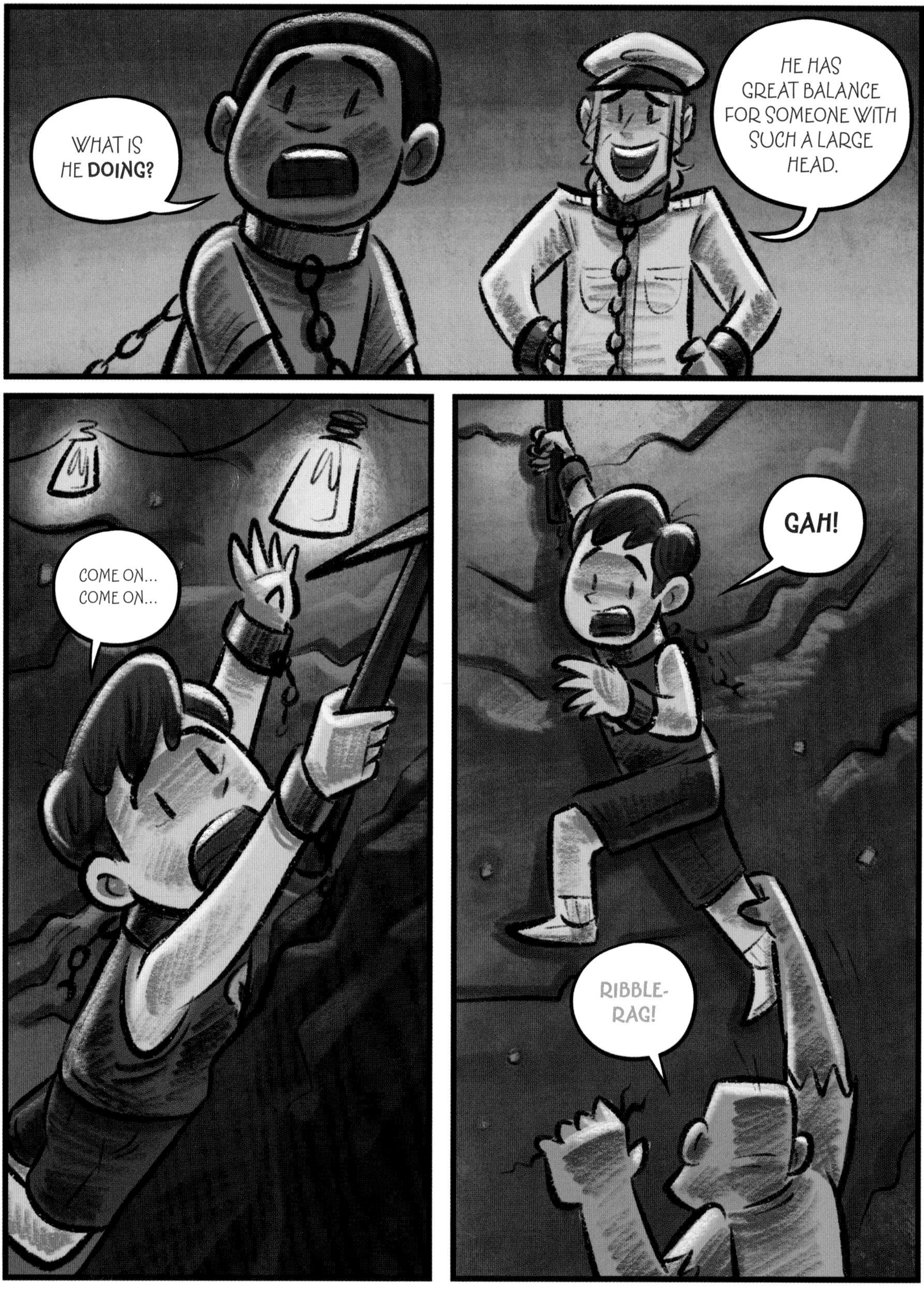
WHAT IS HE **DOING?**
HE HAS GREAT BALANCE FOR SOMEONE WITH SUCH A LARGE HEAD.
COME ON... COME ON...
GAH!
RIBBLE-RAG!

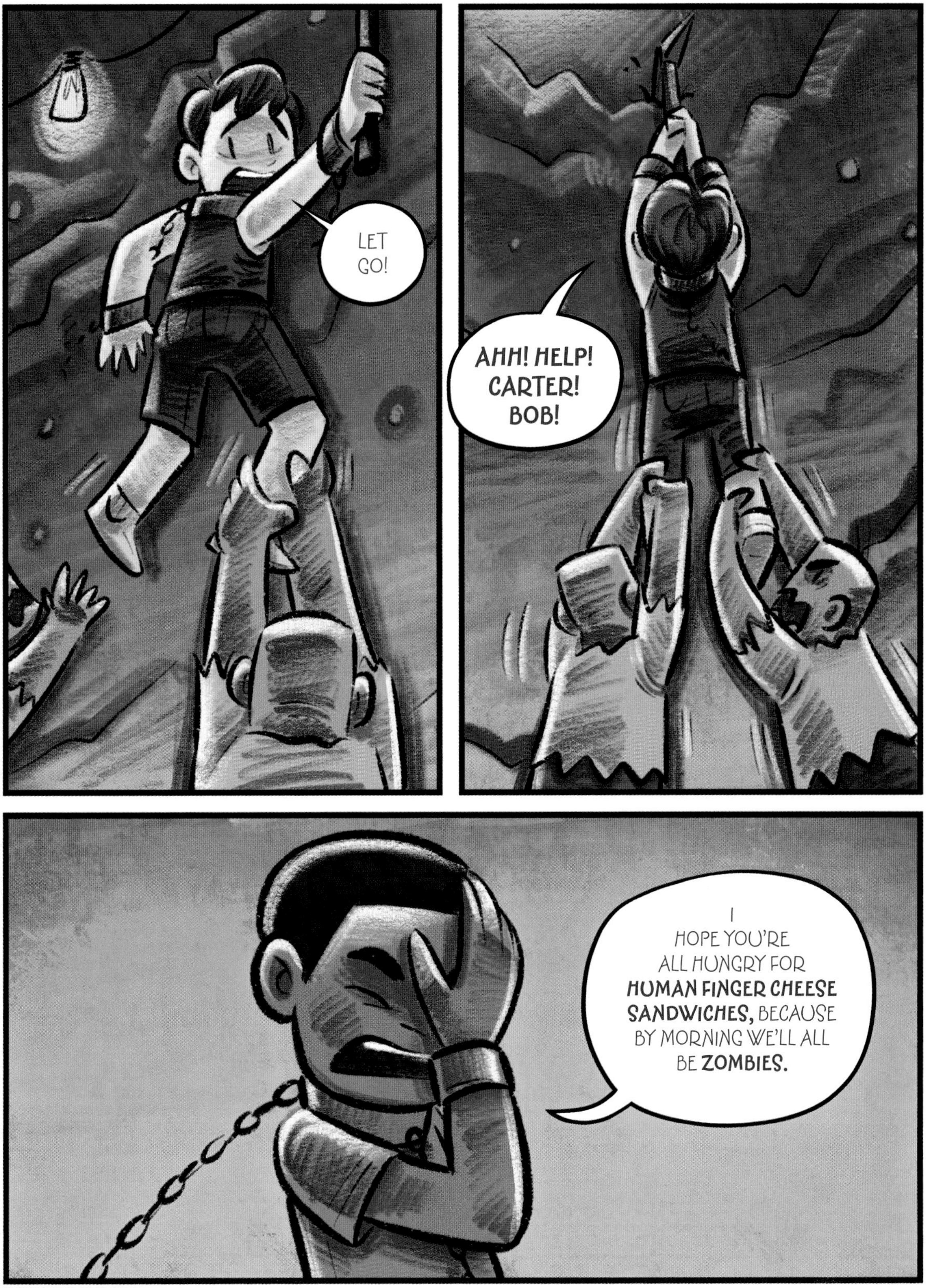
LET GO!
AHH! HELP! CARTER! BOB!
I HOPE YOU'RE ALL HUNGRY FOR **HUMAN FINGER CHEESE SANDWICHES,** BECAUSE BY MORNING WE'LL ALL BE **ZOMBIES.**

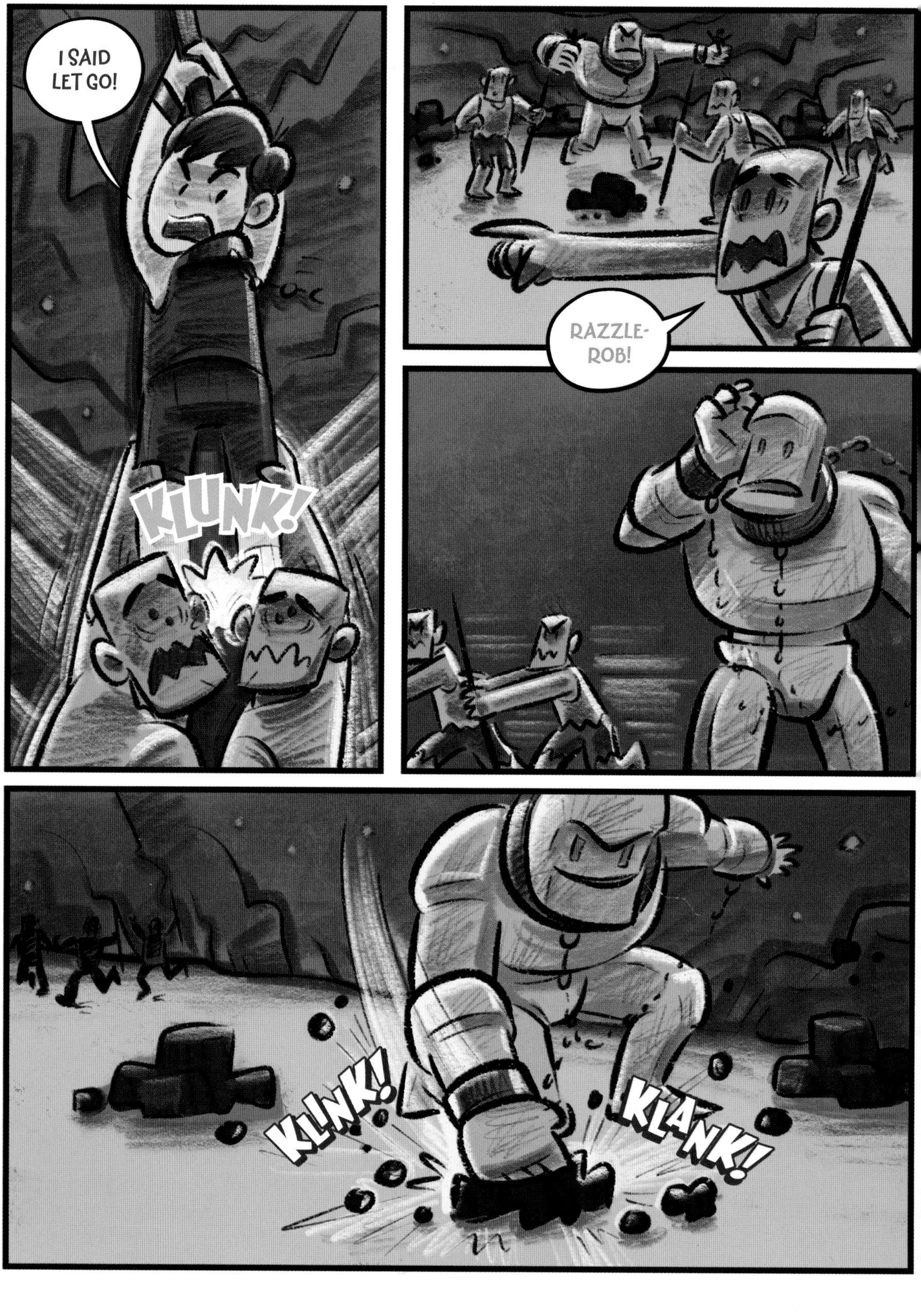
I SAID LET GO!
KLUNK!
RAZZLE-ROB!
KLINK!
KLANK!

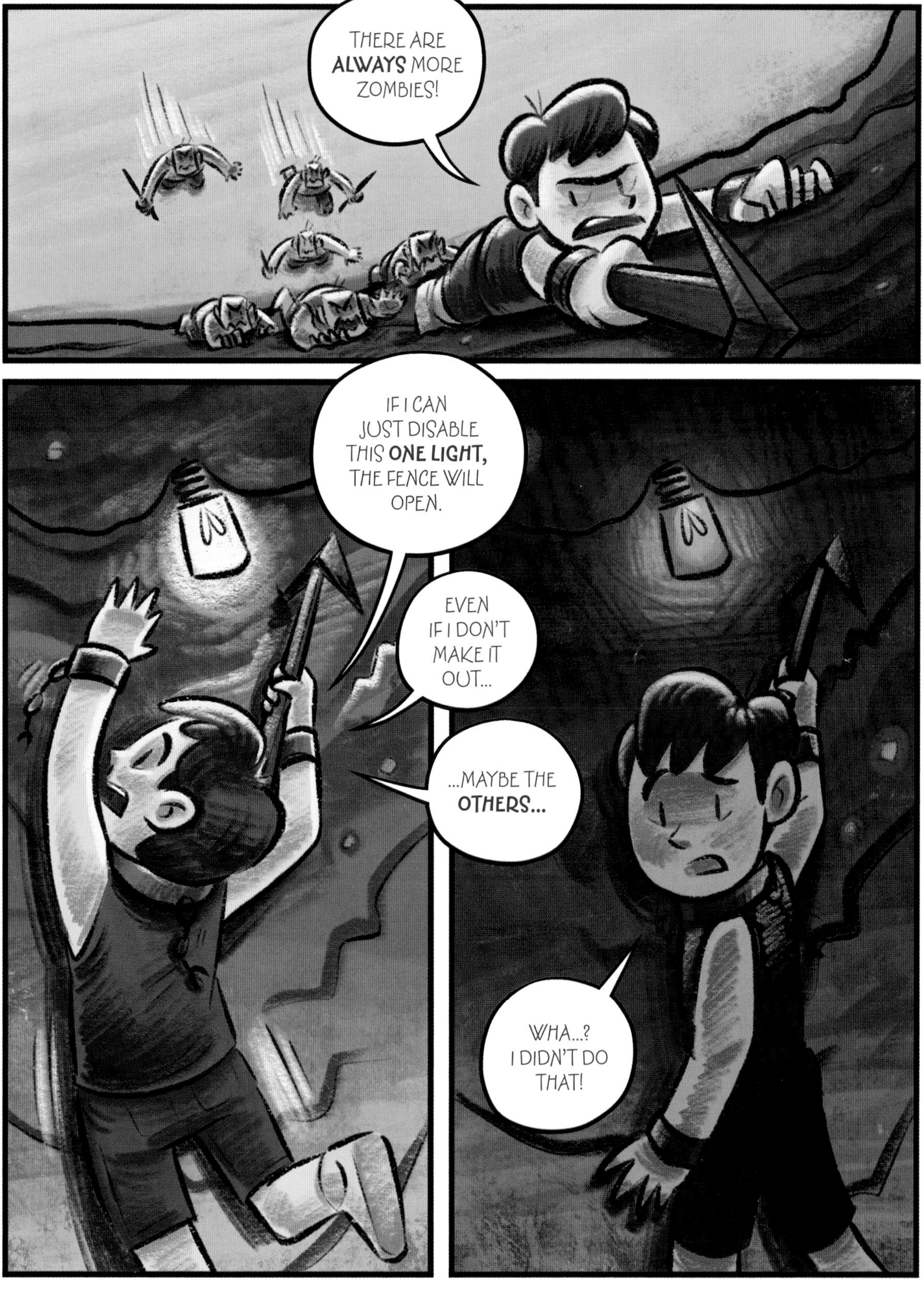
THERE ARE **ALWAYS** MORE ZOMBIES!
IF I CAN JUST DISABLE THIS **ONE LIGHT,** THE FENCE WILL OPEN.
EVEN IF I DON'T MAKE IT OUT...
...MAYBE THE **OTHERS...**
WHA...? I DIDN'T DO THAT!

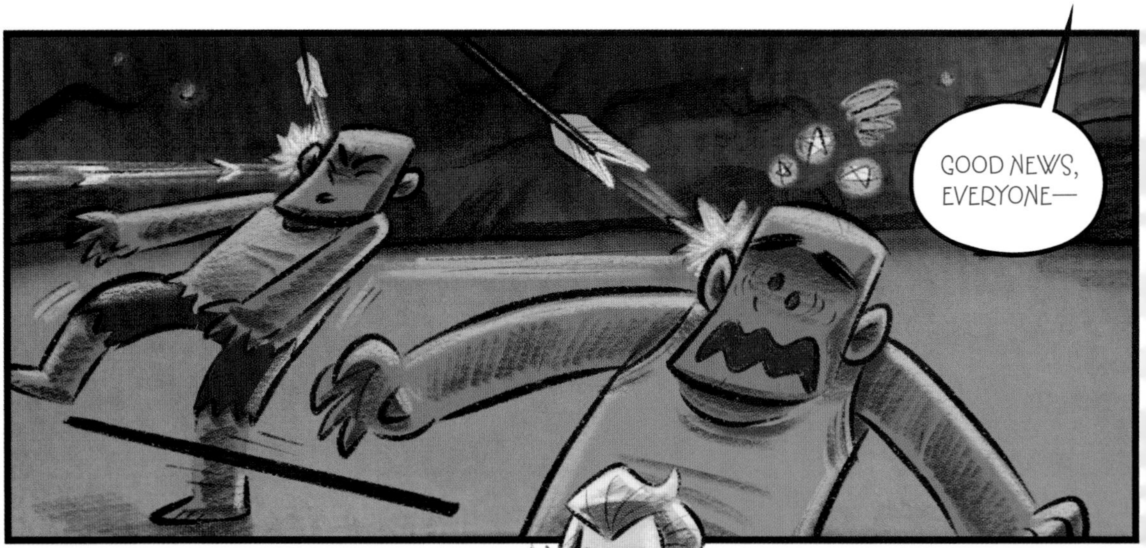
GOOD NEWS, EVERYONE—

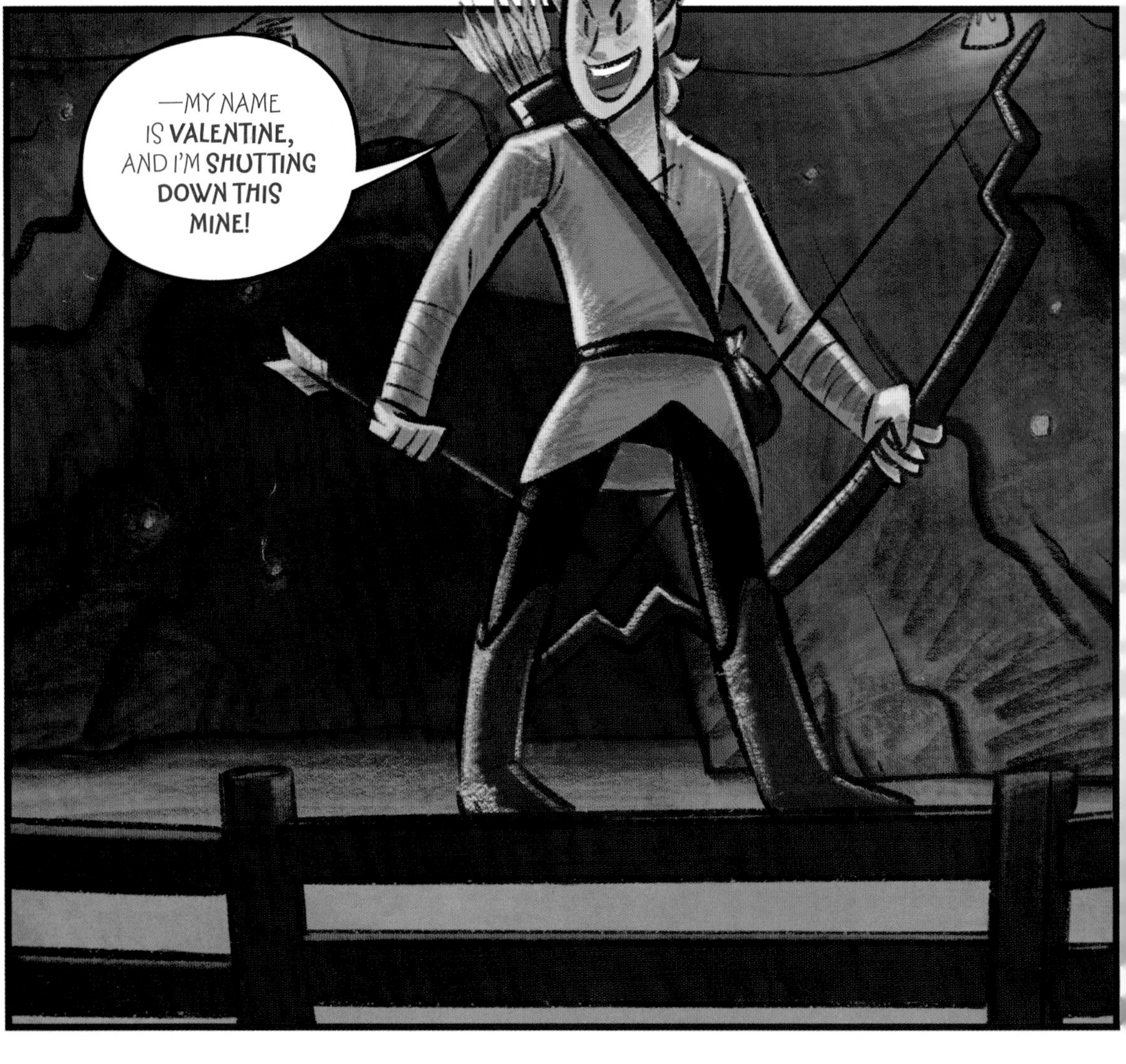
—MY NAME IS **VALENTINE,** AND I'M **SHUTTING DOWN THIS MINE!**

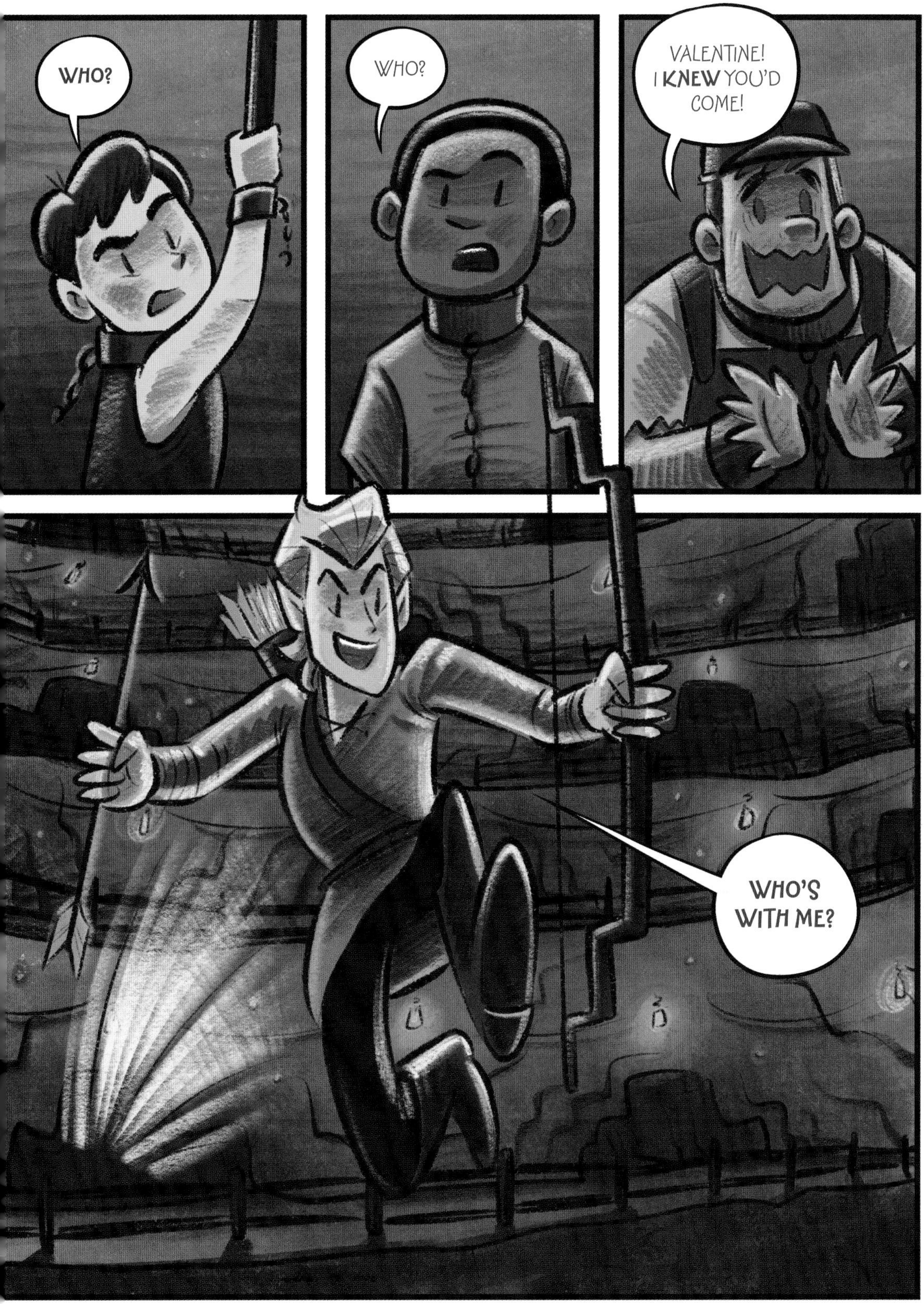
WHO?
WHO?
VALENTINE! I **KNEW** YOU'D COME!
WHO'S WITH ME?

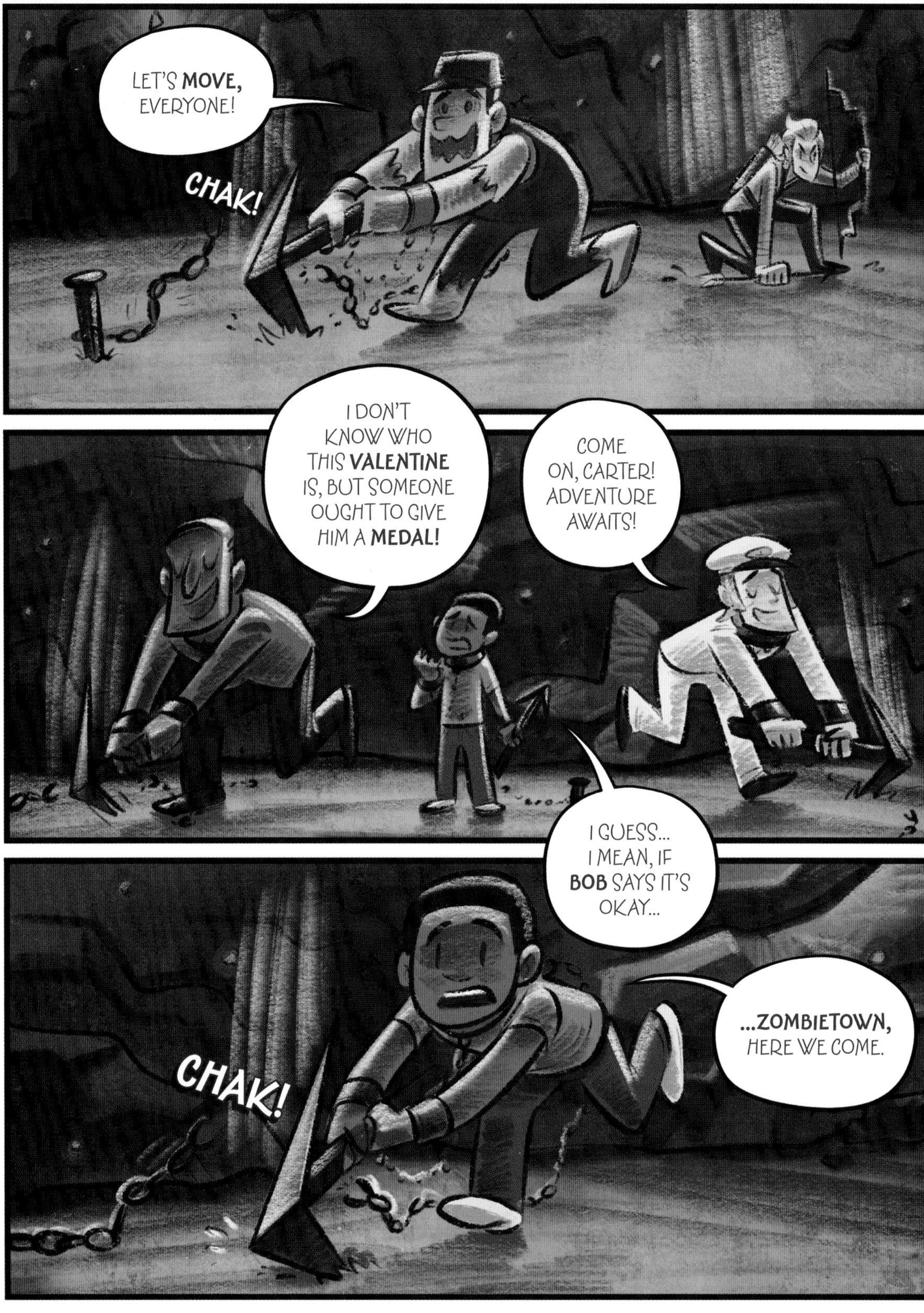
LET'S **MOVE,** EVERYONE!
CHAK!
I DON'T KNOW WHO THIS **VALENTINE** IS, BUT SOMEONE OUGHT TO GIVE HIM A **MEDAL!**
COME ON, CARTER! ADVENTURE AWAITS!
I GUESS... I MEAN, IF **BOB** SAYS IT'S OKAY...
CHAK!
...ZOMBIETOWN, HERE WE COME.

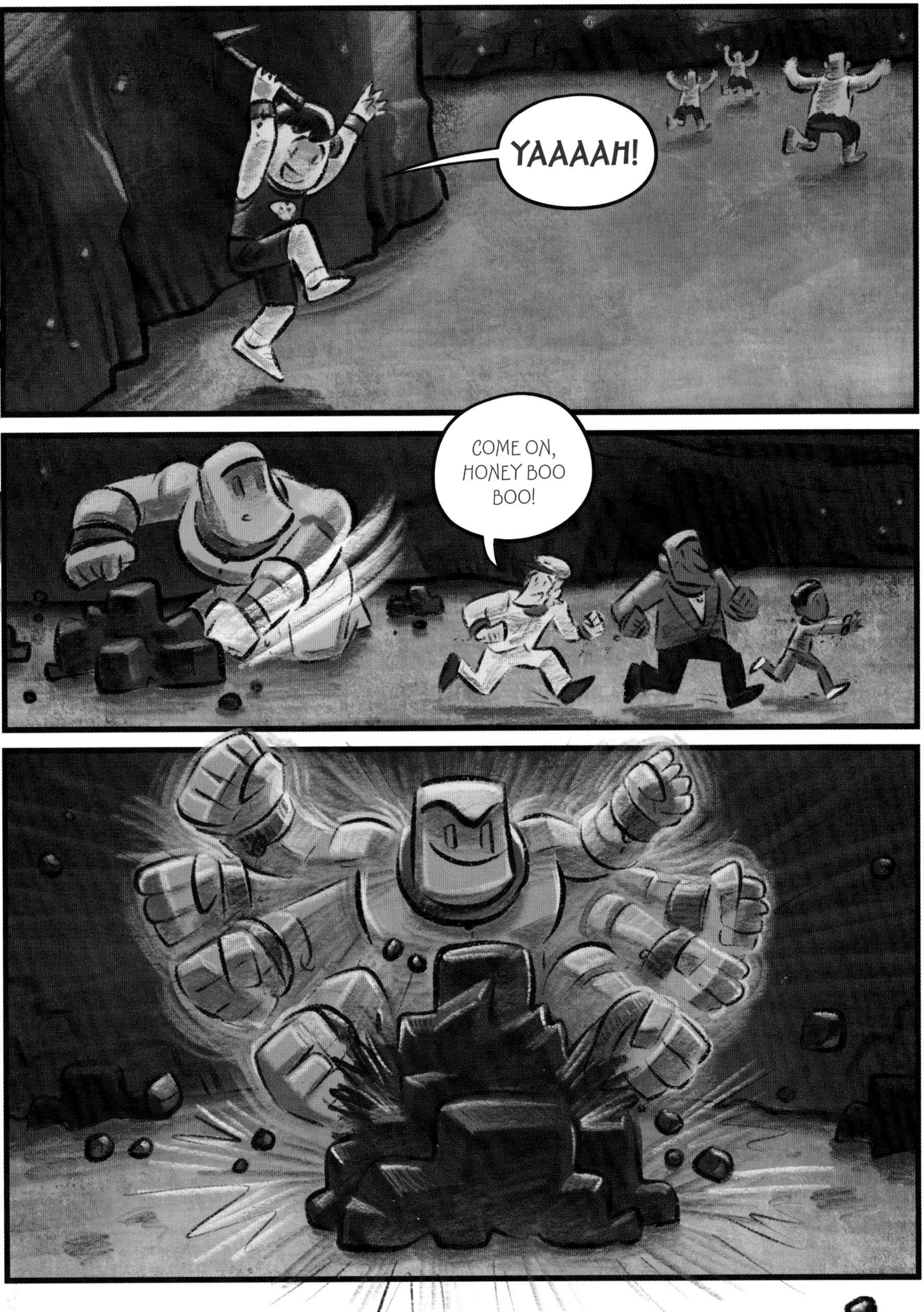
YAAAAH!
COME ON, HONEY BOO BOO!

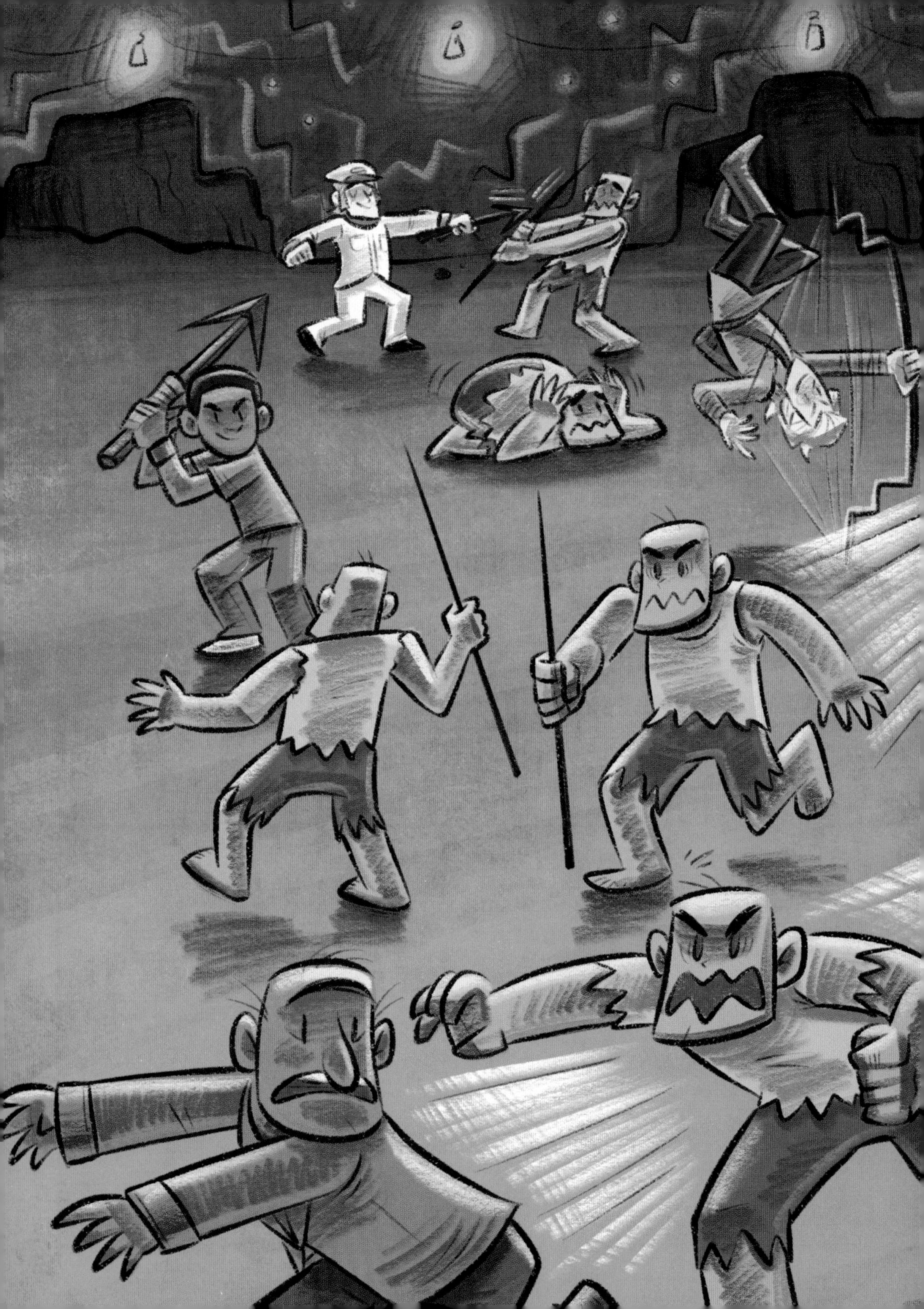

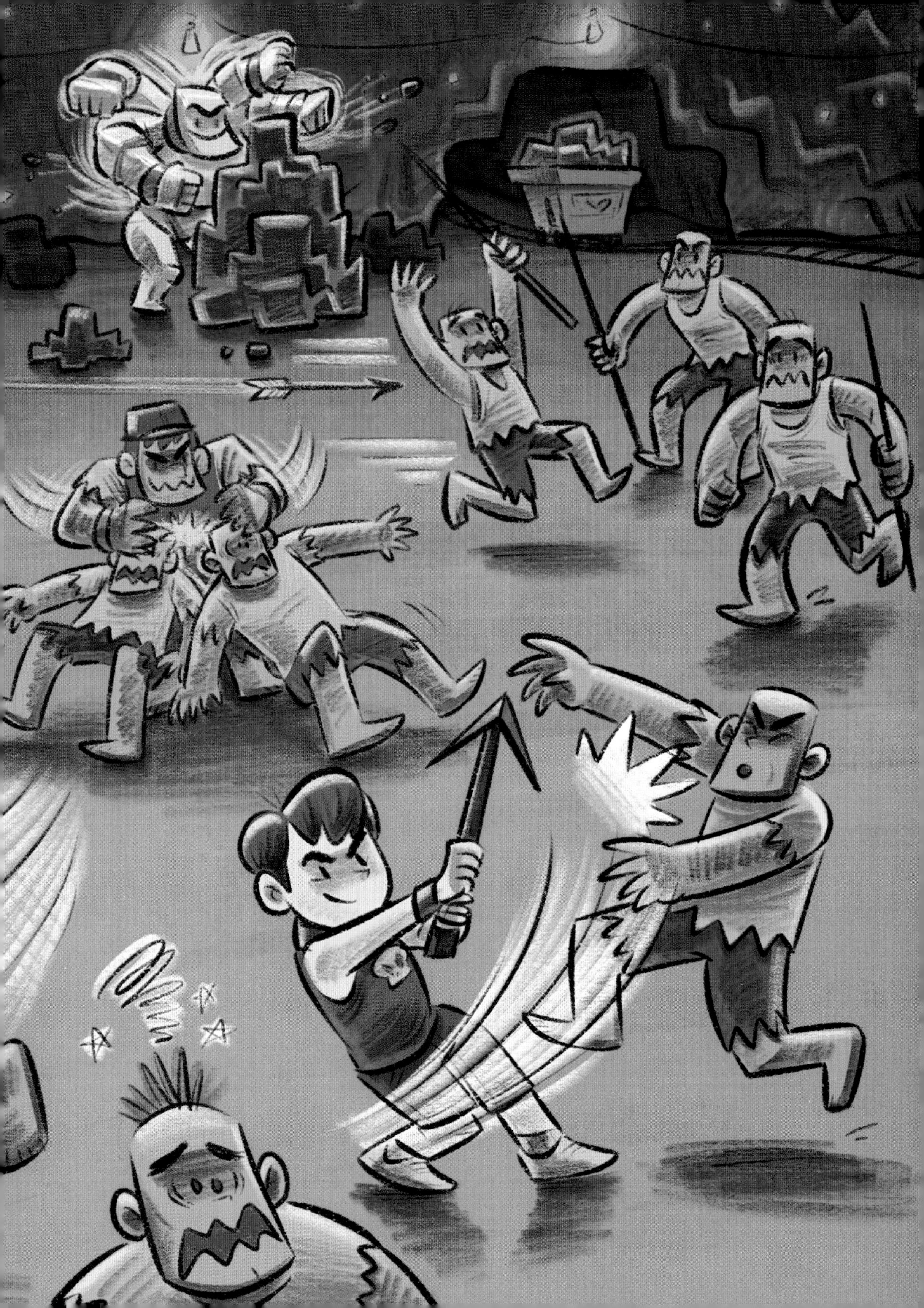

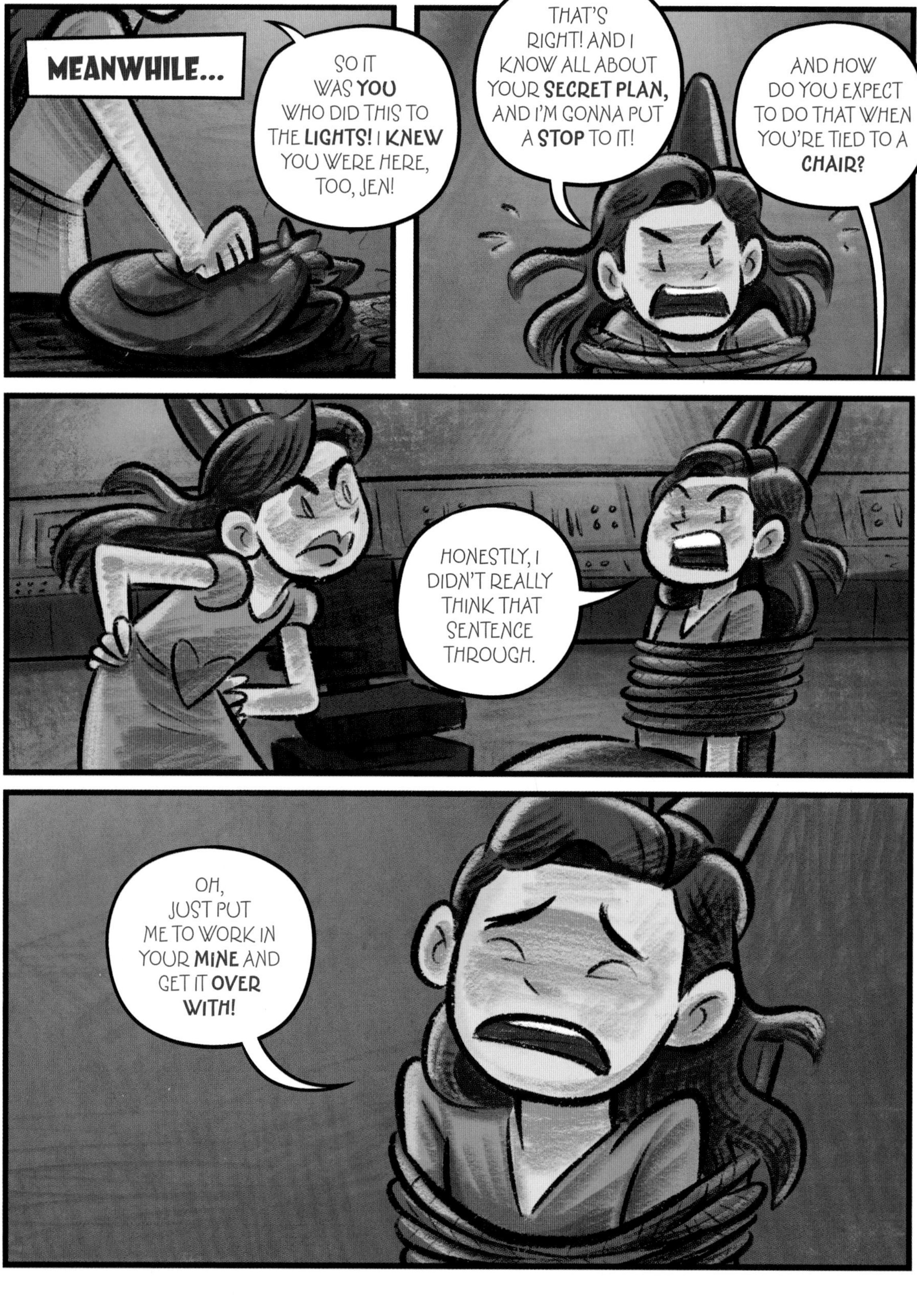
MEANWHILE...
SO IT WAS YOU WHO DID THIS TO THE LIGHTS! I KNEW YOU WERE HERE, TOO, JEN!
THAT'S RIGHT! AND I KNOW ALL ABOUT YOUR SECRET PLAN, AND I'M GONNA PUT A STOP TO IT!
AND HOW DO YOU EXPECT TO DO THAT WHEN YOU'RE TIED TO A CHAIR?
HONESTLY, I DIDN'T REALLY THINK THAT SENTENCE THROUGH.
OH, JUST PUT ME TO WORK IN YOUR MINE AND GET IT OVER WITH!

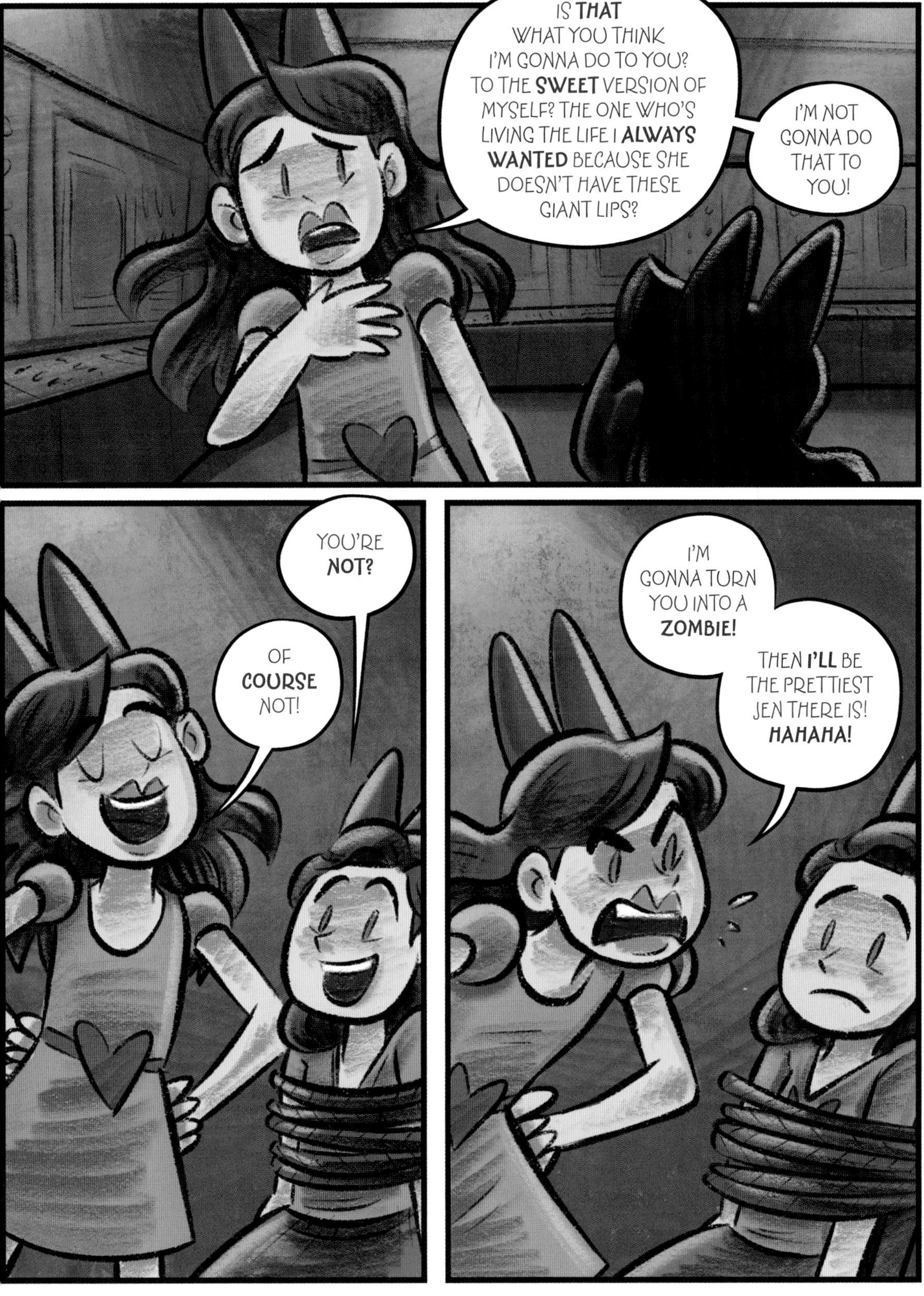
IS **THAT** WHAT YOU THINK I'M GONNA DO TO YOU? TO THE **SWEET** VERSION OF MYSELF? THE ONE WHO'S LIVING THE LIFE I **ALWAYS WANTED** BECAUSE SHE DOESN'T HAVE THESE GIANT LIPS?
I'M NOT GONNA DO THAT TO YOU!
YOU'RE **NOT?**
OF **COURSE** NOT!
I'M GONNA TURN YOU INTO A **ZOMBIE!**
THEN **I'LL** BE THE PRETTIEST JEN THERE IS! **HAHAHA!**

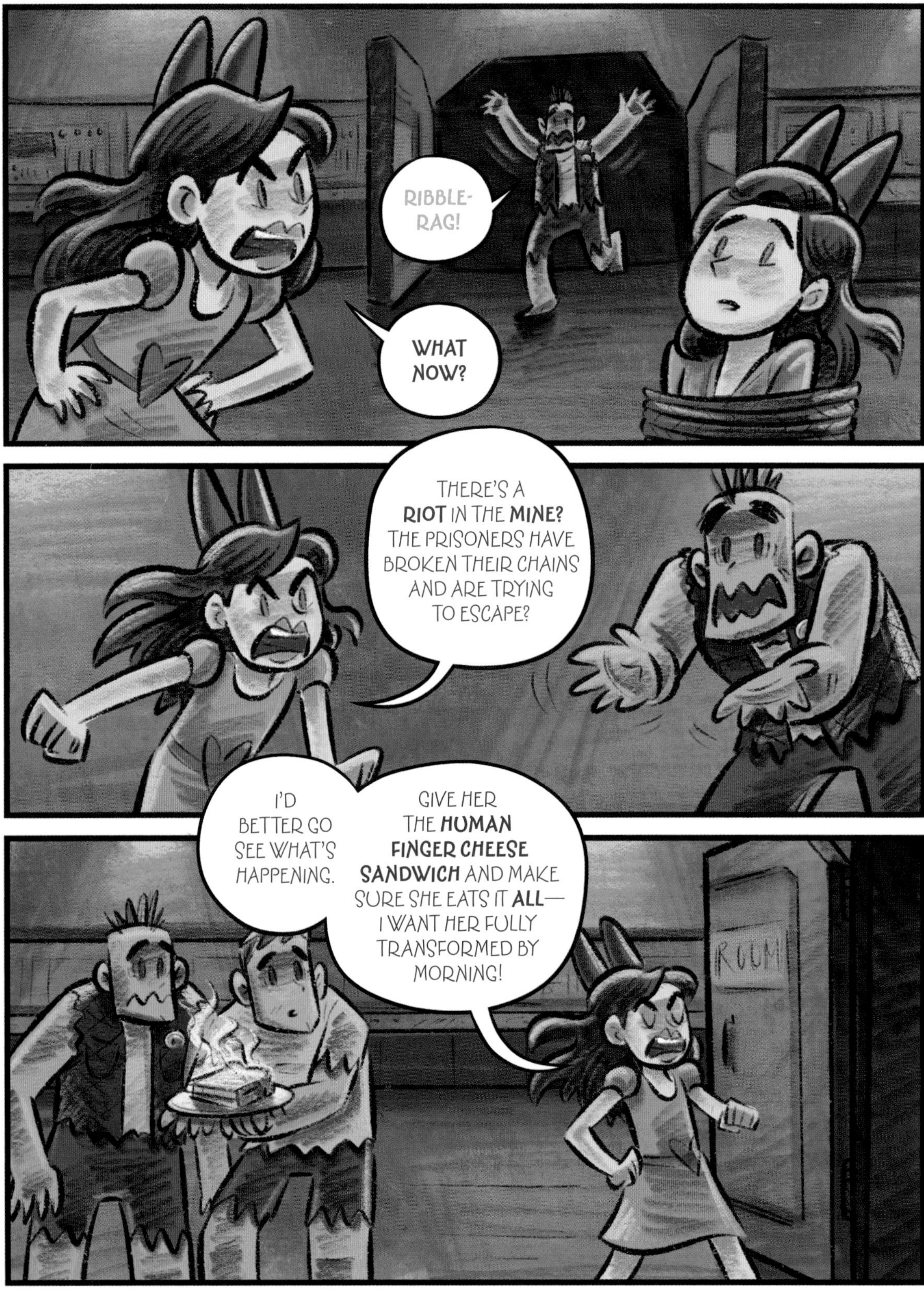

RIBBLE-RAG!
WHAT NOW?
THERE'S A **RIOT** IN THE **MINE?** THE PRISONERS HAVE BROKEN THEIR CHAINS AND ARE TRYING TO ESCAPE?
I'D BETTER GO SEE WHAT'S HAPPENING.
GIVE HER THE **HUMAN FINGER CHEESE SANDWICH** AND MAKE SURE SHE EATS IT **ALL**— I WANT HER FULLY TRANSFORMED BY MORNING!
ROOM

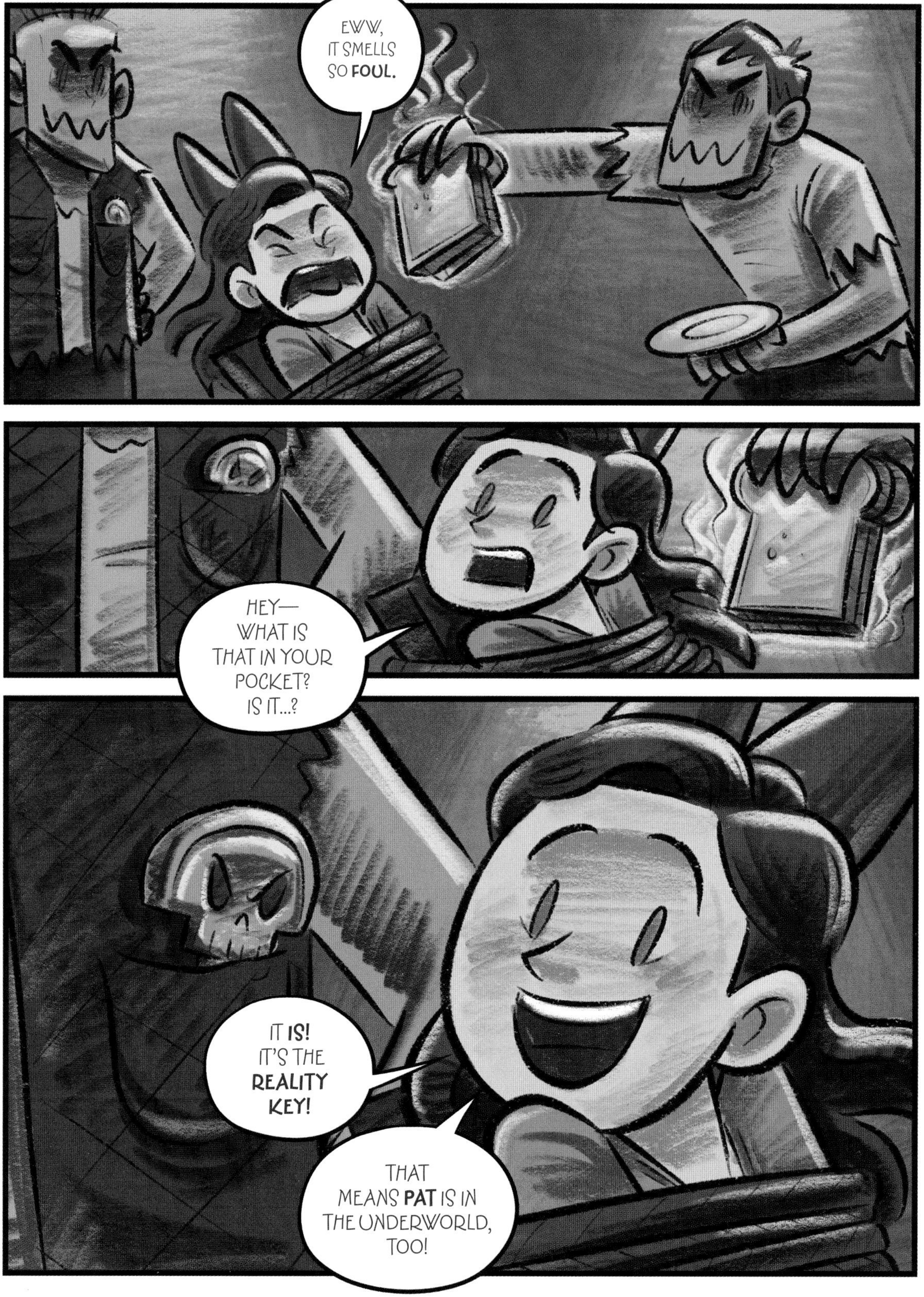
EWW, IT SMELLS SO **FOUL.**
HEY— WHAT IS THAT IN YOUR POCKET? IS IT...?
IT **IS!** IT'S THE **REALITY KEY!**
THAT MEANS **PAT** IS IN THE UNDERWORLD, TOO!

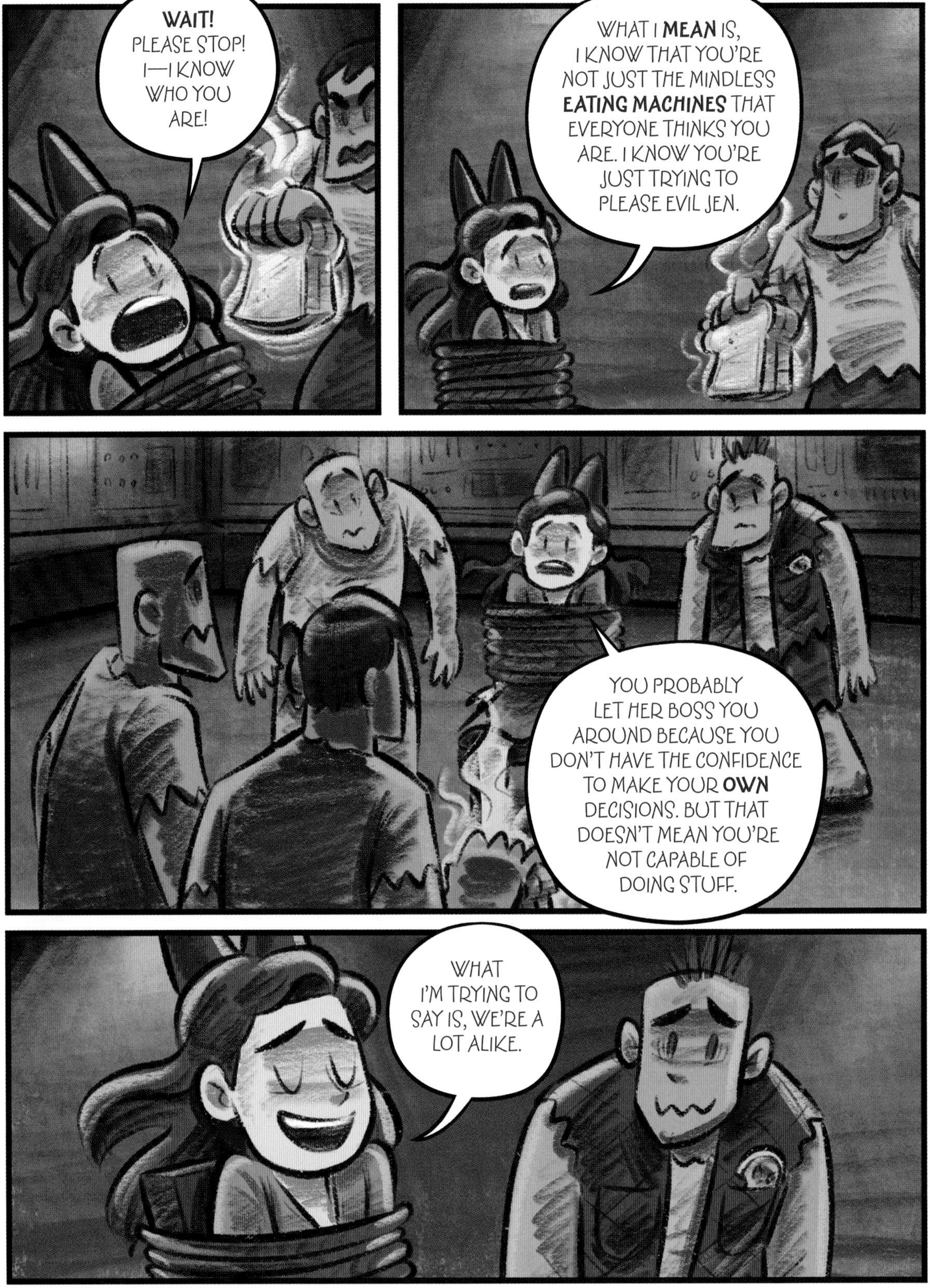
WAIT! PLEASE STOP! I—I KNOW WHO YOU ARE!
WHAT I MEAN IS, I KNOW THAT YOU'RE NOT JUST THE MINDLESS EATING MACHINES THAT EVERYONE THINKS YOU ARE. I KNOW YOU'RE JUST TRYING TO PLEASE EVIL JEN.
YOU PROBABLY LET HER BOSS YOU AROUND BECAUSE YOU DON'T HAVE THE CONFIDENCE TO MAKE YOUR OWN DECISIONS. BUT THAT DOESN'T MEAN YOU'RE NOT CAPABLE OF DOING STUFF.
WHAT I'M TRYING TO SAY IS, WE'RE A LOT ALIKE.

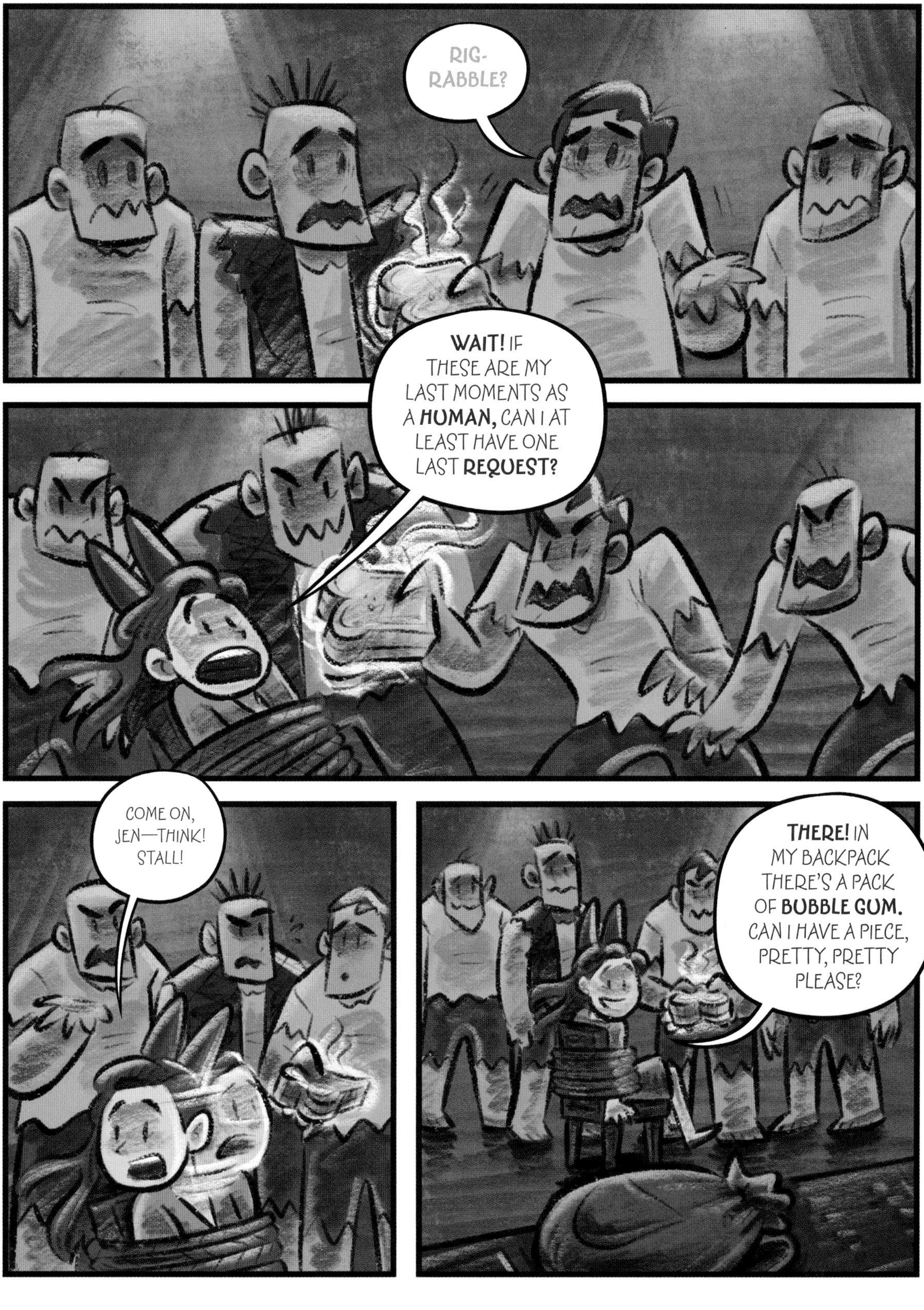
RIG-
RABBLE?
WAIT! IF THESE ARE MY LAST MOMENTS AS A HUMAN, CAN I AT LEAST HAVE ONE LAST REQUEST?
COME ON, JEN—THINK! STALL!
THERE! IN MY BACKPACK THERE'S A PACK OF BUBBLE GUM. CAN I HAVE A PIECE, PRETTY, PRETTY PLEASE?

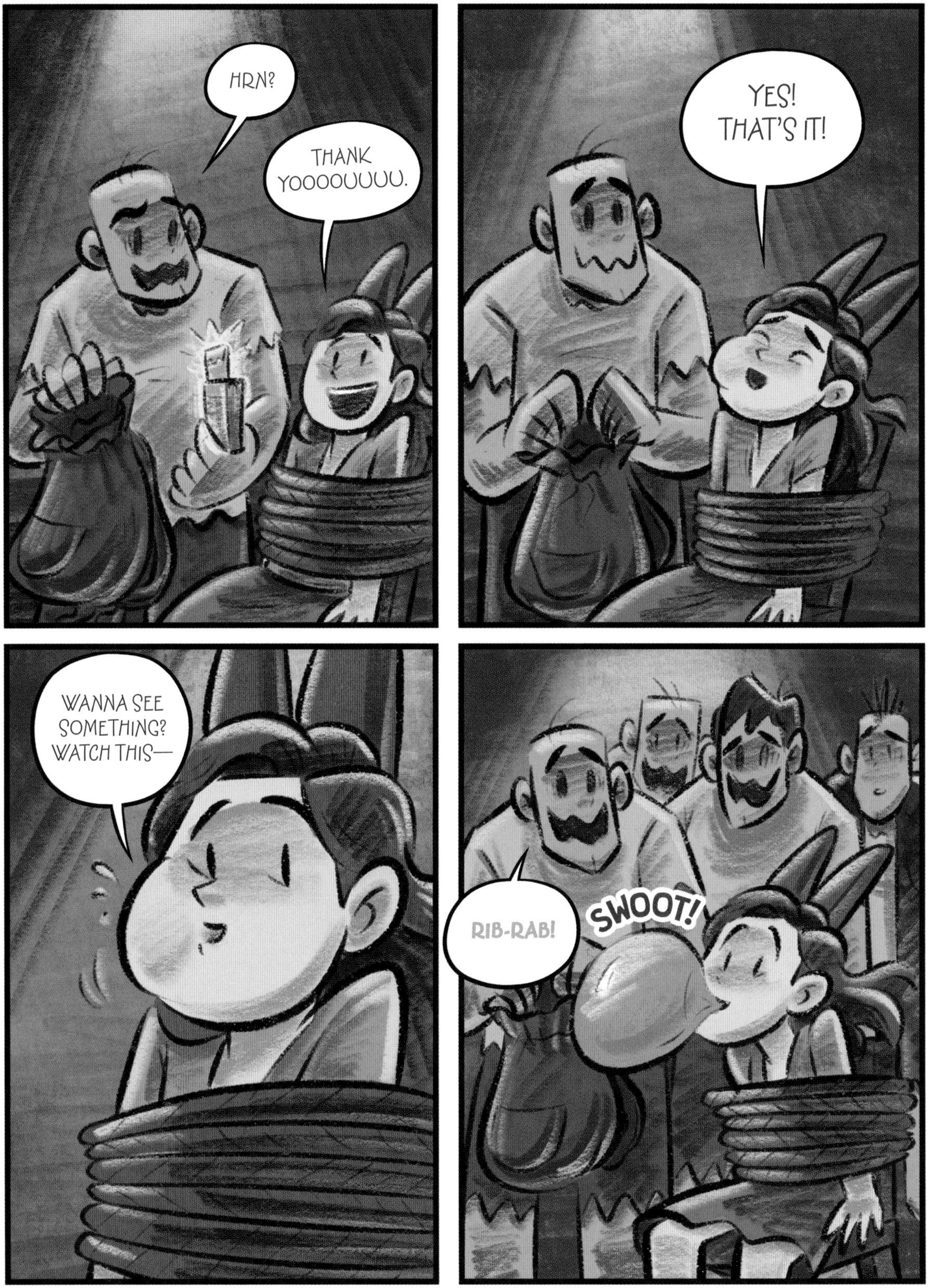
HRN?
THANK YOOOOUUUU.
YES! THAT'S IT!
WANNA SEE SOMETHING? WATCH THIS—
RIB-RAB!
SWOOT!

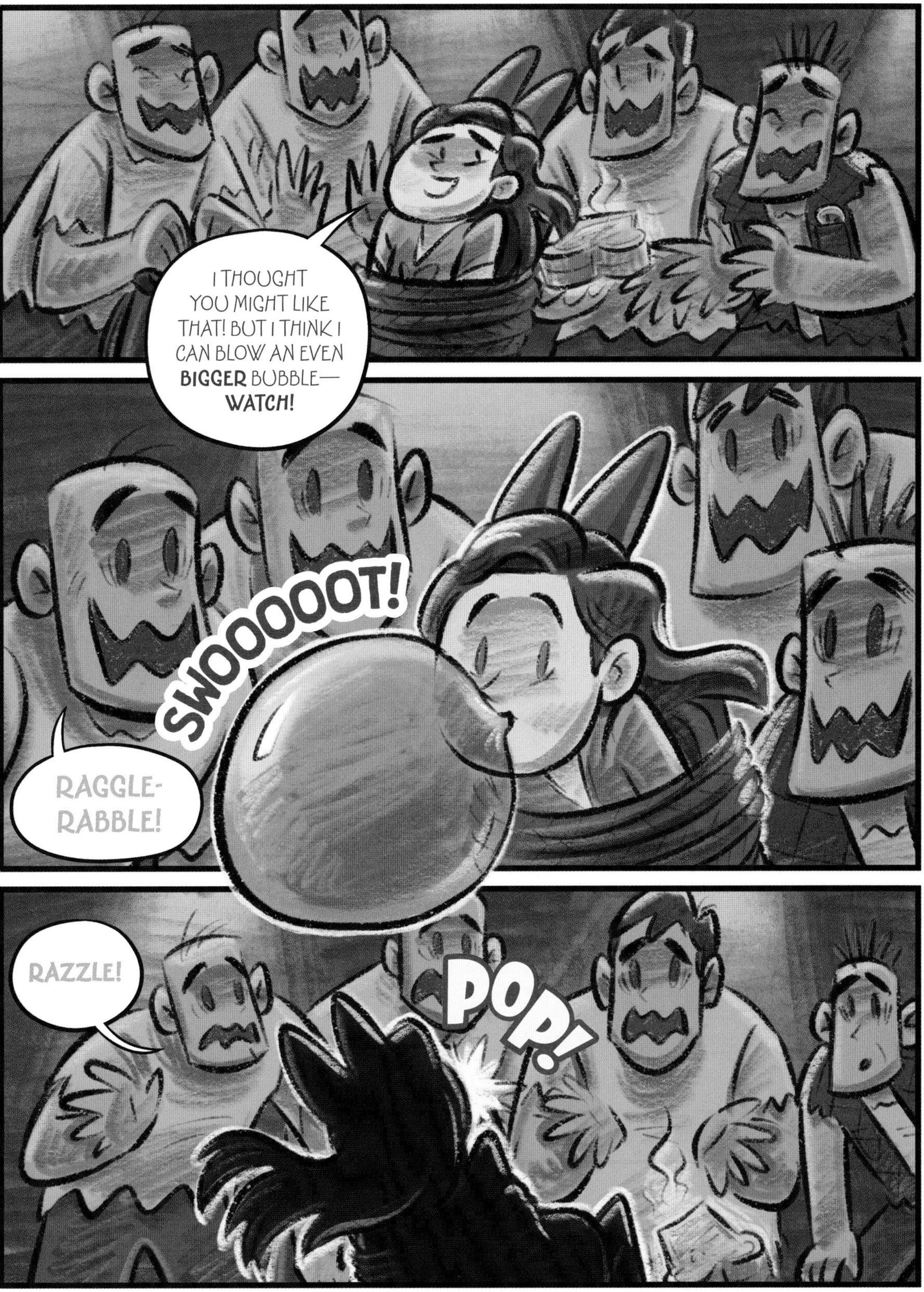
I THOUGHT YOU MIGHT LIKE THAT! BUT I THINK I CAN BLOW AN EVEN **BIGGER** BUBBLE—**WATCH!**
SWOOOOOT!
RAGGLE-RABBLE!
RAZZLE!
POP!

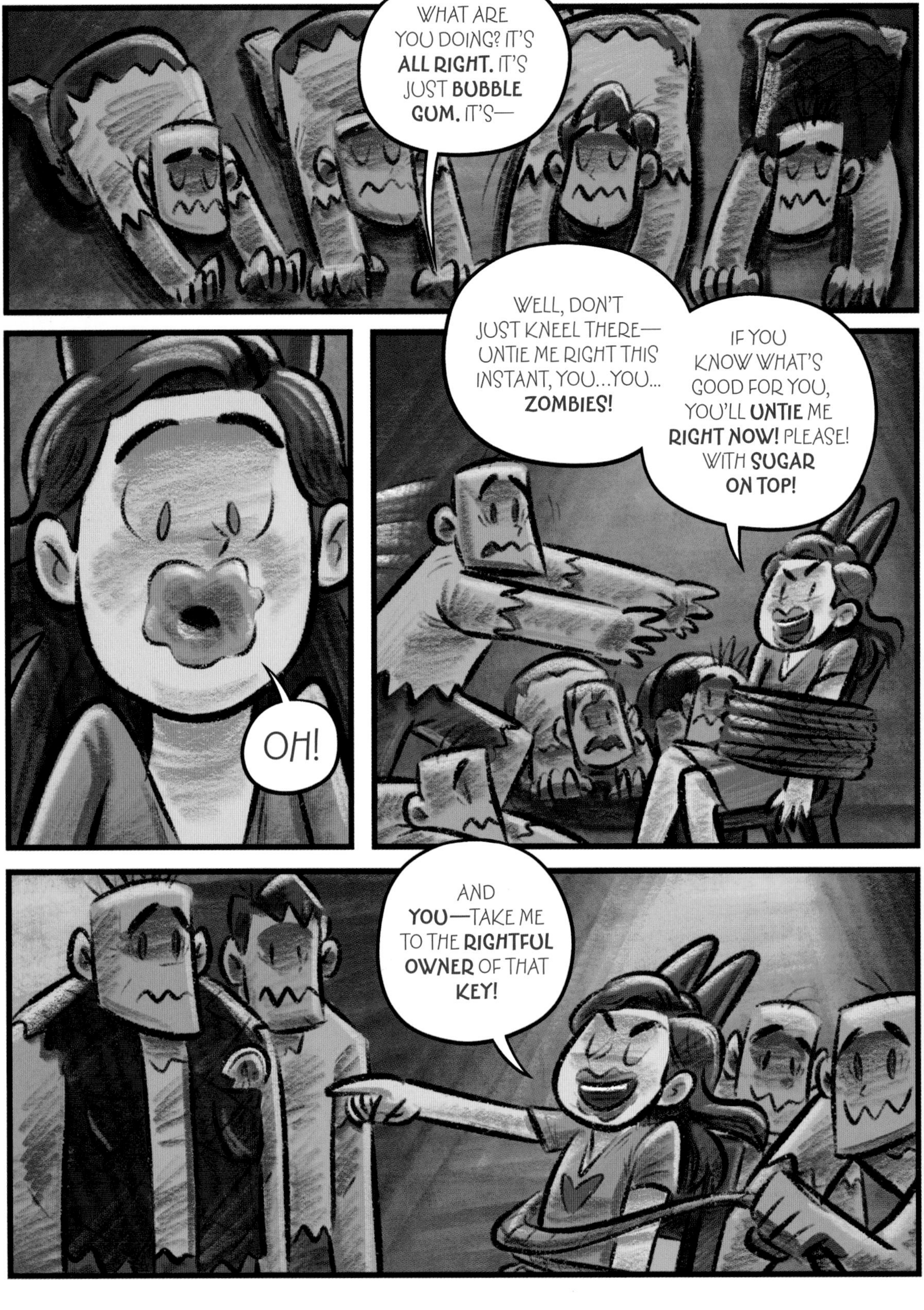
WHAT ARE YOU DOING? IT'S **ALL RIGHT.** IT'S JUST **BUBBLE GUM.** IT'S—
OH!
WELL, DON'T JUST KNEEL THERE—UNTIE ME RIGHT THIS INSTANT, YOU...YOU... **ZOMBIES!**
IF YOU KNOW WHAT'S GOOD FOR YOU, YOU'LL **UNTIE** ME **RIGHT NOW!** PLEASE! WITH **SUGAR ON TOP!**
AND **YOU**—TAKE ME TO THE **RIGHTFUL OWNER** OF THAT **KEY!**

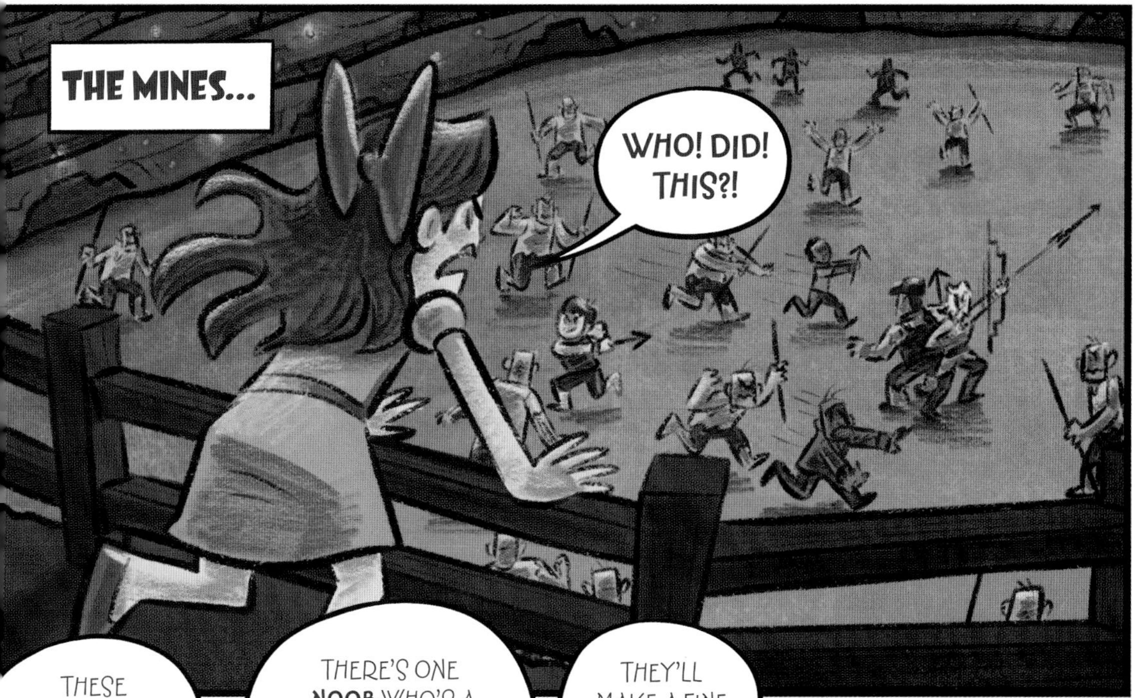
THE MINES...
WHO! DID! THIS?!

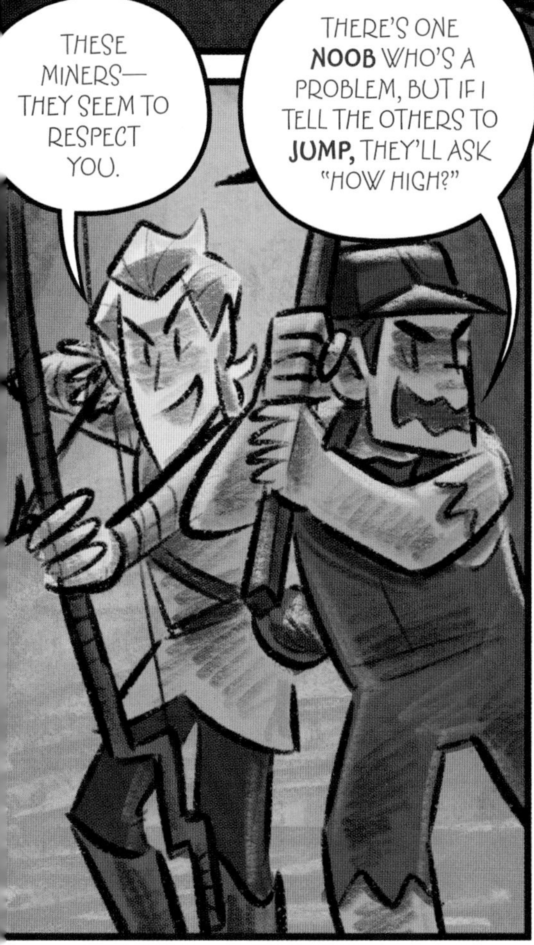
THESE MINERS—THEY SEEM TO RESPECT YOU.
THERE'S ONE NOOB WHO'S A PROBLEM, BUT IF I TELL THE OTHERS TO JUMP, THEY'LL ASK "HOW HIGH?"

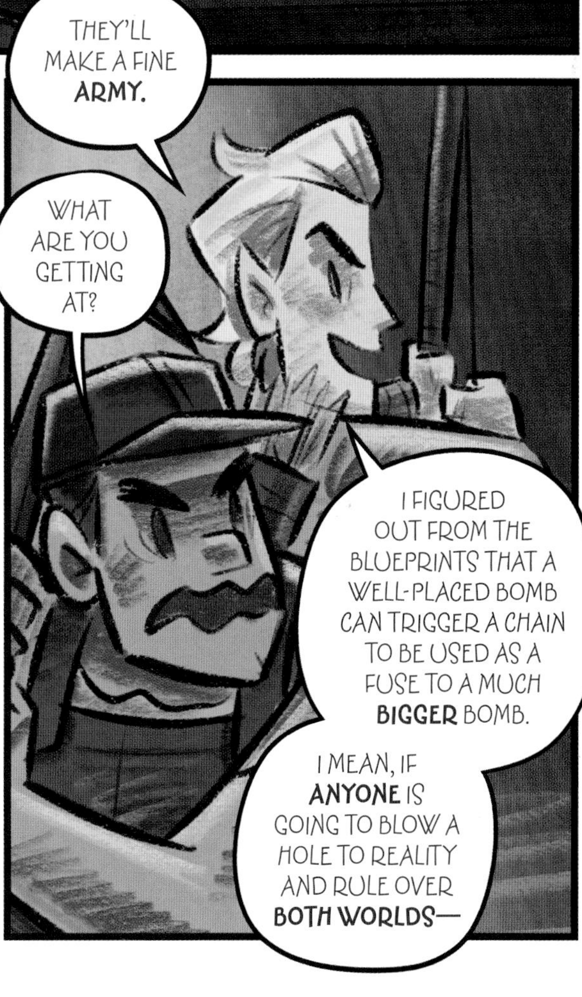
THEY'LL MAKE A FINE ARMY.
WHAT ARE YOU GETTING AT?
I FIGURED OUT FROM THE BLUEPRINTS THAT A WELL-PLACED BOMB CAN TRIGGER A CHAIN TO BE USED AS A FUSE TO A MUCH BIGGER BOMB.
I MEAN, IF ANYONE IS GOING TO BLOW A HOLE TO REALITY AND RULE OVER BOTH WORLDS—

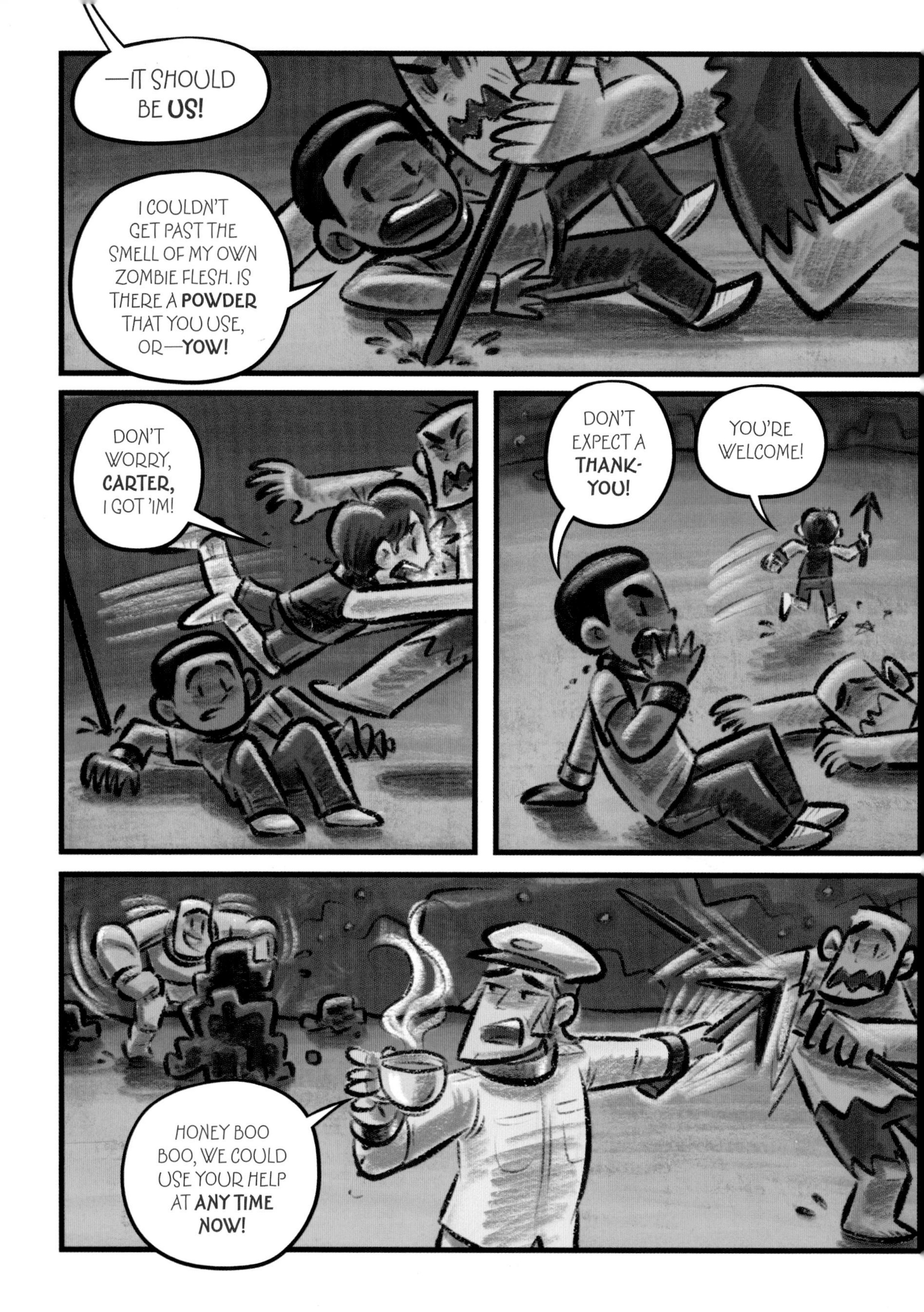
—IT SHOULD BE **US!**
I COULDN'T GET PAST THE SMELL OF MY OWN ZOMBIE FLESH. IS THERE A **POWDER** THAT YOU USE, OR—**YOW!**
DON'T WORRY, **CARTER,** I GOT 'IM!
DON'T EXPECT A **THANK-YOU!**
YOU'RE WELCOME!
HONEY BOO BOO, WE COULD USE YOUR HELP AT **ANY TIME NOW!**

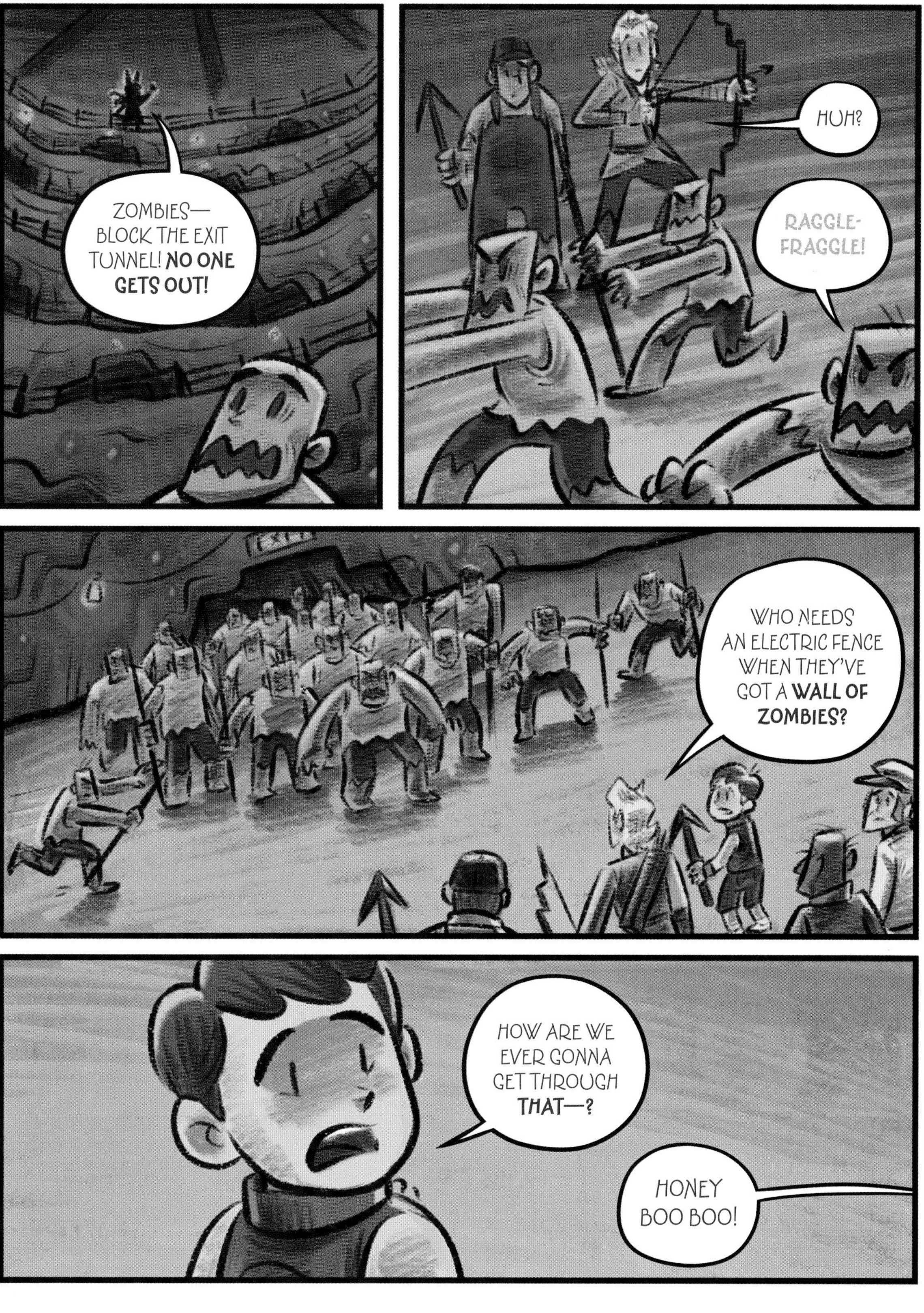
ZOMBIES— BLOCK THE EXIT TUNNEL! NO ONE GETS OUT!
HUH?
RAGGLE-FRAGGLE!
WHO NEEDS AN ELECTRIC FENCE WHEN THEY'VE GOT A WALL OF ZOMBIES?
HOW ARE WE EVER GONNA GET THROUGH THAT—?
HONEY BOO BOO!

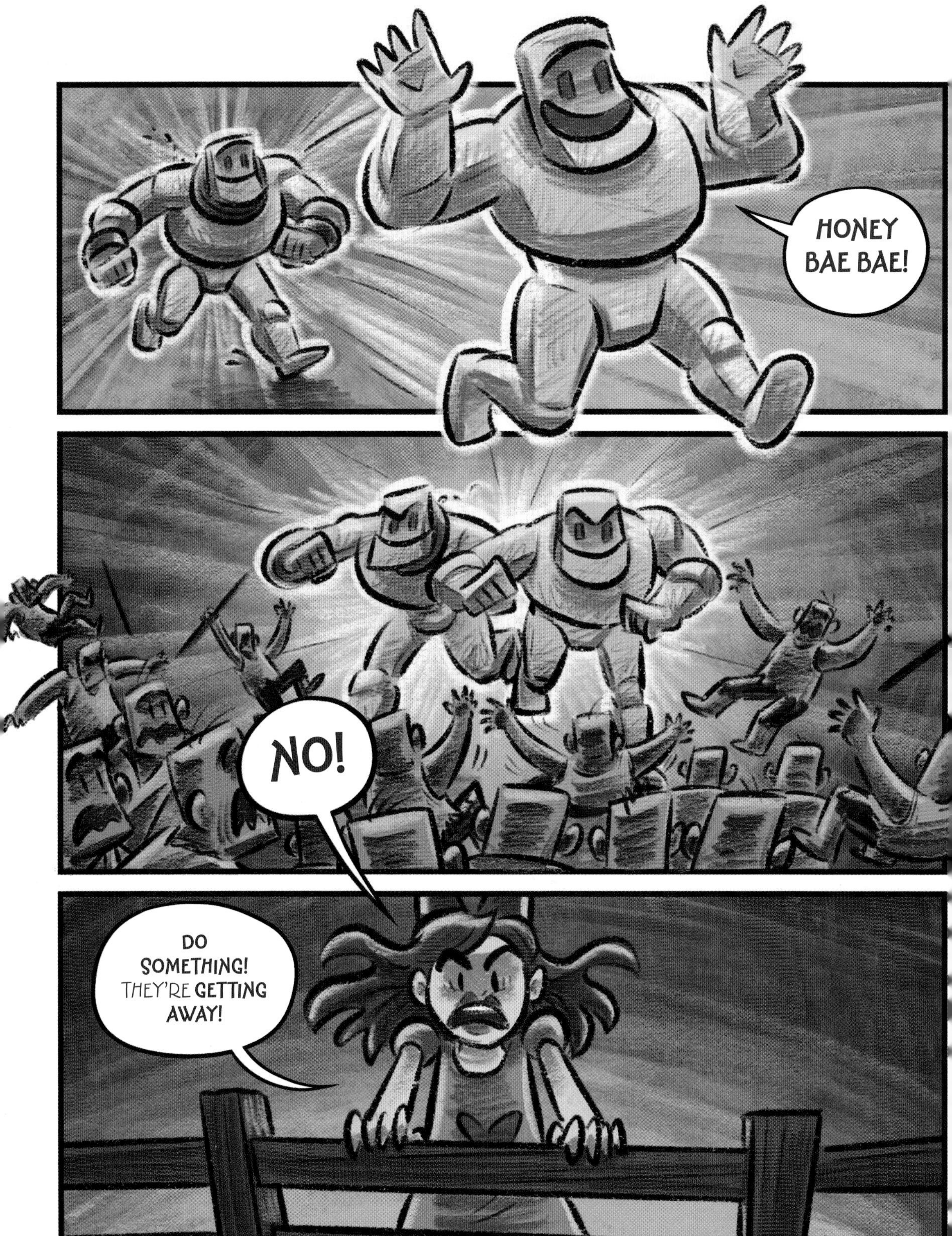
HONEY BAE BAE!
NO!
DO SOMETHING! THEY'RE GETTING AWAY!

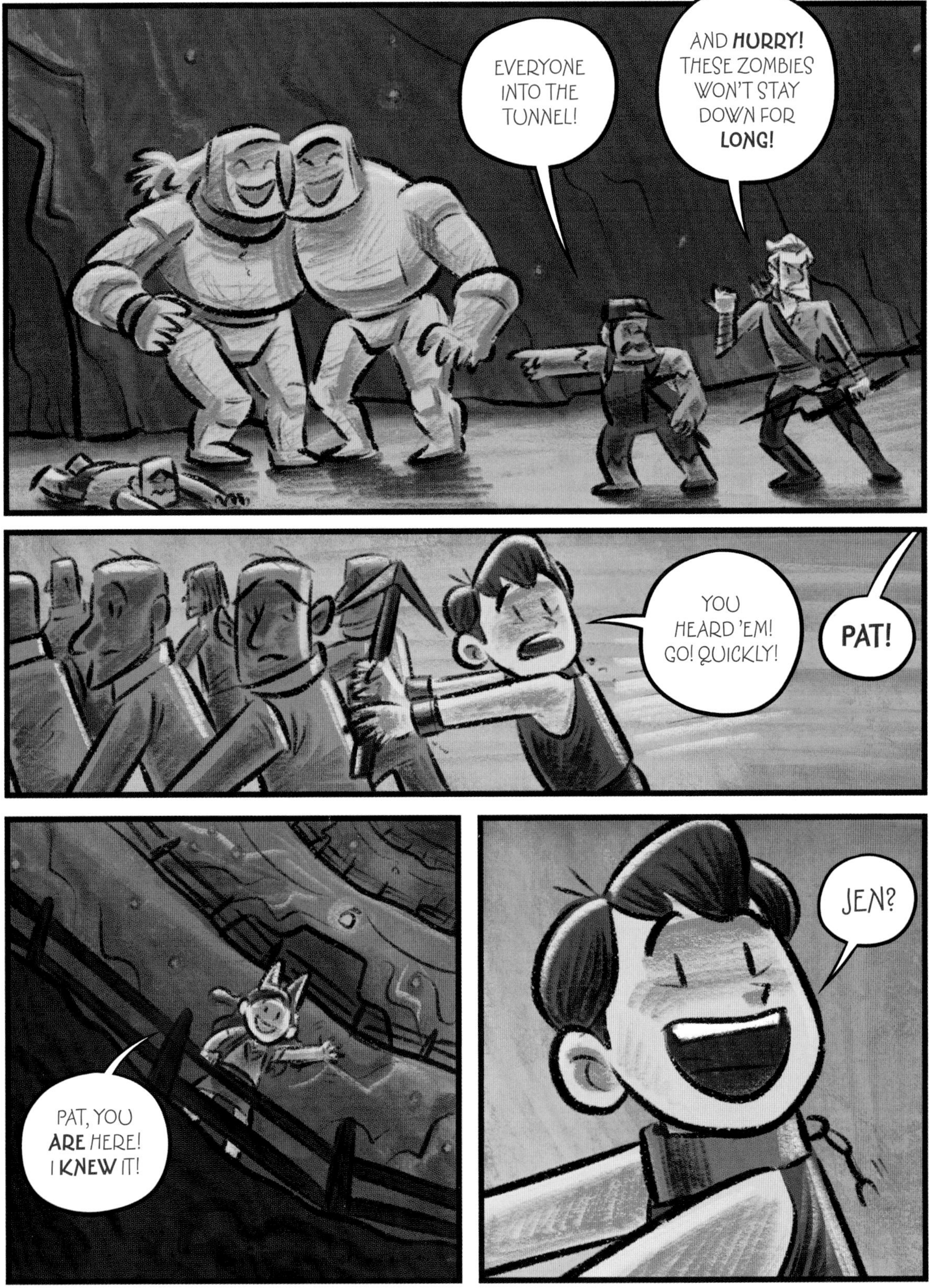
EVERYONE INTO THE TUNNEL!
AND **HURRY!** THESE ZOMBIES WON'T STAY DOWN FOR **LONG!**
YOU HEARD 'EM! GO! QUICKLY!
PAT!
PAT, YOU **ARE** HERE! I **KNEW** IT!
JEN?

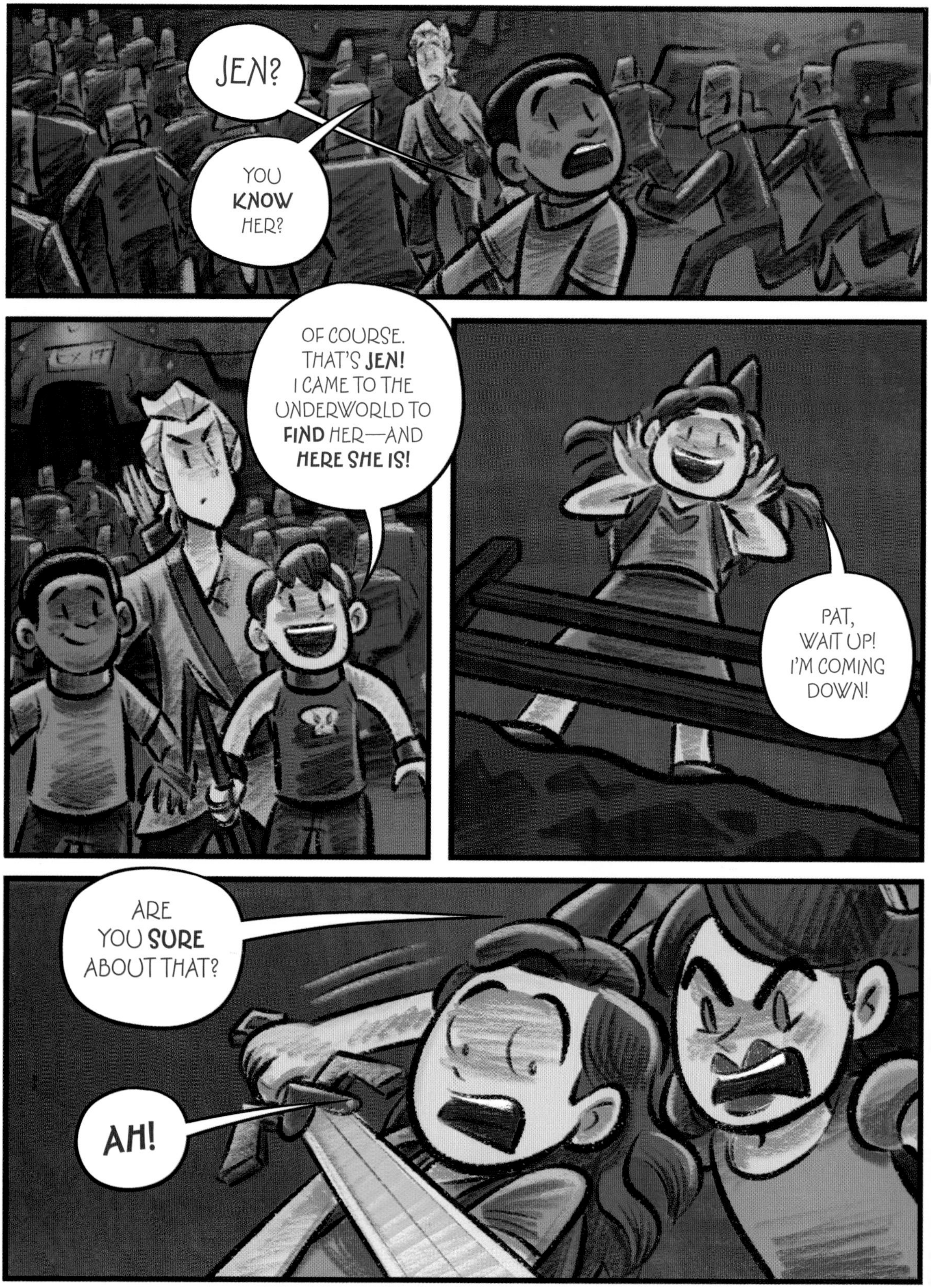
JEN?
YOU **KNOW** HER?
OF COURSE. THAT'S **JEN!** I CAME TO THE UNDERWORLD TO **FIND** HER—AND **HERE SHE IS!**
EXIT
PAT, WAIT UP! I'M COMING DOWN!
ARE YOU **SURE** ABOUT THAT?
AH!

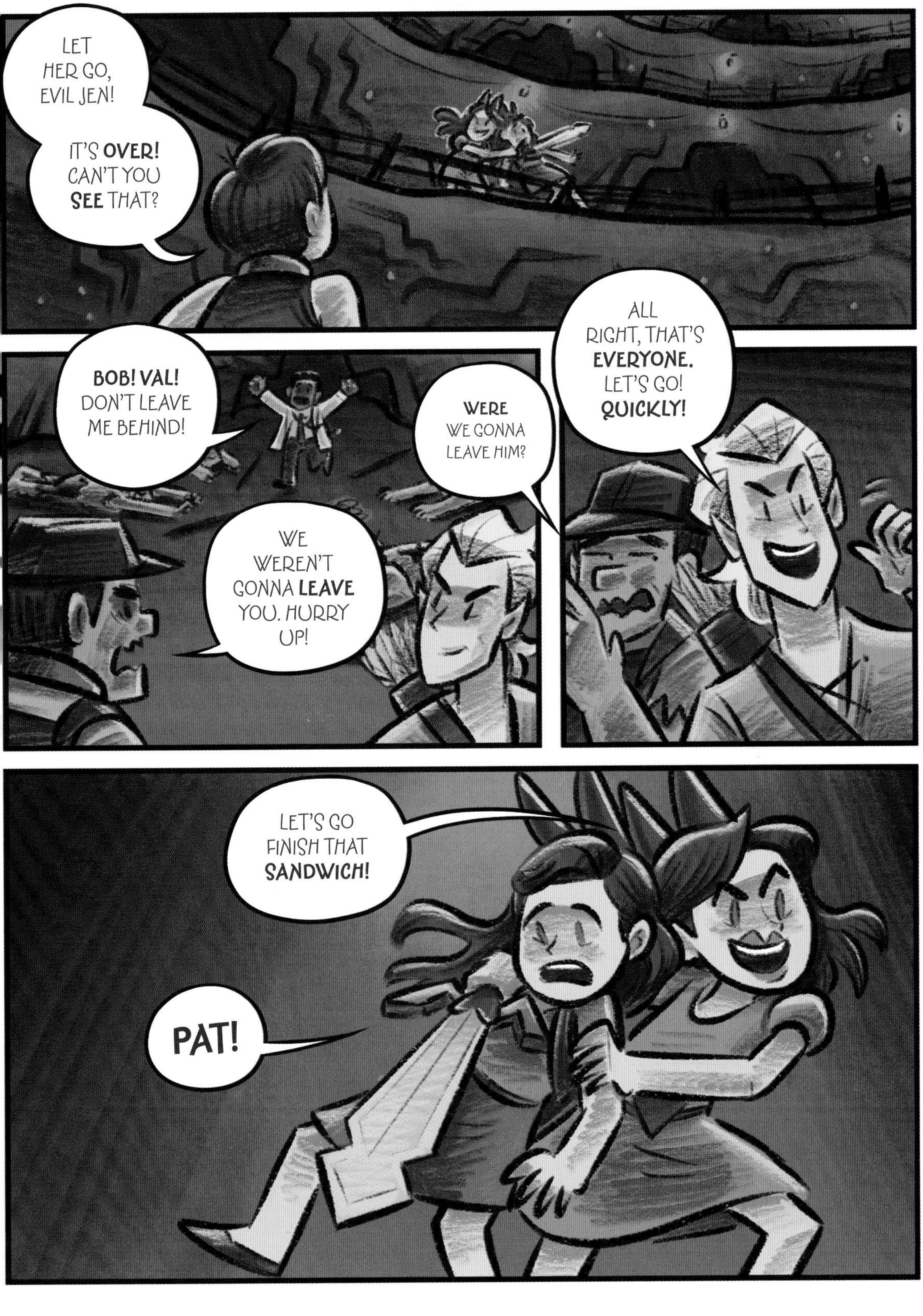
LET HER GO, EVIL JEN!
IT'S OVER! CAN'T YOU SEE THAT?
BOB! VAL! DON'T LEAVE ME BEHIND!
WE WEREN'T GONNA LEAVE YOU. HURRY UP!
WERE WE GONNA LEAVE HIM?
ALL RIGHT, THAT'S EVERYONE. LET'S GO! QUICKLY!
LET'S GO FINISH THAT SANDWICH!
PAT!

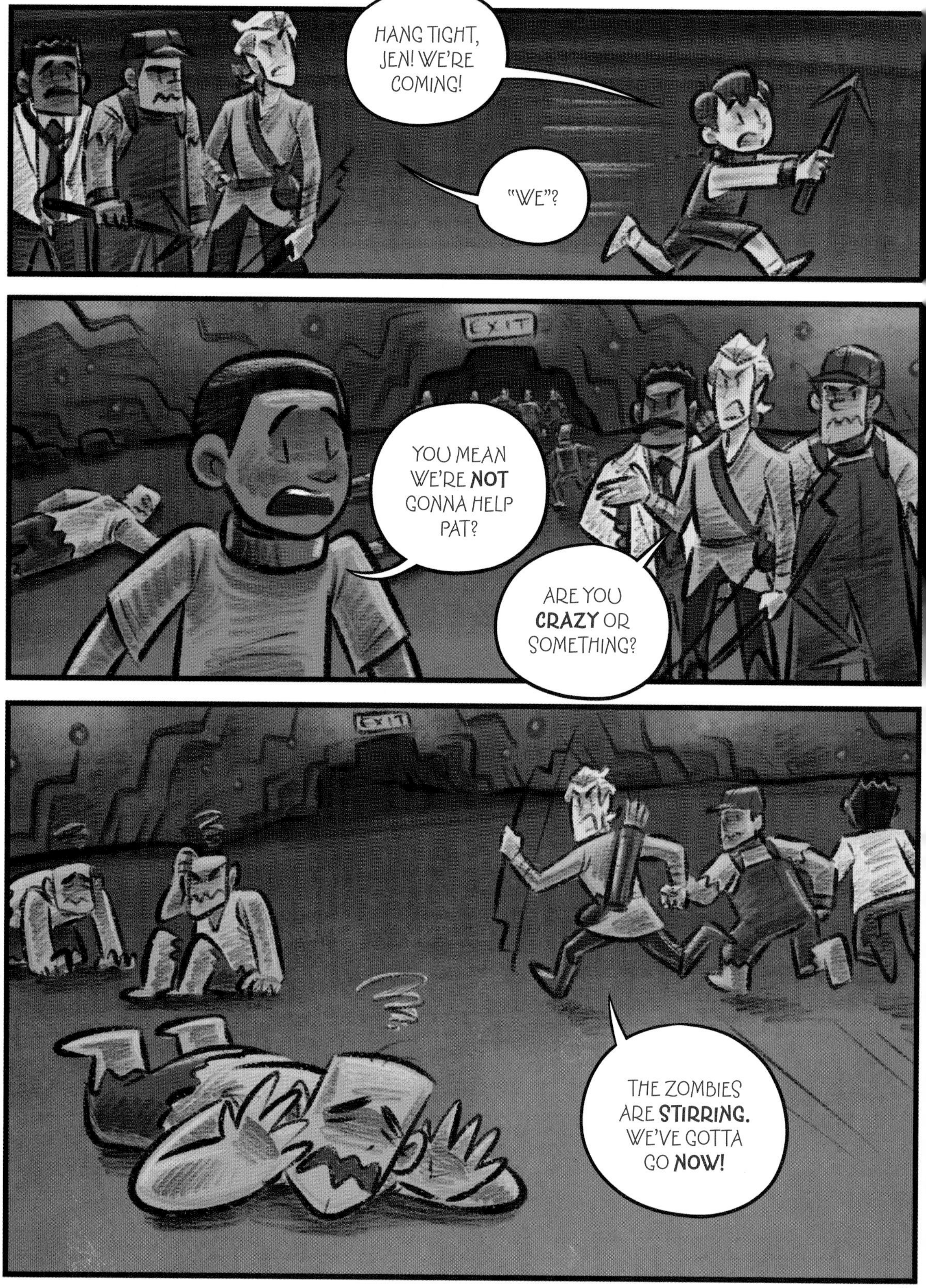
HANG TIGHT, JEN! WE'RE COMING!
"WE"?
YOU MEAN WE'RE **NOT** GONNA HELP PAT?
ARE YOU **CRAZY** OR SOMETHING?
EXIT
THE ZOMBIES ARE **STIRRING.** WE'VE GOTTA GO **NOW!**

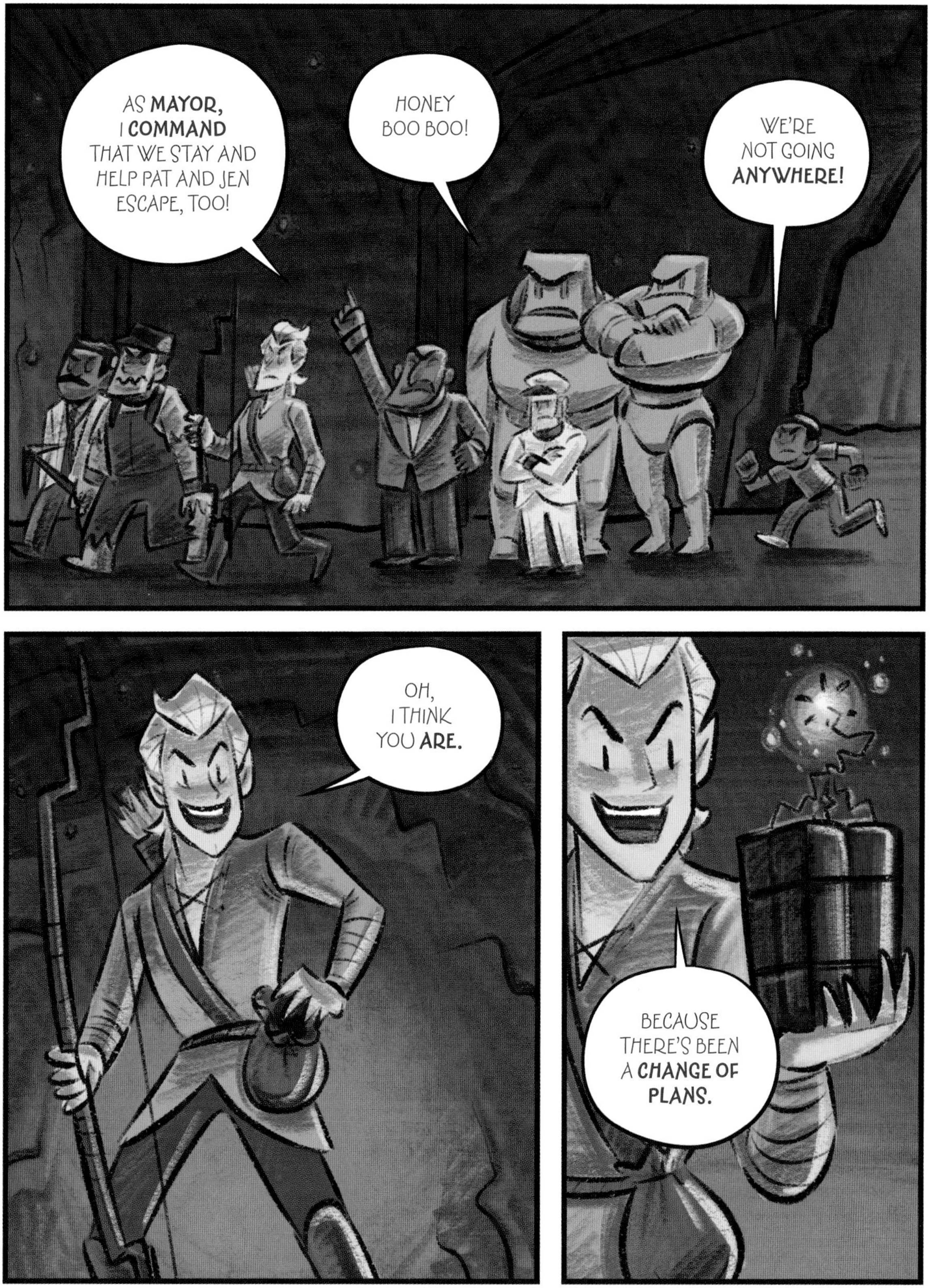
AS MAYOR, I COMMAND THAT WE STAY AND HELP PAT AND JEN ESCAPE, TOO!
HONEY BOO BOO!
WE'RE NOT GOING ANYWHERE!
OH, I THINK YOU ARE.
BECAUSE THERE'S BEEN A CHANGE OF PLANS.

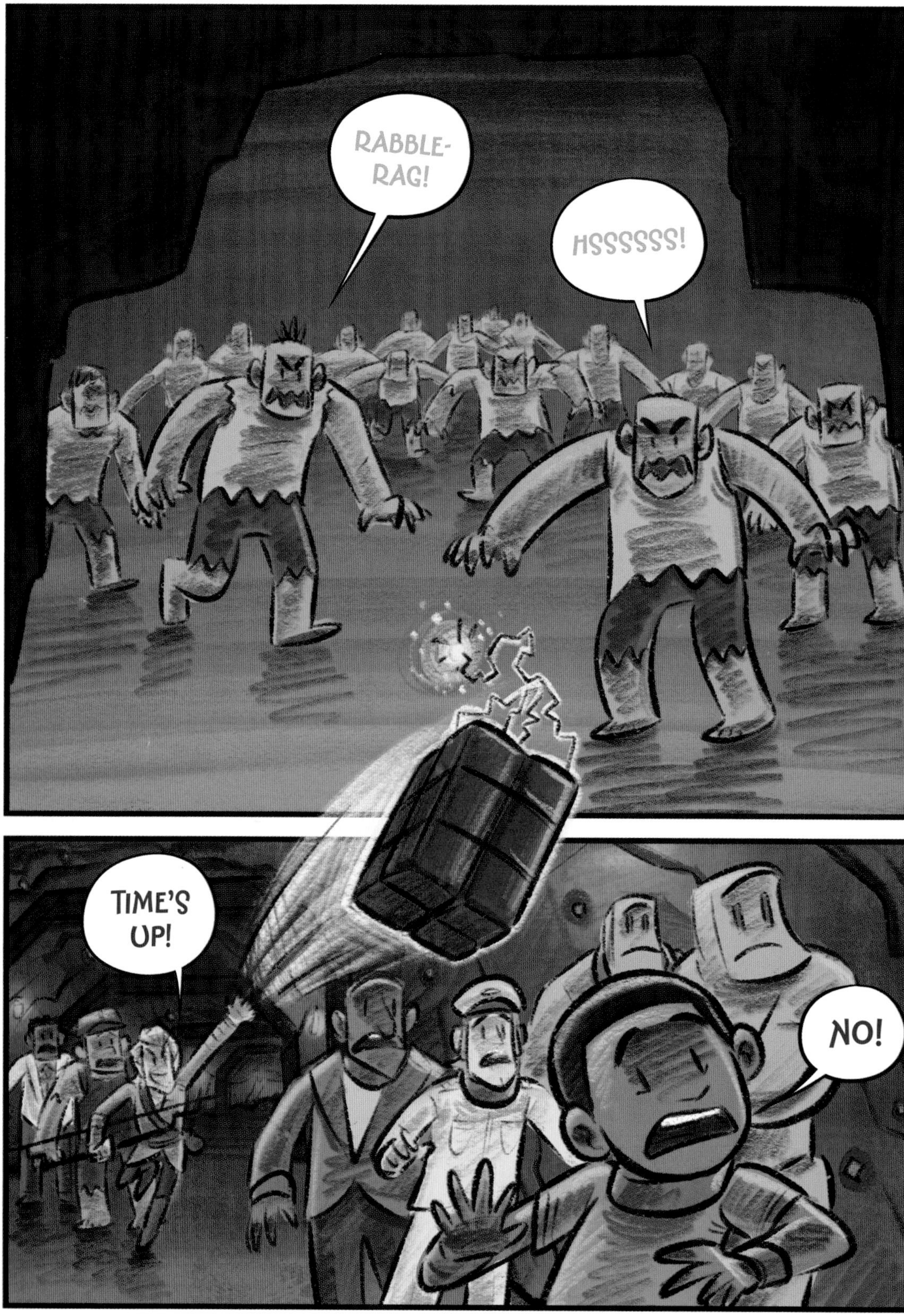
RABBLE-RAG!
HSSSSSS!
TIME'S UP!
NO!

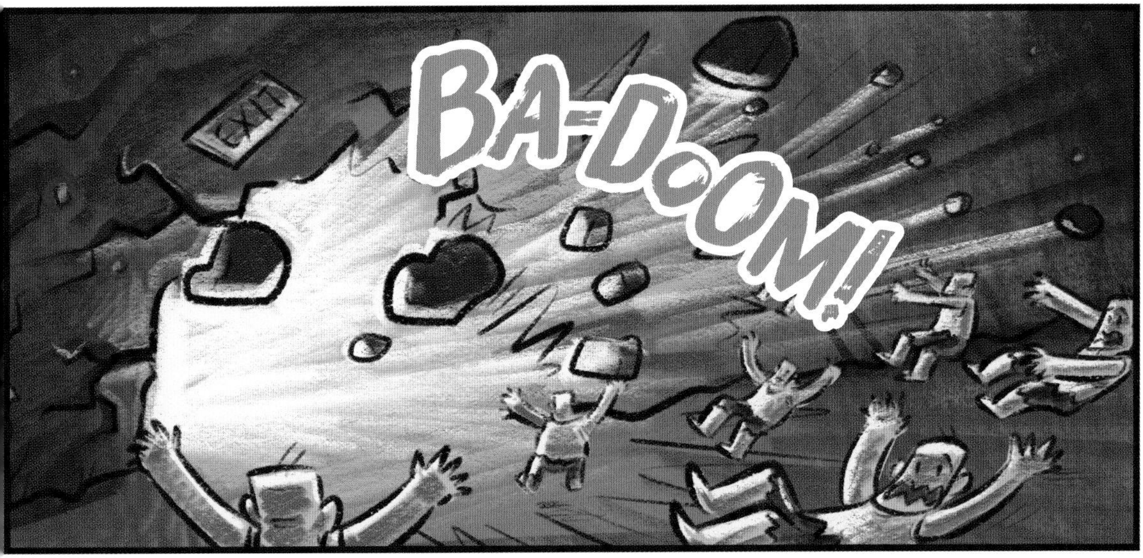
EXIT
BA-DOOM!

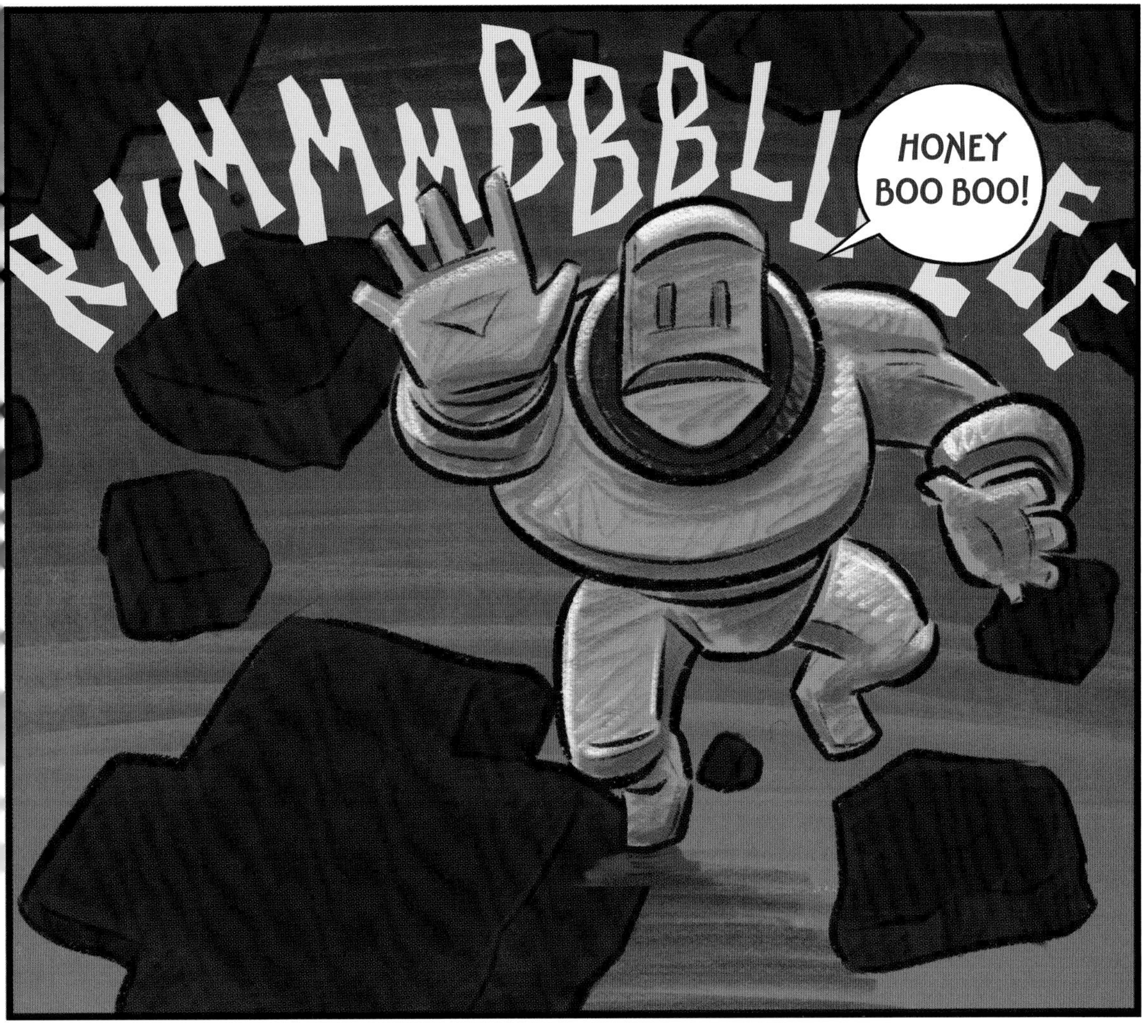
RUMMMBBBLLEE
HONEY BOO BOO!

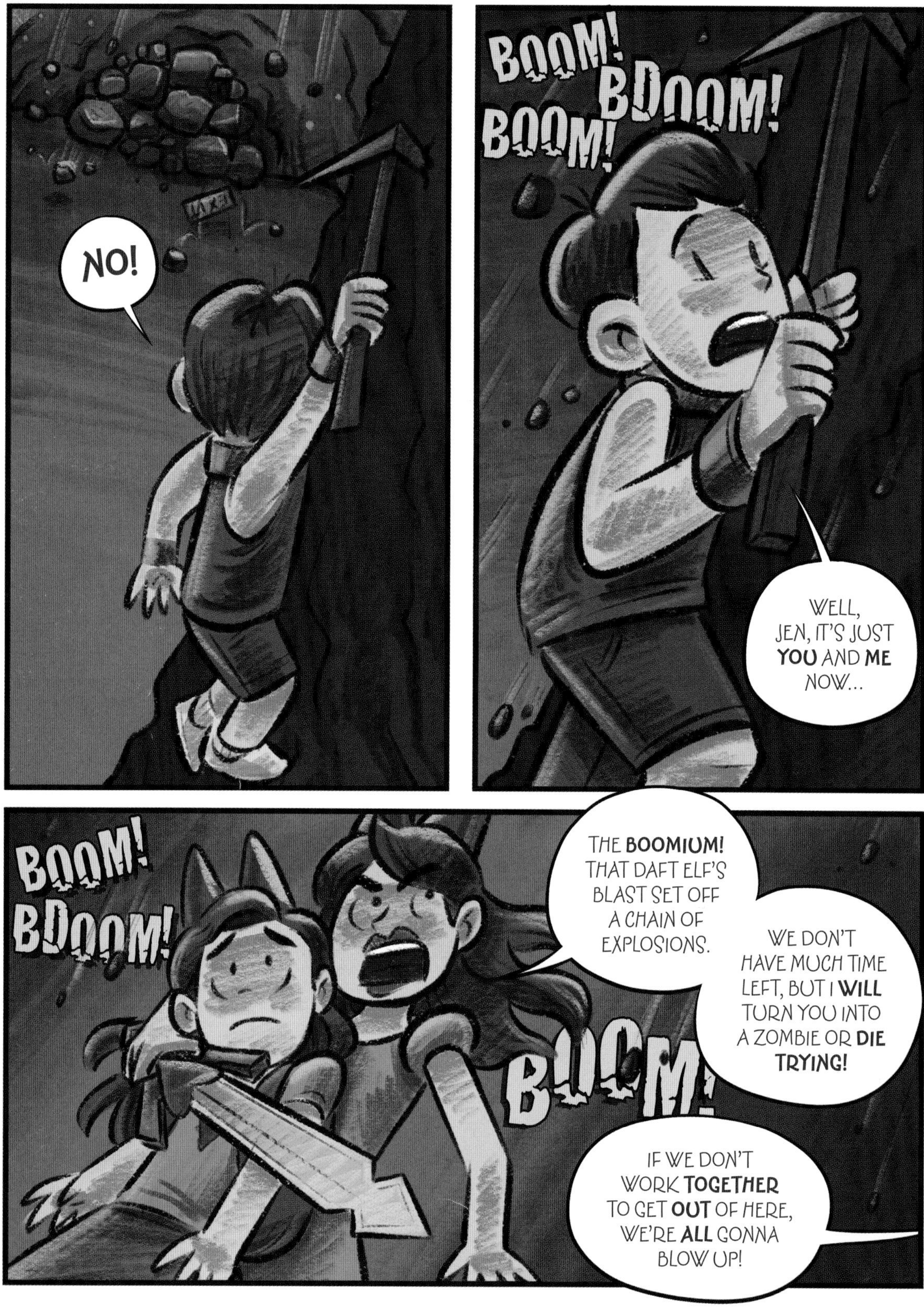
NO!
BOOM! BDOOM! BOOM!
WELL, JEN, IT'S JUST YOU AND ME NOW...
BOOM! BDOOM!
THE BOOMIUM! THAT DAFT ELF'S BLAST SET OFF A CHAIN OF EXPLOSIONS.
WE DON'T HAVE MUCH TIME LEFT, BUT I WILL TURN YOU INTO A ZOMBIE OR DIE TRYING!
BOOM!
IF WE DON'T WORK TOGETHER TO GET OUT OF HERE, WE'RE ALL GONNA BLOW UP!

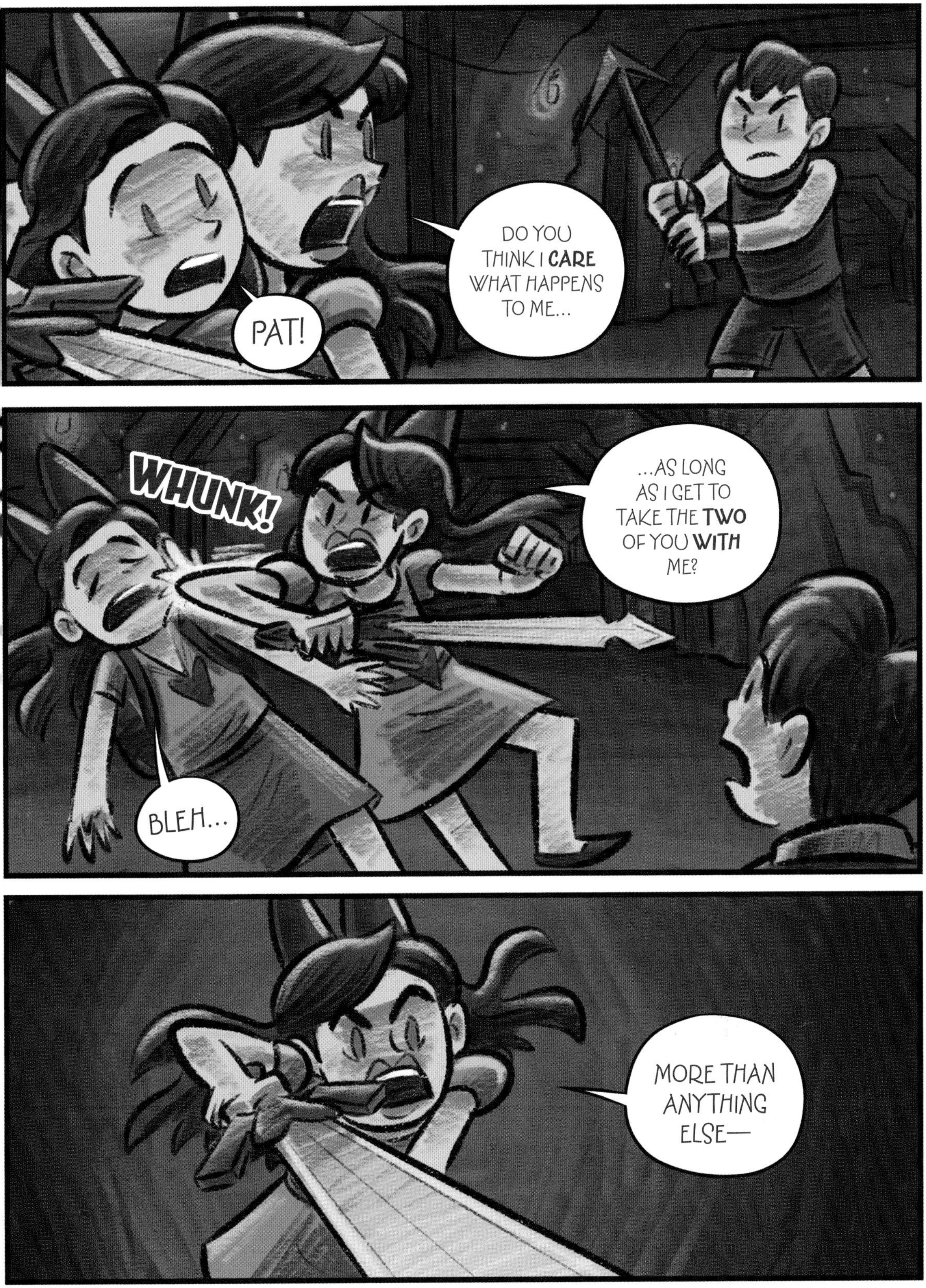
PAT!
DO YOU THINK I CARE WHAT HAPPENS TO ME...
WHUNK!
...AS LONG AS I GET TO TAKE THE TWO OF YOU WITH ME?
BLEH...
MORE THAN ANYTHING ELSE—

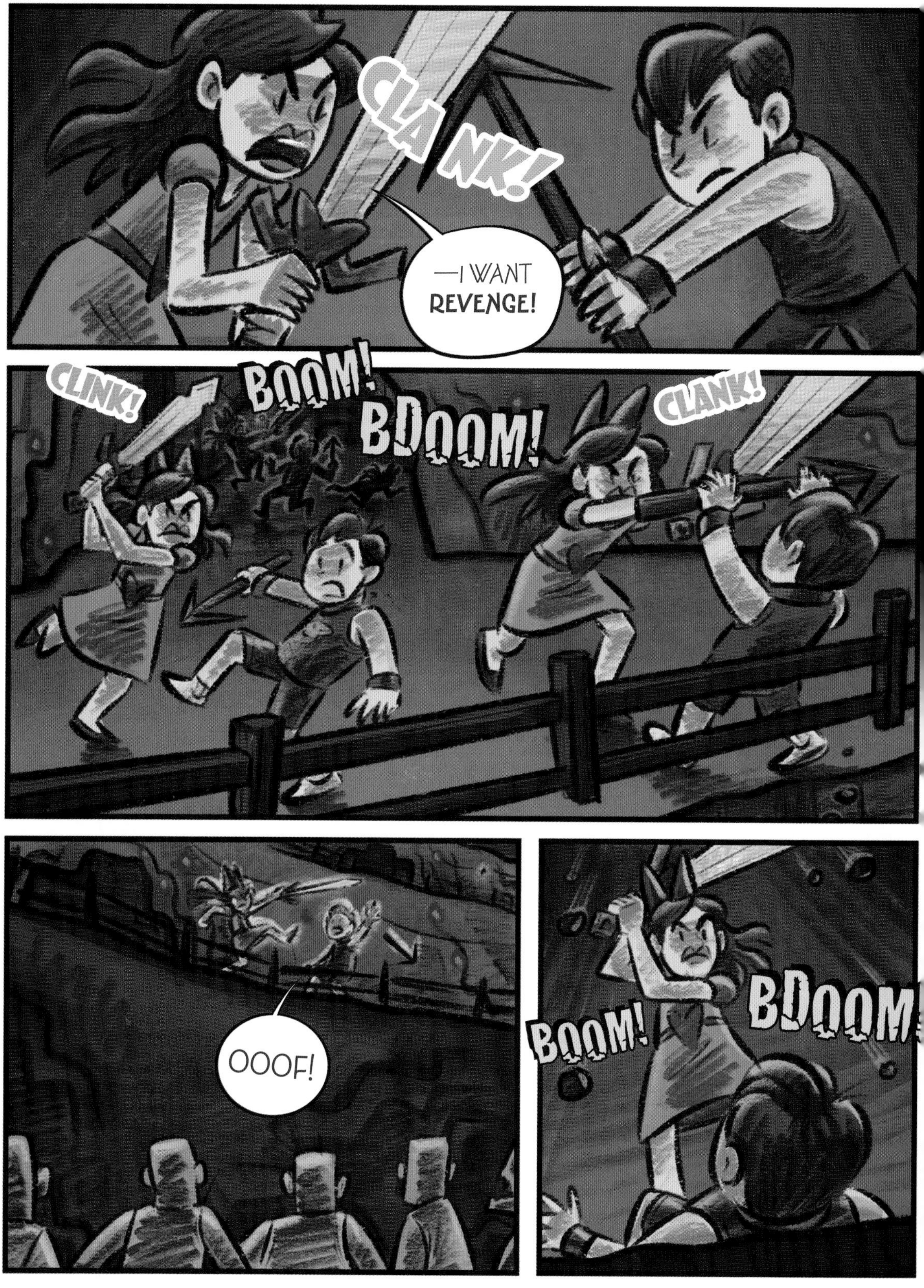

CLANK!
—I WANT REVENGE!
CLINK!
BOOM!
BDOOM!
CLANK!
OOOF!
BOOM!
BDOOM!

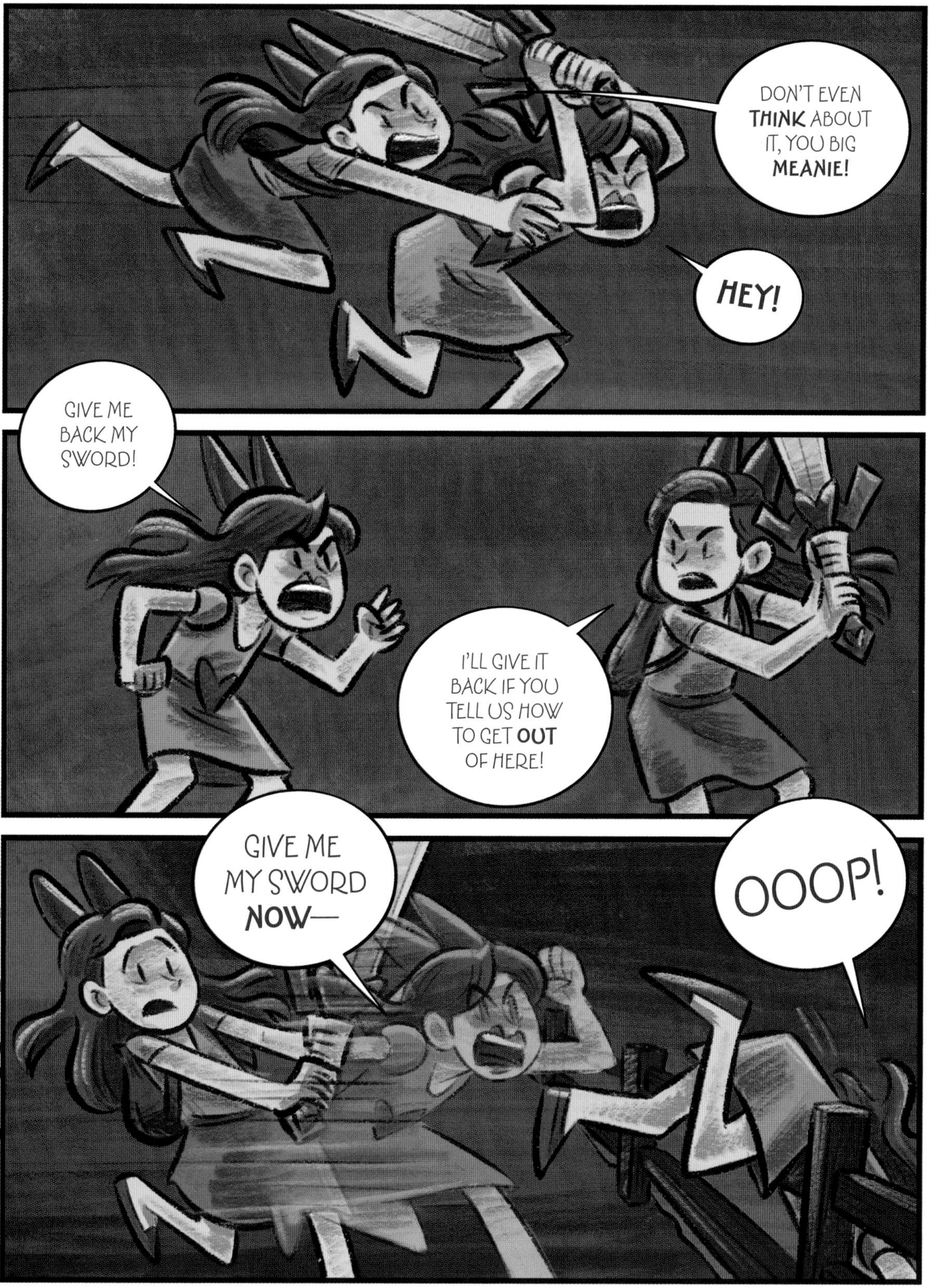
DON'T EVEN THINK ABOUT IT, YOU BIG MEANIE!
HEY!
GIVE ME BACK MY SWORD!
I'LL GIVE IT BACK IF YOU TELL US HOW TO GET OUT OF HERE!
GIVE ME MY SWORD NOW—
OOOP!

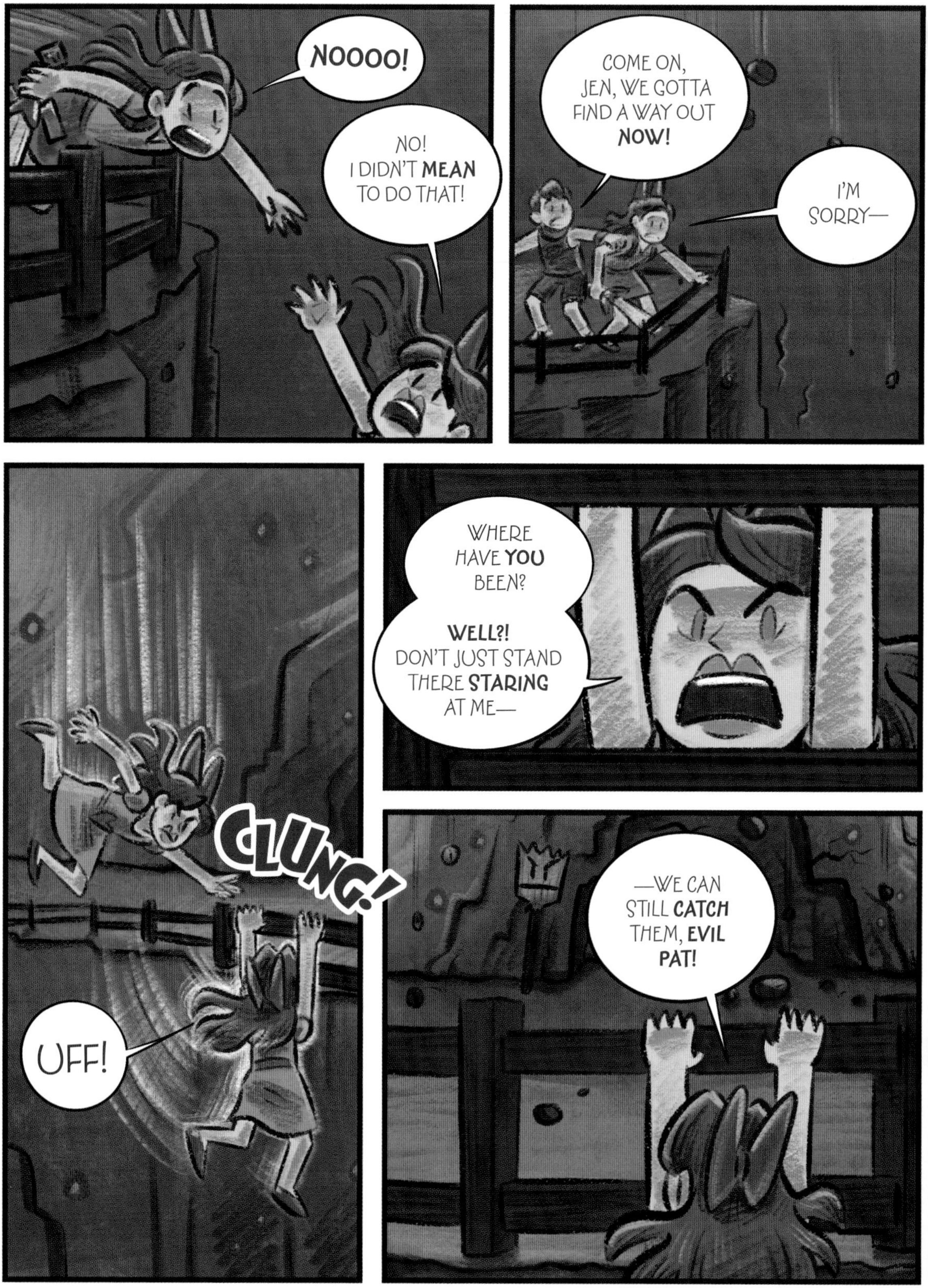
NOOOO!
NO! I DIDN'T MEAN TO DO THAT!
COME ON, JEN, WE GOTTA FIND A WAY OUT NOW!
I'M SORRY—
CLUNG!
UFF!
WHERE HAVE YOU BEEN?
WELL?! DON'T JUST STAND THERE STARING AT ME—
—WE CAN STILL CATCH THEM, EVIL PAT!

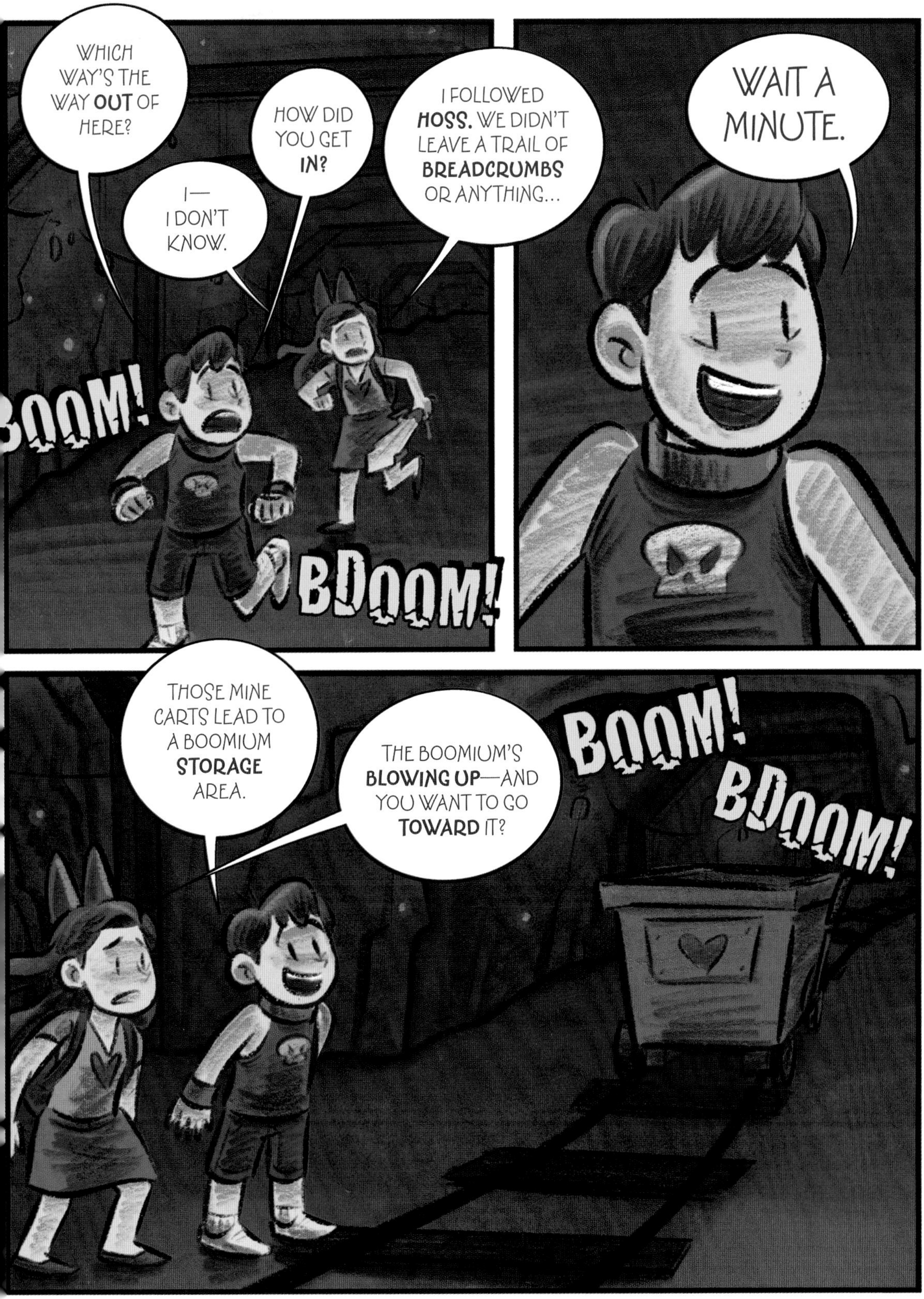
WHICH WAY'S THE WAY **OUT** OF HERE?
I— I DON'T KNOW.
HOW DID YOU GET **IN?**
I FOLLOWED **HOSS.** WE DIDN'T LEAVE A TRAIL OF **BREADCRUMBS** OR ANYTHING...
BOOM!
BDOOM!
WAIT A MINUTE.
THOSE MINE CARTS LEAD TO A BOOMIUM **STORAGE** AREA.
THE BOOMIUM'S **BLOWING UP**—AND YOU WANT TO GO **TOWARD** IT?
BOOM!
BDOOM!

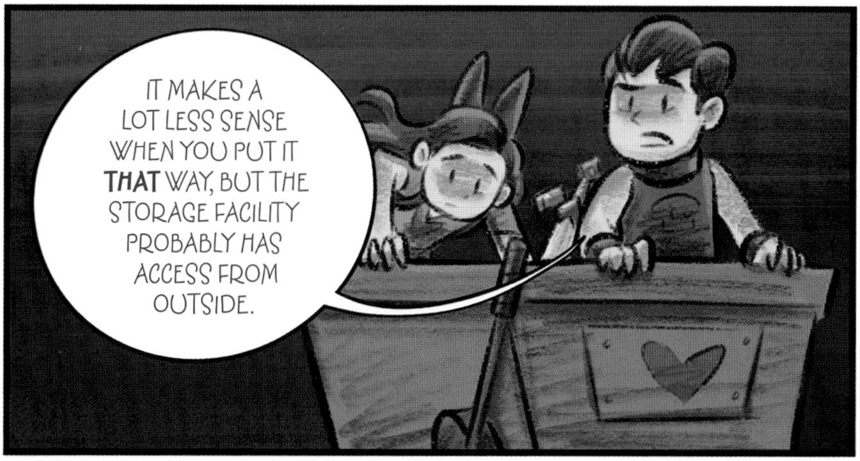
IT MAKES A LOT LESS SENSE WHEN YOU PUT IT **THAT** WAY, BUT THE STORAGE FACILITY PROBABLY HAS ACCESS FROM OUTSIDE.

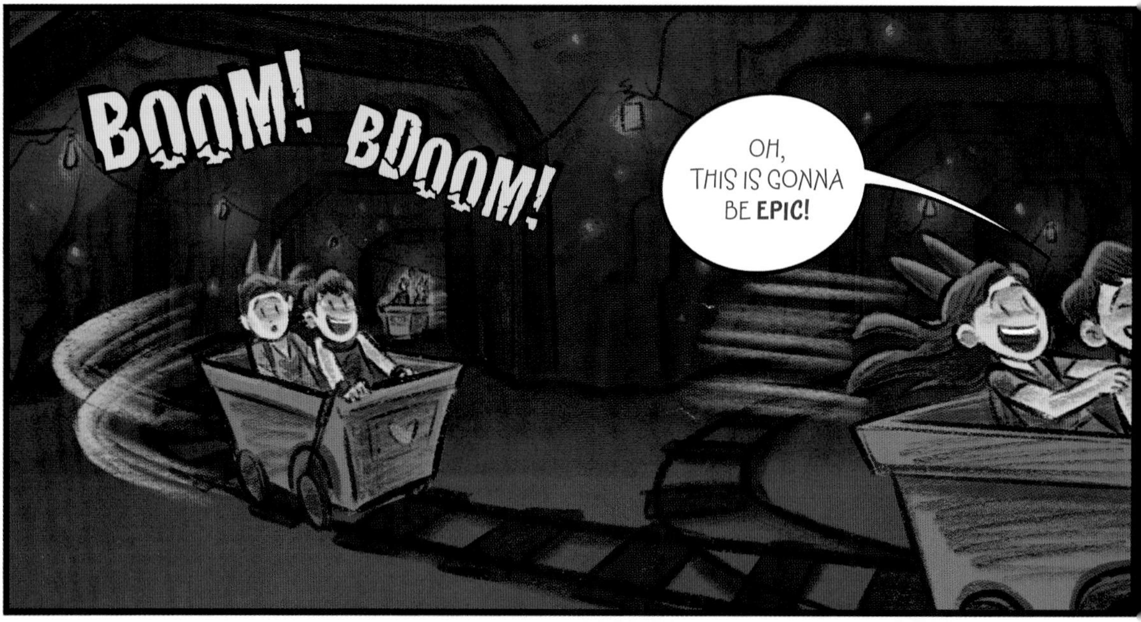
BOOM!
BDOOM!
OH, THIS IS GONNA BE **EPIC!**

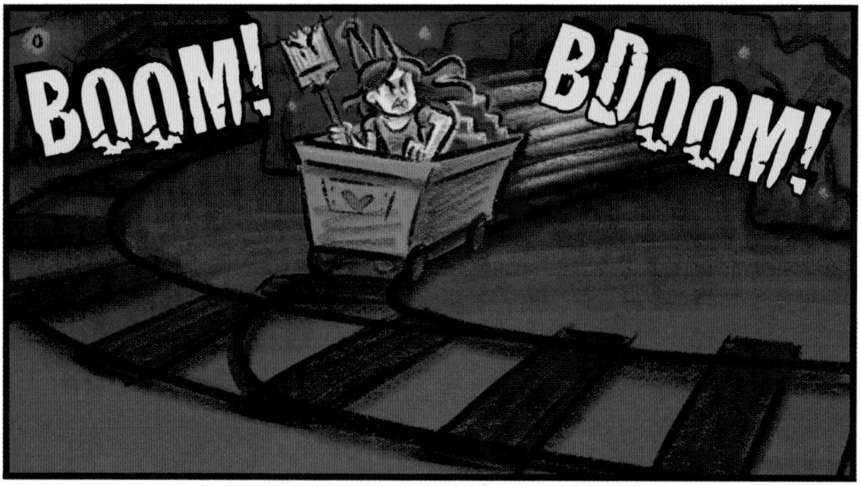
BOOM!
BDOOM!

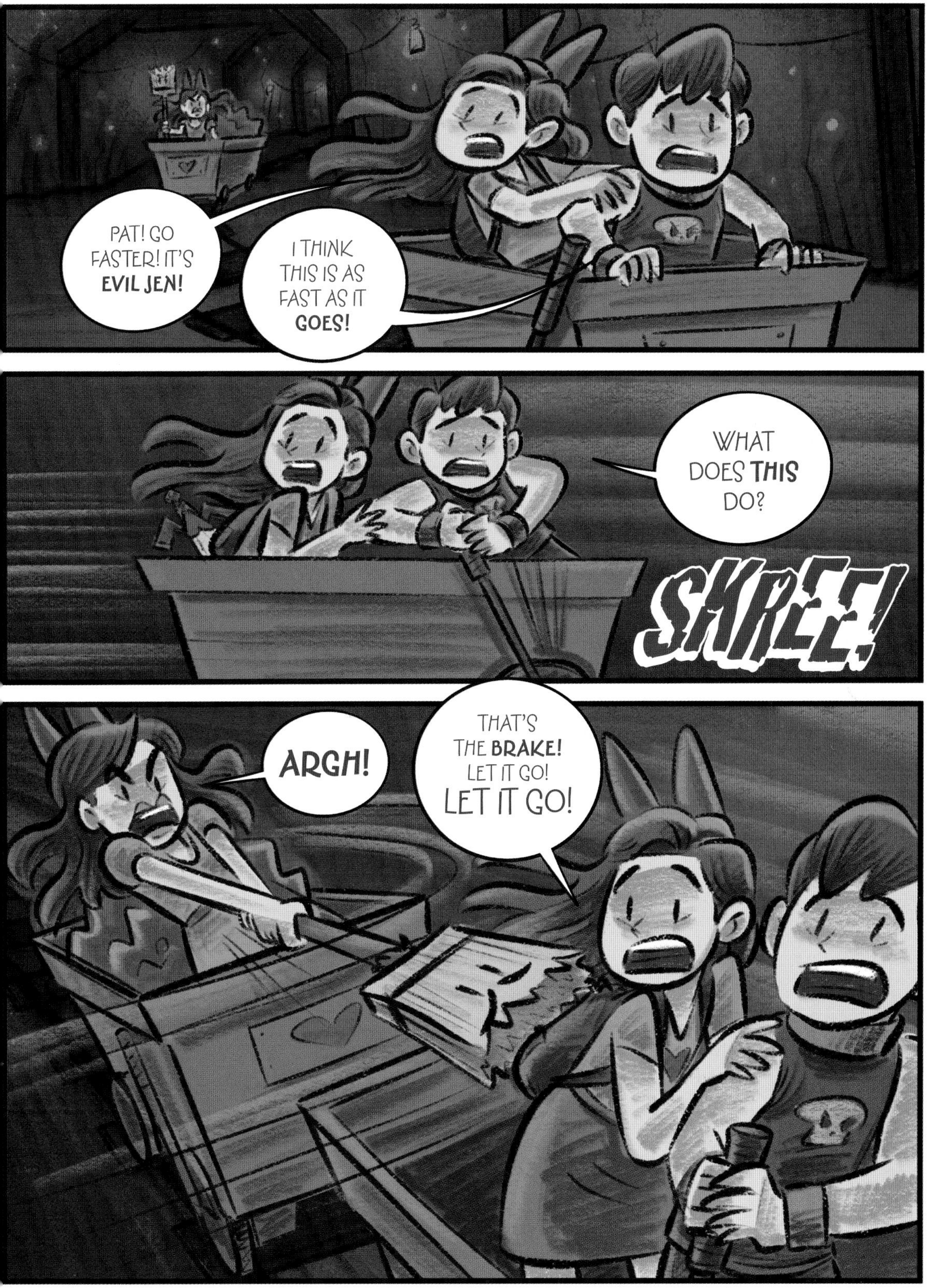
PAT! GO FASTER! IT'S **EVIL JEN!**
I THINK THIS IS AS FAST AS IT **GOES!**
WHAT DOES **THIS** DO?
SKREE!
ARGH!
THAT'S THE **BRAKE!** LET IT GO! LET IT GO!

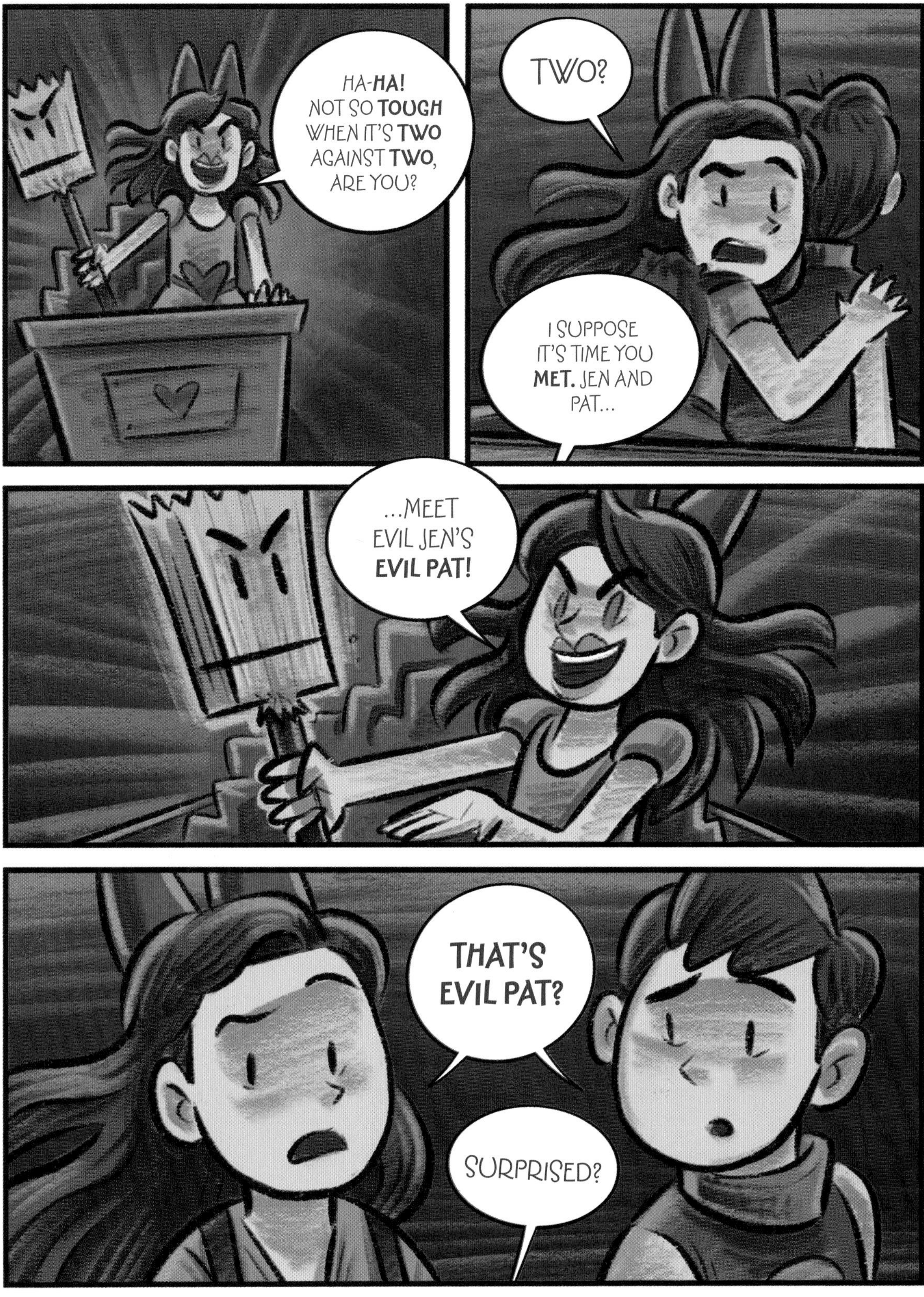
HA-**HA!** NOT SO **TOUGH** WHEN IT'S **TWO** AGAINST **TWO,** ARE YOU?
TWO?
I SUPPOSE IT'S TIME YOU **MET.** JEN AND PAT...
...MEET EVIL JEN'S **EVIL PAT!**
THAT'S EVIL PAT?
SURPRISED?

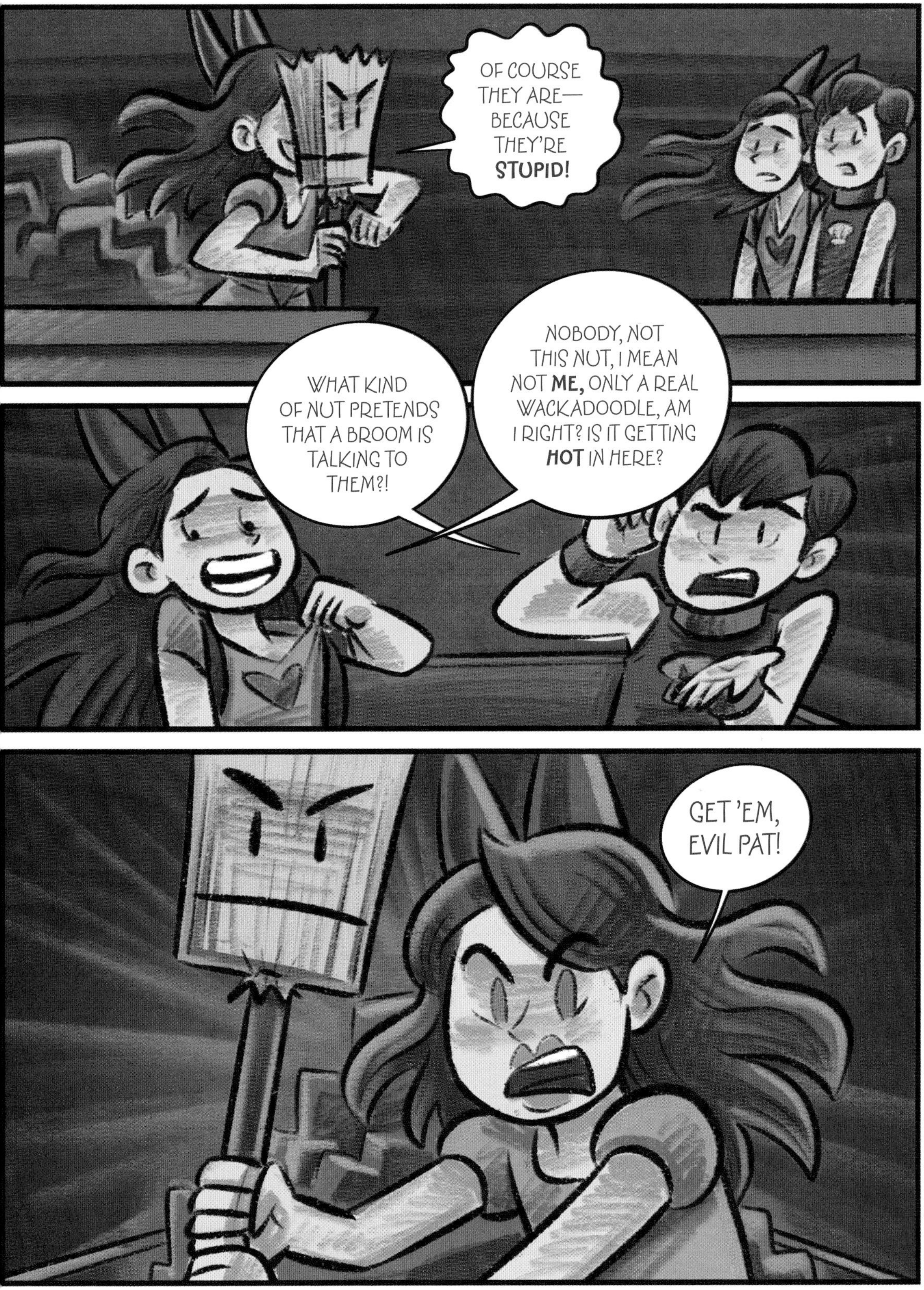
OF COURSE THEY ARE— BECAUSE THEY'RE **STUPID!**
WHAT KIND OF NUT PRETENDS THAT A BROOM IS TALKING TO THEM?!
NOBODY, NOT THIS NUT, I MEAN NOT **ME,** ONLY A REAL WACKADOODLE, AM I RIGHT? IS IT GETTING **HOT** IN HERE?
GET 'EM, EVIL PAT!

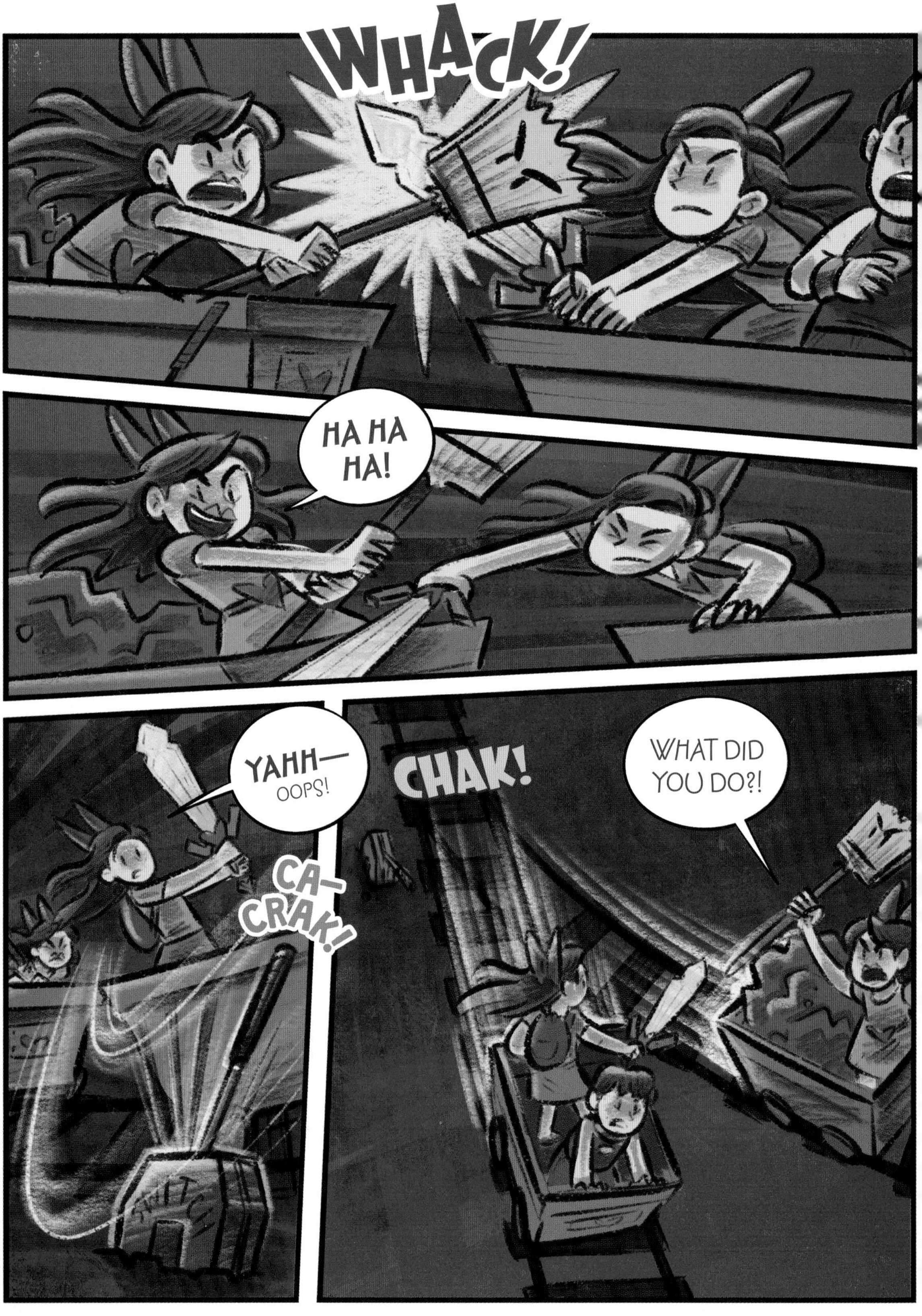
WHACK!
HA HA HA!
YAHH—
OOPS!
CA-CRAK!
CHAK!
WHAT DID YOU DO?!

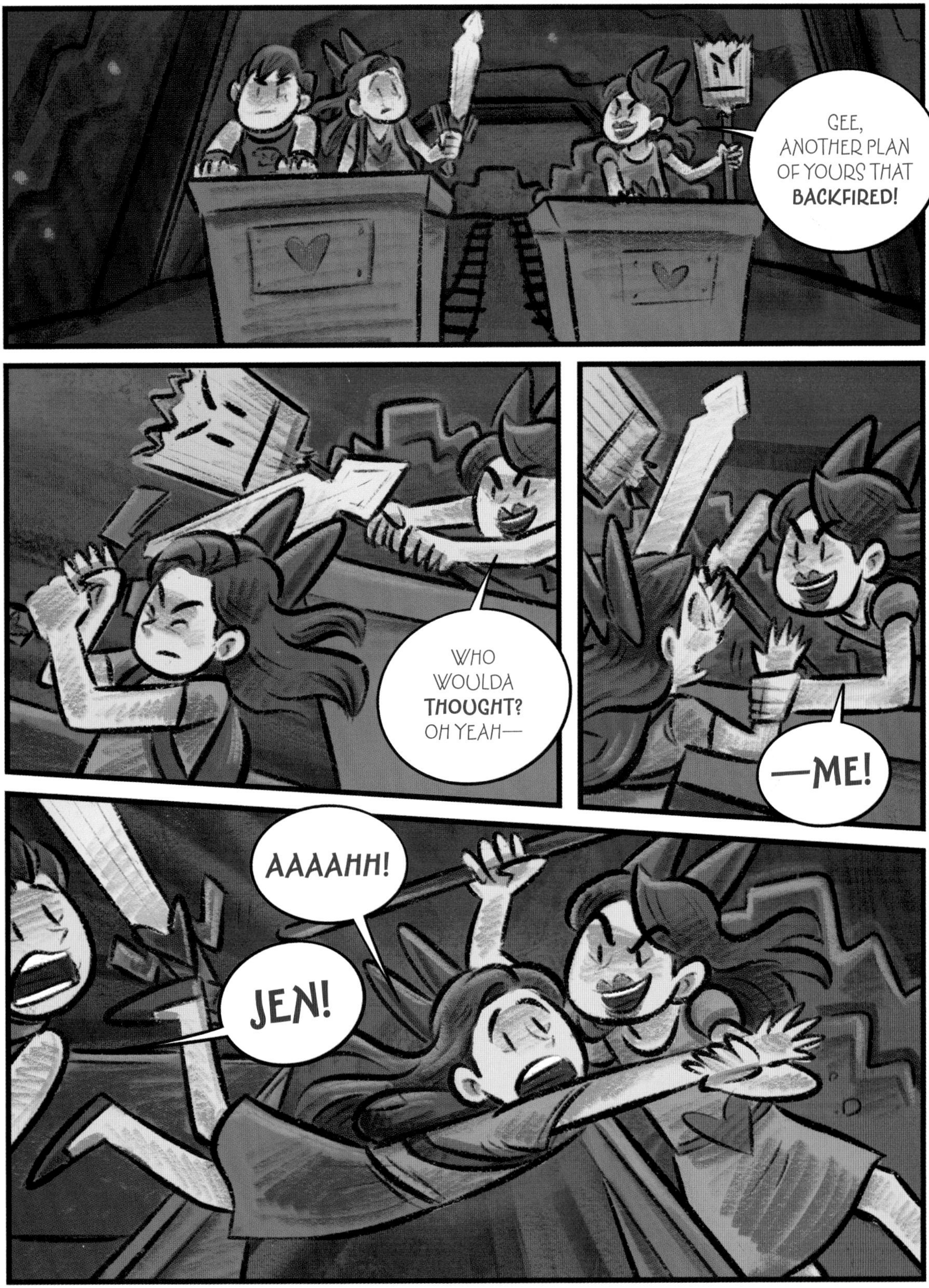
GEE, ANOTHER PLAN OF YOURS THAT BACKFIRED!
WHO WOULDA THOUGHT? OH YEAH—
—ME!
AAAAHH!
JEN!

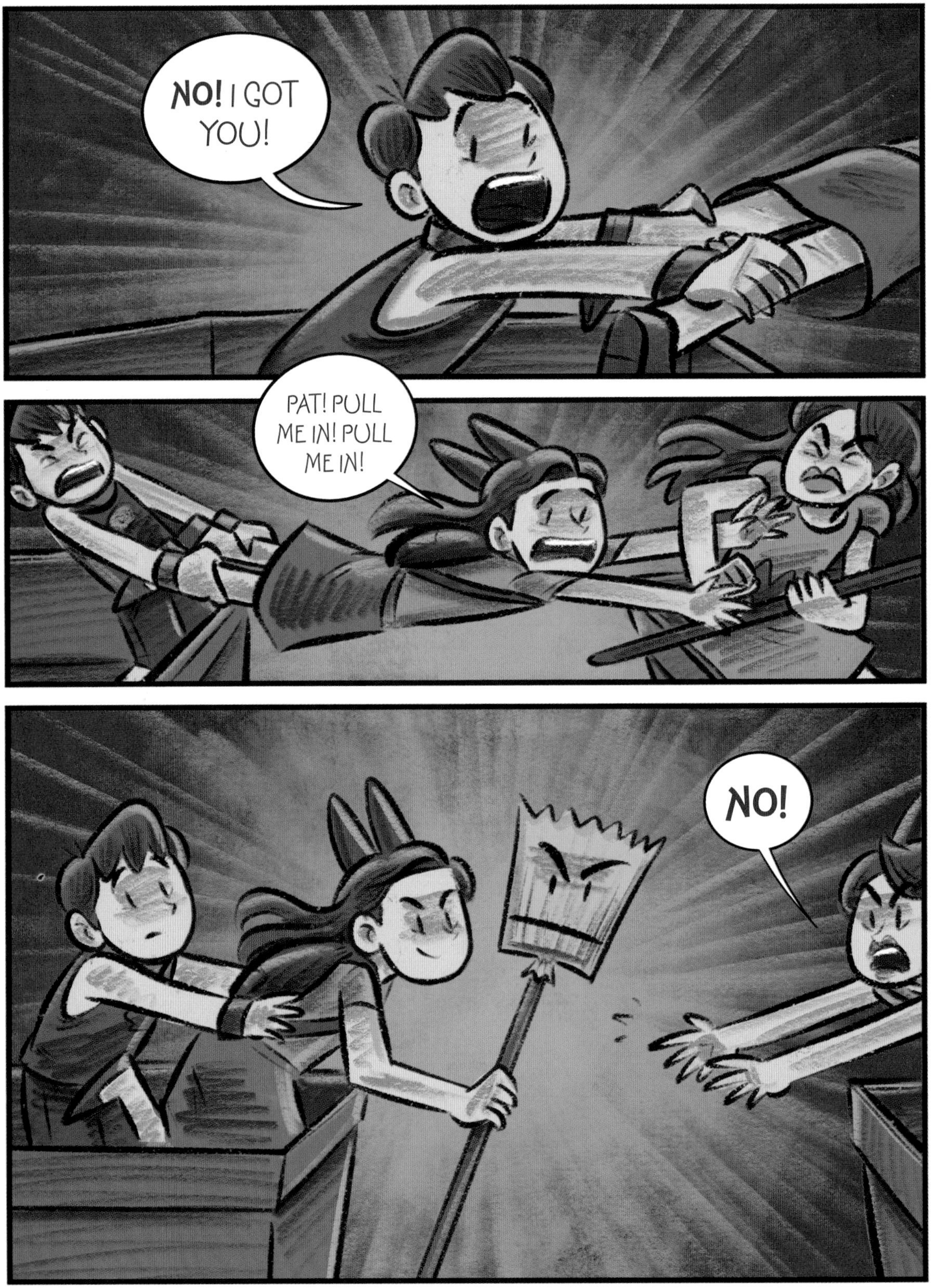
NO! I GOT YOU!
PAT! PULL ME IN! PULL ME IN!
NO!

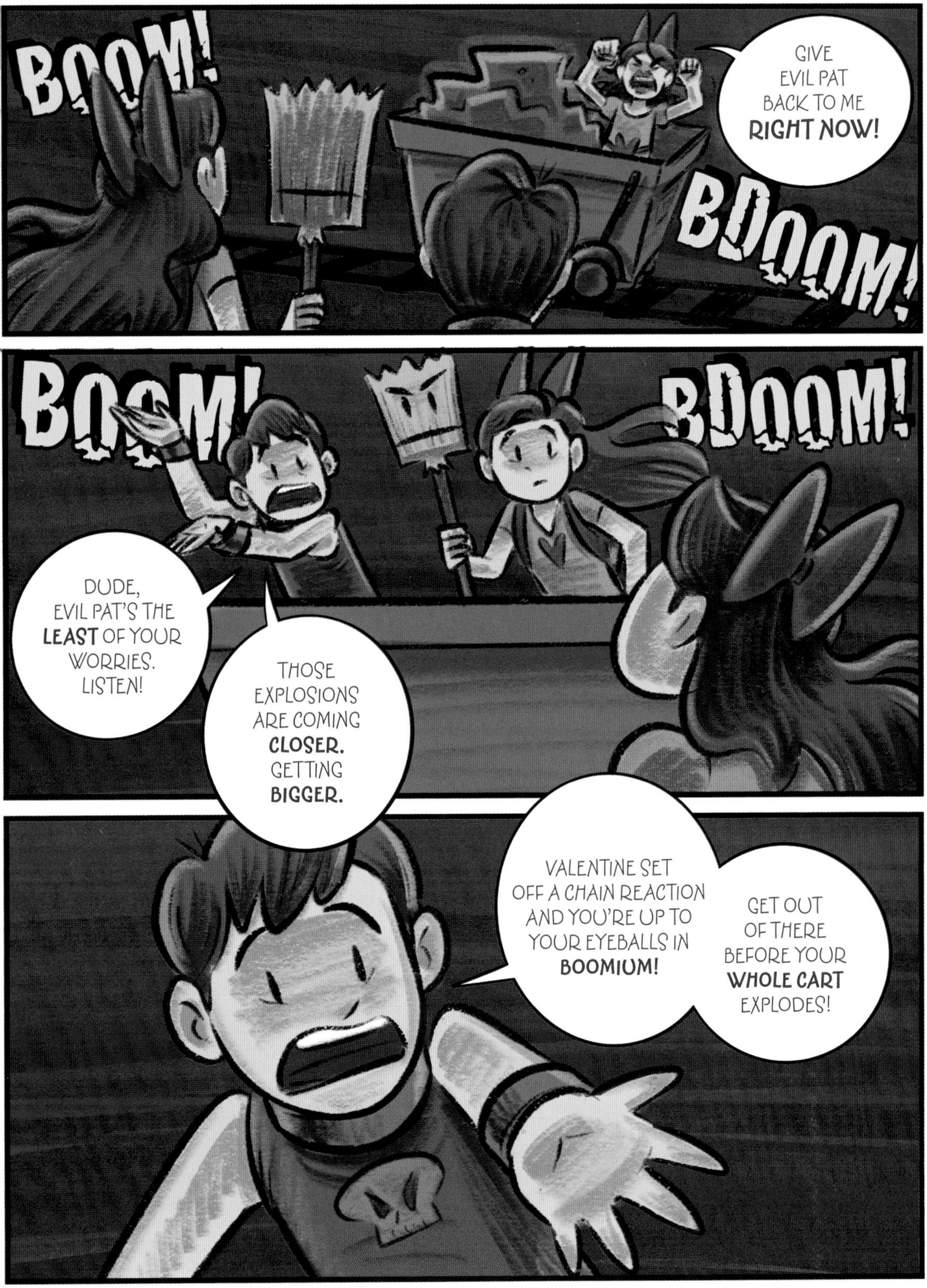
BOOM!
GIVE EVIL PAT BACK TO ME **RIGHT NOW!**
BDOOM!
BOOM!
BDOOM!
DUDE, EVIL PAT'S THE **LEAST** OF YOUR WORRIES. LISTEN!
THOSE EXPLOSIONS ARE COMING **CLOSER.** GETTING **BIGGER.**
VALENTINE SET OFF A CHAIN REACTION AND YOU'RE UP TO YOUR EYEBALLS IN **BOOMIUM!**
GET OUT OF THERE BEFORE YOUR **WHOLE CART** EXPLODES!

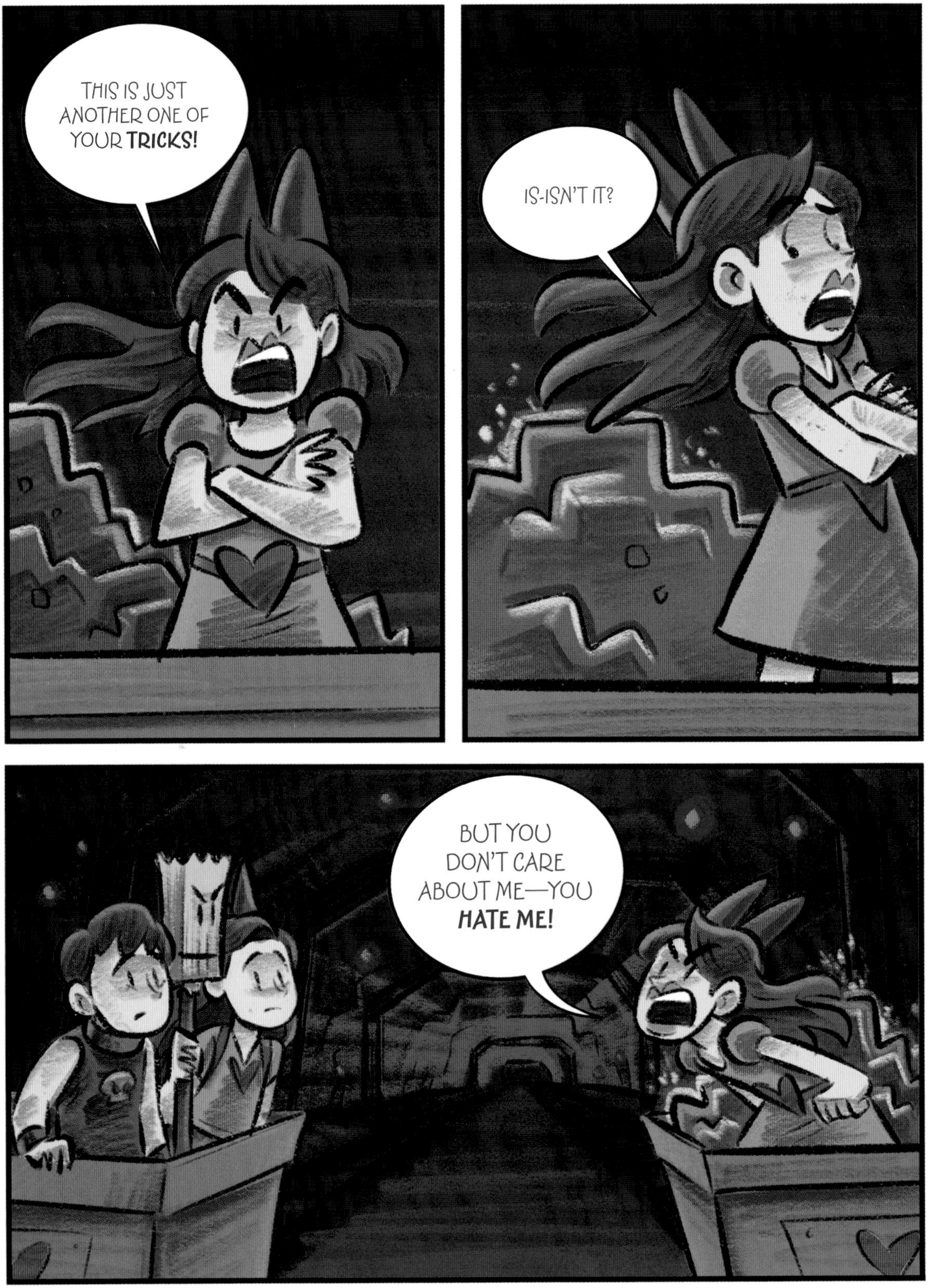
THIS IS JUST ANOTHER ONE OF YOUR **TRICKS!**
IS-ISN'T IT?
BUT YOU DON'T CARE ABOUT ME—YOU **HATE ME!**

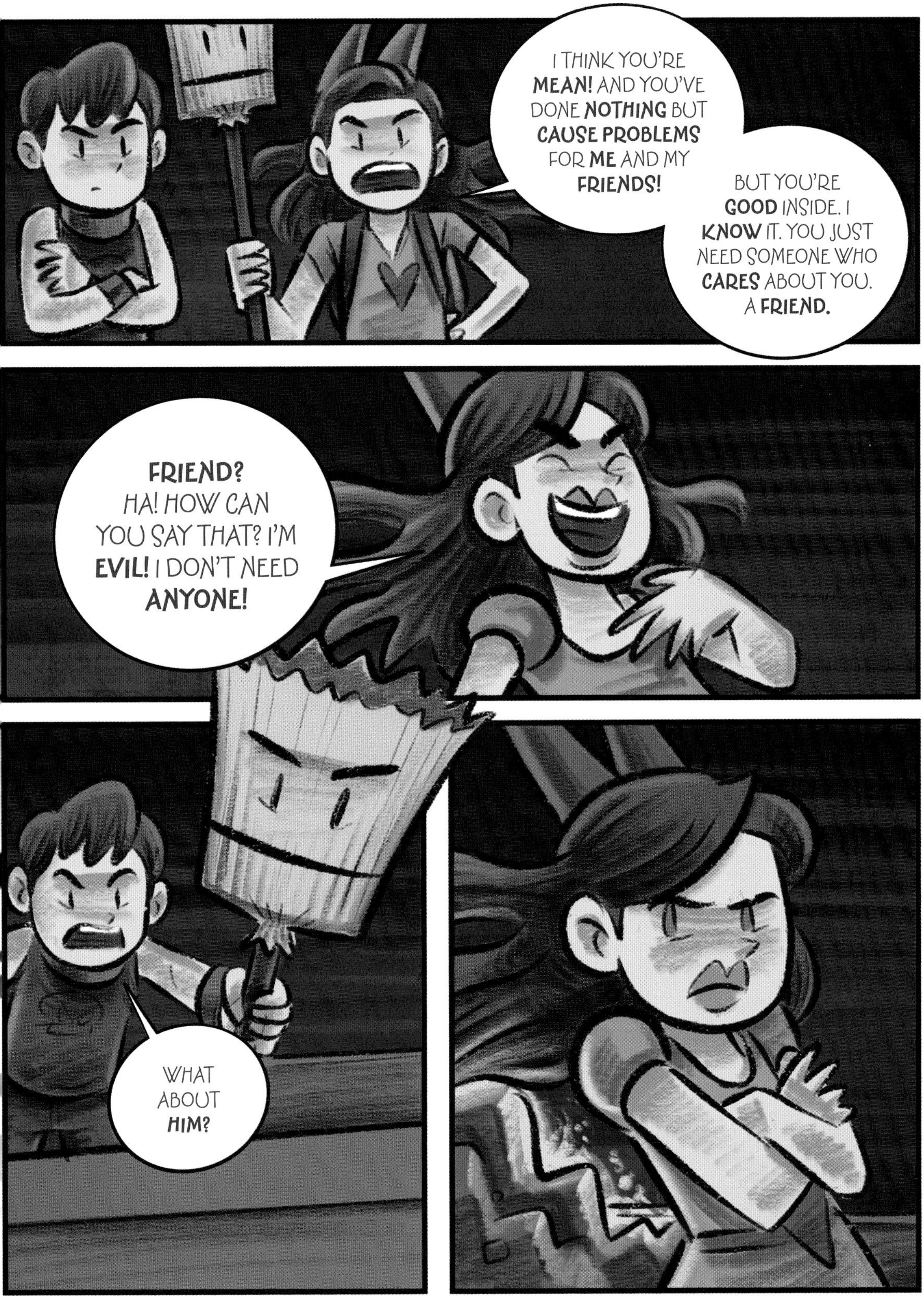
I THINK YOU'RE MEAN! AND YOU'VE DONE NOTHING BUT CAUSE PROBLEMS FOR ME AND MY FRIENDS!
BUT YOU'RE GOOD INSIDE. I KNOW IT. YOU JUST NEED SOMEONE WHO CARES ABOUT YOU. A FRIEND.
FRIEND? HA! HOW CAN YOU SAY THAT? I'M EVIL! I DON'T NEED ANYONE!
WHAT ABOUT HIM?

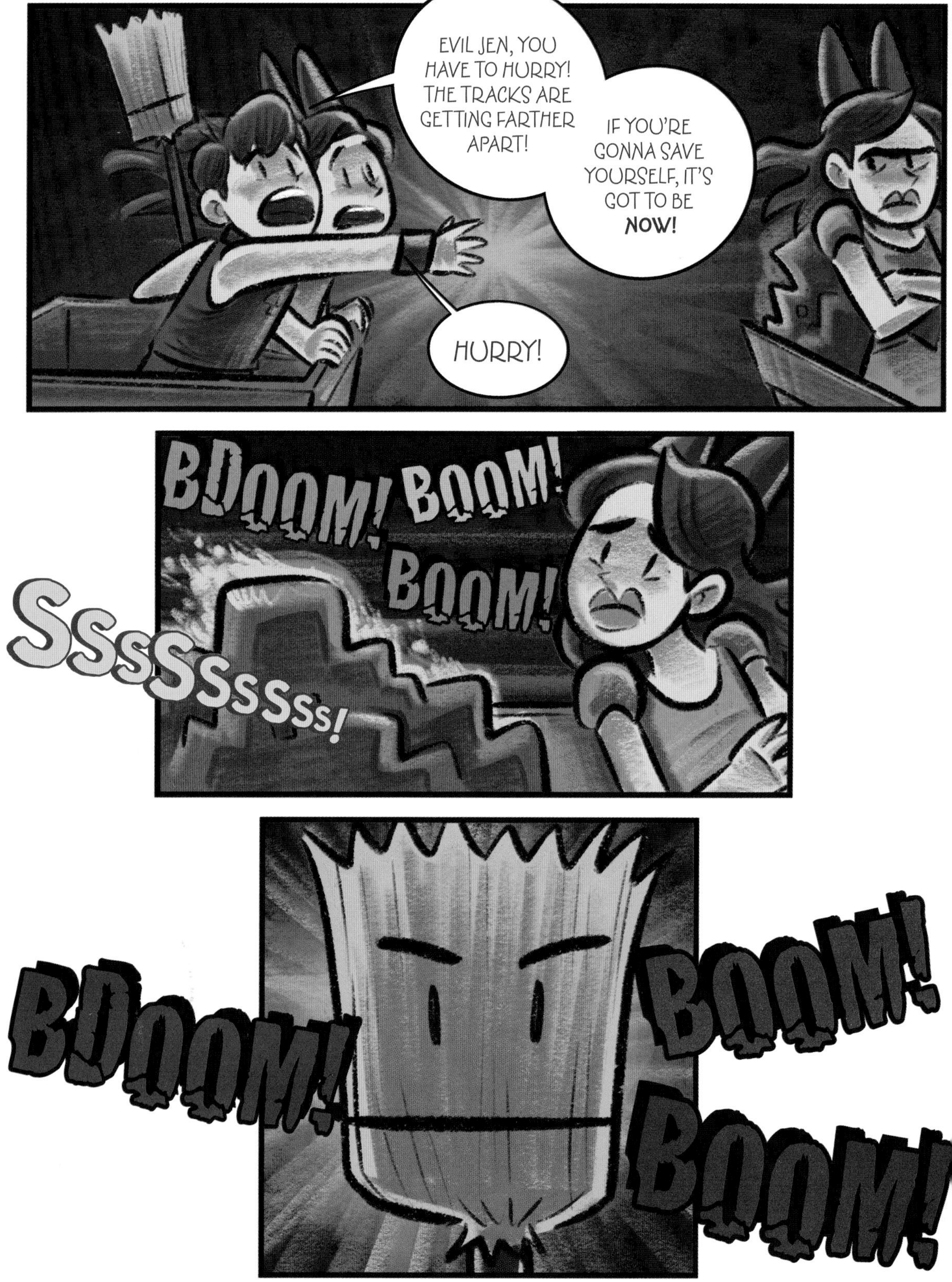
EVIL JEN, YOU HAVE TO HURRY! THE TRACKS ARE GETTING FARTHER APART!
IF YOU'RE GONNA SAVE YOURSELF, IT'S GOT TO BE **NOW!**
HURRY!
BDOOM! BOOM!
BOOM!
SsssSsssss!
BDOOM!
BOOM!
BOOM!

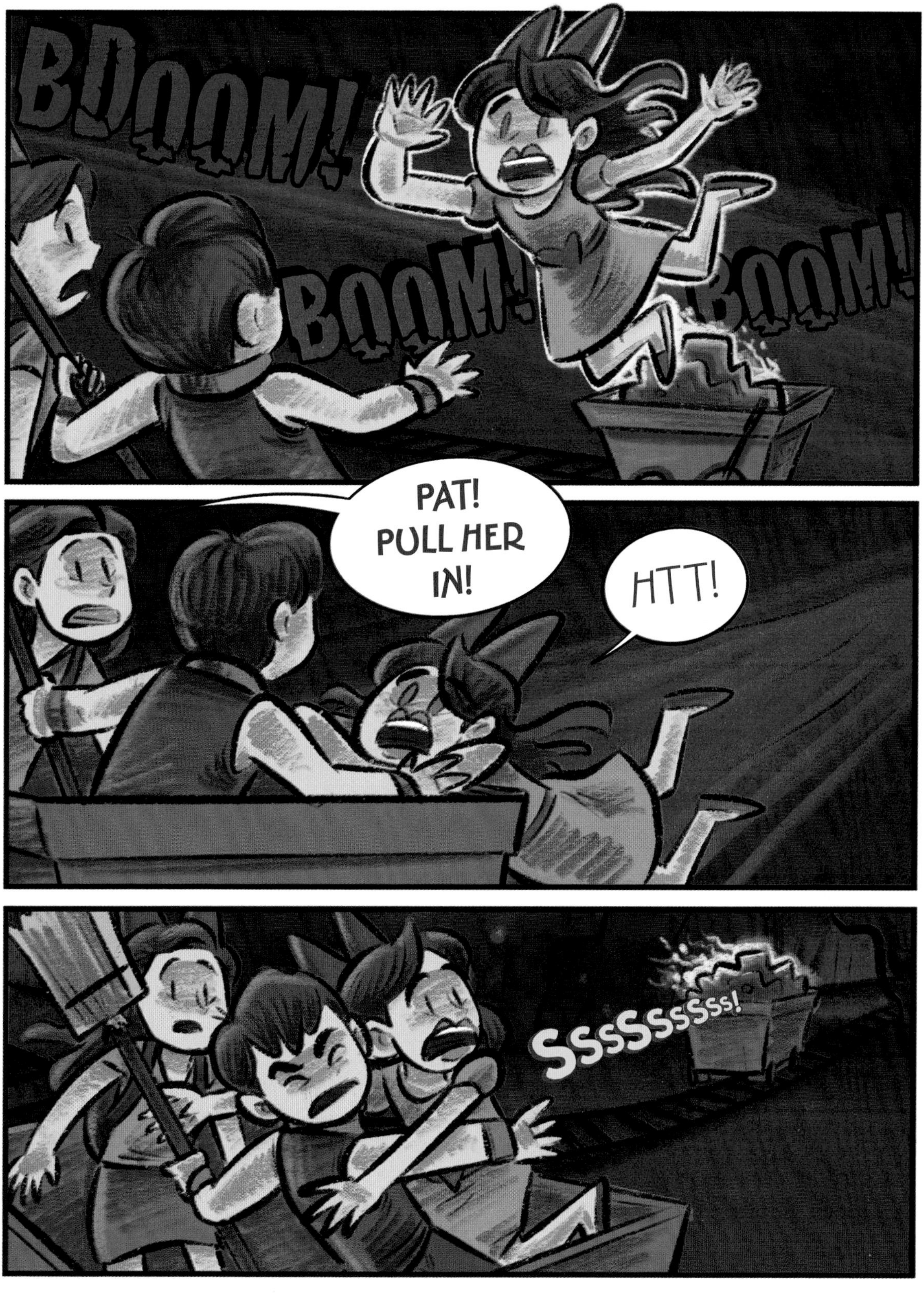
BDOOM!
BOOM!
BOOM!
PAT! PULL HER IN!
HTT!
SSSSSSSSS!

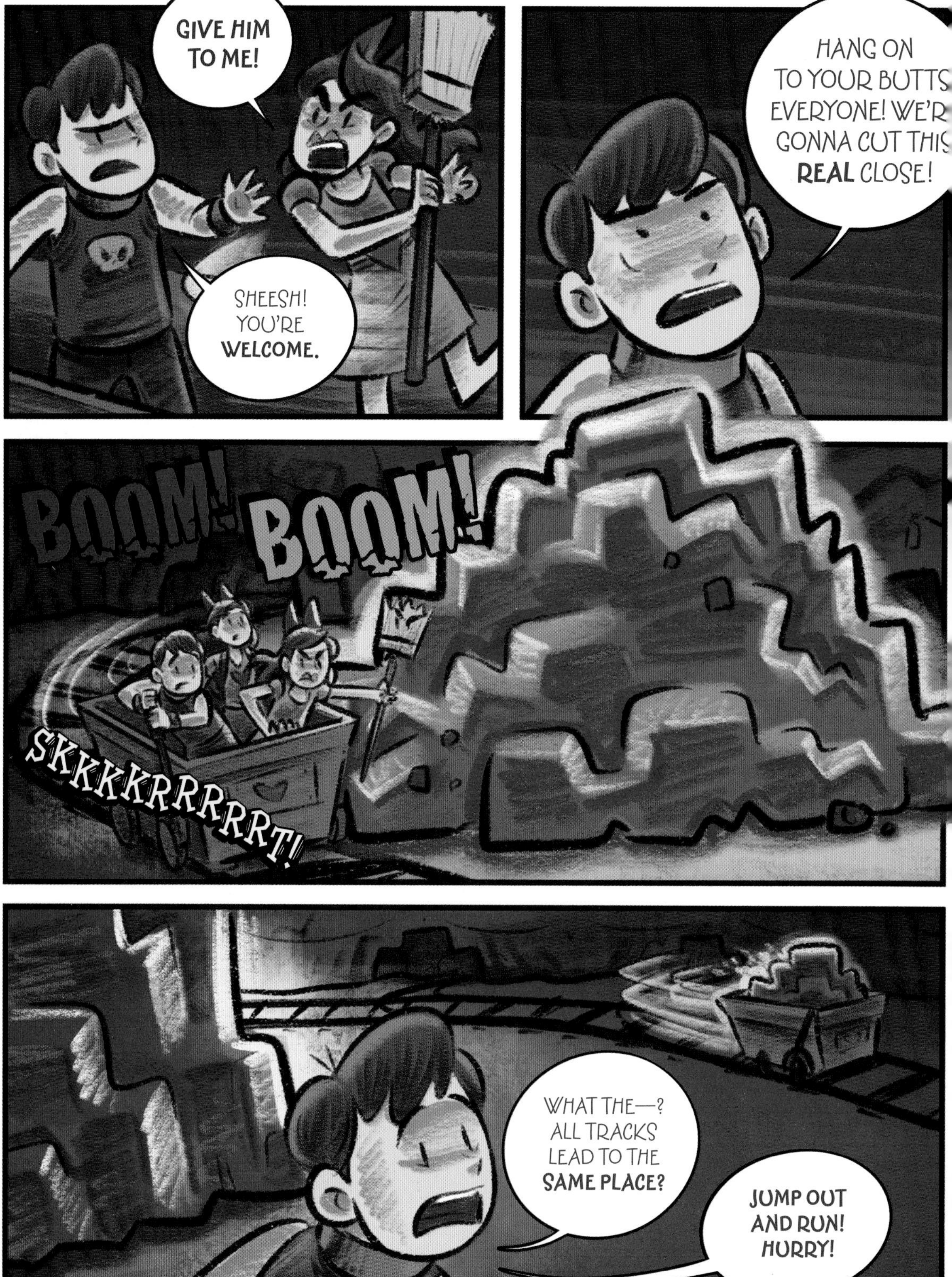
GIVE HIM TO ME!
SHEESH! YOU'RE **WELCOME.**
HANG ON TO YOUR BUTTS EVERYONE! WE'R GONNA CUT THIS **REAL** CLOSE!
BOOM! BOOM!
SKKKKRRRRRRT!
WHAT THE—? ALL TRACKS LEAD TO THE **SAME PLACE?**
JUMP OUT AND RUN! HURRY!

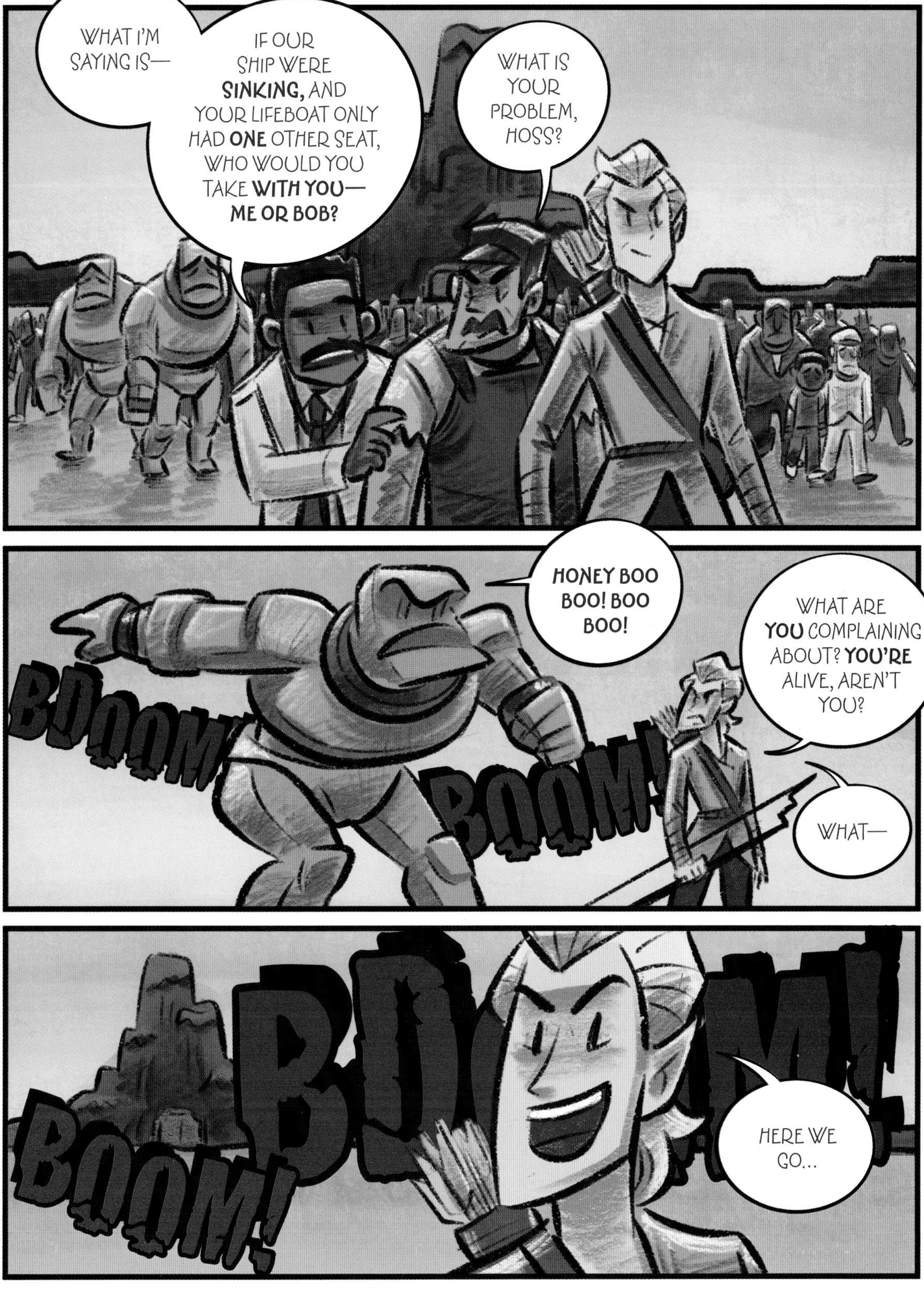
WHAT I'M SAYING IS—
IF OUR SHIP WERE SINKING, AND YOUR LIFEBOAT ONLY HAD ONE OTHER SEAT, WHO WOULD YOU TAKE WITH YOU—ME OR BOB?
WHAT IS YOUR PROBLEM, HOSS?
BDOOM!
HONEY BOO BOO! BOO BOO!
BOOM!
WHAT ARE YOU COMPLAINING ABOUT? YOU'RE ALIVE, AREN'T YOU?
WHAT—
BDOOM!
BOOM!
HERE WE GO...

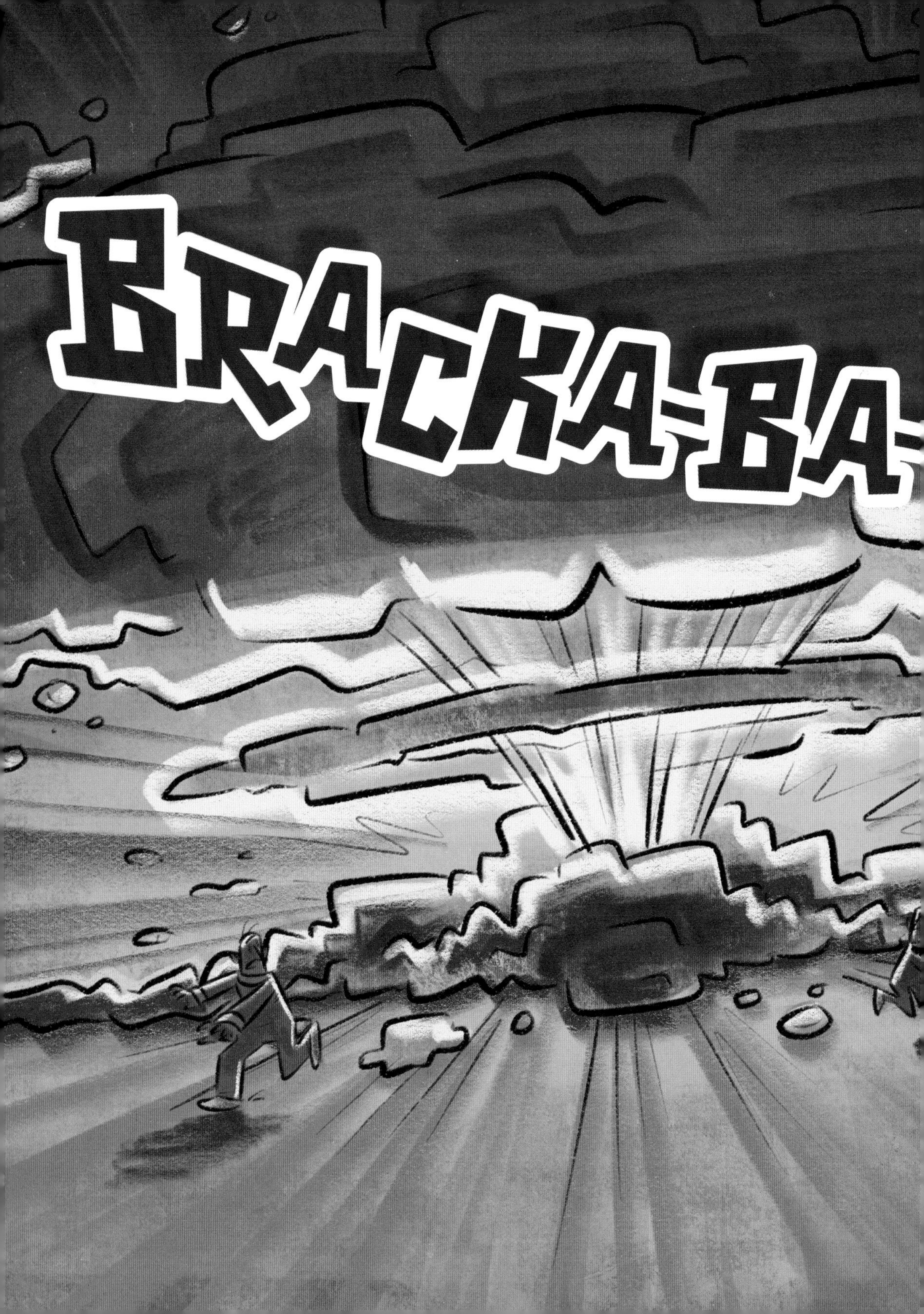
BRACKA-BA-

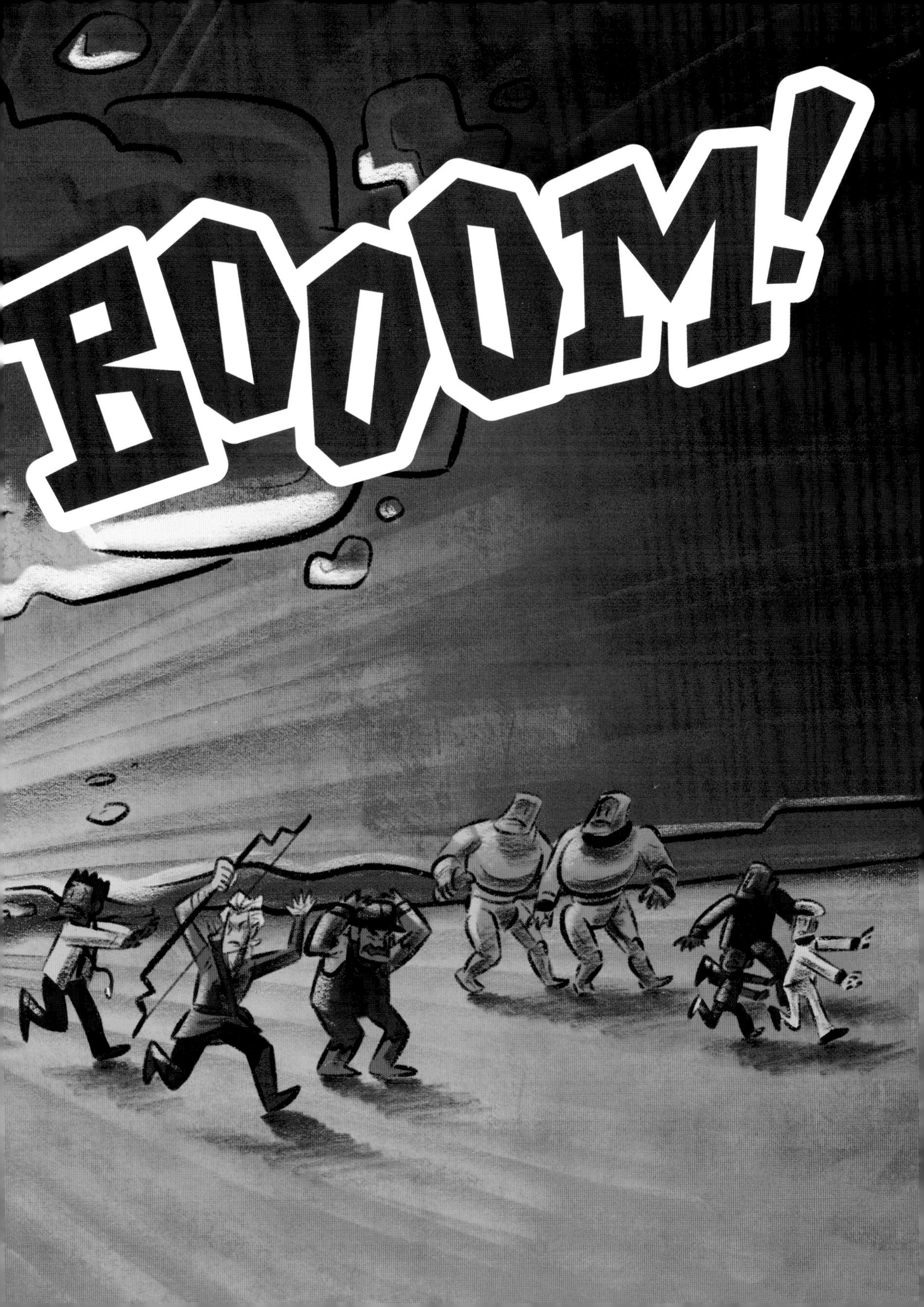
BOOM!

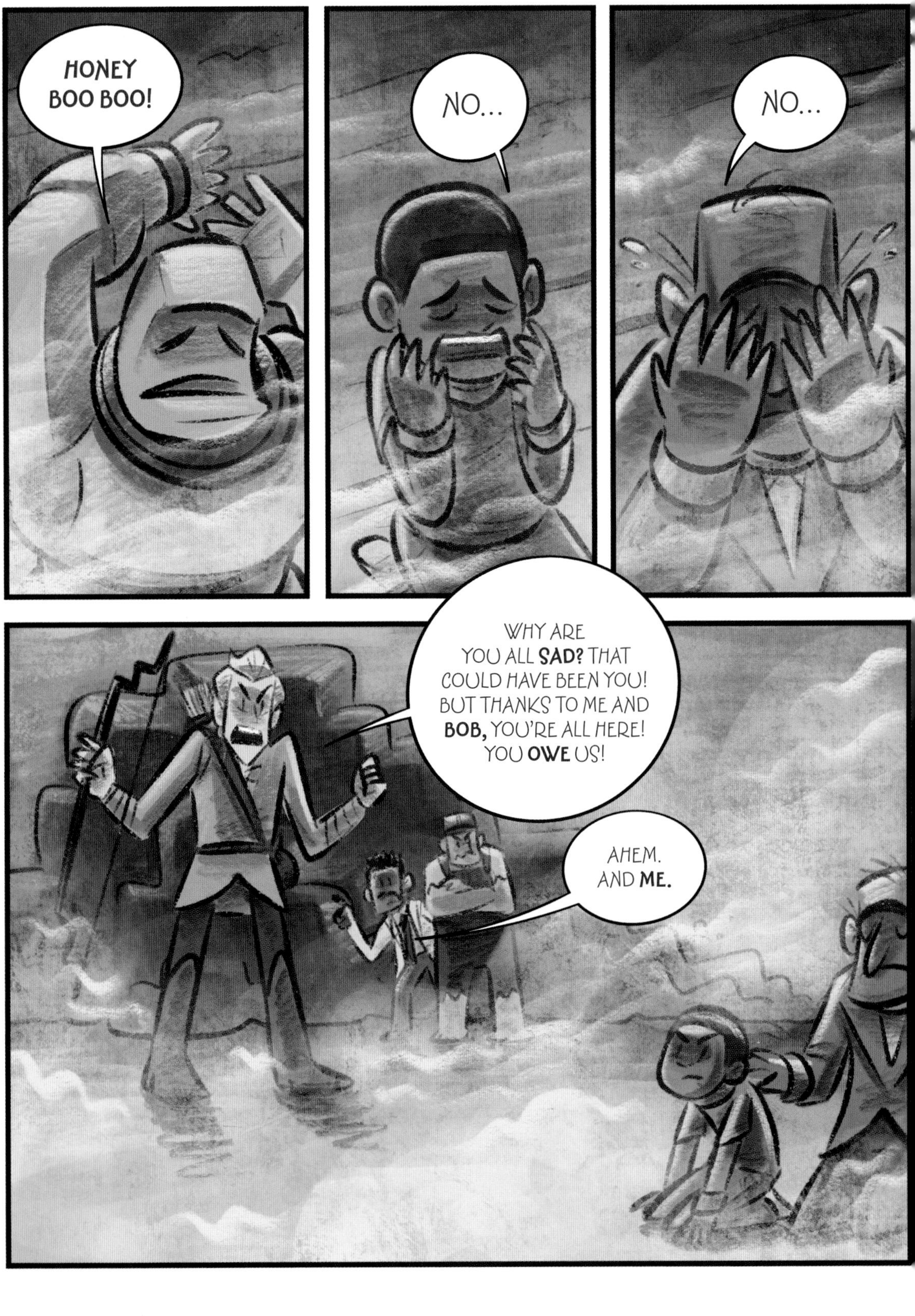
HONEY BOO BOO!
NO...
NO...
WHY ARE YOU ALL **SAD?** THAT COULD HAVE BEEN YOU! BUT THANKS TO ME AND **BOB,** YOU'RE ALL HERE! YOU **OWE** US!
AHEM. AND **ME.**

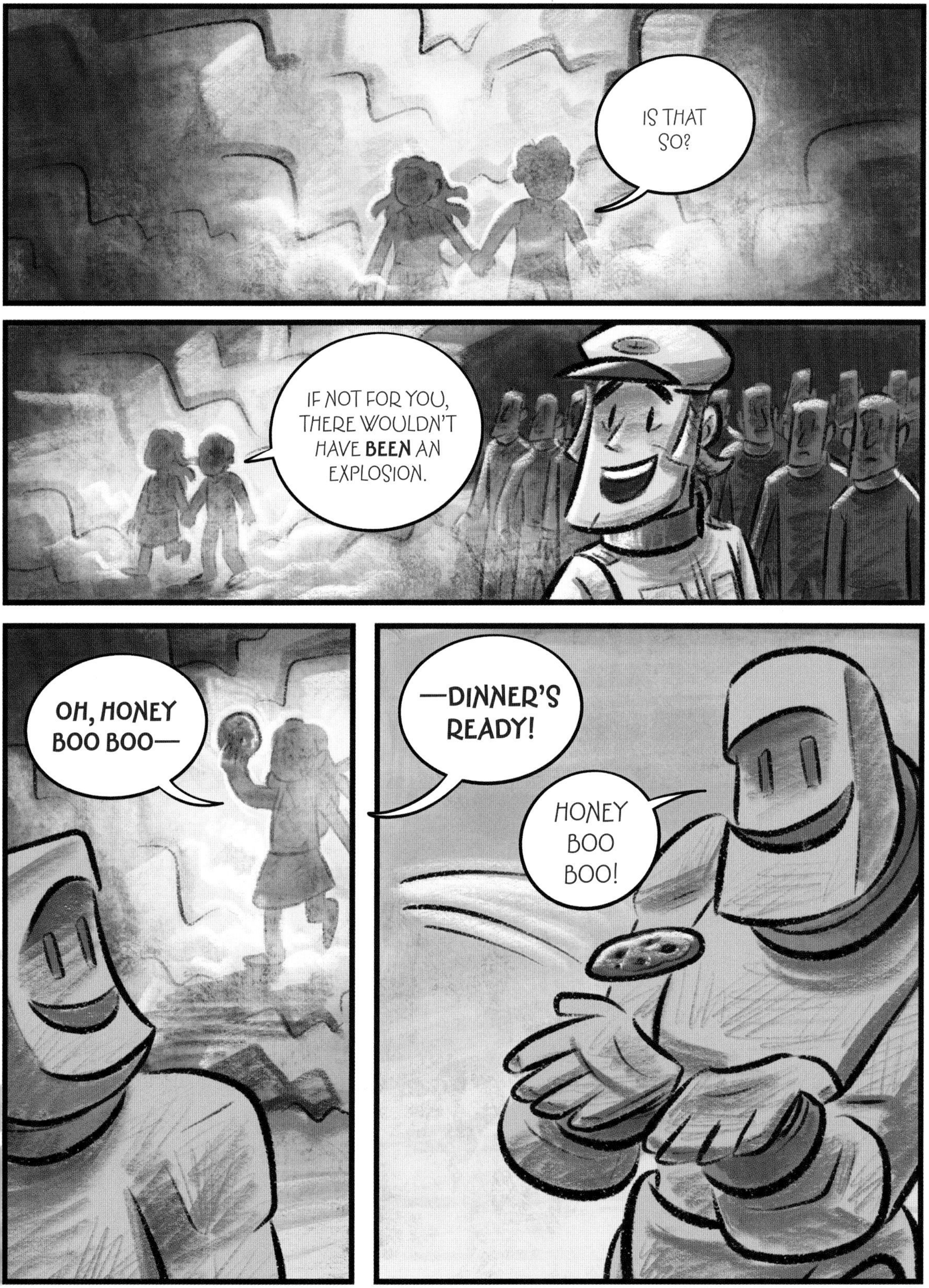
IS THAT SO?
IF NOT FOR YOU, THERE WOULDN'T HAVE BEEN AN EXPLOSION.
OH, HONEY BOO BOO—
—DINNER'S READY!
HONEY BOO BOO!

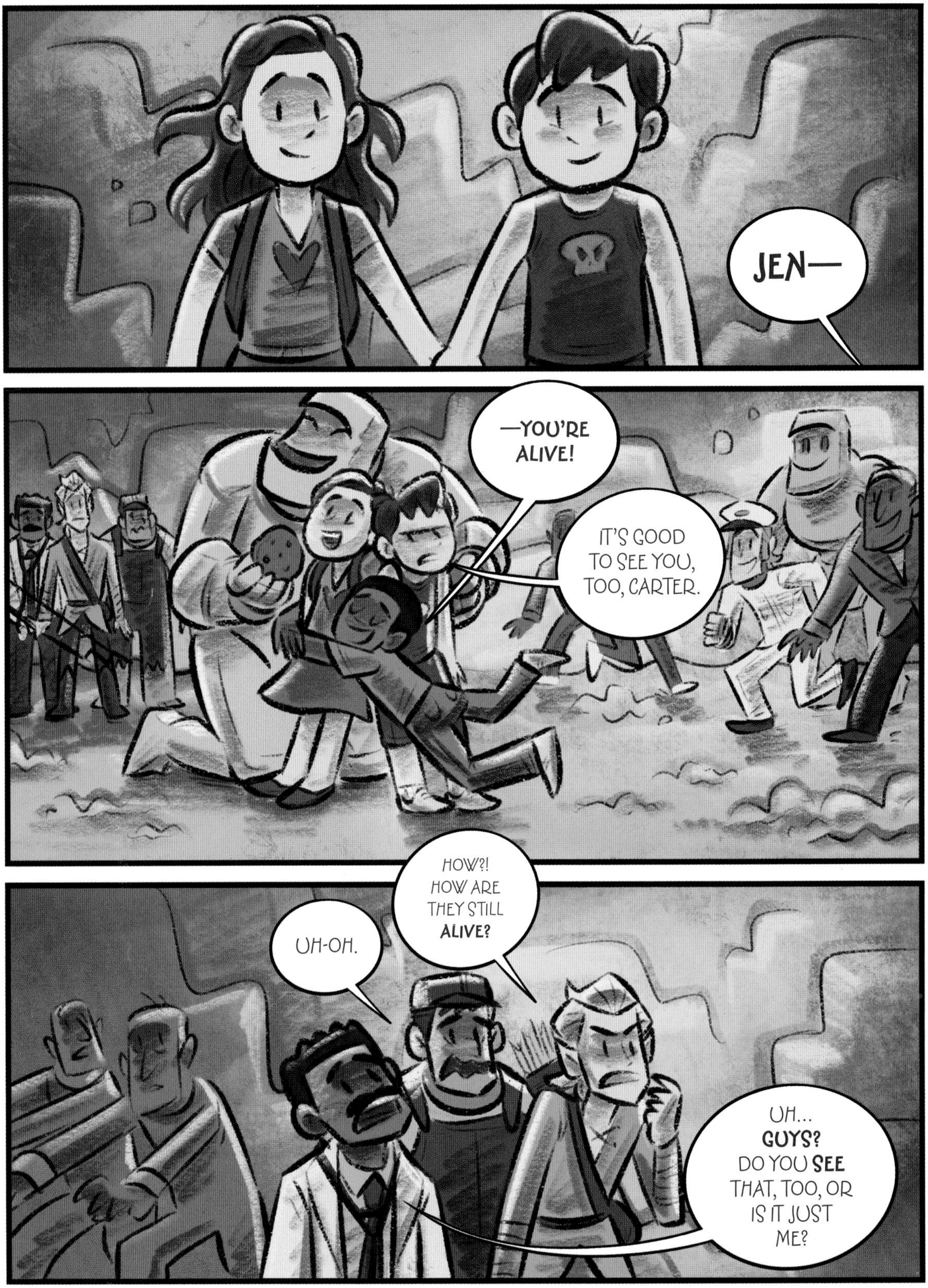
JEN—
—YOU'RE ALIVE!
IT'S GOOD TO SEE YOU, TOO, CARTER.
UH-OH.
HOW?! HOW ARE THEY STILL ALIVE?
UH... GUYS? DO YOU SEE THAT, TOO, OR IS IT JUST ME?

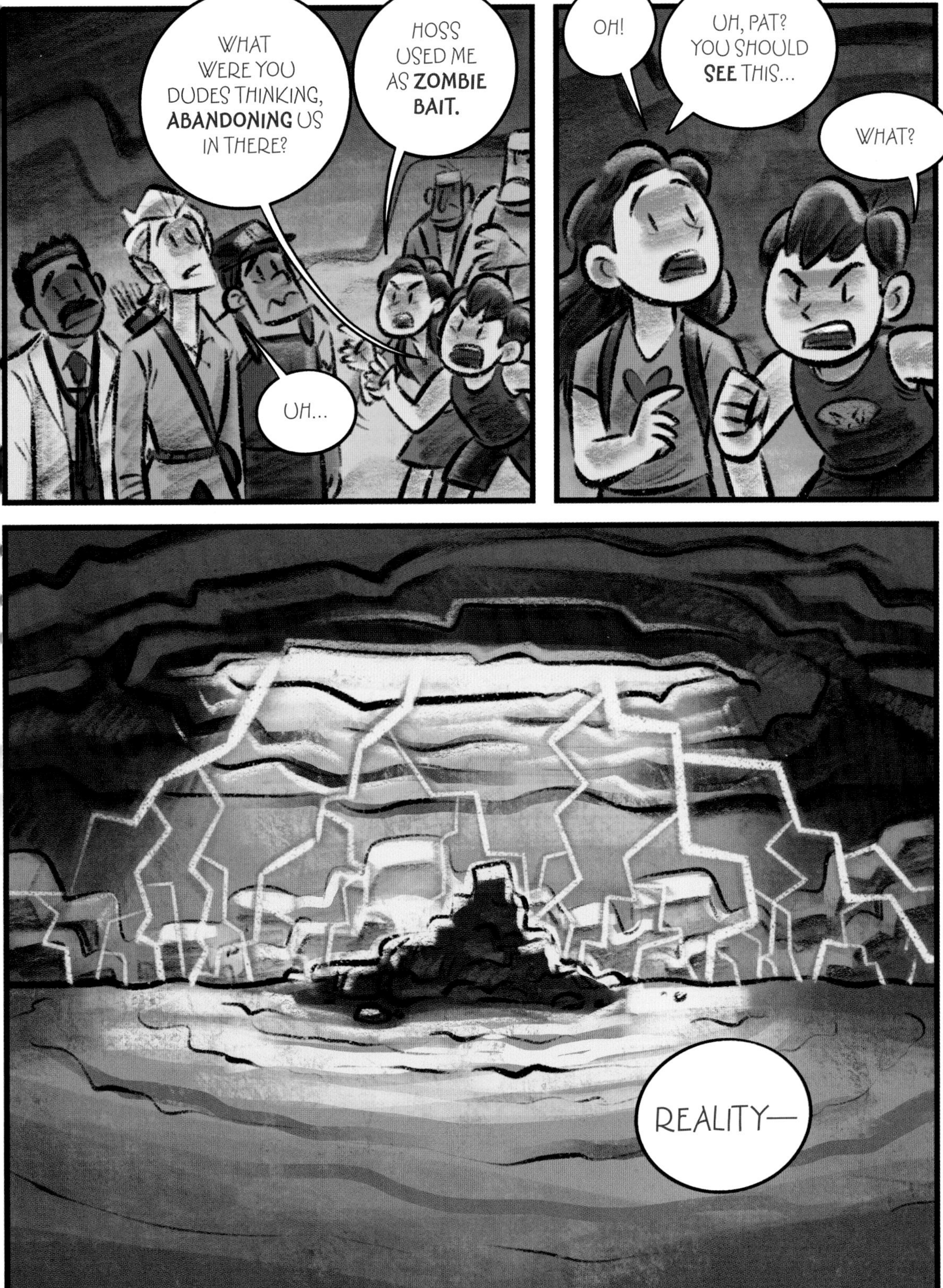
WHAT WERE YOU DUDES THINKING, **ABANDONING** US IN THERE?
HOSS USED ME AS **ZOMBIE BAIT.**
UH...
OH!
UH, PAT? YOU SHOULD **SEE** THIS...
WHAT?
REALITY—

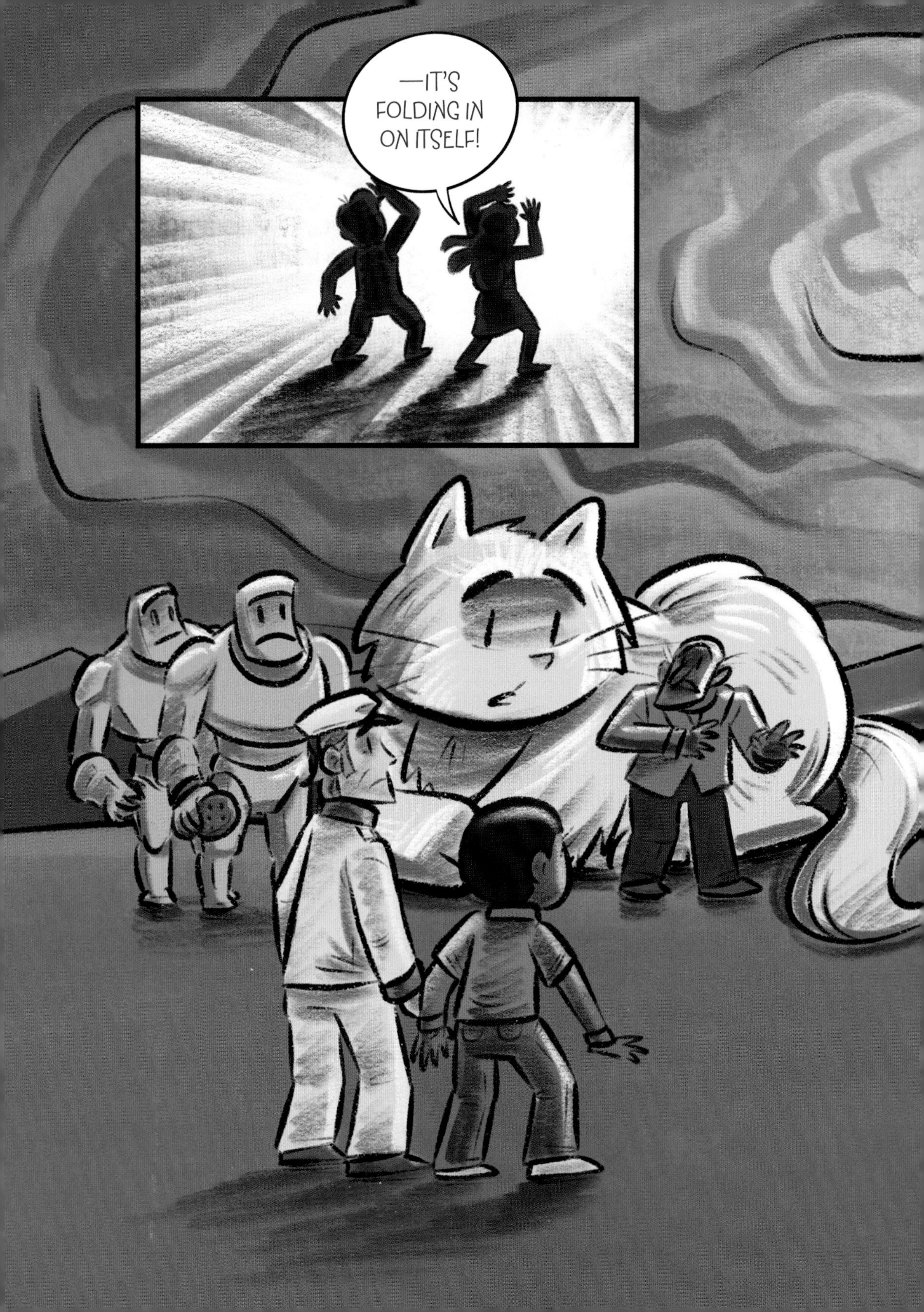
—IT'S FOLDING IN ON ITSELF!

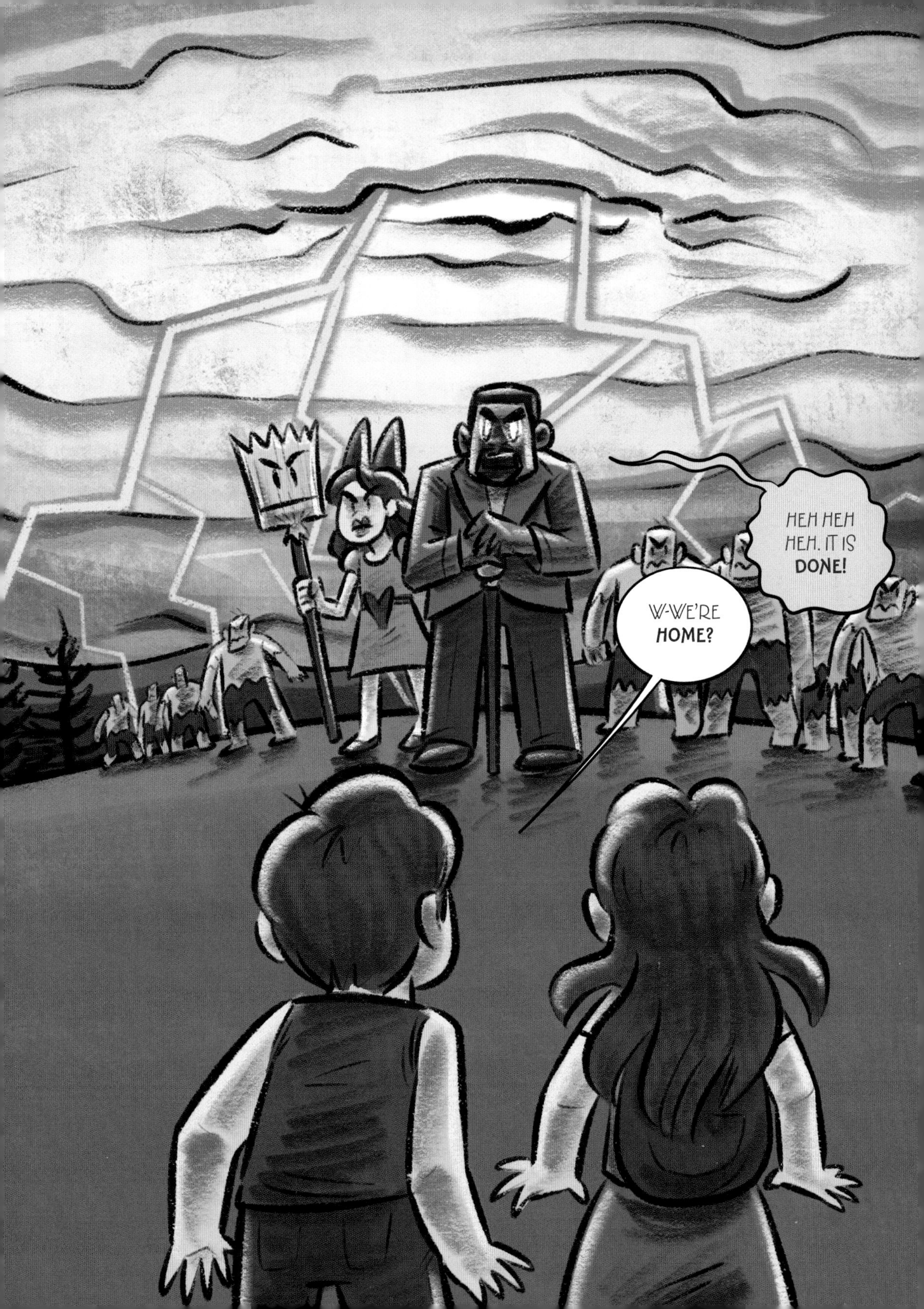
HEH HEH HEH. IT IS **DONE!**
W-WE'RE **HOME?**

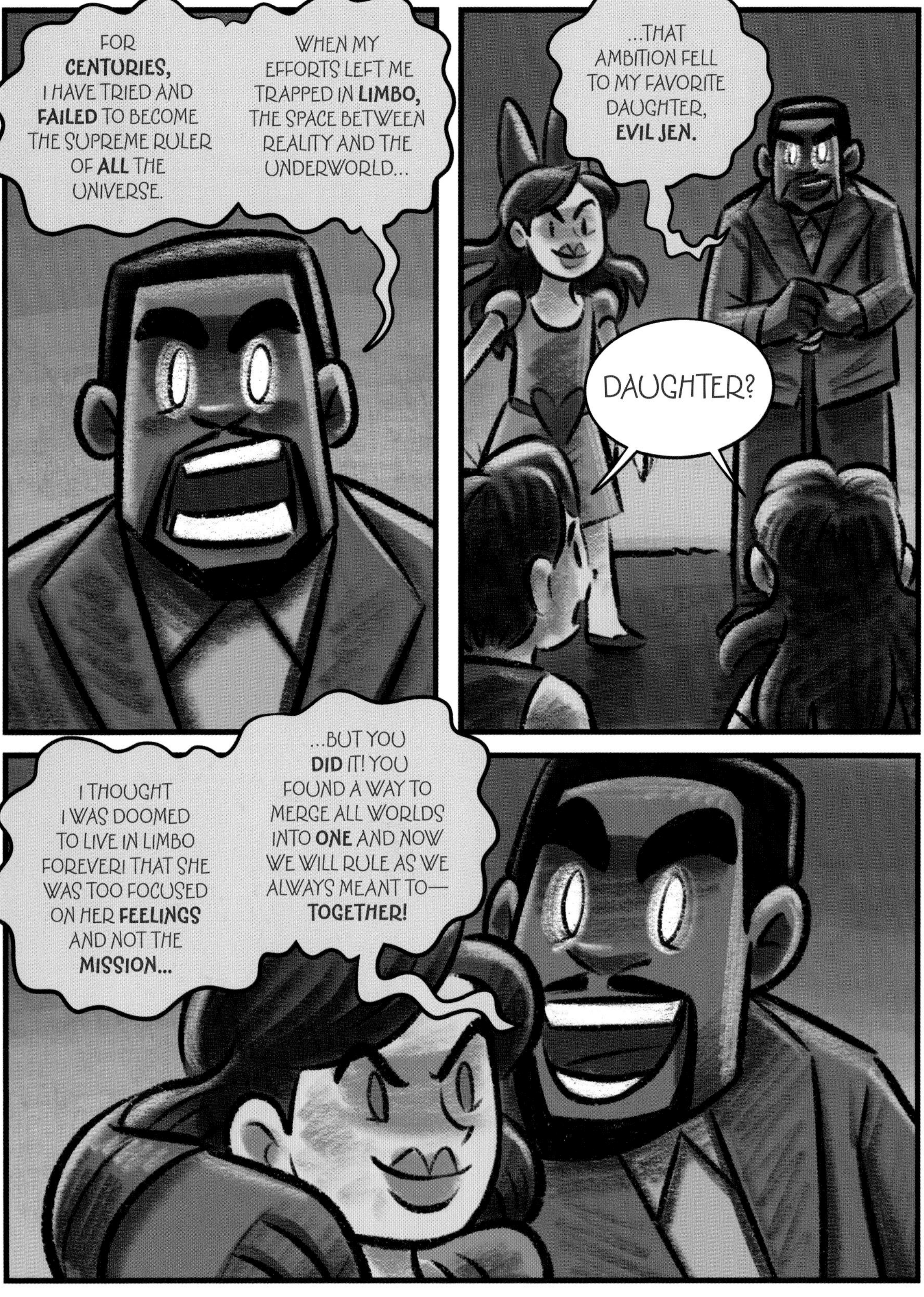
FOR CENTURIES, I HAVE TRIED AND FAILED TO BECOME THE SUPREME RULER OF ALL THE UNIVERSE.
WHEN MY EFFORTS LEFT ME TRAPPED IN LIMBO, THE SPACE BETWEEN REALITY AND THE UNDERWORLD...
...THAT AMBITION FELL TO MY FAVORITE DAUGHTER, EVIL JEN.
DAUGHTER?
I THOUGHT I WAS DOOMED TO LIVE IN LIMBO FOREVER! THAT SHE WAS TOO FOCUSED ON HER FEELINGS AND NOT THE MISSION...
...BUT YOU DID IT! YOU FOUND A WAY TO MERGE ALL WORLDS INTO ONE AND NOW WE WILL RULE AS WE ALWAYS MEANT TO—TOGETHER!

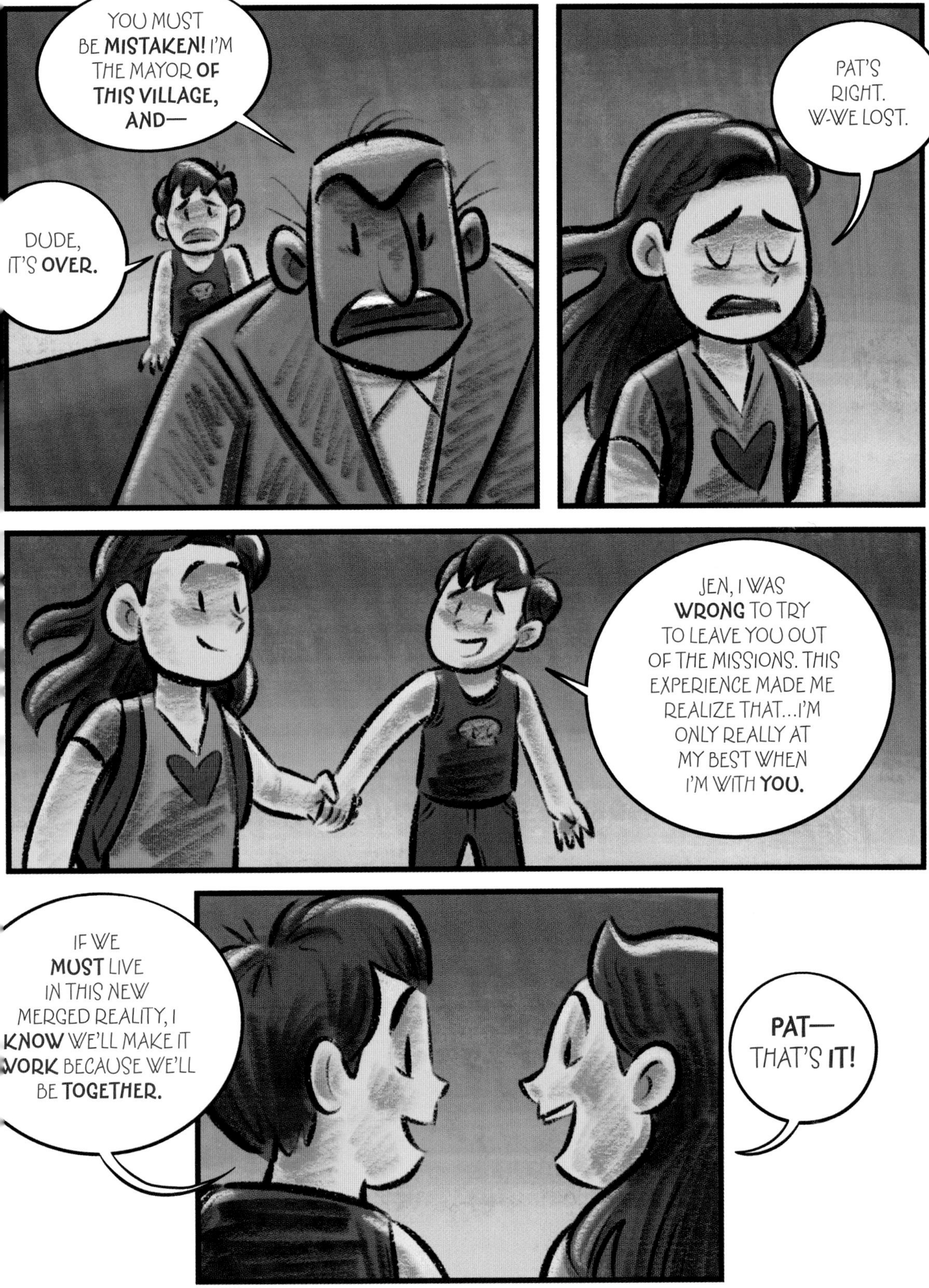
YOU MUST BE MISTAKEN! I'M THE MAYOR OF THIS VILLAGE, AND—
DUDE, IT'S OVER.
PAT'S RIGHT. W-WE LOST.
JEN, I WAS WRONG TO TRY TO LEAVE YOU OUT OF THE MISSIONS. THIS EXPERIENCE MADE ME REALIZE THAT...I'M ONLY REALLY AT MY BEST WHEN I'M WITH YOU.
IF WE MUST LIVE IN THIS NEW MERGED REALITY, I KNOW WE'LL MAKE IT WORK BECAUSE WE'LL BE TOGETHER.
PAT— THAT'S IT!

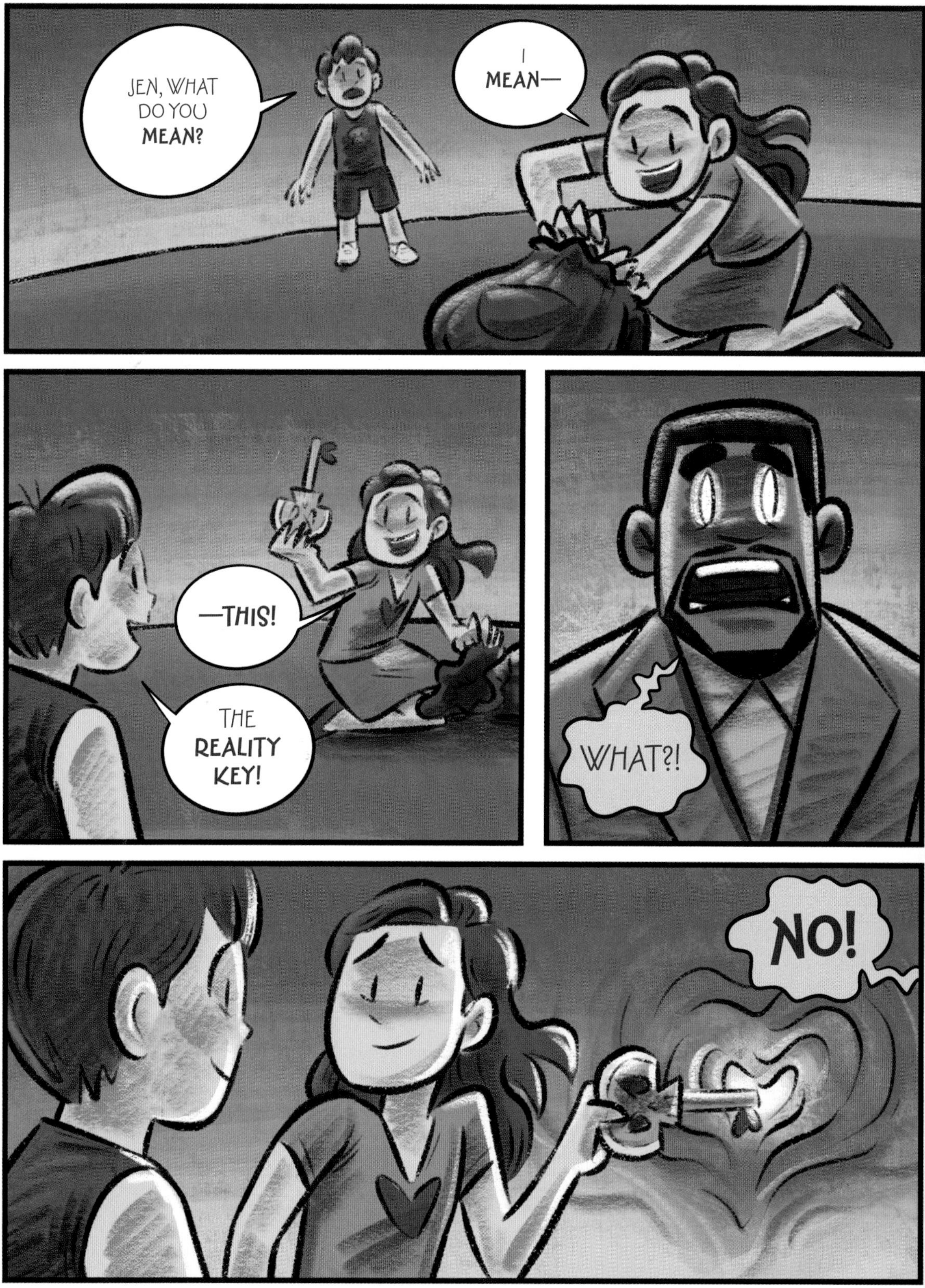
JEN, WHAT DO YOU **MEAN?**
I **MEAN—**
—THIS!
THE **REALITY KEY!**
WHAT?!
NO!

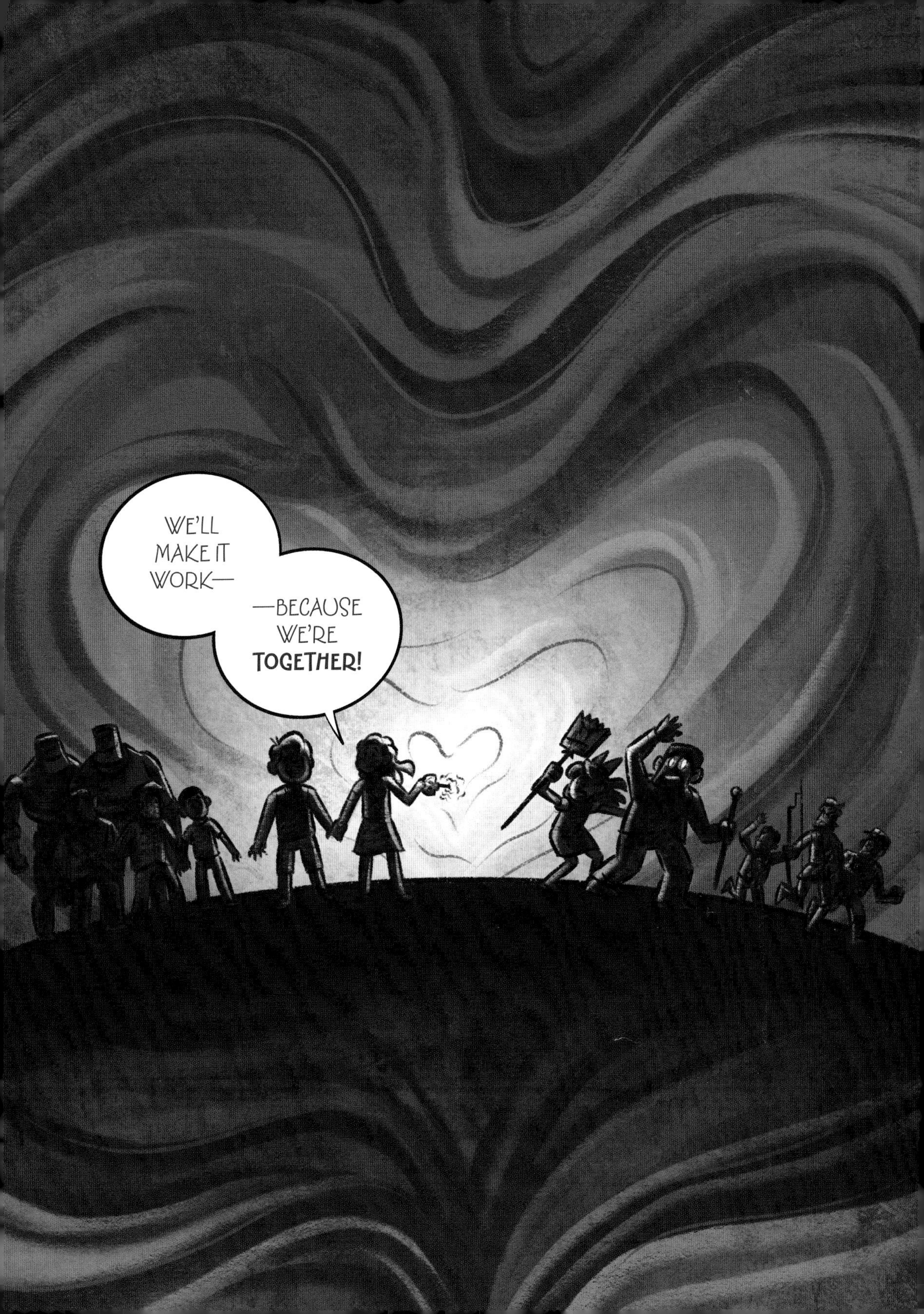
WE'LL MAKE IT WORK—
—BECAUSE WE'RE TOGETHER!

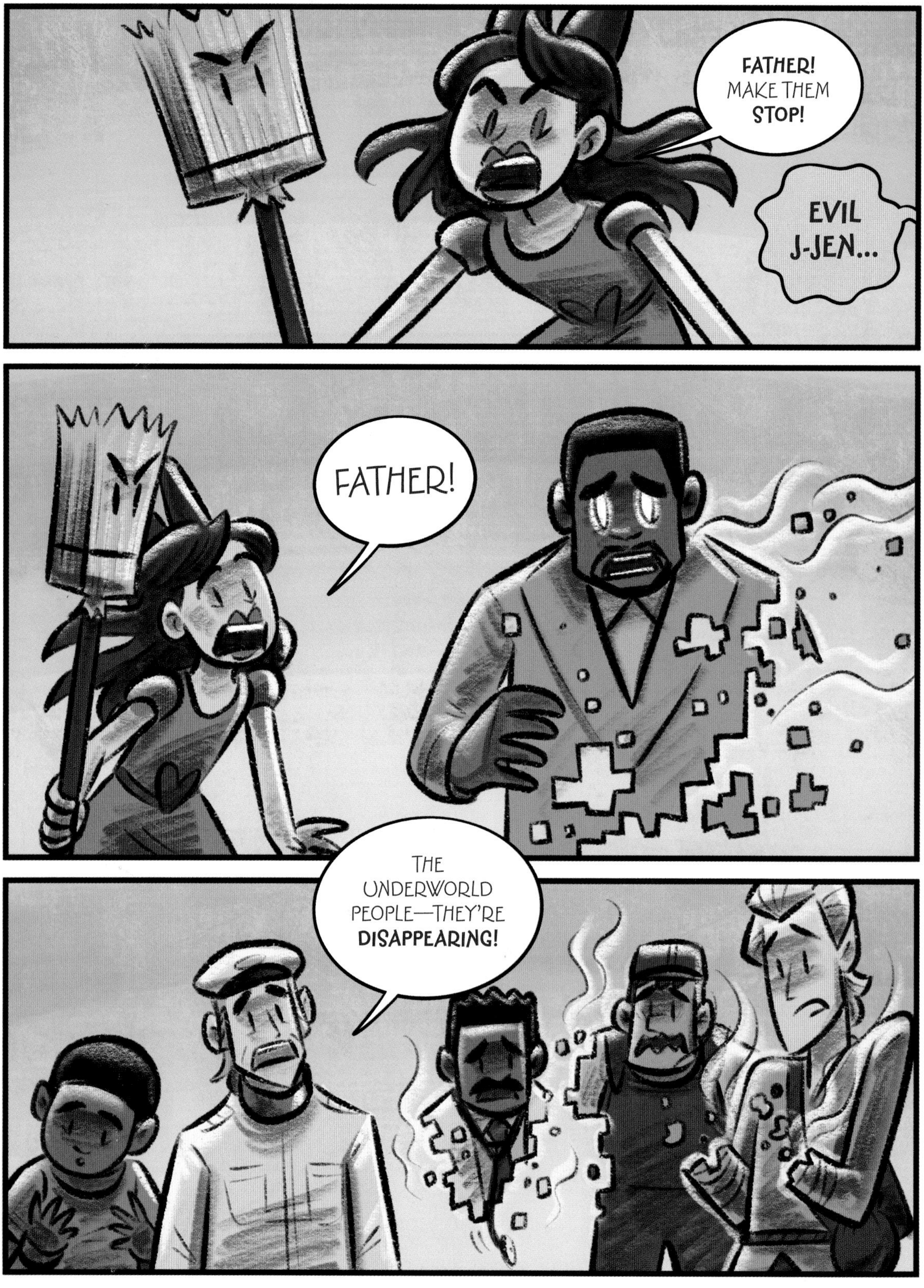
FATHER! MAKE THEM STOP!
EVIL J-JEN...
FATHER!
THE UNDERWORLD PEOPLE—THEY'RE DISAPPEARING!

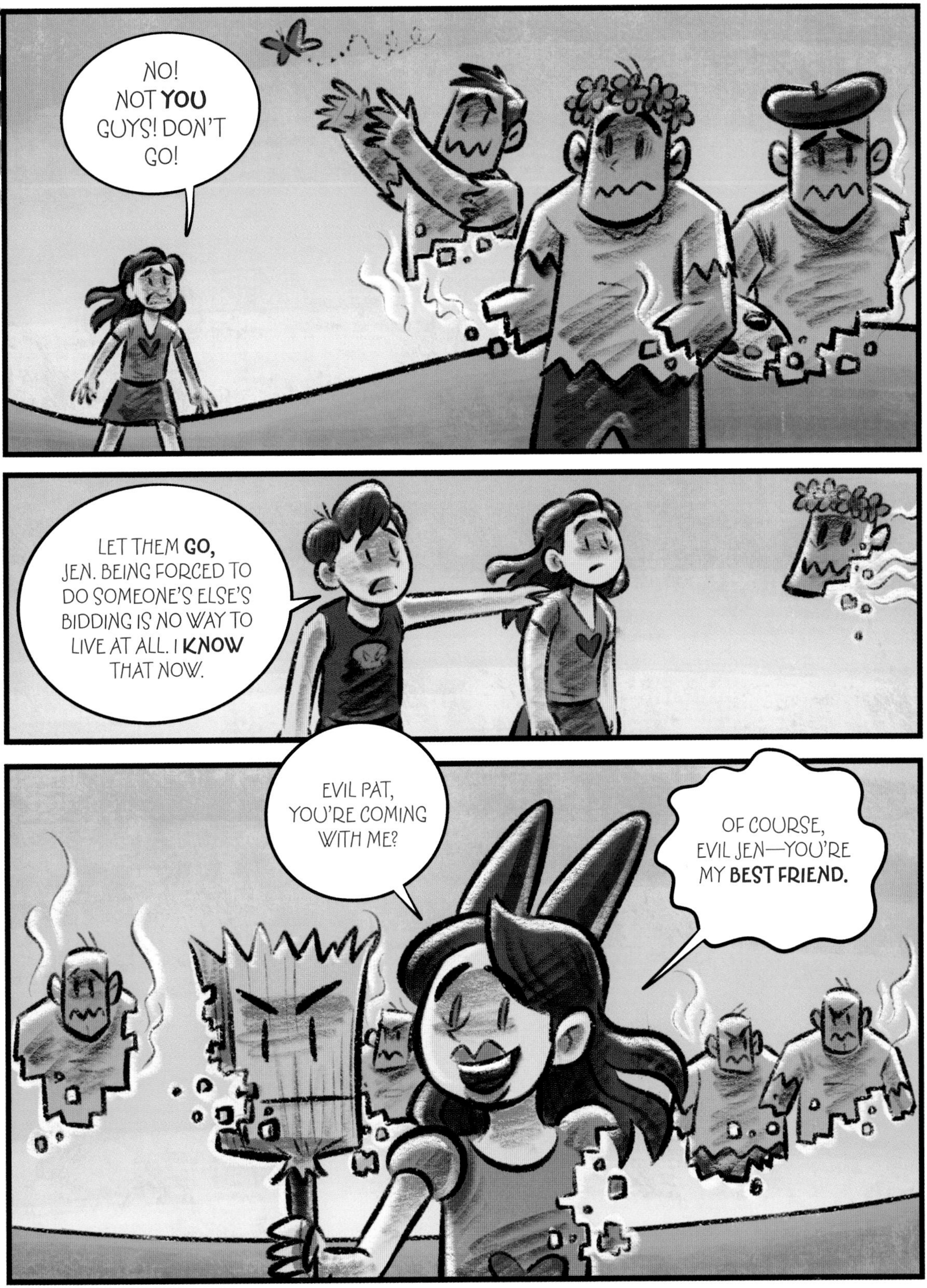
NO! NOT **YOU** GUYS! DON'T GO!
LET THEM **GO,** JEN. BEING FORCED TO DO SOMEONE'S ELSE'S BIDDING IS NO WAY TO LIVE AT ALL. I **KNOW** THAT NOW.
EVIL PAT, YOU'RE COMING WITH ME?
OF COURSE, EVIL JEN—YOU'RE MY **BEST FRIEND.**

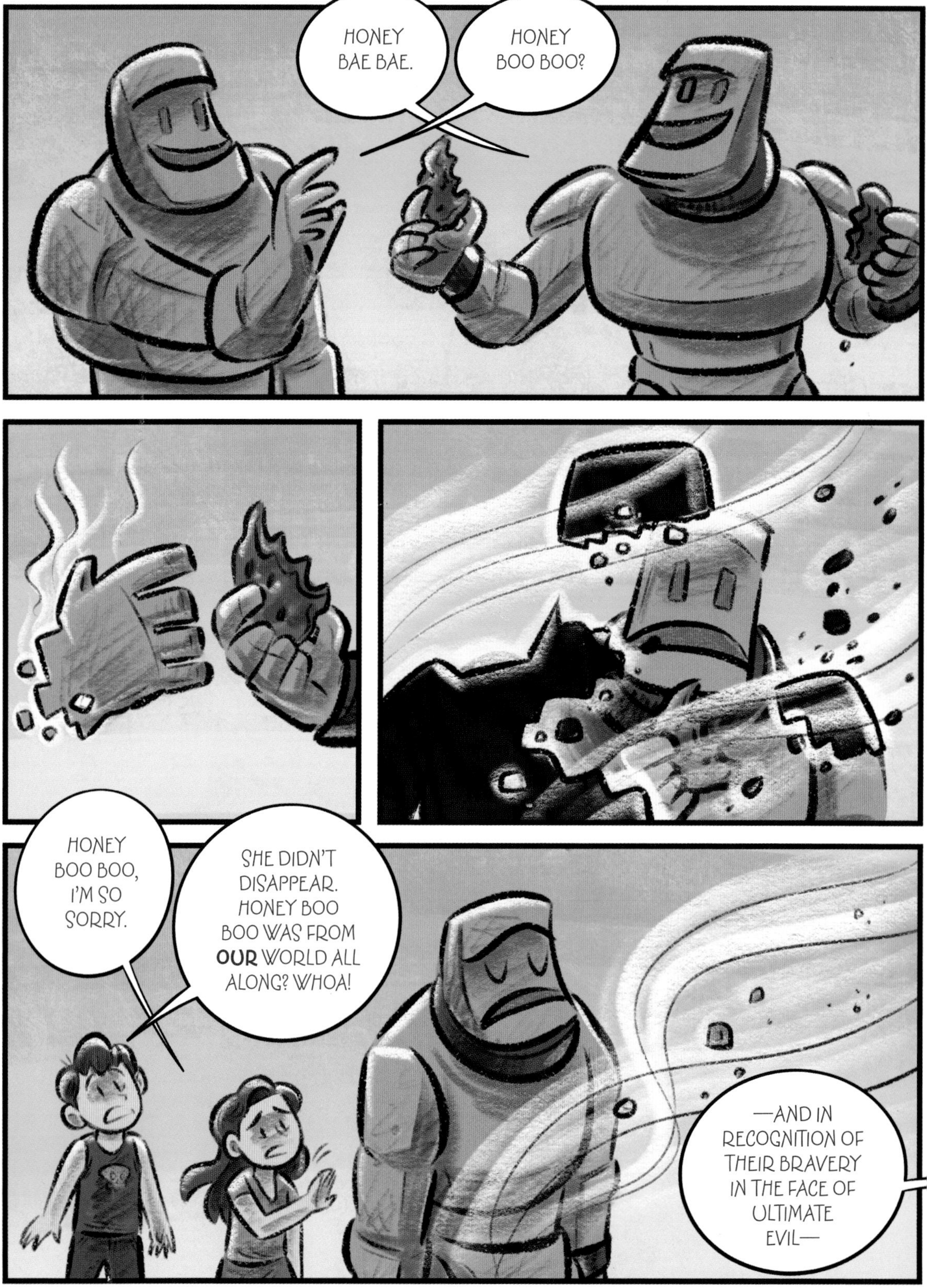
HONEY BAE BAE.
HONEY BOO BOO?
HONEY BOO BOO, I'M SO SORRY.
SHE DIDN'T DISAPPEAR. HONEY BOO BOO WAS FROM **OUR** WORLD ALL ALONG? WHOA!
—AND IN RECOGNITION OF THEIR BRAVERY IN THE FACE OF ULTIMATE EVIL—

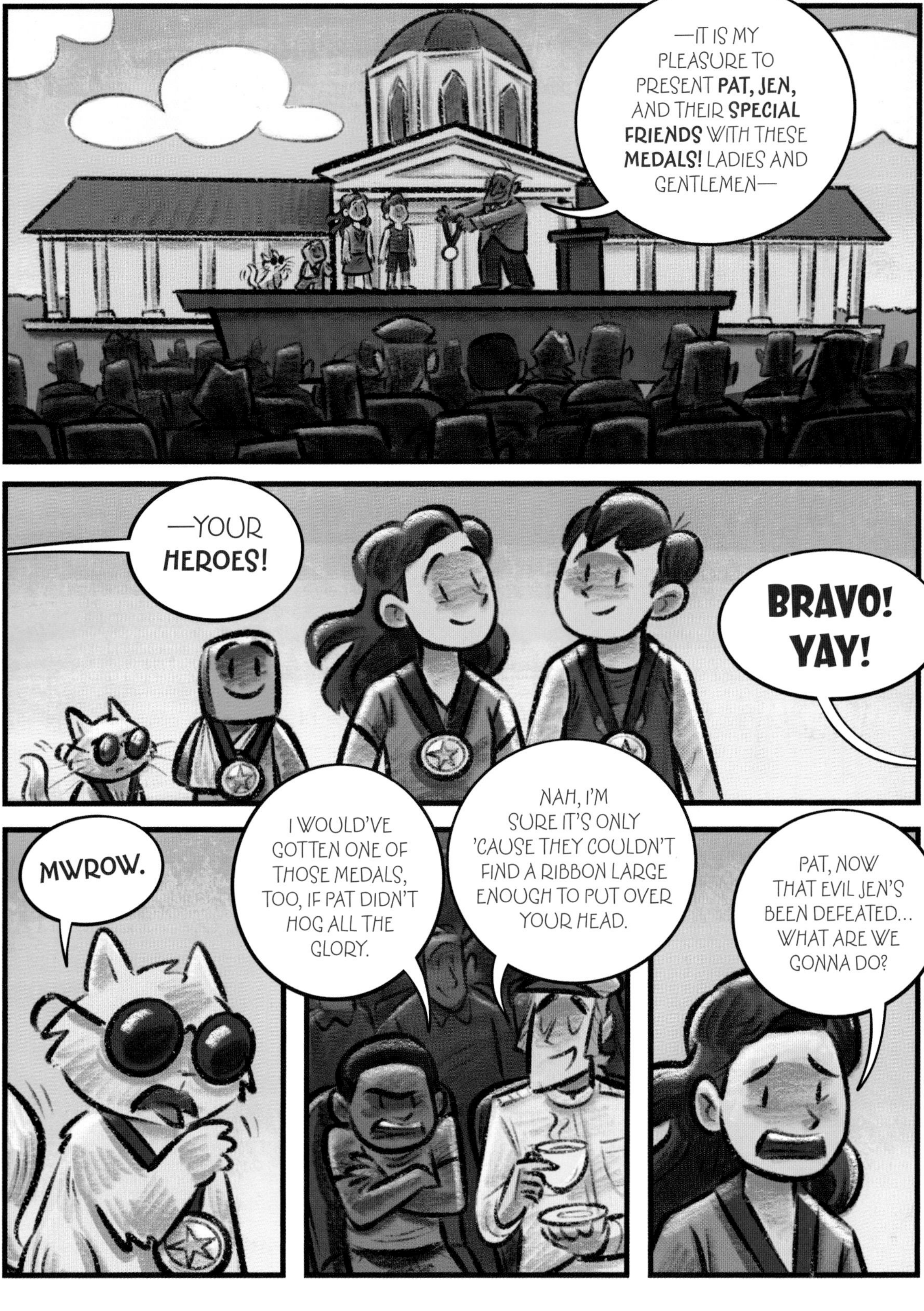
—IT IS MY PLEASURE TO PRESENT **PAT, JEN,** AND THEIR **SPECIAL FRIENDS** WITH THESE **MEDALS!** LADIES AND GENTLEMEN—
—YOUR **HEROES!**
BRAVO! YAY!
MWROW.
I WOULD'VE GOTTEN ONE OF THOSE MEDALS, TOO, IF PAT DIDN'T HOG ALL THE GLORY.
NAH, I'M SURE IT'S ONLY 'CAUSE THEY COULDN'T FIND A RIBBON LARGE ENOUGH TO PUT OVER YOUR HEAD.
PAT, NOW THAT EVIL JEN'S BEEN DEFEATED... WHAT ARE WE GONNA DO?

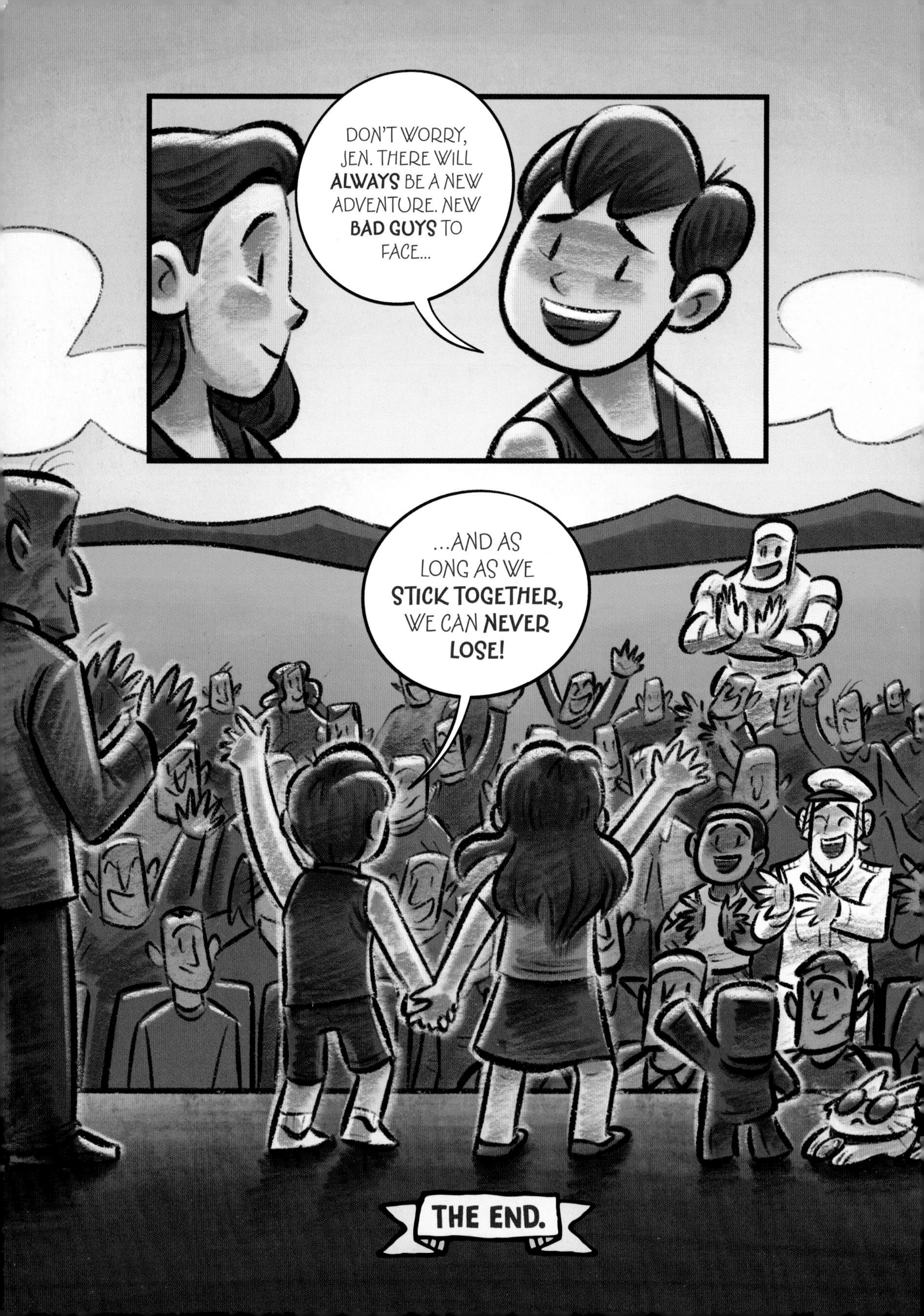
DON'T WORRY, JEN. THERE WILL **ALWAYS** BE A NEW ADVENTURE. NEW **BAD GUYS** TO FACE...
...AND AS LONG AS WE **STICK TOGETHER,** WE CAN **NEVER LOSE!**
THE END.